EGO &
ENDURANCE

by
KAREN EISENBREY

For Kathy

Karen Eisenbrey

"By endurance we conquer"

To John and Isaac,
my resident science advisor
and worldbuilding consultant,
and two of my favorite
nonfictional characters

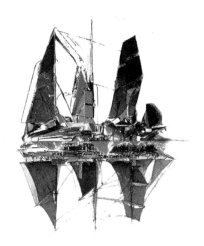

Chapter 1

2124/08/24: This ship is not pretty, but she'll be a fine home-very-far-away-from-home. In that sense, she's beautiful.

— Commander Ladd's Expedition Journal

It was love at first sight.

The ship, blocky and basic and bristling with greebles, wasn't anyone's idea of pretty. But to Ruby Ladd, she was the only thing on the whole Moon worth looking at. This ship meant Ruby could finally get back to the work she was best at. Maybe even redeem the past.

Diagrams and models couldn't compare to her first glimpse of the real thing. Ruby bounded across the bright, pale surface for a closer look. The Salish-class cargo transport *Polaris* had been completely remodeled for this expedition. The long-range communications laser and shorter-range antennas were currently angled forward, pointing like a sailing ship's prow toward a distant goal. Solar panels faced into the sunlight while thermal radiators, black against the white hull, were turned to be in shadow. The solar sail's housing formed a ridge the length of the ship. Just behind the forward viewport, in crisp black letters, the ship displayed her new name: *Endurance.*

On a mission this long, they'd need it.

Ruby presented her credentials to the guard at the entry hatch. "Commander Ladd, reporting for duty."

The guard saluted and opened the hatch. "Welcome aboard, Commander."

Ruby entered the airlock. When the light changed from red to green, she opened the inner hatch and stepped into the ship proper. A bright white passage ran forward to the bridge and officers' quarters, aft to the galley, mess, and access to the cargo deck. The outer wall matched the curve of the hull, and the rounded corners were less likely than square to collect debris. Large black arrows indicated "up" in relation to the ship, and bright yellow handholds at regular intervals would assist with zero-gravity movement when the time came.

Ruby removed her helmet and hung it next to three others on a rack beside the hatch. She made her way to her quarters in the forward section. The captain and first officer had the cabins to either side of Ruby's. The commander's relatively spacious cabin would also serve as her office. The rest of the expedition party would sleep in private cubicles converted from cargo space, just large enough for a sleeping bag and storage locker.

Ruby appreciated the potted succulents tucked into her quarters to add a touch of nature and improve air quality, though her favorite feature was either the private toilet facilities or the large forward viewport. She caught herself space-gazing, so her vote for now went to the viewport. But Ruby had work to do. She stashed her bags and spacesuit in the locker. She liked this new generation of suit — bright white as before, it had a sleeker profile than she was used to, and it was designed so an individual could put it on without help. A patch with the SCEI logo adorned the front — a chain of planets with a stylized spaceship. Ruby preferred the mission patch on the shoulder that represented the real ship she was now aboard.

She peeled out of the bright blue pressure suit and changed into the close-fitting but comfortable working uniform of dark blue pants and shirt with sky blue jacket.

Ruby clipped her SkyComm to her belt and adjusted the wireless earpiece. As she headed to the bridge, a faint thud drifted up the passage from the direction of the galley. She moon-hopped back along the passage to investigate. A maze of transport bins slowed her down — fresh and pre-cooked food that had not yet been stowed. Ruby cast an impatient glance at this disorganization but didn't resent the meat and produce. They would be on packaged rations soon enough.

"How long do you estimate it will take to put all this away?" Ruby called as she entered the galley. "We launch at —"

A disheveled white man in a spacesuit sprawled on the deck. Stubble shadowed his chin. He inhaled with a resonant snore that might have roused the dead but did not wake him. He clutched an empty tequila bottle like a teddy bear.

"Hey!" She shook his shoulder. He snorted and peered at her through half-opened eyelids. "What are you doing here?"

"I'm the cook," he slurred.

"I'm the cook, *ma'am.*"

His brows drew together in a puzzled frown. "No, you're not, I am. And don't call me ma'am. G'night." He closed his eyes again and rolled onto his side.

Before he could snore again, Ruby nudged his ribs with her booted foot. "I'm the Expedition Commander. *You're* supposed to call *me* ma'am."

He opened his eyes wide. "Oh. Shit. You're Ladd?" He sat up.

"Yes. And you are …?"

"Green. Ma'am. Lloyd Green. I'm the cook."

"You mentioned that. You're also drunk."

"Yes, ma'am. As a skunk, ma'am. I was … nervous. Never been on a … on such a long mission before. Not as far as we're going. It won't happen again."

"You're right about that. Please leave the ship at once, Mr. Green."

"Yes, ma'am. When shall I report back for launch?"

"You misunderstand. You're fired."

He stared at her a moment, then struggled to his feet. He staggered out of the galley. Transport bins thumped and clattered as he bumped into them on his way down the passage, and again as he returned. "Commander Ladd, ma'am? I have to tell you … something." He frowned and scratched his head.

"No, you don't. Now get off my ship."

She escorted him to the airlock, personally secured his gloves and helmet, and made sure the guard knew Green was not allowed back on *Endurance*. The guard took Green's elbow and steered him back toward the base.

Ruby met no other obstacles on her way to the bridge, where the non-disheveled white man she intended to see was waiting. Frank Anderson also wore the blue working uniform, but he had removed his jacket. He grinned and rose from his seat. "Welcome aboard, Boss."

"I like the sound of that."

"You've earned it." He opened his arms for a hug.

Ruby shook her head. "Sorry, Skipper, you work for me now. Hugs fall into the category of *inappropriate touch*." She squeezed his shoulder and gripped his hand in a firm handshake.

"Even between friends?" Anderson sighed. "A pity." He smiled down at her. Like most adults, he was a good deal taller than Ruby. A little older, too — mid-thirties now. His cropped brown hair was beginning to gray around the temples, but his light brown eyes had lost none of their mischievous sparkle. He glanced out the viewport. "It's a beautiful day on the Moon."

She smiled. "It's always a beautiful day on the Moon, Skipper. This'll sound strange, but I feel like I can breathe again." She tried and failed to stifle a yawn. "I'm sleep deprived and still on Pacific Time, though, so excuse me if I'm not too bright-eyed."

"You should've slept on the shuttle."

"I tried, but ..." She shook her head.

"Not sick, were you?"

"Not ... much. Just excited, I think. I haven't been off the rock in five years!"

"Cutting it a little close, though. We launch tomorrow — I was afraid we might have to leave without you." He winked.

"Ha ha. I was a little worried myself, but the bean-counters had to balance the books before they'd let me go." She frowned. "Remember how I wanted the whole party to train and quarantine together?"

"Yeah, I wondered about that. What happened?"

"Too extravagant for SCEI. They tried to turn it into a compliment: 'Your officers and crew are all consummate professionals — they need no more than a refresher course, if that.'" Ruby shook her head ruefully. In recent years, the Space Colonization and Exploration Initiative had tilted more heavily toward a business mindset than scientific. "I suppose I should be grateful they allowed the mission specialists to train together, but I really hoped we could gel as a team before launch."

"You'll get us there," Anderson said. "Please tell me you at least got laid before quarantine. Marie was worried."

"I was this close." Ruby held up thumb and forefinger a centimeter apart. "Triathlete, great dancer, stamina to burn … and in training for a big race. No booze, no junk food, and no fooling around."

"Not even with a space commander?"

"I couldn't persuade him. He wanted to make a date for tomorrow night, but …" She shrugged.

Anderson made a sad-clown face. "Poor Ruby, such a martyr to the cause. So what's this paragon's name?"

Ruby guffawed. "I don't remember."

"I hate to think what'll happen if you ever sleep with someone you actually care about."

"Who says I haven't? But I'd rather hang out on a spaceship with my best friends." They both sat and faced the forward viewport, gloriously filled with the bright moonscape against the black of space. "So, how do things look?"

"Excellent. I can hardly wait to take this ship out." He beamed.

"It's the same class of ship we've both piloted dozens of times, delivering supplies and cleaning up space junk," she teased. "It's a trash hauler."

"A souped-up trash hauler with lots of cool new toys," Anderson corrected. "No more puny orbit missions. We're going deep this time; getting real."

"You could have gone before this."

"Not until they let you go, too. SCEI needs to make it right."

"What, you think Wesley James is going to apologize?"

Anderson shrugged and didn't answer. But just being with him improved Ruby's attitude. They'd survived the Chickering Expedition together. He knew better than anyone what that ordeal had cost her, but he also knew how to cheer her up.

"Here's the final expedition roster." He brought up the list:

Ladd, R.: Expedition Commander
Anderson, F.: Captain
Wild, P.: First Officer
Nguyen, B.: Second Officer; Navigator/Communications
Crean, J.: Mission Specialist (Phys.)
Curley, A.: Mission Specialist (Geol.)
Eyestone, J.: Mission Specialist (Rob.)
Mack, Y.: Mission Specialist (Biol., Med.)
Gunner, H.: Documentarian
Green, L.: Cook
Keith, L.: Administrator
Nielson, C.: Engineer

A party of twelve? Funny — Ruby had been thinking eleven. She could put faces to most of the names on the list. She had selected the captain and first officer herself, and trusted Anderson to put together a solid crew. She also knew half the science staff already and accepted their recommendations for the others. But ...

"S'pose my reputation has preceded me?" She tried to sound casual, even humorous, but she could hear the subdued tone in her own voice.

"Are we talking about the hyper-competent leader who puts her people's welfare ahead of her own?" Anderson asked.

"Not that reputation, Frank. The other one."

"It's possible," he admitted. "But six of us have served with or instructed you. We know better. Any doubts among the rest won't last long."

"I hope you're right." Ruby returned her attention to the roster. "Nielson, huh? Are you sure about that?"

"Best engineer in the Corps," Anderson replied.

"No question. But he doesn't play well with others, and this is a long trip."

The Skipper chuckled. "Exactly — long trip. I'd rather have the most skilled engineer than the most charming. And he knows you. I think he'll behave."

"I hope so."

"I've met with just about everyone in the past few days," Anderson said. "You know Wild better than I do — is he good?"

"He's a rock. I'd trust him with my life." She flicked her eyebrows up. "There was a time I had my doubts about you, Skipper, but never about Wild. He'll be an excellent First Officer."

"My ears are burning!" a deep voice said.

"Pete!" Ruby sprang from her seat, her arms open to hug another old friend. She remembered in time and gave him the warmest handshake she could muster.

Peter Wild was even taller than Anderson. His face was the faded pink of a peeled, healing sunburn. He had close-cropped blond hair and piercing blue eyes, softened by a perpetual look of calm and good humor. A lithe middle-aged woman with short black hair stepped up beside Wild. Her golden-brown skin hinted at her southeast Asian roots.

"And Betty!" Ruby hadn't seen her spaceflight instructor in years, but she had changed little in that time. "How long has it been?"

Betty Nguyen beamed as she clasped Ruby's hand. "Too long ... Commander."

That sounded so good and so strange at the same time. The heat rose in Ruby's cheeks. She turned to Wild to hide her flustered pleasure. "How's Marcus?"

"Well, we got some excellent news while I was in quarantine," he replied. "Marcus was just awarded full custody of his niece. We're starting formal adoption procedures."

"Congratulations!" Ruby said. "Nia must be what, four now?"

Wild nodded. "She's been with us half her life. I've just about learned how to braid her hair."

"And now you're running off to space," Anderson said.

"Well, no point wasting a good quarantine." Wild grinned. "But this will probably be my last long mission. Anyway, sorry we're late," he added. "We had to wait for the guard to return to his post and let us in."

"What did we miss?" Nguyen asked.

"Not much, Betty," Anderson assured them. "We were just going over the final roster. "There was a bit of a problem with the cook."

Ruby snorted. "Tell me about it!"

He frowned. "You heard already?"

She hesitated. "Maybe not. What was your problem?"

"I had somebody all lined up, very experienced. She was supposed to meet us here a week ago. The day before she was scheduled to leave for Upham, she fell down some steps in front of her house and tore up the ligaments in her knee." He shook his head and grinned with disbelief. "Can you imagine if we had to scrub the mission because we didn't have a cook?"

"The role isn't exactly mission-critical," Ruby said. "Most of the food is heat and serve."

"Regulations, though. We're required to have someone with the right permits. It worked out, anyway — I was able to hire one of the cooks here at Armstrong, a guy named Lloyd Green. He comes highly recommended."

Ruby felt a pang of doubt. Now her count was down to ten. "Yeah, about that ... I just fired him. That's why the guard was away from his post. Sorry."

Anderson stared. "But we launch tomorrow! There's no time to find another."

"Then we won't find another."

"Who'll do the cooking, then?"

Ruby shrugged. "I will, if necessary. It's not that hard."

"But — the permits!"

Wild snorted and covered his mouth, unsuccessfully hiding a smile that threatened to turn into a laugh.

"Funny thing." Ruby held up her SkyComm and displayed a document. "Is there still a problem?"

"I ... guess not." Anderson sighed and allowed himself a smile. "What are you doing with a food handler's permit?"

"You wouldn't believe all the permits and certificates I have."

"I would," Wild said. "Ready for anything, that's you."

"But where do you find the time?" Betty Nguyen asked.

"I have no life. And every time I get fed up with the suits at SCEI, I earn or renew another certificate. It keeps me sane and out of trouble."

Anderson shook his head. "So you really just boarded the ship and fired the cook?"

Ruby patted his shoulder. "Green wasn't going to work out. He was dead drunk in the galley, and we're not even underway. Said he was nervous about the trip."

"That's only natural."

She frowned. "You say he came highly recommended. What missions has he been on?"

"None. He was cooking here at the spaceport for the last month. Before that, he worked in several restaurants planetside."

She groaned and leaned back in her seat. "Well, no wonder he was nervous. Still, it's just as well, if he was that scared."

"You fired him because he was scared?" Anderson asked.

"No, we all know this kind of work can get you killed." She sighed. "I'm sorry. I should have talked to you first, Frank."

He shook his head. "I'll back you on this one. You're the Boss. But why did you fire him, then?"

"Because he lacked discipline."

"Come on, we're not military, you know."

"He wasted an entire bottle of tequila. *Our* tequila, from the supplies, and not that synthetic rotgut, either." Alcohol and other nonessentials were limited to one small locker in the galley. Ruby had selected such luxuries with care and forethought. "Shared out in a month's time, it could have been bottled morale. But worse than that, he lacked optimism."

Nguyen snorted a laugh. "Optimism? What, believe hard enough and everything will work out fine?"

"Believe it, and then do everything in your power to see that it does," Ruby replied. "Make a plan that looks as far ahead as possible. Control what you can. Have a contingency for what you can't."

Wild grinned. "Disciplined optimism. That's how you'll run this show, isn't it?"

"You know I will. Green couldn't even organize his supplies. In the long run, we're better off without him. Now, who's this Gunner?"

"I thought you knew," Anderson said. "The name seems familiar, but I didn't hire him. Why do we need a documentarian? I can tell you now, we don't have room for a whole camera crew."

Ruby gazed at the name on the roster and thought back to her meetings with the money people. That was the extra person. They had an idea for making a profit even if the expedition failed. But this was beyond anything she'd imagined.

"I might know," she said. "I just hope I'm wrong."

Chapter 2

2124/08/24: We have several talented amateur musicians aboard. While I would have chosen different instruments, I am grateful for the current fashion in live performance with as little processing as possible. A do-it-yourself mentality will serve us all well.

— Commander Ladd's Expedition Journal

Commander Ladd and Captain Anderson returned to the galley in search of coffee while Wild and Nguyen moved into their quarters. Ruby found it in the locker above the hot-drinks unit, which actually came as something of a surprise.

"Green must have put this away before he pickled himself." She handed a package to Anderson.

He glanced at the label. "Huh. Somebody upgraded us to the good stuff."

"You're welcome." Ruby flashed a quick grin.

He laughed. "I'm glad you know what's important, Boss."

Ruby checked the bins still scattered along the passage and stowed anything that looked immediately perishable. They could deal with the rest of it later.

Anderson started the coffee brewing before the rest of the expedition party arrived, and Ruby located the locker for nonessentials — the "morale locker" — from which she extracted a package of cookies. There wasn't time to offer more than modest hospitality, but even a small treat would start things on the right tone. To make this first meeting more of an occasion, she returned to her quarters and changed into her new dress uniform, a long, fitted white jacket with black and gold trim, worn over narrow black slacks and polished, well-made leather boots. Ruby rarely thought about fashion, but admired the design of this comfortable, becoming outfit.

She returned to the messroom, a relatively large area near the galley where the whole party could gather for meals, meetings, and entertainment. As in their private quarters, pots of hardy plants in a soilless growing medium adorned the mess. She waited as the rest of the group took their places. Ruby stood at the head of the table. "In the name of the Space Colonization and Exploration Initiative, welcome aboard the *Endurance*. For those who don't know me, I am Ruby Ladd, commander of this expedition."

She let the smattering of applause die down. As she drew breath to continue, her comm notified her of an incoming urgent call from SCEI. When she accepted it, the tanned, square-jawed face of SCEI Director Wesley James appeared on the screen. Compared to the spacers in the room, his golden hair was extravagantly long and carefully styled.

"Good afternoon, Commander! I wish to address the entire party. Is this a good time?"

"Yes, sir, we've just gathered for an introductory meeting."

She cast the call to the media module at the other end of the mess. Its camera activated so he could see all of them. Viewed through the augmented reality lens they each wore, his projected image appeared life-size and three dimensional, though translucent.

"Friends, allow me to wish you a satisfying and successful journey from both the commercial and the scientific standpoints," James said. "Your explorations and research will move us closer to our goal of colonization throughout the solar system. Imagine, in ten years, we could go from a small research base on Mars to humans living and working on the moons of Jupiter and Saturn. Perhaps sooner than that, thanks to all of you."

Ruby's smile froze. Even ten years was wildly optimistic. People about a century ago had finally started taking meaningful steps to slow climate change, but that was already too late to avoid catastrophic effects. With the livable parts of Earth shrinking while the population continued to grow, other planets presented a last resort. But ten years? The Mars base had been in operation for only eight and was not yet self-sufficient, even for its small population. James had come from the business sector, though, where unrealistic timelines were the norm.

"Thank you, Director James," Ruby said. "You can count on us to do our jobs well."

She returned the call to her private comm. She was about to end it when James spoke again.

"What do you think of my surprise? Quite a coup, getting Gunner. With him along, the expedition will pay for itself. So be sure to treat him well."

"I'll see to it that everyone is treated well. We'll be in touch before launch." Ruby ended the call before James could add more. She stowed her comm. "Let's proceed with the introductions. Peter Wild will be my second in command. Mr. Wild? Any words of greeting or advice?"

Wild unfolded his lanky frame and stood to greet the assembly. "Listen to the Boss," he said. "She's always right." He resumed his seat amid chuckles.

Ruby barely managed to keep a straight face at her old friend's dry humor. "Thank you, Mr. Wild. And Second Officer Betty Nguyen is our navigator and communications officer, as well as a skilled space pilot." Ms. Nguyen rose and smiled at the group. "Captain Frank Anderson has charge of the ship itself. Whether I was planning a road trip or a space journey, this is the man I'd want at the helm. Skipper, will you introduce your crew?"

Anderson gave her a nod and rose to his feet. "A ship like this requires only a small crew to operate it. On this expedition, we have Chip Nielson as engineer and all-around Mr. Fix-it." A compact man with a lined, leathery face half stood and acknowledged the polite applause. "In addition to Ms. Nguyen, Mr. Wild and Commander Ladd are also qualified to pilot the ship, if necessary." Anderson started to sit but quickly straightened. "My apologies! It wouldn't do to forget our administrator, Lee Keith." He gestured toward a small, pale man at the other end of the table, dressed in the green uniform of a crewmember. His almost colorless hair had been parted and combed with precision. "He'll monitor the supply inventory to make sure we don't run out of anything critical."

"Just what we need, a damned bean counter. I'll be sure to log every bolt and screw," Nielson muttered.

Ruby frowned but otherwise ignored the remark. "Thank you, Captain. As you all know, our ultimate destination is the Asteroid Belt, where our assignment is to assay and tag asteroids for eventual mining, if we find enough large ones to be worth the effort." A thrill ran through her, and it was difficult to maintain a professional demeanor. Not about asteroids in particular — she knew there wouldn't be much to see out there, though her dreams were filled with pop-culture images of tumbling space rocks. The thrill was about going out again, this time farther than any crewed mission to date. "Probes have been able to target only one asteroid at a time," Ruby continued. "Those on their way somewhere else rarely came near any at all, so we may have to chase them down. Fortunately, *Endurance* has plenty of speed and almost unlimited power from the reactor. We won't run out of fuel in our lifetimes."

Dr. Yvonne Mack, the ship's physician, raised her hand. She was about fifty, her dark brown face just beginning to show lines. Her black hair was threaded with gray and worn in short, tight curls. "Just as long as one of them doesn't chase us!" She smiled widely at her joke.

"They're not as close together as you might think," Anderson replied. "There's usually plenty of space."

"Usually?" the doctor asked.

"May I take this one?" The expedition's physicist, Dr. Jamie Crean, stood up. His dark, hairless scalp shone under the lights. At fifty-five, he was the eldest member of the party. Ruby had worked with him in the past and remembered his practical jokes as much as his science lectures. "Asteroids do collide with each other relatively frequently — in astronomical terms. Every million years or so, give or take a few thousand. We're aiming for a relatively populated area of the Belt, but even there, we should be fine."

"Thank you, Dr. Crean," Ruby said. "This is as good a time as any to introduce the science staff. In addition to the commercial component, this expedition will include ongoing research. I mean, there's no reason to send this many people into space unless you plan to send a lot more. This asteroid chase is a good opportunity to study the effects of long space journeys on the human body and mind, as well as a practical test of some new technology that could be useful in colonization — everything from our power plant to our laundry facilities. Dr. Mack is along to treat any illness or injuries that occur. She'll also be studying *us*."

Dr. Mack stood. "I'll be looking at the effects of long-term low-gravity conditions on the human body. I feel lucky to have such a diverse sample — a wide age range, a mix of men and women, several ethnic backgrounds. So don't be surprised if I request a sample of some fluid or other bodily materials from any of you." Nervous laughter met this comment.

Ruby turned to Jamie Crean. "We've already heard a little from Dr. Crean, our resident physicist. What is your specific project?"

"We'll be testing a newly designed solar sail, and I, too, will be looking at gravitational issues, though I am unlikely to ask for any fluids."

"Dr. Aaron Curley is our geologist and metals expert. He'll be working closely with roboticist Dr. John Eyestone to ready the team of robots for asteroid duty."

The geologist, a white man in his early thirties with wavy, dark-blond hair, lifted his hand but turned down the opportunity to speak. Dr. Eyestone stood and smiled around at the group. He was a good deal younger than anyone else in the room — twenty-five at the oldest. He wore blue jeans and a blinding tropical print shirt in orange and green. With his brown skin and black hair, floppy and boyish, he could get away with it. "I designed a team of seven neural-net robots for this expedition," he said. "To a limited extent, these are learning robots. They'll benefit from interaction with as many people as possible, so feel free to visit the robotics lab and just hang out with us."

"I second that suggestion," Ruby said. "Some of us have been out to Mars before. For those who haven't, here's a warning: this trip is going to be long." Her listeners laughed and nudged each other at this statement of the obvious. "The lab coats predict that sometime soon, we'll be able to make these long shots in some kind of stasis or hibernation — go to bed on the Moon and wake up on Mars, or some more distant world, without any experience of the intervening months or years. We're not there yet. We get to experience every day of this journey.

"We can learn from our ancestors who crossed oceans on sailing ships and a continent in covered wagons. Keep the mind active, keep the body active, stay engaged. Everyone will have daily work to do. Due to unforeseen circumstances, we find ourselves without a cook, but this may be a blessing in disguise. It's one more way to keep busy. We will also hold regular training sessions and drills to ensure we are prepared for whatever may occur."

Ruby drew her comm from its holster to the extent of the retractable cord and held it up. "Everyone should have been issued a SkyComm for use on this expedition."

In answer, the other members of the party held up their palm-sized communicators — like hers, Space Corps blue, except for one. The man at the far end of the table displayed a comm in matte black, like his clothing. She didn't know him, but she knew who he was. Already, he had to try to stand out.

The little comms, regardless of color, would allow the party to communicate with each other over the ship's network. More importantly, they could connect with the ship's communications laser to send messages and data back to Earth. They also had excellent storage capacity and processing power, not to mention the latest in augmented reality graphics.

Ruby stowed her SkyComm. "For leisure hours, we have a library of books and videos available for download — see Mr. Wild after the meeting if you need the network access code. There are multiplayer and single-player games on the network, too, and we have a collection of magnetic table-top games if we get sick of screens. Everyone is required to use the ship's array of exercise equipment to prevent muscle and bone loss in low gravity. And anyone with a talent to share is welcome to perform for our entertainment, teach a skill, or start a club."

"The refit crew left a basketball hoop and ball in the cargo hold, and there's just about enough space for a half-court game," Wild added.

Ruby glanced at him and tried not to smile. She could imagine how the cargo area, once pressurized but still empty, would have made a tempting playground. A jumpshot on the Moon? Epic. "I don't know how well that will work in zero G, but you're welcome to try." She looked around the room and made eye contact with the man at the other end of the table. There was no putting it off. "I probably don't need to introduce our resident celebrity, Mr. Harte Gunner. The SCEI execs sent him along to document the expedition."

Gunner stood and took a little bow to the applause that followed. Ruby hadn't met him before, but like all of them, she knew his face. He was even better looking in person than in his publicity shots. He wore a turtleneck and designer jeans, both black. Like he was some kind of *auteur*, but she had to admit, the outfit looked good on him. He was not as tall as Wild, but better filled out. He had a full head of lustrous dark hair and a beautifully groomed mustache. He was almost as deeply tanned as Wesley James. He looked like a man from another time — Tesla, maybe. They all knew his work and his reputation. He'd made a name for himself with AR documentaries that put the viewer in the middle of all kinds of breathtaking events and locations. He took absurd risks to get his shots, but so far, those risks had paid off. He had no trouble getting production money — or commissions like this one.

Ruby was not opposed to documenting the expedition. SCEI clearly expected her to feel honored that they had graced her mission with such star power. But they hadn't even asked. Maybe they knew they wouldn't like her opinion. Gunner had a reputation for recklessness and arrogance. He could jeopardize the whole expedition.

"Thank you for that kind welcome," he said. "But I'm not the only one who's had my name in the news, Commander. It's a privilege to be part of your first command."

"Second, technically."

He lifted an eyebrow and smiled. It was a charming smile, but it didn't fool Ruby. If he thought she would talk about that first command, on camera or off, he was sadly deluded. But she shouldn't have said anything.

"I'm very excited to be a part of this historic expedition," he said. "I've done a space picture before, but nothing like this. We're going to make a real hit, I'm sure of it."

"Thank you, Mr. Gunner." Ruby forced a gracious smile onto her face. "I'm sure you're right."

"But don't even think of doing anything that smells like a publicity stunt," the Skipper added. "The Boss would confiscate your equipment and probably confine you to quarters. Right, Boss?"

"Absolutely," Ruby replied. "But we won't have to worry about that, will we?"

"No, Ma'am!" Gunner saluted as he resumed his seat.

He would bear watching, but for now, she chose to go on with her talk. "We have one stop planned — we're taking supplies and equipment to the Columbia research base on Mars, so we'll have that opportunity to stretch our legs. I imagine they'll be glad to see us, too. With technicians, administrators, and support staff, I think they're up to a population of about thirty, which is still an awfully small town. But that's months off, so get used to this ship. Feel free to settle into your quarters now. Small as they are, we each get our private space — no entry except by permission." Scattered chuckles greeted this announcement. "It may sound funny now, but trust me, in a week or two, you'll know the value of that little bit of space to yourself." Ruby ran a hand over her head. "Two more things before we break. You'll notice all of us professional spacers have our hair cut short. I need to ask everyone else to do the same — four centimeters in length, max."

Half the mission specialists groaned and protested.

"I know, I know," Ruby said. "On a short mission or with fewer people, it would be less of an issue. But we can't afford to have long hair tangled up in equipment or floating around where someone might breathe it in. This is for the good of the whole party. We have vacuum clippers available in each of the toilet cubicles, or if you don't want to do it yourself, Mr. Wild is a capable barber, and I'm not bad myself. Good? Good. Now I need a volunteer to help me make supper." Dr. Mack raised her hand. "Thank you. This meeting is adjourned. If you need anything from the base, go get it and come right back. We'll sleep aboard tonight."

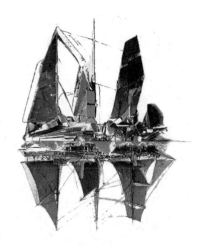

Chapter 3

2124/08/24: This documentary is, by definition, an unscripted feature that runs the risk of being one damn thing after another. If I'm lucky, a compelling narrative will emerge, though I suspect it may lie in the past ...

— *Harte Gunner's Production Journal*

During the introductory meeting, Harte Gunner watched Commander Ladd with interest. He'd looked up her history as soon as he was accepted for the expedition, but it hadn't registered that she was no older than he was. Prodigies were almost expected in his field but seemed rare in hers. She had already been part of events that would make a prize-winning feature. She was attractive enough to star in it, too. Her published head shot didn't do her justice. Her hair, which looked sometimes brown and sometimes red, was shorter than he liked, but all these Space Corps types seemed to favor a close-cropped look. And she had the bone structure to pull it off. Her stature came as a surprise. It was rare to encounter someone so small in a position of authority, especially one who didn't try to compensate. Ruby Ladd looked commanding even in low-heeled boots.

She didn't act like someone with a blot on her record or something to prove. But there was a mysterious hole in the official record that Harte hoped to fill. She had hinted at the answer with her comment about this being her second command.

As the others left to move into quarters or retrieve gear from the base, he followed the commander and physician to the galley. It was a narrow passage with handholds along the floor and ceiling, as well as between the many storage lockers. These handholds weren't needed yet, but they would be. He could hardly wait.

Commander Ladd and Dr. Mack were laughing about something but broke off abruptly when he entered. Up close, he could tell the Commander's close-cropped hair was definitely at the red end of brown, and her alert eyes at the green end of hazel. She had sculpted cheekbones and an athletic build with modest but obvious curves in all the right places. She had removed her jacket. Her sleeveless black top accentuated her toned arms, and the cut of her slacks hinted her legs were equally toned. It was hard not to stare, but he wouldn't complain about the effect of low gravity on the female form.

"You must have worked together before," Harte said. "You were laughing like old pals catching up after a long absence."

"We go waaaay back," the doctor said with a laugh.

"Yvonne was a mentor to me early on," the commander said. "I made sure she was on the planning team for this mission."

"May I be of assistance?" he asked.

"No pictures!" Dr. Mack cried, but she was smiling.

"But I must take your picture." He had left his camera in his cabin but held up his hands as if framing a scene. "You'll all be characters in a real-life drama."

"As long as you make me look beautiful," the doctor teased with a coquettish look.

"That will be the easiest job I could imagine, my dear doctor." It wasn't mere flattery, though he wasn't above using it. Her lovely skin color spoke of the African diaspora filtered through generations in North America. She was older than the commander and more generously endowed, with a warm smile that hinted at a solid foundation and joy in life. If he were her patient, it would be easy to trust her care. "But in all seriousness, perhaps I should start recording tonight. I need to capture scenes of daily shipboard life. What do you think, Commander Ladd?"

She had her head in the refrigerated compartment. Standing upright, she announced, "I think you're going to have to take off at least eight centimeters of hair before we launch."

Harte touched his carefully gelled locks. "You're kidding, right? Putting one over on the rookies?"

"I'm afraid I'm quite serious," the commander said. "There's no room for vanity on this trip. You can grow it back when the mission is over. The good news is, we're having fish tonight." The Commander reached into the compartment and produced a pan of salmon fillets, hatched with grill marks and speckled with dill and pepper. "I had these sent ahead in advance to be prepared for us at the base. I'm so glad Green didn't leave them out to spoil! And there's a tub of salad greens and fresh veggies, obviously for tonight — salad's a mess in zero gravity, so enjoy it now. How are your knife skills, Mr. Gunner?"

He was happy to accept the task, just to stay in the galley and eavesdrop. He longed to interview her, ideally on camera, about what really happened on the Chickering Expedition. But there was plenty of time, and she wasn't going anyplace without him.

He looked over the tools available. "Only one knife?"

"How much do you think we'll be cooking from scratch on this trip?" the commander asked. "We're more likely to need a sharp tool to get through a stubborn package."

"I'll … make do." He removed the knife from the magnetic utensil rack that included a large spoon, a pair of shears, and a metal mixing bowl. A miniature herb garden grew in pots above the utensils, the hint of nature a relief in the otherwise sterile white environment. The knife was also connected to the rack by a cable. You didn't want something like that wandering around by itself in zero gravity. He began to cut up vegetables. Next to him, the commander slid the pan of salmon into the small oven to reheat.

"Not bad." She looked over his shoulder at the paper-thin cucumber slices and uniform wedges of miraculously ripe tomato.

He suspended the knife and half turned toward her. "There was a time when I was undecided between Media Production and Culinary Arts, so I did both. You never forget how to chop."

She smiled, and he wished he had his camera. "Must be useful in the editing booth."

Encouraged, he dared ask a question. "You've progressed quickly in your career. Some would say you've rocketed to the top — the youngest officer in Space Corps history. To what do you owe your success?"

The smile vanished, replaced by a guarded look. "Is this an interview?"

"Conversation. I'm interested, that's all. I'm not recording, and if I use anything you say in the doc, you'll get final approval." He emptied the tub of greens into the bowl and added the chopped and sliced vegetables. The bottled vinaigrette smelled bland when he poured it over the salad. He snipped parsley and thyme and added them before tossing it all with the big spoon.

"My success, huh?" Commander Ladd said. "That's a funny word for it, when I've been grounded for five years over my one big failure."

That failure was precisely what he wanted to hear about. Five years ago, she was second-in-command, and one of the few survivors, of the disastrous 2119

Chickering Expedition to Mars. Six officers, including Commander Chickering, had died during a summit attempt on the massive volcano Olympus Mons. The purpose of that venture was unclear, but Harte knew one thing: Ruby Ladd had not been part of it.

As the highest-ranking survivor, she assumed command of what was left of the expedition. The subsequent investigation cleared her of all wrongdoing, which implied she was under suspicion, though the official report was ambiguous as to details. Rumors hinted at incompetence, sabotage, mutiny, even murder. Anything she might have said in her defense was not part of the public record; neither did SCEI place responsibility on anyone else. The disaster was deemed an accident and the case closed. All Harte knew for sure was that Ruby Ladd had been grounded for five years. Then, as if back from the dead, she was given command of a major, high-profile expedition. Which she wore as comfortably as those low-heeled leather boots.

Harte hid his eagerness behind a mask of professionalism. "But you were quite young even when you served under Chickering, and now you have a command of your own. Someone must believe in you." She pressed a hand to her chest in what seemed an unconscious gesture. "I'm sorry, Commander; are you all right?"

She glanced at her hand, then dropped it to her side. "I'm fine. Dr. Mack can attest to that."

"The Boss is the fittest person aboard." The doctor's low, velvety voice distracted Harte for a moment with thoughts about narration. It was a voice to instill both comfort and confidence.

"So, my so-called success. You'd be amazed where you can get just by showing up on time and doing your work."

Great. A grinder. No fun at all. He kept his face impassive. "I'm sure there must be talent involved, too."

"Possibly. Mostly hard work and motivation, though. I powered through school and received my astronautics degree at nineteen."

"You must have had great plans. What did you want to do?"

"This." Her gesture took in the whole ship, or for all he knew, the whole solar system. He was certain she didn't mean the galley. "I always wanted to fly spaceships and see as much of the universe as I could. I wanted to be part of something important, something that could make a difference. My greatest fear was they'd cancel SCEI before I got to be part of it." She pronounced it *Sky*. He'd heard that before and thought it pretentious and forced, but coming from her, it sounded right.

"But they didn't cancel it, and you achieved your goal quickly. I'll bet your parents were proud."

"Don't bet much, because you'd lose. They thought it was just a phase. They wanted me to go into law or politics."

"What halfway decent parent wants *that* for a kid?" The joke failed; she scowled at him. "Sorry, I'm no comedian. But why did they want that?"

"You have to understand, my parents were activists — idealists. I was born the year after the States broke up."

"Really! Me, too — San Francisco. But I'm based in Seattle now."

Her expression warmed a trifle. "That's my hometown. Mom and Dad were part of the movement that organized the Northwest Union."

"How exciting!" Harte said, though he cared little about the politics of his adopted country. "What did they do?"

"Dad was on the Sustainability Committee. He was one of the drivers behind our farm co-op system. Mom formed committees, led marches, and probably drafted legislation to guarantee no family lacked food, shelter, health care or childcare."

"That's ... a lot. I see where you get your drive."

She frowned. "They both wanted me to do my part to help humankind; they didn't understand what good I might do away from the planet. But ironically, their drive to ensure all children had the same advantages I did meant I was on my own a lot. I was free to pursue my own interests even if my folks didn't share them."

"Such as?"

She gave him a long look. "Space travel." She had the grace not to add, "duh." He bit his tongue and tilted his head to signal interest. "Cooking." He smiled. "Basketball." It was impossible to hide his surprise on that one, but he kept quiet in hopes she'd spill something unusual. "Religion, for a while." Dr. Mack shook her head and continued slicing a baguette.

"Your family didn't share that?"

"They were too busy believing in the movement. Still — mostly, just space travel. Before I even started high school, I had it all mapped out: how to join the Commercial Space Corps, what kind of college program would best get me into pilot training, what courses and grades I would need in high school to get into that program." She folded her arms. "By the time my folks figured out what I was up to, it was too late."

She was warming to the subject, and Harte wanted to keep her going. Maybe she'd tell him what he wanted to know without any coaxing. Maybe she'd smile again. "Wow. Makes me wonder what I might have accomplished with some kind of plan."

"There are other kinds of success."

"You speak of your parents in the past tense — are they still living?"

"Dad is. He's retired now."

As they talked, a savory odor of grilled salmon filled the galley. Harte's mouth watered and his stomach growled. A tone signaled that the fish was hot.

"I hope we can continue this conversation another time … Boss."

She gave him a smile so sweet it had to be fake. "You can hope, but I know what you're after. The answer is no."

He pretended to be hurt. "Don't you like me, Commander Ladd?"

"I admire your work, Mr. Gunner. You take nice pictures. But there are some things I don't talk about. Get used to it."

The entire party took Ruby's cue and dressed up for their first meal together. Harte Gunner put on a black cashmere sport coat over his turtleneck. Dr. Eyestone still wore a tropical shirt, but this one was made of silk in shades of blue and purple.

"Now why is it I shouldn't wear the red one?" he asked.

"Seriously bad luck," Betty Nguyen said. She wore a dress uniform similar to Ruby's, but with less gold trim.

"Anybody puts on a red shirt is asking to be fucked up," Nielson added.

"Oh, please." Lee Keith said with a prim shake of the head. "Superstition, plain and simple."

"Of course it's superstition!" Nielson sputtered. "Where do you think superstitions come from? Bad shit goes down, you don't do that again. Wearing a red shirt gets you killed, period. So don't."

Ruby shook her head. Whether you sailed the sea or the stars, you couldn't escape that kind of logic. She didn't share the superstition. Then again, she hadn't packed anything red, either.

Dr. Mack looked to Ruby before they began to pass the dishes of food. "May I say grace?"

Ruby glanced around the table. Gunner raised his eyebrows, Wild watched her with a knowing smile, the others looked variously positive, baffled, or uncomfortable. "Let's observe a moment of silence."

She closed her eyes and tried to clear her mind, but it raced with preparations and excitement about the upcoming expedition.

"Amen," Dr. Mack whispered.

Ruby smiled at her and nodded. She admired the physician's faith, even if she didn't share it anymore.

The dinner was a great success. The salmon runs were beginning to recover, but it was still a special treat. In addition to the fish, she allowed each person one glass of wine. They wouldn't get king salmon and wine every night, but there were other little luxuries squirreled away for later in the expedition. Morale was key on these long missions, and this would be the longest yet.

Ruby made sure Harte Gunner sat near her for the meal. Although he seemed honest and transparent, she wanted to be aware of any "casual conversations" he struck up, at least for now. It hurt nothing to stroke his ego by seating him with the leaders of the expedition. She couldn't afford to let one man's vanity endanger the mission, when it was easy enough to keep him happy. Confined to a ship this way, diplomacy was as important as morale.

"If this is a party, how about some music?" Chip Nielson asked after the table was cleared. Without waiting for an answer, he pulled a harmonica from his pocket and launched into a lively tune. Several members of the party clapped and stomped along. Nguyen and Crean got up and danced. Curley grinned and darted out of the mess.

Ruby had decided to tolerate Nielson's prickly personality in light of his gifts as a mechanic. She had suppressed any memory of his harmonica playing until now. He was a competent musician, but the harmonica was one of her least-favorite instruments, second only to the …

"Banjo!" Dr. Curley burst in, wielding said instrument.

Ruby sighed and forced a smile onto her face. Curley knew what he was doing, and his shyness disappeared when he played. Then Gunner started to sing. He had a fine, strong baritone voice that encouraged others to join in. Ruby sang along on a few songs herself. In spite of the instrumentation, so much music and laughter at the outset had to bode well for the expedition.

She went to her quarters in a good mood, undressed, and lay down in her bag. It was nice to know where "down" was, even with only one-sixth Earth gravity. She hoped she wouldn't be too excited to sleep. It was always difficult the night before launch. Space travel never got old — though space sickness did. But maybe this time would be different.

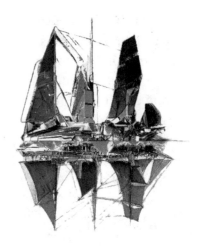

Chapter 4

2124/08/26: You can't play basketball in zero gravity.

— Commander Ladd's Expedition Journal

Ruby rose early on launch day with plans to make breakfast for the whole party. Her good mood improved when she arrived in the galley. Someone had stowed all the fresh food and neatly stacked the empty bins by the airlock. That kind of initiative was exactly what she wanted to see on this expedition.

She removed two dozen huckleberry muffins from the freezer compartment and set them in the oven to warm. While they heated, she brewed coffee and filled a lidded beaker that reminded her of children's sippy cups, only more tightly sealed. You pumped the beverage in through one valve, then drank it through another — no leakage, and thanks to the ultrasonic cleaning unit in the galley, easy to sanitize and reuse.

She took the cup to Betty Nguyen on the bridge. She had been on watch overnight and wouldn't get to sleep until after the launch.

"Good morning," Ruby said.

The navigator leaped to her feet. "Good morning, ma'am."

"No need for formality. Here, I brought you coffee."

Nguyen took the beaker. "Thanks, Boss." She sipped and sighed.

"Ready for launch?" Ruby asked.

"I can't wait! I know we're supposed to be adults, but on the first day of a mission, I'm like a kid on Christmas."

Ruby smiled. "I know the feeling."

Nguyen sipped her coffee and gazed out the viewport. "I still wonder why the Skipper hired me. He barely knows me, except that I'm 'by the book' and ..."

"And he's not," Ruby finished for her. "My guess is that's why. People like us balance people like him. You might not remember, but I was in your spaceflight class about ten years ago."

"Oh, I remember," Nguyen said with a laugh. "I've kept an eye on you ever since. Always figured I'd be working for you one day. I actually thought it would happen sooner than this. You seemed to know where you were headed from an early age. Younger than I was, anyway."

"This time I had to wait for the powers to agree with me," Ruby said. "But you must have figured out your own path in good enough time, too."

"After several detours. I was supposed to be a dancer."

"*Supposed to be?*" Ruby asked.

"I took ballet lessons when I was little, and my mom got the idea I was good enough to dance professionally," Nguyen explained. "I kept trying after I no longer enjoyed it. Then I took an astronomy class for the science credit. Changed my major and my life, and here we are."

Ruby smiled. "I look forward to working with you, as a colleague this time. I'm sorry I couldn't give you nice quarters like the rest of the officers. These ships don't usually fly with more than three people."

"Oh, I know this class of ship well," Nguyen replied. "I'm happy to be here, even if I have to play housemother."

Ruby grinned at that. "Shall we wake the others?"

Nguyen flipped a switch. She jumped as a recorded rooster crowed from every speaker on the ship.

The commander laughed at her reaction. "Sorry, I didn't know it would be that loud. Good thing your coffee cup has a lid."

"Is this how we'll wake up every day?" the navigator asked.

"Not likely. I had them put in an assortment of random alarms, so it shouldn't be the same two days in a row. I'll send up your relief. Then you can come have breakfast."

She met Captain Anderson in the galley. He had taken the muffins out, and they filled the narrow space with their aroma. "This is a treat," he said. "But are you sure you should eat before a launch?"

"Very funny. That's not for hours, and we all deserve a good breakfast."

"True." He was quiet for a long time. "How do you feel about going back to Mars?"

Ruby braced herself for a twinge, like a lump in the throat but lower down, nearer the heart. She'd lived with this chronic ache, for which there seemed no physical cause, since that last mission. It was a heavy stone in her chest that sometimes cut like shards of glass. She gave it a name — the Pearl, as if it were her evil twin — and did her best to work around it. She didn't have to pretend with the Skipper, but she still took her time before answering.

"On the one hand, I wish it wasn't part of the mission." She tried to smile. "On the other hand, it's probably good to go back and get it over with. But I'm glad we're not staying. I'm glad we get to go past it."

"I'm with you on that. I can't wait to surf the Belt."

He took a muffin and went to relieve Nguyen on the bridge. Ruby found two vacuum-sealed pouches of pre-cooked scrambled eggs in the small refrigerator, each the equivalent of a dozen eggs. She emptied all of one and half the other into a dish for heating and returned the remainder to the refrigerator to be part of a future meal.

When the rest of the party gathered for breakfast, Ruby was pleased to see they'd all complied with her request for shorter hair. Dr. Eyestone had shaved his head bald, which made him look older, though his face still struck her as boyish. They greeted the muffins and scrambled eggs with enthusiasm.

"These blueberry muffins taste homemade," Gunner said. His newly clipped hair looked to be the maximum allowable length, and carefully styled. "Who do we have to thank for that?"

"My bet's on the Boss," Wild said.

She gave him a nod. "And they're huckleberry." She had baked them weeks ago, and sent them ahead, frozen, with the rest of the supplies.

"So you bake, too?" Gunner reached for another muffin.

"And she probably picked the berries," Dr. Mack said.

"When did you have time to learn to bake, on top of everything else?" Gunner asked.

Ruby laughed. "I made time, as soon as real food became readily available."

"You taught yourself?"

"Sure. My dad's work sparked an interest in food, but he didn't cook."

"And your mother?"

Wild chuckled. "I never saw Minnie in the kitchen."

"Minnie?" Gunner asked.

"My mom — Minnie Bowman. And Wild's right, she never cooked a meal from scratch in her life. But they didn't have much to work with when she was young. You grow up with synthetic food, your first real huckleberry is a revelation!"

"Amen to that," Gunner said. "Sometimes I just want to settle down somewhere and plant a big garden. I'm not sure it would make a good doc, though."

Ruby stood to address the entire party. "Let's clean up here, and then if you haven't called home yet, take care of that before you secure your belongings. Launch protocols require that everyone wear the full spacesuit and helmet. Please allow time to change. We'll meet on the bridge by 1400 hours."

The rest of the morning passed in a blur of preparations. Everyone with family on Earth called home, most likely the last live calls they'd make for a long time. The farther away they got, the more energy required to transmit and the longer the delay. Except in an emergency, recordings and text messages would take the place of live calls. Ruby made no calls, but she sent a brief message to her father.

> *Dad,*
> *I thought you should know I'm going out again — Mars, then the Asteroid Belt. I'm the Boss this time, and I have a good group with me, so I hope to stay out of the news with anything but glowing reports. If you want to check in, you know how to reach me.*
> *-Ruby*

She thought about changing the signature to one of her old nicknames. When she was small, he used to pretend to forget her name, and call her "Onyx," "Jasper," or her favorite, "Sapphire." But that was a long time ago. Now he didn't call her anything.

The garbage and transport bins were unloaded and all gear secured for launch. At 1400 hours, Ruby finally assembled the entire expedition party on the bridge.

"Boss, there's still a helmet on the rack."

"Thank you … Dr. Eyestone." Ruby had to read the helmeted figure's name badge to know who it was. The white suits were identical except in size. "It may be an extra, but I'll take roll call before we launch, just to be sure."

When all eleven were accounted for, they strapped into the two rows of blue upholstered seats behind Captain Anderson and the navigator. Ruby made a discreet check of the pocket on the side of her seat to make sure it contained at least one valved space-sickness bag, just in case. Matter went in but could not come out. Some things you definitely did not want floating around.

The Skipper ran through a checklist with the base. He received the OK and a tractor towed *Endurance* into position to be launched by the spaceport's mass driver.

Ruby gripped her armrests as the ship's smooth acceleration pressed her into her seat. Though many things could go wrong on a space mission, launch was generally considered the most dangerous point, closely followed by landing. But the ship lifted flawlessly from the Moon's surface. When they were clear of the base, Anderson lit the main engines to get into a higher orbit. They accelerated around the Moon before shooting away into space.

"That's odd." Nguyen studied a display panel.

Ruby couldn't see what she was looking at. "Problem?"

"Probably not, but this says our mass is off from calculations by about fifty kilos."

"Too much or too little?" Ruby asked.

"Too much," Nguyen replied. "We subtracted Mr. Green and added the last load of supplies. Could be the fresh food, though. It's not as consistent as packaged."

"I blame the burgers at the base." Wild's comment got a laugh. The burgers at the Armstrong cafeteria were notorious calorie bombs.

They remained strapped into their seats as long as the rockets fired. Once they were aimed in the right direction, Anderson shut down the engines. "And that's what I call a launch," he announced. "Please feel free to remove your helmets and float about the cabin."

Ruby was only too happy to get out of her helmet. Space sickness and helmets did not mix. So far, she felt all right, but it was early. She unfastened her harness and floated out of her seat. With an expert kick off the armrest, she propelled herself to Anderson's position and stopped herself with a touch on his seatback.

"Nicely done, Skipper." They shook hands and grinned at each other. Now the expedition was officially underway.

Nielson immediately started a pool for their arrival date on Mars. Lee Keith tutted about gambling, but nearly everyone got in on it.

"We should get Crean up here," Anderson said. "I'm about to deploy the sail."

Ruby beckoned to the physicist, who appeared to be enjoying zero gravity as if this were his first mission, not his tenth. He and Harte Gunner were turning flips in mid-air, with no apparent dizziness. "Mr. Gunner, you'll want to see this, too."

Both men joined her and watched as Anderson deployed the solar sail. It had its own panel of instruments, including a video screen to display images from an external camera. As they watched, the sail unfurled like a vast shiny wing.

"Beautiful," Dr. Crean murmured. He consulted the other instruments. "And working perfectly. Look, it's already adding a little acceleration."

"How does that work?" Gunner asked.

"Light pressure — photons hitting the sail," Dr. Crean explained. "It's not enough for us to feel, but it'll add up over the long distance we'll travel. If all goes well, this solar sail could cut months off our travel time."

"Can I get a copy of the video feed for my doc? That was a very striking shot."

"It was, wasn't it?" Ruby shook her head as he did a backflip. He was a show-off, but he had a good eye.

Even by-the-book Betty Nguyen rose from her seat and executed ballet moves in midair. A tone sounded and she pushed herself back into her seat. "SCEI is on the line."

"On speaker," Ruby said. They had called the ship, not her.

"Beautiful launch, *Endurance*, or so I'm told," the voice of Wesley James said.

"You didn't watch the feed?" Ruby asked.

"I was in a meeting that ran long. Have you deployed the solar sail?"

"Jamie Crean says it appears to be working perfectly, already adding some acceleration."

"Excellent! With technological advances like that, we'll be colonizing in no time. Keep me posted."

"Will do."

The call ended and the members of the party not suffering from nausea continued to play. Ruby herself took great care to remain oriented to the ship's up and down. She had always suffered from space sickness to some degree. How would Wesley James sell that aspect of space life to aspiring colonists? But so far, she had only a mild headache and queasiness, an improvement over past missions. She wasn't the only one feeling off. Dr. Mack retreated to her quarters with the onset of nausea. Eyestone went to the robotics lab, claiming he needed to work, though he took a space-sickness bag with him. Dr. Curley, the geologist, became quieter than usual and remained towards the rear of the bridge, gazing out the forward viewport. The administrator, Mr. Keith, looked the queasiest, but he insisted on working even though he obviously felt awful.

"Commander Ladd, how many eggs did you use at breakfast?" he asked.

"Almost all of them."

"*All* of them?!"

"Don't panic — we didn't *eat* all of them. I put some away for tomorrow."

Dr. Crean tumbled past them and bumped Keith in such a way that the administrator flipped upside down.

Wild and Anderson tried not to laugh; Nielson guffawed openly.

"Oops, sorry there! I'm out of practice," the physicist called. "Everything about us is evolved for one G. Surprisingly tricky to adjust." He shrugged and left the bridge.

Before Ruby could right Keith, Harte Gunner had done it. Mr. Keith's face had a greenish cast, but he maintained his composure. "Thank you, Mr. Gunner," he said, a slight tremor in his voice.

Ruby took his arm and helped him move away from the bridge. "When you're feeling better, will you set up a schedule for use of the exercise equipment? We need to keep everyone in good condition. And while you're at it, we'll need a cleaning schedule for the common areas."

He brightened immediately. "I'll get on it right away."

The next morning, Ruby woke to a bugle call and the sense that she had no limbs. Even when she opened her eyes and could see them, they had no obvious connection to her body. As soon as she willed her arms to move, they did, and their relationship to her returned — only to disappear again as soon as she relaxed. It was also unclear whether she was lying down or dangling from a wall, but at least the nausea had passed. She climbed out of the sleeping bag and pulled herself into what passed for a bathroom: no running water and a disconcerting suction thing for a toilet. That was something she hadn't missed when she was grounded. But all these things meant they were finally on their way.

She took a sponge bath, washed her two centimeters of hair with rinseless shampoo, dressed in her work uniform, and went to breakfast. She was startled to find Harte Gunner serving it up, but then again, he had been to cooking school. So far, no one else had signed up for meal-prep duty. She supposed she would have to ask Keith to make a schedule for that, too. Or she could ask Gunner to take it on permanently, though he'd probably be insulted. But she liked his cooking. He had put together breakfast burritos with cheese, the remaining eggs, and some pre-cooked chorizo sausage. It was exactly the kind of self-contained, hand-held meal that worked in zero gravity.

After breakfast, she stayed in the messroom and started a log of the expedition so far. A data recorder on the bridge would automatically log technical details of the ship's performance, to which Captain Anderson could add his own notes, as needed. Ruby's task was more subjective and anecdotal — to make observations on morale, interpersonal relationships within the party, and general well-being. The intangibles that could mean success or failure in a mission this long. She planned to send monthly digests of these notes to SCEI and use them to compile her final report at the conclusion of the expedition. It was too early to have much to report, but she noted the minor problem regarding the cook, as well as the camaraderie of their first evening.

Before she had finished entering her observations, her comm buzzed loudly to announce an urgent incoming message.

Ruby frowned as she read it. "Mr. Nielson, this is your area. I'm forwarding the details. Please tell me it's nothing."

Nielson read over the information. "Fuck," he muttered. He checked another document and frowned. "Aw, double fuck."

Harte Gunner was the only one to appear shocked at the matter-of-fact vulgarity. Ruby kept her own expression neutral.

Nielson looked up at the assembled party. "Anybody with tech skills, come with me."

Harte leaped to follow Nielson. He liked to tinker with anything electronic or mechanical, or just to watch someone else with skills. Dr. Crean and Dr. Eyestone fell in after him. Nielson pulled himself out of the mess, through an open airlock, and down a sloping passage to the cargo deck. He stopped outside a locked compartment and glanced at his followers. "I'm not surprised to see these two, but why is the camera guy here?"

Harte bristled. Camera guy? "The name's Gunner, and I have a few repair skills."

Nielson nodded. "Ever fix a fusion reactor?"

Harte's jaw dropped. He didn't even try to answer.

Nielson unlocked the hatch, and they went inside. The reactor was smaller than Harte expected, about the size of a large passenger vehicle. "The manufacturer just notified us of a recall of some turbines. I checked the serial number on their list against my specs, and sure as goddamn, ours is one of the defective ones. It's not all bad news, though, because we have a spare and it's not on the list. Otherwise, we'd have to limp back to Armstrong and sit on our asses till they sent us a good one. Which would probably mean losing our launch window."

"I didn't realize this ship was fusion powered," Harte said.

Nielson scowled. "Well, it is. This is the goddamned power plant for the whole ship, including the main engines. New compact design, supposedly idiot-proof. It better be, because, without reliable electricity, we can't go anywhere."

Following the manufacturer's step-by-step instructions, they were able to swap the turbines without stopping the reaction, which would have been a challenge to restart. By the time the repair was complete, Harte was shaking from the strain. Nielson slapped him on the back. "You were right, Gunner. You do have some skills. Welcome aboard. Now let's have some fun."

Ruby closed her expedition journal as an appointment popped up — it was her turn to use the gym. She returned to her quarters and changed into a T-shirt and shorts, then made her way to the cargo hold, where she found Wild, Crean and Nielson attempting to invent a new sport — Zero-G Basketball. Lee Keith begged to join, too, so he must have been feeling better since the previous day. Gunner recorded their antics, though he was laughing so hard he could barely hold the camera still. He soon put it aside and joined the game. It wasn't really basketball. Everything that made basketball what it was — running, dribbling, shooting — required gravity. Dribbling and running were impossible. Passing had interesting consequences for the passer. Shooting required shoving or spiking the ball straight into the hoop. Mostly, the players were spinning helplessly, laughing and swearing as they caromed off one another. Nielson's language was particularly salty, especially toward the hapless Lee Keith, who seemed to have little experience of the game under any conditions.

"Hey, Boss! Stow your comm in that locker and join us!" Wild called. "We're a player short of three-on-three."

Dr. Crean looked at her, then at him. "Are you sure?"

"Don't let her size fool you. Our commander was a devastating point guard in her youth. She always could call the plays. Besides, it might make Nielson watch his language!"

Ruby grinned and removed her comm holster from her belt, adding it to the collection in the storage locker. "And it doesn't look like height is an advantage in this game." She pushed off and stole the ball from Gunner as she passed him. "Who's on my side?"

She had Wild and Keith on her team, against Gunner, Crean, and Nielson. With practice, they gained control, though Keith had sluggish reflexes and seemed unlikely ever to come up to the level of the others. It didn't help that Nielson continued to taunt him, but at least he used a less vulgar idiom.

It was remarkable how much effort was required to move so slowly, but they were all sweating and breathing hard. Ruby was grateful for the reclamation system that distilled their excretions and exhalations into an emergency water supply. She didn't like to think about drinking it, but without it, the humidity would have been unbearable.

The score was 10-6 in her side's favor when the PA crackled to life. "Commander Ladd and Mr. Wild to the bridge," Ms. Nguyen's unruffled voice said. "An urgent situation requires your attention."

"Wouldn't you know, just when we were winning!" She pushed off from a bulkhead and returned to the locker to collect her comm, then made for the exit, Wild right behind her. She arrived at the bridge still out of breath. "What's up, Skipper?"

The attempt at zero-G levity did not draw a smile from Anderson. He looked grim. "I don't know how it happened, Boss. We have a stowaway."

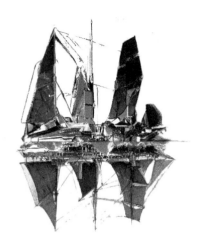

Chapter 5

2124/08/26: I didn't know a robot could be cute. I believe they will add unexpected charm and comedy to the documentary. Still looking for the narrative …

— Holden Gunner's Production Journal

"Here's our extra fifty kilos." Behind Captain Anderson, Betty Nguyen gripped the stowaway's wrist with one hand, a handhold with the other.

Even this level of restraint seemed unnecessary. The skinny captive somehow managed to slump in zero gravity, dejected and resigned.

The stowaway lifted her gaze to meet Ruby's. She was definitely more girl than woman. Her face had a washed-out greenish tinge to it. Most of her long hair was almost equally light with obvious dark roots. The bleached tresses floated around her head.

"Thank you, Ms. Nguyen. You may return to your duties."

The navigator released the stowaway. The girl rubbed her arm but made no move to flee.

"Well, Skipper? What's the story?" Ruby asked.

"Betty, you want to tell it?"

"Yes, *Captain*." Nguyen gave Anderson a pointed look. He shook his head, smiling, and gestured for her to continue. "I came out of my quarters and saw someone I didn't recognize sneak out of the head, on her way to the galley. Our young friend here is not as adept at navigating in zero G, and I caught her easily. But how she got aboard, I have no idea."

Ruby turned to the girl. "I'm Commander Ruby Ladd, and this is Mr. Wild. You have some explaining to do. Let's start with your name and age."

"Amelia Blackborow, ma'am. I'm … almost eighteen. And just so you know, if I barf, it's nothing personal."

Ruby tried to maintain a severe expression, but it was difficult not to smile with sympathy. "Thank you for the warning. The feeling should pass soon. But just in case — Skipper, will you give Ms. Blackborow a bag, please?"

The captain reached into the pocket of the nearest seat for one of the valved space-sickness bags. The girl accepted it with a grateful smile, but Ruby doubted she would need it. She already looked more comfortable.

"Now tell me, if you will, how you happen to be with us on *Endurance*. Stowing aboard would be one challenge, but how did you even get on the Moon shuttle?"

"I was with Lloyd Green, ma'am. He was allowed to bring an assistant when he came up to cook at Armstrong. He was waiting for her at the launch loop, but she flaked out before quarantine. So he gave me the ticket, we quarantined together, and I worked with him in the cafeteria at the base. When he got this job, I helped bring over the supplies. I might have mentioned that I wanted to go on a space mission someday, and he had the idea that I should stay aboard — I could be his assistant, just like I was at the base. I'd just have to stay out of sight until it was too late to send me back."

Ruby held her head. They were barely underway and already things she hadn't planned — people she hadn't even met — were complicating the expedition. Green substituting for the injured cook, this stowaway substituting for his wayward assistant ... Just how many cooks did it take to fill one almost unnecessary position?

"That's the thing he needed to tell me. And the extra helmet ..." She looked at the stowaway. "You know I fired him, don't you?"

Amelia nodded. "I thought something like that must have happened, when I didn't see him for so long."

Ruby snapped her fingers. "*You* put away the supplies!"

"Yes, after everyone went to bed. I didn't want anything to spoil." She glanced at the Skipper, Nguyen, and Wild, then back at Ruby. "So what happens now?"

That was a good question. This girl was a minor and should be returned immediately. But turning back would lose them more than just the four or five days' travel time. They would have to resupply and get on the schedule for the mass driver again, but that delay would be nothing compared to the bureaucratic quagmire surrounding an underage stowaway. While they waited, the solar system would keep circling. Mars would move out of easy range. They could lose their shot, maybe for good.

Ruby looked the girl in the eyes. "When's your birthday, Amelia?"

"August 30. Why?"

"Do you have a food-handler's permit?"

"Sure, I needed it to work at Armstrong. Why?"

Ruby turned to Captain Anderson. "Skipper, let the log show that we discovered an eighteen-year-old stowaway … four days from now."

"Commander, I don't think —" Nguyen began.

Anderson raised a hand to cut her off. "Let's hear her out. Are you sure about this, Boss?"

"I will not risk losing this expedition. And she has the right attitude."

"The girl's underage," Nguyen objected. "She's had no training, no physical exam. This breaks so many rules."

Anderson looked at the First Officer. "Wild?"

"It's the Boss's decision," Wild said. "I support her."

"I take full responsibility," Ruby assured the other officers. She grinned. "And we needed a cook." She held out her hand to the girl and they shook on it. "Welcome aboard, Ms. Blackborow. Provided you pass your physical, you're a member of the crew. Come with me and I'll show you the galley and your quarters."

Blackborow grabbed a handful of her straw-colored mane. "Can we do something about my hair? It's too long, and I'm sick of this color."

"Absolutely." Ruby was relieved that she didn't have to suggest it. "We'll do that first."

Harte soon dropped out of the basketball game, but recorded as Crean, Nielson, and Keith continued to play. It would be good footage for the final doc, though he regretted that he hadn't gotten any shots while Commander Ladd was playing. She brought a spark of athletic intelligence to the game that none of the others could match. Not to mention she was more photogenic by far — especially in shorts.

"That's enough recreational footage," he said. "I should try to find somebody actually working."

Grabbing a handhold, he propelled himself to the other end of the remodeled cargo hold. Labs had been set up on the port side, sleeping quarters to starboard. He headed down the port passage. Dr. Crean was out, of course, but he found Dr. Mack setting up microscopes and scanners of various kinds.

"May I have permission to film your lab, Dr. Mack?"

She looked around with a welcoming smile. "Go ahead. Just don't touch anything."

"Have you ever done voiceover work?" Harte asked. "You have a beautiful speaking voice."

She gave a throaty laugh. "Thank you. I haven't, but I was into musical theater in my teens. For work, I've never been anything but a doctor."

"Have you always been a space doctor?"

"No, I was in primary care for almost twenty years. But I stayed involved with research, too. And one night, when my son was about fifteen, he caught me gazing at the Moon and said, 'Go for it, Mom. You know you want to. We'll be fine.' So I looked into it, and the next thing I knew, I had a position with SCEI."

"That must have been quite an adjustment for your family."

"They're very supportive. This will be the longest I've ever been away, though."

"How did you get involved with this expedition?"

"Ruby asked me early on, back in the planning stages."

"You call her Ruby?"

"Force of habit. Commander Ladd, I should say. The Boss. We've worked on projects before, but this is our first long mission together."

"Is it an issue at all, working for someone so much younger?"

"Not with her. She's ... ageless. She thinks of everything, and then has two or three alternatives in her back pocket, just in case. That invites confidence."

"So I've seen already. Was that always the case?"

Dr. Mack frowned. "I'm not sure I follow you."

"You know — on the Chickering Expedition, for instance."

She smiled and shook her head. "Sorry, I wasn't part of that one. The captain was, and Mr. Nielson, I believe. You'd have to ask them."

"Thank you for your time, Doctor."

Harte got no answer at the geology lab but found the geologist in the robotics lab. Ancient pop music filled the room, adolescent boys singing in close harmony. Dr. Curley and Dr. Eyestone had both put on special boots that allowed them to get on the floor with the robots.

"How do the robots stay attached to the floor?"

Dr. Eyestone glanced at Harte with a grin. "Their feet have gecko pads, just like our boots — they can cling to smooth surfaces. I'll have one move for you. Samson, walk."

"Samson?" Harte asked.

"We have to call him something, right? This is Delilah, that's Hercules, and over there is Sally. I call this one Sir Ernest — he's got that whole stiff-upper-lip thing going on — and behind him is Slag. He's a punk. I haven't decided what to call that other one."

Harte couldn't tell one from another, but he was happy to film the seven spherical, knee-high bots. They had four legs and a single round sensor at what he took to be the front. He expected insect or spider-like movements, but the exaggerated care of each step evoked nothing so much as an arthritic dog.

"Will an asteroid be smooth enough for the pads to cling?"

"No, but they have extendable spikes to help them grip — like cleats or crampons. Delilah, give me your foot. Thank you. Now, extend." The resulting bristle of spikes was like the claws of an enraged, eight-toed cat, without the hissing.

"So they respond to voice commands," Harte observed. "Do they talk?"

"Not in words, but they're capable of a range of tones that can be used to signal a human or another bot." A chorus of beeps and hoots ensued.

"How will they function on an actual asteroid?"

"Various tools extend from hatches in the body as needed. They can dig or scrape the surface, then assay the material on site. They'll communicate the results to me, and Curley here can take a closer, in-person look at any promising asteroids."

Harte turned the camera on the geologist as Dr. Curley laid an ore sample in front of one of the robots. A hatch opened and a tool extended to scratch the sample. The taciturn scientist watched without speaking.

"Dr. Curley, this isn't a silent film. Since you didn't bring your banjo, maybe you should say something."

He glanced at the camera with a shy smile. His raincloud-gray eyes should have belonged to a stormier personality. "What about?"

"I don't know! Rocks, I guess."

"Can you be more specific?"

"Well, what are we looking for? What do you hope to find in the Asteroid Belt?" Harte asked.

"Any asteroid worth analyzing," Dr. Curley replied.

"I heard Dr. Crean saying they weren't close together," Harte said. "Is it likely we won't find any?"

"We'll be actively looking for them with radar, so we should be able to chase down quite a few," Dr. Curley said. "Will they be big enough to be worth it? I hope so! Once we find them, I'm interested in a number of resources. There are three basic types of asteroids: C, M, and S — carbonaceous, metallic, and silicate. All useful materials, depending on what you want them for."

"So it's sort of a treasure hunt," Harte said.

Dr. Curley scratched his head. "I guess you could say that. We're not likely to find gems on this trip. They're what first got me interested in geology, though."

"What, like rubies and sapphires?"

Dr. Eyestone chuckled. "There's only one Ruby on this expedition."

"Oof, one striver like that is plenty," Harte said. "Sorry, no offense. You probably know her better than I do."

The two scientists exchanged a glance and shook their heads. "Not really," Dr. Eyestone replied. "Dr. Crean recommended me for the mission. I wasn't about to pass up the opportunity, no matter who was commanding the expedition."

"So you're not concerned about her … reputation?" Harte asked, silently hoping for something juicy and dramatic.

"Her reputation for not dying, you mean?" Dr. Curley said. "I can't speak for John here, but I don't follow gossip. But I don't see how any of that stuff with Chickering was her fault."

"Fair enough," Harte said. "Let's get back to gemstones, then. Ruby happens to be my birthstone. July 9."

"Chemically, they're an aluminum oxide, AL2O3, the red form of the mineral corundum," Dr. Curley said. "Any other color is sapphire — bet you didn't know that. Rubies can be brownish or purplish, but blood-red is the most prized. Rarer than diamonds, almost as hard, but prettier, in my opinion. But if we're really lucky, we might find ice."

"Ice? In the Asteroid Belt?"

"Sure, you crash an ice asteroid onto Mars, and you've got a source of water vapor for an atmosphere. Or the ingredients of rocket fuel."

"OK. So once you find an asteroid you like, then what happens?"

"Then I send the robots out to verify composition," Dr. Eyestone said. "Those with the right make-up will be tagged with beacons so they can be located later. Then we collect the robots and repeat the process until supplies get low enough that we need to head for home."

Harte lowered his camera. "Thank you for your time, gentlemen. I'll see you later."

He left the lab area, his mind awhirl with images of asteroids and gemstones. One in particular. He agreed with Curley's assessment — rarer than diamonds, and prettier — but almost as hard. He had the bruises to prove it.

Ruby showed Blackborow how to efficiently propel herself along the passages. She took the girl to her own quarters for a haircut. She snipped off the bleached length with scissors, then neatened what remained with trimmers attached to a vacuum pump that drew the clippings into the waste system.

The girl gazed out the large viewport. "Are we really going to Mars?"

"Yes, and beyond. The real meat of this expedition is in the Asteroid Belt."

"Wow." Blackborow drew the word out in dreamy fashion. She looked older with her brown hair cut short, but still sounded like the teenager she was.

Ruby found it encouraging that Blackborow's sense of wonder had survived a couple days of space sickness, but it was probably time for a reality check. "I hope you're not just looking for a thrill ride. You do know that you've signed on for a long mission — a year, eighteen months?" They left Ruby's quarters and made their way to the galley.

"The longer the better. This is what I've always wanted."

"You don't get homesick?"

Blackborow barked a derisive laugh. "I'm a runaway. I got over that already."

"Where'd you run away from?"

"Hoquiam. Do you know it?" Blackborow shook her head dismissively before Ruby could answer. "My mom put me on the train to spend the summer with Dad in Portland, but I changed the ticket and just kept going."

"After a year or so, you might miss the rain. And your parents must be worried."

"They both probably still think I'm with the other one. Anyway, they don't get me."

"Parents never do."

Blackborow scowled. "I'm serious! I don't think they believed I really wanted to be in the Space Corps. This'll show them I meant it."

"Even so, don't cast them off so easily. Do you have a comm?"

With an exquisite teenage eyeroll, Blackborow reached into her pocket and extracted a glittery purple unit.

"OK, not regulation, but it'll do. Call them, or at least send a message." Ruby thought about this for a moment. "On your birthday, or after."

"Yeah, OK."

"It's probably late to be asking this, but have you even finished high school?"

"I dropped out and got my GED in April. I was *done* with school, you know?"

Ruby hadn't dropped out; she had powered through and graduated at sixteen. "I do know." They had reached the galley. "I guess you're already familiar with some of this, but let's go over where everything is."

She opened various compartments to reveal chilled and frozen perishables, a fraction of the supplies, along with the larger volume of shelf-stable, self-heating MessPaks. "Those can be served as-is, or if you're feeling creative, you can open several and combine ingredients, or even sprinkle in some herbs." She pointed out the herb garden. "The MessPak meals are all sticky enough to stay in the tray in zero G. The trays and wrappers go into the composter afterwards."

Blackborow frowned. "What do you need with compost on a spaceship?"

"It's not for us," Ruby explained. "We'll add it to the greenhouses on Mars when we get there. OK, when this supply of MassPaks runs out, there are cases of them on the cargo deck." Ruby opened another compartment to display a supply of dense, high-nutrition NutriCubes. "We call 'em *dice*. I don't know why they make so many flavors; they all taste the same. But we won't be getting into those unless we absolutely have to. They'll keep you going, but ..." She made a face at the memory of the strong vitamin taste.

"I know. I had a couple while I was ... hiding." Blackborow peered into the freezer compartment. "Why so many tortillas?"

"A lot of carbs in a small volume, for one thing," Ruby replied. "And you can wrap pretty much anything in one and have a tidy, hand-held meal. Or use the sandwich press for a nice quesadilla. For variety, there are also frozen waffles. Mr. Keith, our administrator, is keeping an eye on the supply inventory, so be aware of what you're using. We can afford to eat well, but don't overdo it the first month out. Delay the NutriCubes as long as possible."

"You don't have to tell me twice."

"It will also be your responsibility to clean and sanitize this area after every meal," Ruby said. "You won't believe the stuff that floats around and gets trapped in odd corners. We all take turns cleaning the common areas. I'll have Mr. Keith add you to the rotation."

Blackborow peeked into all the lockers, familiarizing herself with where things were and what was available. She tugged on one door that wouldn't open. "Is this one stuck or locked?"

"Locked," Ruby replied. "I call that the morale locker. I have the access code for when we've earned a treat or a stronger drink than coffee."

"That's like something my mom would do," Blackborow said. "Don't you trust your people?"

Ruby considered her answer. "I ... don't know everyone well enough to guess how they'll respond to the challenges we're sure to face. Think about it — Lloyd Green drank a whole bottle of tequila before the expedition even began, because he was nervous. And also had a problem."

"Yeah, I never saw him drunk while he was working, but in the evenings ..." Blackborow shook her head.

"I doubt anyone in our party would drink up our whole supply," Ruby said. "Or eat all the cookies, or whatever. But when those kinds of treats come out, it will be because we all need or deserve them. We will always share. Because we're in this together."

With Ruby's input, Blackborow decided on menus for that day's lunch and dinner, and the next day's breakfast. "After this, I'll rely on you to decide," Ruby said. "You should move into your quarters now."

Blackborow gave her a sheepish smile. "I kind of already have. Green had me hide in his cabin, so my stuff is already there."

"I hate to ask. You weren't … sleeping with him, were you?"

"With Green? God, no!"

Ruby smiled. "That's a relief. We're not ready to risk pregnancy in low or zero gravity."

"You mean *nobody's* had sex in space yet?"

"Oh, I'm sure somebody's tried, but not me. And not you, either, if you want a future in the Space Corps."

Blackborow reddened. "Green wanted to, I'm sure, but he had … issues… I didn't need that."

"Neither did I. That's why I fired him." She shook the girl's hand again. "I think you're going to work out fine. Feel free to rest awhile, before you start lunch. And if you have any questions, don't hesitate to ask."

Blackborow looked like she might cry. "Are you sure? I mean, I appreciate it. But you're the *commander*. I'm just the cook."

"And on a shorter mission, we'd probably rarely even speak. But on something as long as this, we really are all in it together. Besides, I'm responsible for you. It's in my interest to know what's happening."

"Thank you, Commander. You won't be sorry."

Ruby escorted Blackborow to her quarters, then headed off with the intention of actually using the exercise room this time. When she reached the basketball court, the game had ended and all but one player had left. Lee Keith rotated despondently about a meter from the hoop.

"Need any help there, Mr. Keith?"

"Oh, Commander Ladd! I didn't see you come in. No, I'm fine. I'm just —"

She ignored his protests and pushed off. His back was to her as she collided with him, and she slammed him face first into the opposite bulkhead. "Sorry about that. Are you hurt?"

"Only my pride. I had everything under control, but I thank you for your help."

"What happened with the game?"

"Nothing much. After you and Mr. Wild left, Mr. Gunner dropped out to continue filming. Dr. Crean and Mr. Nielson offered to teach me the game — I don't know if you noticed, but I haven't had much experience. Somebody bumped into me and set me spinning."

That seemed familiar. On the bridge after launch, Dr. Crean had bumped Keith and flipped him over. He apologized afterward, so it was probably unintentional, but Ruby knew the physicist as something of a practical joker. She wouldn't put it past him to goose the rookie. But it was also clear that Nielson and Keith didn't much like each other. And what about Gunner? Was he the type to invent drama for the sake of his project?

"I'm sure it was an accident," the administrator continued, "but by the time I spun around, everyone had gone. But that's all right. It's very peaceful down here, all by oneself."

"So it is. If you don't mind, I'd like to experience that peace myself now. You may return to your duties, Mr. Keith."

He crept along the bulkhead to the locker to collect his comm, and from there to the exit. Ruby clung to a handhold and thought about things. One or more of the basketball players had left a shipmate alone and out of reach of a surface. That would not do.

But how to prevent a recurrence without a major confrontation? She didn't know who was to blame and didn't want to create unnecessary conflict this early in the mission. She made her way to the exercise room. Exercise always helped her think. She couldn't say she liked Lee Keith, but his function aboard *Endurance,* no matter how annoying, was as important as anyone's. She wouldn't have him, or anyone else, mistreated. They had too far to go.

Harte left the lab area, pleased with this latest footage. The intimate looks at the scientists in their labs would provide a nice contrast to the grand, sweeping space vistas he planned to include. He was especially happy with the robot segment. The little machines were oddly appealing, and he was sure audiences would love them.

A tone from his comm announced an appointment. He didn't know he had any. A message instructed him to report for daily fitness training. He understood the importance of regular exercise in low gravity conditions but rebelled against the regimentation. Still, he was near the designated workout area, and already in gym clothes from the basketball game. He used a handhold to change direction and propelled himself into the exercise room.

He wasn't alone. Commander Ladd was jogging — no, running — on a treadmill fitted with a vacuum device that simulated Earth gravity. He stowed his camera in a locker, settled himself on the seat of the exercise bike, fastened the seatbelt, and began to pedal.

"So, you're back," he said. "Everything all right on the bridge?" She glared at him. At least he hadn't been staring at her legs, obscured as they were by the equipment. He decided to delay asking for an on-camera interview. "What's up, Boss? You look troubled."

She gazed at him so long without saying anything that he was about to apologize and retract his question, harmless though it seemed. Then she took a deep breath, as if reaching a decision. "I'm pondering what someone might gain from bullying Mr. Keith. You, for example — stirring up drama?"

He blinked and forgot to pedal for a moment. "I'm not aware that I've bullied anyone." He resumed his workout. "Did something happen after I left the game?"

"You left the … Then I beg your pardon." Her smile looked forced, but at least she no longer seemed actively hostile. "At least that narrows it down."

"What happened?"

"I'm not sure. I came back and found Mr. Keith alone and stranded. Even you could not have gotten out of that without help, and he has nowhere near your skill at maneuvering in zero gravity."

"I'll take that as a compliment."

"That does not surprise me."

Not hostile. Still hard. "So you rescued him?" He was beginning to breathe heavily.

"Of course I did! But I hate to think either Crean or Nielson would do something like that on purpose." She ran faster.

Harte didn't have strong feelings on the subject, but it offered an opening to get into the commander's good graces. "Between us, we can make sure it doesn't happen again."

"Thank you, Mr. Gunner, but I don't think I need your help to manage my crew."

"I'm sure you don't, but I'll do what I can. So, what was the emergency on the bridge?"

She smiled mysteriously. "You'll find out soon enough. But I may have found a way to relieve you of cooking duties. Will you excuse me? I need to find Dr. Crean, and then I have a surprise to prepare before lunch." She stopped running, switched off the vacuum pump, and emerged from the machine.

In spite of the smile, there was a finality in her voice that forced him to swallow any further questions. At least she was still speaking to him. A mysterious emergency and a surprise could add some needed zing to his doc. That, and the glimpse of her in shorts, would have to be enough for now.

Harte finished his workout and returned to his quarters to clean up and get dressed. His wardrobe consisted of black T-shirts and turtlenecks, to be paired with jeans or slacks, also black. The all-black look came across as arty and serious, but the real reason for it was simple: it saved him from deciding what to wear.

Appetizing aromas wafted through the messroom when Harte arrived, so the commander was telling the truth about him being off cooking duty. She was the only person not present. Did that mean she had taken the job back? When she emerged from the galley, he was sure he'd guessed it, though it didn't seem like much of a surprise.

"Lunch will be ready soon," Commander Ladd said. "I have some interesting news to share before we begin. I'm bending a rule here, so I need to ask for your cooperation. Especially from you, Mr. Gunner. No video or audio recording while I make this announcement."

He raised both hands to show they were nowhere near his camera. Everyone else agreed, murmuring about what the news might be. The commander returned to the galley for a moment.

She came back smiling. "*Endurance* party, allow me to introduce your new cook. Meet Amelia Blackborow."

The person who followed the commander from the galley looked like a child to Harte. Her brown hair was cut short, almost but not quite as short as the commander's, almost but not quite as if she'd done it herself. The green crew uniform she wore was at least two sizes too big — a hand-me-down with rolled cuffs at wrist and ankle. Large eyes in a light olive-toned face gazed around the group, her smile uncertain.

"Ms. Blackborow managed to stow away and was not discovered until this morning," the commander explained. "And before anyone asks: Yes, she is underage, but not for long. She turns eighteen on the 30th — four days from now. Rather than risk the whole mission by returning to Armstrong, I have added her to the crew."

Wild and Anderson smiled serenely. "She's smaller than Mr. Green," Wild said. "Ms. Blackborow, let me know if you need help taking in your uniform so it fits better."

"Th-thank you, sir."

Nguyen scowled and shook her head, but also looked unsurprised. This must have been the emergency on the bridge.

"Oh, hell no," Nielson muttered.

"So when you said you were 'bending a rule,' you meant shattering it completely," Keith said. "This is highly irregular."

Nguyen nodded vigorously. "Right?"

"But we supplied with a party of twelve in mind, and that's what we have," the commander said. "It shouldn't affect your records."

"Epic practical joke," Dr. Crean said. "I salute you both."

"I'm happy not to be the baby of the group," Dr. Eyestone said. "Welcome, Ms. Blackborow."

"Provided she passes her physical exam," Dr. Mack put in. "I assume it isn't required for stowaways, but it is for crew."

"Correct," Commander Ladd replied. "And, for the next four days, we must make sure she does not appear in any date-stamped recordings or reports — no logs, no messages home, no casual videos, no documentary footage. Is that clear?"

Harte bristled at being told what or what not to film, but he loved the narrative aspect. Now this was a juicy story! He wouldn't think of jeopardizing the mission now. Would anyone else?

The Boss listened to the mix of enthusiastic and reluctant assent. She raised the hatch of the service window between the galley and the messroom. "All right then, we have an assortment of pre-heated MessPaks for your lunching enjoyment. Come and get it."

Chapter 6

2124/08/27: I'm training our less experienced members in more advanced spacer skills. There's no real need for it, but it passes the time, and perhaps it will benefit them in their careers.
— Commander Ladd's Expedition Journal

The next day, Ruby invited the rookies of the party to the cargo deck for training: Amelia Blackborow, Lee Keith, John Eyestone, Aaron Curley, and Harte Gunner. She also included Chip Nielson, though he was an old hand.

"Good afternoon, everyone. Thank you for coming." She had them arrange themselves along the wall with the basketball hoop so she could examine the confidence — or lack thereof — with which each moved in zero gravity. Nielson was a pro, Gunner was surprisingly adept, and the others were improving. "I'm calling this Space Skills 101. Everyone who came up through the Corps has already received extensive training in all aspects of spaceship life, as have Dr. Crean and Dr. Mack. With the exception of Ms. Blackborow, the rest of you received some basic instruction and training when you were selected for this expedition. Now that we have nothing but time, I intend to bring everyone's skills up to a professional level."

Gunner gave a dismissive eye roll, but Blackborow nodded eagerly.

"We'll start with basic movement in zero gravity. You've already discovered that it's nothing like walking around on Earth. But within the ship, it's not that difficult, either. In the passages and cabins, there's always something within arm's reach to grab or push against if you need to start, stop, or change direction. But here on the cargo deck, there's enough space to get into trouble, as we've already seen."

Keith's face reddened, and Nielson turned away to hide a laugh. Blackborow looked puzzled. Dr. Eyestone whispered something to her, and her look of confusion turned to shock.

"What the hell am I doing here?" Nielson asked. "I already know this shit."

"You're going to help me with a demonstration," she explained.

"Why me, though?"

"You don't get dizzy."

He puffed up proudly. "That's true, I don't."

Ruby held the basketball. "Follow me — not too fast." She nudged away from the wall and faced Nielson as they drifted out. She passed him the ball for a training exercise she had performed hundreds of times. The force of the pass added a little to her backward momentum, while canceling his forward momentum.

Nielson hung suspended just beyond reach of anything that could help him move or change direction. "Should I pass you the ball or what?"

"Not yet." Ruby bumped against a container of equipment for the Columbia Base on Mars. She grabbed hold so she wouldn't drift back out. "That was basic Newtonian physics — Nielson had more mass than the ball but not much momentum. I threw the ball just hard enough to stop him." She moved along the container to the bulkhead until she judged the angle to be right. She launched herself at Nielson and glanced off his shoulder, bumping him enough to set him spinning in place, while she continued to the opposite wall. "Try to stop spinning."

He flailed around and contorted his body, but only succeeded in flipping himself over. The whole group laughed at his predicament — all except Nielson himself. Maybe he did get dizzy, after all.

"OK, now you can throw the ball."

The force of the throw imparted enough momentum to get him moving, though he still rotated upside down in relation to the rest of the group. He came to rest near Ruby, breathing hard. She flipped him over so they were the same way up.

"What's the big idea?" he sputtered.

"Not so fun, is it?" she whispered back. A quick conversation with Dr. Crean had confirmed he had returned to his lab while Nielson and Keith were still playing ball. Nielson was the culprit. "I'm only going to say this once: I will not tolerate bullying aboard this ship. Got it?" To the whole group, she said, "Let's have a round of applause for Mr. Nielson. Thank you for being a good sport."

"So is the lesson that we should always carry a basketball, just in case?" Gunner asked.

Ruby narrowed her eyes at him. "The lesson is that exaggerated movement can get you into trouble. That's doubly true outside the vehicle." Nielson's face turned gray. "Small, controlled movement is the key." She spoke into her comm. "Mr. Wild, please bring down the harnesses and training tethers."

Wild arrived moments later with a locker module. "Did I miss the physics demonstration? I always enjoy that one." Nielson made a disgusted noise. Wild ignored him and opened the locker. He distributed harnesses to the participants.

Gunner examined his harness. "Looks like rock-climbing gear."

"Very similar," Ruby said. "Go ahead and put those on. Help each other, if necessary."

"I prefer free climbing, myself," Gunner said. He slipped his harness on with no difficulty, though some of the others struggled. Wild offered expert help where needed.

"I've seen your rock-climbing doc," Ruby said. "There's no way you were free-climbing and holding the camera at the same time."

He gave her a smug grin. "I didn't say I do it when I'm filming. Just that I prefer it."

She chose not to dignify his remarks with further comment. "If you needed to work outside the ship, you would be secured on a tether."

"What, no jetpack?" Gunner asked.

"No, Mr. Gunner. No jetpack. That would be far too advanced and far too costly. So ... you would be secured on a tether — a strong cable like this one." She held up a slender line. "The actual EVA tethers are housed in the main airlock, where they're attached to reels that can be played out or retracted as needed. These training tethers are not as long, but they'll give you a chance to practice and get a feel for it. One end locks onto your harness, the other end has an electromagnet to attach to an interior surface. Everybody, give it a try, and remember — small, controlled movement."

Blackborow was almost immediately upside down and facing the wrong way. Dr. Eyestone moved with as much care as one of his robots and mastered the technique in short order. He helped Blackborow. Dr. Curley fumbled around at first, too, but got himself out of trouble. Mr. Keith seemed afraid to move at all. Gunner was a natural, which vexed Ruby for reasons she couldn't name. But he offered to help Keith, so he must not have been feeling too superior.

"Thank you, everyone. That's enough for today," she announced when they'd practiced for twenty minutes. "Pull yourself along the tether, back to the wall. Next session, we'll try it with suits and helmets."

Wild collected the harnesses and tethers. "But if you should find yourself outside the ship without a spacesuit, don't panic."

"Sure, because what's the fuckin' point?" Nielson asked. "Instant Chip-sicle."

"Actually, no," Wild said, in his unperturbed way. "It takes a long time to freeze in a vacuum. You'd pass out and asphyxiate long before that. And contrary to what you might have heard, your eyeballs wouldn't pop, either." He stroked his jaw, apparently unaware of the appalled stares all around him. "The oxygen would be drawn out of your blood through your lungs; that can't be pleasant. But if somebody can get to you in about a minute and a half and bring you back inside, you'll be fine. So don't panic." He smiled and left the cargo deck without another word.

Ruby's eyes watered with the effort not to laugh. "Thank you, Mr. Wild. Everyone — same time tomorrow, in full suits."

The next day after breakfast, Harte dawdled over coffee and the latest news feeds. "Glad I'm not in China," he muttered. A nasty Frankenflu was spreading through several cities, overwhelming health officials' efforts to contain the outbreak and develop an effective vaccine. It was already responsible for thousands of deaths and threatened to become a global pandemic.

"What an old-fashioned way to go! Glad I'm not on Earth." Tensions in the Confederate States of America were heating up; armed conflict between factions was expected to break out any day, though it could have been nothing but saber rattling. Predictions of a heavy storm season further complicated matters, but maybe it would offer a chance for cooler heads to prevail. Harte had been planning a doc on the brewing conflict before this better opportunity arose. Meanwhile, news from the Northwest Union seemed light by comparison. Legislators had voted to replace the word "marriage" with "domestic union," and the words "wife" and "husband" with "spousal partner," throughout statute law.

"Waste of time, if you ask me. What difference does it make what you call it?" Harte asked.

"*Marriage* is a loaded term for a lot of people, with religious or patriarchal overtones," Dr. Mack said. "Some folks are offended that the institution is open to anyone, others are offended by the history of exclusivity."

"Then why didn't they take it out to begin with?"

"My mother wished they would," Commander Ladd said. "But they were in a hurry to get the documents written, so they copied a lot of existing language straight across."

"So your mother didn't want to be married?"

The Boss smiled. God, she had a great smile! "She was very happy with the relationship. It's just —" A signal interrupted her — six loud beeps and a sustained tone. "Lifeboat drill," she said before he could ask.

The captain's voice came over the PA. "Your attention, please. We are conducting an emergency drill. Please change into spacesuits as quickly as possible and assemble near the hatch to the shuttle bay."

"We have a shuttle bay?" Harte asked. "Where is it?"

"Cargo hold," the commander replied. "You'll have no trouble finding it because the crew and I will be there before you."

So it was a race, was it? They all grabbed their helmets from the rack by the main airlock and proceeded to their own quarters to change. Harte's cabin was a narrow cubicle with a locker, a sleeping bag, and a potted plant. Not even a window. No, these spacers called it a *viewport*. Whatever you called it, he didn't have one.

As quickly as he could, he stripped off his clothes and squeezed into the snug pressure suit, a challenge in zero gravity. The heavy, stretchy fabric mimicked one atmosphere of pressure all over the body, except the face. The pressurized helmet took care of that. He strapped on the life-support pack and donned a roomier, insulated white jumpsuit over it. Harte was grateful for the coverage. Besides being skintight, the pressure suit was bright blue and shiny — not really his look. At least the snug hood couldn't mash his hair, the one good thing about the enforced haircut. He put on the helmet, grabbed his camera, and pulled himself along the passage to the cargo area.

True to her word, the Boss was already at the designated assembly area, with Anderson, Wild, Nguyen, Nielson and Crean. At least Harte wasn't the last to arrive. When the whole party had gathered, the captain opened a hatch. One by one, they pulled themselves through into an airlock that held them all with no room to spare. This in turn led into a larger but still cramped space. Harte filmed as much of the drill as he could, carefully avoiding shots that included Blackborow's face. It was uncomfortable and not very exciting, but it was a look at space travel the majority of his audience would never have even considered.

He grasped a handhold and slowly panned across the scene. His shipmates were crowded into an area smaller than the messroom. Three rust-colored seats ran down each of the long sides. There was an open area at one end, and at the other, two more seats and an instrument panel.

Now the Boss's comment about a "lifeboat drill" made sense. This was another ship — a tiny one, but a ship. With the whole party inside, it felt more like a clown car.

"This is our lander shuttle," the captain announced. "In an emergency, it could also serve as an escape vehicle over a short distance. We won't climb in here every time we have a drill, but I wanted you to see it this first time. Thank you for your cooperation, and next time, try to be faster."

They crowded back into the airlock and returned to the cargo deck. "Space Skills class, please remain here," the Commander announced. "Mr. Nielson, would you bring the harnesses down? Then you're free to go."

As Nielson left, one of the robots trotted across the deck and followed him. It didn't move like the others

Harte had seen. He didn't get a good look at it, but it seemed looser and faster. Two more robots emerged from the passage. One continued boldly into the middle of everyone, while the other hung back and watched from a distance. If "watched" was the right word. Harte still didn't know what the big round sensor was for.

Dr. Eyestone chuckled. "I guess I left the door to the lab open when I went to put my suit on. Is it all right if they watch us?"

"I don't think they can get into much trouble out here," the Boss said, her voice slightly distorted over the helmet speaker. "Just be sure to round them up afterwards. All right, everyone, please glance at the upper left of your visor. That's your heads-up display, or HUD. It gives you information on communication channels, your air supply, heart rate, respiration, the temperature of the environment, and so on — the kind of data that can keep you alive in hostile circumstances. You have a second, gold-plated visor that can be pulled down." She demonstrated and they all followed suit. "It protects you from radiation. Outside the ship, you'll want to use it, but you don't need it in here." She pushed hers back up. "If there are no further questions about the suit, let's continue our training."

The training was the same as the previous day, with harnesses and tethers. It was a little more awkward in the spacesuit, but Harte had already mastered the techniques. "Commander, how would it be if I filmed this session?"

She watched him for a moment. "You seem to know what you're doing," she allowed. "Go ahead, as long as you —"

"Yeah, yeah, no identifiable shots of Blackborow."

"Right, you get it," she said. "But I know you want to document all our activities, and this might be interesting to folks."

He moved off to the side to get a good angle on the proceedings. Commander Ladd moved among the other four, offering assistance or advice as needed. She never lost patience or scolded, even with Lee Keith. He needed the most help, but he seemed marginally less hopeless than in the first class. Blackborow had made a surprising amount of progress; she was almost as adept as the two scientists. Before long, everyone was chattering and laughing.

"This is a good time to talk about the headset in your helmet," the Commander said. "You are now on the public channel 1, but you have the option of speaking over a private channel. Use the control on the left side of your helmet and watch your heads-up display for the number you've selected. Blackborow and Eyestone, use channel 2; Keith and Curley, channel 3. Gunner, I guess you're stuck with me on channel 4."

Harte adjusted the setting and watched his HUD. As he moved off channel 1, the other voices went silent. The Commander's voice returned on channel 4. "… copy, Mr. Gunner?"

"I … uh … yes, I copy, Commander."

"So talk to me."

He'd been wanting to talk to her for days, and now he couldn't think of a single question. "Well, Boss, what do you do for fun?" he blurted at last.

She cocked her head. "You don't think this is fun?"

A joke? He didn't know her well enough to be sure, but he thought she almost smiled. "It's all right, I guess. Not how I expected to spend my free time." He glanced at the others. He couldn't hear them, but he could see their lips move. Both pairs were in animated conversation. That wasn't surprising with Eyestone and Blackborow, who were both outgoing and lively, but the other two both seemed pretty shy. "Maybe I should rephrase the question: what do you do to relax when you're not on duty?"

"I don't think that's any of your business." She waited a beat. "You have free time? Maybe I should have put you to work in the galley."

He shook his head. "Maybe. You know, you're very good at this, Commander."

"Thank you, Mr. Gunner. It means so much to me that you approve of how I do my job."

Sarcasm again. He hadn't heard her use it with anyone else. "I said that wrong. I meant this whole training thing. You're teaching advanced skills to people who most likely won't ever need to use them, but you're taking it, and them, seriously. You have good people skills."

He couldn't see her expression clearly through the visor, but it seemed she was beginning to smile again. "It's an important part of being a leader."

"Maybe I can pick up some tips from you. My staff thinks I'm an ogre."

"Then you probably are. You don't bark orders, do you?"

"Sometimes." He considered. "Maybe more often than that."

"How many assistants have left in tears, or a huff?"

"Um ... two huffs, three tears. Why?"

She shook her head. "You might pretend you're not paying them; that you need them more than they need you; that they're individual human beings with their own lives."

"That sounds like a lot of work."

"Then maybe you should hire someone to do it for you. Then you'd only have to worry about alienating one person."

"You know, I like that idea. What are you doing when this is over?"

"Hah! Sorry. It'll be a warm day on Mars before I work in an office again."

"Can't blame me for asking. And I made you laugh."

"But you can't make me work for you." She waved her hand toward the others. "You seem to have some aptitude for this, though."

"I have good body awareness."

"That figures."

"What? No, I mean by training. I used to do parkour when I was young. You have to know where all your parts are."

"I see. So why aren't you a spacer?" she asked.

He laughed. "They didn't offer it at my community college."

"I had no idea. I assumed you went to a prestigious media school."

"That was later, when I was already on a path." This was more like it — a friendly exchange, free of sarcasm. He could imagine her granting an interview in this mood. "But I'm glad my path crossed yours."

"And if you mind your manners, neither of us will have to regret it."

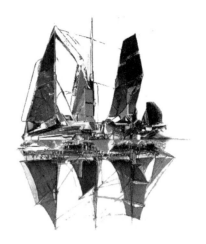

Chapter 7

2124/08/31 We are far from our goal and must keep our spirits up and our minds engaged in the months ahead. It is not enough for me to encourage my people. They must own this expedition.
— Commander Ladd's Expedition Journal

Ruby left the exercise area, muscles pleasantly burning from a good workout. The exertion had done nothing to relieve her anxiety about the event taking place in Dr. Mack's lab/exam room. She was on her way there when Aaron Curley pulled himself into the passage. Ruby reached for handholds on either side of her to stop her progress. Dr. Curley managed to grab only one, swinging into the wall for a gentle face plant.

The geologist straightened himself out. "Oh! Hello, Boss. They, um, said you were in the gym."

"I finished early. Is there something I can help you with?"

"Yes. That is, if you're not busy." He glanced at the nearest door. "Do you have a meeting with Dr. Mack?"

"I'm waiting for her, but I don't know when she'll be finished. She's giving Ms. Blackborow her physical this morning."

"Really, they didn't do that already?" Curley asked.

"Regulations prohibit administering a space physical to a minor without the permission of a parent or guardian," Ruby explained. "They had to wait for Blackborow's birthday."

"Oh! I hope she passes."

"You and me both," Ruby murmured. The outcome of the examination could decide the future of the expedition. If Amelia passed, she would be an official member of the crew, graduating from the acting capacity she had filled (cheerfully and surprisingly well) since they had discovered her. If she failed, the expedition was over. They couldn't take an unfit, unofficial crewmember on a year-plus journey, much less a passenger. Ruby would be forced to report the stowaway and return to Armstrong.

"She's been kind of unofficially assisting John and me," Dr. Curley continued. "Transcribing voice notes, helping with the robots ..."

"I gathered something like that was going on. I'm glad you're keeping her busy." With food preparation at a minimum, Blackborow's main official duties were cleaning the galley and keeping the food inventory up to date for Mr. Keith's records. "Just don't go getting a crush on her."

Dr. Curley laughed. "Don't worry, I don't get those. Anyway, Amelia reminds me of my youngest sister: similar enthusiasm, curiosity, native smarts." He shook his head. "Hard to believe she dropped out of school."

"She got her equivalency degree," Ruby said.

"And we're like her college! You're teaching her space skills, John and I are sharing technical and scientific stuff … Of course, she's teaching us Spanish. Turns out she and John both have *abuelas* from Mexico, but he never picked up the language. I had it in high school, but it's been a long time."

"How … interesting." This was by far the longest conversation she'd had with the shy geologist. "What did you want to ask me? Is it related to all that?"

"Yeah, kind of. At the intro meeting, you said something about sharing talents and teaching skills. So … would it be OK if I offered … banjo lessons?"

She stared. Why did it have to be the banjo? But it had been her idea, and at least it wasn't bagpipes.

"I know," he said. "It's a silly idea. I won't be hurt if you say no."

She smiled. "It's a great idea. You're the first to show any interest, but that's exactly what we need. I'll announce it at lunch."

"I'm not sure it needs a big announcement. I'll just put a message on the network."

"I'm not talking just about banjo lessons. Like you said, we're each other's college. I'm talking about *electives*."

With a smile, Dr. Curley continued to his lab, leaving Ruby more grateful than he could have guessed. She'd made the suggestion about sharing talents, then heard nothing from anyone on the subject. Maybe it only needed time. They were less than a week into the mission, but the novelty was already wearing off. The experienced hands knew to be deliberate in how they filled their days, but everyone aboard would soon need variety. Official tasks, required training, and exercise filled only so much time, and could not scratch every itch. Electives could help bring this disparate group together, not just as shipmates, but as a real team.

Provided, of course, Blackborow passed her physical. No. She *would* pass. The alternative was almost unthinkable. How could Ruby give up this expedition after living it in her head for years? She was still thrilled to wake every morning and find herself on a spaceship, commanding a mission. She was happier than she'd been in ages, except for this one lingering anxiety. The only other blot was that intrusive know-it-all documentarian, Gunner, and even he had proven reasonably cooperative.

The door slid open, and Dr. Mack emerged. "Aw, look who's hovering. Don't tell me you were worried, Boss."

Ruby smiled. "I just wanted to be the first to offer congratulations ... if they are due?"

The doctor waved Blackborow out. "Say hello to your newest crew member. Amelia is in excellent physical health, and psychologically fit for space duty."

"I never doubted it." Ruby shrugged. "Well, not much. I'm relieved to make it official, though."

"Sorry I complicated things," Blackborow said.

"If everything had gone too perfectly, I would have been waiting for the first big disaster," Ruby said. "Good to get it out of the way early. Welcome aboard, crewmate."

"Thanks, Boss! I need to tell John and Aaron before lunch. And the robots, of course."

After notifying SCEI about their stowaway who was conveniently of age and physically and mentally fit to remain with the expedition, Ruby joined the others in the mess. Once everyone had lunch, Ruby called for their attention. "Dr. Curley has reminded me of an idea for keeping occupied. I call it Endurance College. Anyone who wishes may suggest an activity or offer instruction in a subject of their expertise. This will keep life fresh and help us work together in different ways."

"What's the procedure?" Mr. Keith asked. "Do we apply to you for permission, Boss, or should we go through Mr. Wild?"

"Permission is not required," Ruby said. "If you want to try something and it doesn't go against our official mission, put the word out. If people are interested, they're free to join in. Let's just see what happens."

Mr. Keith, she knew, was not a fan of informal organization. Yet even he soon wore the smile of someone cooking up a revolutionary idea.

Harte listened to the Boss's announcement with interest. At first, he thought she was talking about more space-training classes or other practical instruction. Then Dr. Curley offered banjo lessons, and it became clear that any member of the expedition could propose any kind of class, club, or recreational activity, and lead it if they felt capable.

"In that case, I want to start a weekly prayer meeting," Dr. Mack said. "I'd like to have it on Sunday mornings because that's what I'm used to, but everyone's welcome — any faith, or none." She glanced at the Boss, who almost imperceptibly shook her head. Harte doubted anyone else even caught it.

"What this ship needs is a book club," Dr. Crean announced.

"Then start one," the Boss replied.

"What do you think I'm doing? This is the first meeting. Nobody's required to stay, but everyone's welcome."

"I'm on duty," Captain Anderson said, "but I'll catch the next one." He excused himself and returned to the bridge, but everyone else stayed. Harte raised his camera to record the first meeting. He made sure to include Blackborow in as many shots as possible.

"There won't be much to see," the Boss said.

"You never know. Maybe the audio will be good."

"What's the point of having a club with the same people we do everything with?" Nielson asked.

"The point is this," Dr. Crean replied. "We have a wealth of reading material and a lot of time to fill. A book club will give us a chance to discuss what we're reading, share interpretations, and get some good out of the material rather than just passing the time."

Nielson curled his lip. "Sounds too goddamned educational to me."

"I say we give it a try," Dr. Eyestone said. "What's the book?"

Dr. Crean nodded thoughtfully. "Before we choose a book, I thought we could take some time today for everyone to share what they're reading now and what they like to read. That might point us to a common interest. Commander, would you like to go first?"

"I'm just a spectator," she said. "I don't want to unduly influence your choice. Anyway, I don't get to read much for pleasure."

Dr. Crean smiled at her. "I'll admit, you've been busy. What was the last thing you read?"

"*Fundamentals of Astrodynamics*."

Harte snorted. "For *fun*?"

"No, no, it's a classic," Crean said. "What other topics interest you?"

She considered the question before answering. "Leadership."

No surprise there. They went around the group and each person shared. They had wide-ranging tastes, without a lot of obvious overlap. Crean was simultaneously reading up on the latest work in astrophysics and enjoying *Huckleberry Finn*.

"That would be an interesting book to all read together," he suggested. "We're sort of on a raft here, separate from the rest of society." When they didn't all eagerly climb aboard, he raised his hands and smiled. "There's no hurry, though. What about you, John?"

It was no surprise that the roboticist enjoyed classic science fiction from the likes of Isaac Asimov, Ray Bradbury, and H. G. Wells. But shy Dr. Curley's love of Romantic poets was not what Harte expected.

"Poetry?" Nielson scoffed. "Sounds kinda girly to me."

"You've obviously never met a Byronic hero," Dr. Curley replied.

Nguyen's tastes ran to literary classics; she was re-reading *Pride and Prejudice*. Blackborow liked high fantasy and enthused over something with wizards, dragons, and a feisty sword-wielding princess. It sounded lightweight to Harte, but it took all kinds to make a space expedition.

Dr. Mack was working her way through the Bible. "I'm up to the Psalms, which I can tell you go down much easier than Leviticus! But for variety, I'm perusing a virology journal."

"I usually like something hard-boiled," Nielson said. "Detectives, spies, that kind of shit. But lately, I'm hooked on these old superhero comics. The one I'm reading now has this super smart asshole inventor who makes his own high-tech armor and blows shit up." He grinned. "And it has pictures!"

"What about you, Mr. Keith?" Dr. Crean asked.

"Philosophy. Theology. Right now, I'm reading Kierkegaard. No pictures."

Before Nielson could make a cutting remark, Dr. Crean turned to Harte. "And you, Mr. Gunner?"

"I usually read true-life adventure stories. I'm always looking for ideas for my next documentary — a setting, an event, an over-the-top personality. I've just started a great old mountaineering book, *Annapurna*. Before that, I was reading about polar explorers." He turned to Commander Ladd. "You'd find some good leadership stories there, Boss."

"I don't know, I'm kind of intrigued by Blackborow's sword-swinging princess." Her lips twitched into a challenging little smile. He had half a mind to accept the challenge, if only he knew what it was.

The meeting ended without any definitive choice, but they decided to meet every week, anyway. It was clear that everybody liked talking about their favorites and trying to convert the others. Endurance College was officially in session.

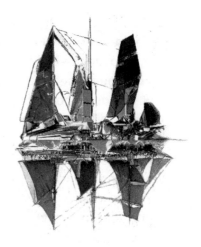

Chapter 8

2124/09/27: I want to be just like the Boss! With one small exception ...

— Amelia Blackborow's private diary

"What the hell is this?" Nielson sniffed the tortilla-wrapped bundle and made a face.

"Language," Nguyen muttered. If Nielson heard, he ignored her.

Blackborow continued passing out lunch to the rest of the party. "I call them jambalaya wraps. I mixed a couple different MessPaks — Spanish rice with chicken and shrimp risotto."

"I thought I smelled fuckin' shrimp," Nielson said.

"Mr. Nielson, I find your language offensive," Nguyen said.

"Tough. And I don't eat shrimp."

Blackborow's eyes widened. "Oh no, are you allergic?"

"No, I just don't like the damn things. Like bugs but in water ..."

Nguyen clenched her fists. "Please. Stop. Swearing. Just for one meal?"

"This is how I talk. If you don't like it, you can ..."

Ruby intervened. "Mr. Nielson, this is what we're having for lunch today. If you don't like it, you can go without or make your own, but no complaints. Next time, Ms. Blackborow will make sure you don't get shrimp. Right?"

"Of ... of course," Blackborow said. "Sorry."

"I, for one, am enjoying the mix of flavors," Gunner said. "It's not quite jambalaya, but it's close enough for me. Just needs some smoked sausage and a little more spice."

"I like that it's a one-handed lunch," Dr. Curley said. He and Lee Keith played chess while they ate. The game board and pieces affixed by magnets to the steel tabletop.

Ruby relaxed, relieved others had stood up for the cook's choice before she set the example. She appreciated the creativity and the break in the monotony. A month into their journey, fresh food was a distant memory and the honeymoon of the first few days was long over. Ruby dreamed of rain, mountain vistas, and her father's face. Everyone must have been missing something from their life on Earth. She hoped this mission would be worth the temporary losses.

Sometimes tempers grew short, but there were also signs of team spirit. In the first month of the expedition, the *Endurance* party had found many opportunities for play in the midst of duties and training, and not only Zero-G basketball. That activity had evolved far from the original game to resemble some kind of rambunctious aerial ballet, especially after Betty Nguyen started to play. Endurance College was established now, with Dr. Mack's prayer meeting, the book club, banjo lessons, and Conversational Spanish. The first night's sing-along had grown into a regular weekly talent night. So far, everyone but Ruby had performed, in at least a supporting role.

She emphasized these moments in her first monthly digest to SCEI HQ, playing down the occasional friction between shipmates. Maybe she could have made more of that aspect, to stress the importance of having the whole party train together in advance of a mission. But on at least one occasion, conflict was due almost entirely to a malfunctioning CO_2 scrubber. No amount of team building would have prevented that. Harmony was restored only after Nielson made the repair. A source of friction was sometimes its cure.

Ruby beckoned Blackborow over. "When you've finished eating, check in the freezer, behind the tortillas. I think we're due for a treat."

After lunch, Blackborow came out of the galley with a case of ice-cream sandwiches, something Ruby had tucked away as a surprise morale booster. They worked in zero gravity as long as you kept the wrapper on and ate the ice cream before it melted. Ruby devoured hers with brisk efficiency, but not everyone was so tidy. Globules of melted ice cream soon floated all over the room, provoking a game.

Dessert was not usually this entertaining. Harte Gunner, with typical vanity, had refused ice cream on account of his mustache (Eyestone and Blackborow happily split his serving), but he filmed the aftermath with great amusement. The players demonstrated a variety of hunting styles. Eyestone crept up on the floating droplets, stalking them, then darted his tongue out chameleon-like to take his prey. Crean liked to push off surfaces and dive onto the globules, while Wild merely waited for whatever drifted his way. Nielson carefully herded globs together into a growing super-glob.

While this was going on, Dr. Curley and Mr. Keith continued their chess game. They were well matched and watched each other's moves intently. It wasn't as much a spectator sport as the absurdity taking place nearby, but Ruby kept her eye on both games. She bit her tongue as first Curley missed an opportunity to put Keith in check, and then Keith overlooked a chance to threaten Curley's queen. It was their game, not hers.

"Do you play chess, Boss?" Gunner asked. "You look like you're dying to offer advice."

"I've been known to play," she said.

"I'd love to challenge you to a game some time."

"You don't want to go there," Wild said. He sucked up a globule of ice cream that came too close. "She can plan eight or ten moves ahead. I've known her almost fifteen years, and I've never won a match."

"Not to worry. A commander shouldn't compete against the people who work for her," Ruby said.

"Hmm." A slow smile spread over Gunner's face, but something distracted him from whatever he was about to say. "That's quite the giganto-blob you've got going there, Nielson."

Ruby was about to agree, when she noticed he was lining it up like a billiards shot — with the side of Keith's head. A puff of breath was all it would take.

"Mr. Nielson," she called. He turned, and the glob remained where it was. "When you've finished your dessert, would you take a look at the water recycling system? It seems a bit humid in here."

"Yes, ma'am." He leaned toward the melted ice cream and slurped it up, then left the messroom without further comment.

"We might need that water someday," Keith said without looking up from the game and with no idea how close he'd come to being splattered.

Something dashed across the floor after Nielson.

"What the —?" Ruby asked.

Blackborow came up beside her. "That was Mrs. Chippy."

"Mrs. Chippy?"

"One of the robots. She likes to prowl the ship, but she particularly likes Mr. Nielson."

"How do you know a robot is a she?" Ruby asked.

"You don't. It goes better with the name, though."

That didn't make any sense, but Ruby let it go. "Is that the same one I've seen in the galley with you?"

"Yeah. She's very curious."

"It … *she* doesn't move like the others." The other robots walked with stiff care, like old dogs. This one managed to slink along, more like a cat.

"John — Dr. Eyestone, I mean — says her joints are loose, and he can't seem to tighten them. She might not be suitable for asteroid duty, but I think she wants to be ship's mascot."

Most of the ice cream had been cleaned up by this time. Gunner stopped filming and went out after Nielson and Mrs. Chippy. "I hope there's more to the doc than this," Ruby said. "It could give people an odd impression of the expedition."

The cook smiled. "I think people will like seeing the fun times." She turned serious. "Can I ask you something?"

"Of course you may, any time. What is it?"

"About the Space Colonization Whatsit Thingy. About — my future."

"In that case, we should include Professor Nguyen, too."

Crean and Eyestone continued to pounce on the last droplets of ice cream. Eyestone spat something out and grabbed it out of the air. "Bleah, whose bandage is this?"

Betty Nguyen shook her head. "Maybe we should go somewhere less goofy."

"My quarters." Ruby led the way out of the messroom.

Thus far, Blackborow had given Ruby no reason to regret her decision to allow the girl to remain on the ship. She had proven herself reliable in the galley, even if she didn't have to do much actual cooking. Meals were always ready on time and in adequate quantities. She was a careful steward of her supplies, which made Lee Keith happy. This in turn made Ruby happy —one less thing to hear him fret about.

They left the ice cream hunt and made their way to the commander's relatively spacious cabin. Blackborow hung for a moment in front of the viewport and gazed out. Ruby dimmed the lights to cut the reflection.

"The stars look different out here."

"There's no atmosphere to distort their light," Ruby said.

"It's more than that. It's like, they're not *them*; they're *us*." She frowned. "That sounded really stupid, didn't it?"

"It sounded like you've been talking philosophy with Mr. Keith," Nguyen said. "Not that there's anything wrong with that."

Ruby joined them and looked out at the blazing specks. One appeared larger, and reddish in color. According to Anderson, they would be there in another five months — maybe sooner. "I think I understand what you're saying. Step away from Earth, and the rest of the universe seems less alien. We're part of the same thing." Ruby waited, but Blackborow didn't say any more. "You wanted to know about SCEI. We're currently in the E-for-exploration phase — finding resources, trying to make planets habitable, establishing research and industrial bases. The colonization phase won't start for at least a decade. Don't tell Wesley James, but I think even that's overly optimistic."

"Who's Wesley James?"

"Right, you missed his little speech the day before launch," Nguyen said. "Imagine if he'd called in just now and seen that lunacy with the ice cream. We'd all have been fired on the spot!"

Ruby laughed. "If he tried that, I'd thank him for the nice ship and fusion reactor. I think Skipper might enjoy turning pirate. We could do the mission on our own, then sell the data to the highest bidder."

"Nobody's answering my question!" Blackborow said. "Who. Is. Wesley. James?"

"Sorry. He's Executive Director of SCEI — my boss," Ruby said. "He's not a spacer; he comes from a business background. He loves projections and deadlines and delivery dates, but I'm not sure he understands how much space there is in space."

Blackborow grinned. "I'm not really interested in living on Mars, anyway."

Ruby smiled. "Neither am I, but maybe you should reserve judgment until you've seen the place."

"Sure," Ms. Nguyen said. "You're still young enough to have a chance at it."

Ruby sighed. "When I first joined the Space Corps, they warned us not to get too excited about the C part of SCEI. Our job was to make things ready. But our children might be colonists. Our grandchildren might be born on other worlds. Not *mine* personally, of course, but I liked that idea — getting something ready for other generations." She thought of Earth, straining under the demands of multiple billions of inhabitants. In spite of her parents' opinion, she *was* doing her part. If it wasn't already too late …

"Why Mars, though?" Blackborow asked. "The Moon's right there."

Nguyen patted Blackborow on the back. "This kid's smart. The Moon is right there, which makes it a good spaceport. And moondust is full of hydrogen and oxygen. But the gravity's too weak for permanent habitation, and even if it could hold an atmosphere, that would complicate launching spaceships. Better to leave it airless and dead."

Blackborow nodded. "I guess I can see that. Do they really think they can make Mars like Earth?"

"That's a tall order, but maybe it could be habitable. It's technically in the Goldilocks Zone."

Blackborow snorted a laugh. "The what?"

"You haven't heard of the Goldilocks Zone?" Ruby asked. "Every solar system has one — an orbital range where conditions are theoretically 'just right' to support life. In our solar system, Earth is in the sweet spot, but Venus and Mars are both in it, too — at the edges, but in it. Venus is atmospherically too out of whack to do anything with now, but Mars is still a possibility, if it's not too small to hold an atmosphere. If that doesn't work, domes or orbiting stations might."

Blackborow nodded. "I don't know if I want to live on a station, either, but I think I want to join the Space Corps. What do I need to do?"

"Take it away, Professor." Ruby gestured for Ms. Nguyen to take the question.

"That depends. Do you want to continue as a cook?"

"Not forever."

"Then you'll have to finish your education. Are you interested in the administrative side of things, like what Mr. Keith does? Or maybe a scientific role?"

"Robotics looks like fun, but I don't think I could hack the math. What I'd really like — is to fly the ships!"

"See, Betty? That's why I wanted you here," Ruby said.

Nguyen chuckled. "There's math there, too, but I think we can both relate. And you've done well in your training sessions." She listed the academic requirements for pilot training, as well as the time and discipline required for the training itself and the job that followed.

"It's a big commitment," Ruby said. "You'd be away from home a lot. You think you could do all that?"

"Sure, but ..." She bit her lip and glanced away for a moment. "Why did you join, Boss?"

"Same as you — I wanted to fly spaceships. I wanted to get *away*."

"From what?"

Ruby chose her words carefully. "The life my parents wanted for me. Don't get me wrong — they were doing admirable work. It just wasn't *my* work, and they didn't understand my ambition. It was convenient that the thing I most wanted to do would take me as far as possible from them."

"Ouch," Nguyen muttered.

"I'm making it sound worse than it was." Ruby gazed out the viewport while she gathered her thoughts. "They were reasonably supportive once they saw they couldn't influence my decision. Once I was in, I found that the life suited me. I liked my work, and I liked the routine, how a lot of the day-to-day decisions were made for me, so I could focus on more important things. I didn't have to think about what to wear or when to eat. I knew what my responsibilities were and who my boss was. It seemed very ... clean."

Blackborow wrinkled her nose. "It sounds like a convent!"

Nguyen laughed. "Well, she's not wrong."

Ruby had never thought about it that way, but the Corps did at times feel like a vocation.

"Is it true what you said before?" Blackborow asked. "About ... no sex?" She blushed.

Ruby was amused, but not displeased, that there were still young people who would blush about such things. "At your age, it's more important to have friends than lovers."

Blackborow raised her hand in the air. "Amen, sister!"

Ruby chuckled. "Maybe at my age, too, especially in this line of work. Anyway, it's not quite *no* sex. Planetside, we can do what we want, as long as we're careful. Anyone with a functioning uterus takes a routine pregnancy test before any launch, and everybody gets a contraceptive injection. I don't know all the science of it, but apparently, it works."

"Dr. Mack gave me one. She said it's good for twelve months and I get to skip those periods, which is a nice bonus. So doesn't that take care of it?"

"I wouldn't trust it. Abstinence is still the only 100% effective method, and out here, we can't afford anything less. So aboard ship, it's kind of monastic."

"Seems like it would be easier to have all men, or all women."

"That wouldn't be any fun!" Ruby objected. "Captain Anderson and Mr. Wild are my best friends anywhere, and the best at their jobs. I wouldn't want to go without them."

Blackborow nodded. "I guess. But isn't it awfully … frustrating?" She blushed again.

"It can be," Ruby admitted. "The injection takes the edge off the libido, which helps. So does having plenty of work to do."

"So, it's for life? You're married to the Corps?"

"Some people do a few missions, then settle on Earth so they can have a family. Others join up after their kids are grown, like Dr. Mack. But some make the Corps their life, permanently."

"That was me," Nguyen said. "Until I met my spouse."

"I didn't know!" Ruby cried. "When did this happen? And how do you make it work?"

"Three years ago. They're a touring musician, so we're used to separations. This was my turn."

"Well, good for you if you can stand it," Ruby said. "Wait, not *she*?"

"When love comes along, I don't let a little thing like pronouns stand in my way," Nguyen said.

Ruby nodded. "I'll probably stick with the Corps; it suits me."

"You don't want a family of your own?" Blackborow asked.

"With whom? That's the trick."

Blackborow frowned. "You shouldn't have any trouble attracting someone."

"That depends on what for. I have standards."

"No surprise there," Nguyen said. "What do you look for?"

"In someone to sleep with? Hygiene and stamina."

Blackborow turned bright red. She stared at Ruby for a moment, then looked away.

"Have I shocked you?" Ruby asked.

"It's just … not what I expected from a space commander."

"And how many of them do you know?"

Blackborow shook her head and didn't answer, but she was smiling again.

"It should go without saying that I don't sleep with anyone I work for, or who works for me," Ruby continued. "So that narrows the field, but not that much. It's not like I expect much conversation. For something long-term, though … that's more difficult. First off, he can't find a strong woman threatening."

"And their egos are so delicate!" Nguyen made a wide-eyed pathetic face. "I assume hygiene and stamina still apply?"

"Perhaps more so, plus personality. I'm drawn to talent, confidence and intelligence, tempered by kindness and generosity, but I can't stand arrogance. Do you know how rare a combination that is?"

Blackborow laughed and nodded. "There's nothing wrong with being a little picky. Still, there must be somebody. What about Captain Anderson?"

Ruby sighed. "He works for me, remember? But he comes close, though I didn't always think so. He's an inspired pilot, but he has a reckless side. He had to earn my trust." She shivered as she remembered how he'd earned it. "He's confident, but not arrogant. And not available. He was already happily married before I met him. He has a couple of kids, too."

Blackborow's eyes widened. "Wow. How do they manage that? He's on a year-plus mission!"

"I know. Marie is a saint, and much better for him than I would be. She … I can't say *grounds*, but she steadies him."

"Well, what about Mr. Wild, then? He's already devoted to you."

"I nearly spoiled that when I was sixteen." Again, she elected not to explain *how*. "And he's not available, either."

"Plus, you're not really his type," Nguyen said.

"True."

"Back up," Blackborow said. "You've known each other since you were *sixteen*?!"

Ruby smiled. "Since I was fourteen, actually. Is that so hard to imagine? We played together in an ecumenical basketball league."

"Ecu-what?"

"You know, a church league. Several faith communities together."

"Really? Then how come you don't come to the prayer meetings? Mr. Wild always does, and even Mr. Gunner, though maybe just for his doc."

"That's all in the past for me," Ruby said. "I mostly went for the b-ball." The Pearl throbbed as if in warning. God talk brought on such an unbearable ache that she'd stopped attending services. She'd never been extremely religious, but she had enjoyed the music, the ritual, the fellowship. She missed it, but there was no comfort there now. "Mr. Wild and I have been friends effectively forever, and that's how it's going to stay."

Blackborow thought hard, then beamed. "Harte Gunner."

Ruby jerked in surprise and stared at her. "You have got to be kidding."

"Why? He's gorgeous, he's smart, he's talented, he works hard —"

"What did I just say about arrogance? He's a celebrity! He's used to people fawning over him. He'd never get that from me."

"That's why it's so perfect!" She gave Ruby a sneaky little smile. "Besides, I think he likes you. He told Dr. Eyestone you're a striver."

"Um, I don't think he meant it as a compliment." Nguyen struggled not to laugh.

"Maybe it means he admires your work ethic," Blackborow said. "I know he can't take his eyes off you."

"No doubt admiring my *work ethic*," Ruby said, and smacked her behind. "Anyway, it's only because he's trying to get me to talk about Chickering."

"Well, why don't you?" Blackborow persisted. "I imagine it's a good story."

"You're too young to know anything about it. Why are we even having this discussion? I thought I was supposed to advise *you* on *your* future."

"And you did! I have a lot to think about." Blackborow moved to the door and opened it. "Thanks for your advice. I think I'll go see the robots before I start supper."

Nguyen followed her out. "Thanks for including me. This has been an enlightening discussion."

Ruby shook her head. Blackborow would probably go far in the Space Corps if she applied herself. So much enthusiasm! She reminded Ruby of herself at that age. But she had no future as a matchmaker. The idea of any sort of personal involvement with Gunner, or anyone, was laughable. That had been part of what drew Ruby to the Corps. Not only did she love her work — she didn't have to waste time trying to meet someone who did not exist. As she had said, it was very clean.

Chapter 9

2124/09/27: Dr. Eyestone has discovered an unprecedented form of entertainment. Morale, while good from the start, is at an all-time high.

— Commander Ladd's Expedition Journal

Harte followed Nielson into the guts of the ship, filming as they went. He hadn't been invited, but he was always on the lookout for new visuals to add and this was a part of the ship he hadn't visited before. Then there was Nielson, a foul-mouthed little SOB, but the master of anything mechanical. As a born tinkerer himself, Harte admired the other man's skills enough to overlook his shortcomings. That said, he didn't envy the commander her task of keeping both Nielson and Keith happy. But for all his faults, or maybe because of them, Nielson was a colorful character. His weathered face and blunt speech would liven up the doc.

So would the detailed look at the inner workings of the ship. They reached a mad-scientist's tangle of pipes, retorts, and reservoirs.

"What is this, a still?" Harte asked.

"You're not far off," Nielson replied. "This is our water reclamation plant and over there are the CO_2 scrubbers. Without them, the air would be clammy and unbreathable pretty damn quick. With them, we don't die, and we have an emergency water supply."

Harte nodded, both disgusted and fascinated to imagine all the exhaled water vapor, evaporated sweat, and excreted urine meeting here to be filtered and distilled into potable water. But as he understood it, they were carrying a substantial supply of drinking water. This reclaimed water was primarily for washing, and not much then — sponge baths and rinseless shampoo didn't require a lot. It would come into use as drinking water only in case of extreme emergency.

The engineer examined displays and put his ear to various parts of the equipment. "Fuck me, the Boss was right — the humidity is up a little, and still increasing. Must be a blocked filter."

"Didn't Mr. Wild say she's always right?"

Nielson barked a laugh. "And here I thought he was just kissing her sweet ass."

"Hey — a little respect for our commander, all right?"

Nielson curled his lip. "*Our*? Anyway, I respect the hell out of the woman — probably more than you do. But don't tell me you haven't noticed her fine form."

"She's ... a very attractive woman."

"With a remarkably sweet ass."

"OK, but tone it down, will you? This is supposed to be a family picture. I'm going to have to censor that whole conversation." Harte watched Nielson work. "So, can you fix it?"

Nielson glanced around. His close-set eyes were the almost colorless gray of dirty ice. "That depends. You gonna take my picture, or you gonna help me out here?"

"I thought that's what the robot was for."

The bot known as Mrs. Chippy bumped against Nielson's leg. He looked down, and Harte could have sworn he almost smiled. "You'd think. She's full of tools and everything, but she doesn't like to follow directions. Underfoot, is all." He gave her a gentle shove. "You're a pest, you know that? Yes, you are."

Harte kept his expression carefully blank. "I'd be happy to assist, Mr. Nielson. What do you need?"

Nielson growled something.

"Pardon?"

"Wrench, goddamn it! From the toolbox behind your damn fool head."

Harte located the tool locker and extracted the wrench. He placed it in Nielson's outstretched hand. The engineer unbolted a cover to the junction between the air return and the condenser unit. He reached in and pulled out a fine mesh filter. It was covered in some kind of whitish goo.

Nielson stared at it a moment, then scraped his finger through it. "What do you suppose this crap is?" He sniffed it, then to Harte's horror, he stuck his finger in his mouth and licked it off. He noticed Harte's expression and grinned. "You're not a fan of ice cream, are you?"

"Is that what it is? How did it get all the way in there?"

"The filters farther up are a coarser gauge, to keep out solid shit — lint, hair, chunks of food, small body parts, shit — but this gunk was a liquid and passed through until it got to this fine filter."

Harte was glad the robots couldn't talk, or Mrs. Chippy would have an interesting vocabulary. Nielson cleaned and disinfected the filter and replaced it. "Can't have Mr. High-and-Mighty dinging me for using a new filter when the old one's still good. Fussy little bastard!"

"He's just doing his job, same as you and me," Harte pointed out.

Nielson made a noise in his throat, and Harte feared he would spit, but he refrained. "So, what message do we have for the cook?"

"Um ... no more ice cream?"

Nielson gave a decisive nod. "No more ice cream. Too bad. I like ice cream."

Harte laughed. "So do I. I just prefer it with a spoon." He smoothed his mustache and turned the camera back on. "So, Mr. Nielson, what do you do when you're not fixing spaceships? Any hobbies?"

Nielson's whole face puckered up when he thought, and Harte cheered silently that he had captured that image. "I like to build shit — pardon me, stuff." He grinned. "Nothing I like better than to take a broken piece of this, a junked piece of that, and make something out of them. Something functional."

"When I was twelve, I built a solar-powered go-kart out of salvaged parts," Harte said.

"So you get it! Not everyone does. Good skill to have out here, where you can't just order a part and have it delivered."

"I never thought of it that way. Is that situation likely to come up?"

Nielson looked straight into the lens. "Stay out here long enough, anything's likely. You can put that in your doc."

At supper, Blackborow offered a choice of two MessPaks — Turkey Tetrazzini or Shrimp Fettuccini. No mixing or creativity, though Ruby appreciated the subtle jab.

"I guess I'll have turkey," Nielson said. "Hold the ice cream."

"That's easy," Blackborow replied cheerfully. "We ate it all. There isn't any more."

"No, we didn't eat it all. Enough got away to gunk up a filter in an important system."

Blackborow's eyes widened. "I didn't know! Was it — ?"

"Exactly. You didn't fucking know, because what do you fucking know? Why are you even here?"

Blackborow stared at him, her mouth open but with no words. With a sob, she swung around and returned to the galley.

"Mr. Wild, please check on Ms. Blackborow," Ruby said. "Mr. Nielson? With me. You may bring your supper." She took her own meal and led him to her quarters. She closed the door and turned to him with a smile. "Thank you for fixing the water recycler. We're lucky to have someone so able." Tact was key. He might be bad-tempered and a bit of a bully, but he was as important to the expedition as anyone on the ship. She needed his cooperation.

He swallowed a mouthful of turkey and wiped his mouth on his sleeve. "It wasn't much — I pulled out a filter and rinsed off some gunk. Gunner could have done that. You're the one who noticed something was wrong."

"A lucky guess. I have to say, though, I wish you had let me talk to Ms. Blackborow about the ice cream problem. Your ... *direct* approach seems to have upset her."

"I can't be worrying about how I might hurt some kid's feelings. She needs to know there's consequences!"

"On a venture as long as this one, trust me, she will. But in this case, the blame needs to be spread around. She served the ice cream, but I ordered it. And any of us could have closed the air return as soon as the first drop got loose, but nobody did. Not even you."

He bristled. "So now it's my fault?"

"Not at all. None of us saw what was happening. It caused a slight problem, but now it's fixed. It's my job, not yours, to prevent it from happening again." She hated to pull rank on him. She preferred a more casual attitude about hierarchy. It was better for morale and worked beautifully when everyone felt they were part of the same cause. But when someone started assuming authority he didn't have, she couldn't let it go. Even if she had once tried it herself. "I shouldn't have to point out that Blackborow doesn't answer to you. You and she both answer to Captain Anderson, to Mr. Wild, and to me. If either of you has a problem with the other, it should go through one of us."

"Seems like a waste of time to bother you or the captain for this puny shit," he said. "Maybe I just won't talk to her at all."

"Now you're being silly. Feel free to make conversation, compliment a meal, even suggest — politely — a change of seasoning. But orders and instructions need to come from above. It may seem inefficient but trust me — it'll be better all around."

"Hmph," he grunted.

They returned to the mess, where the others had finished their meal and now chatted and sipped hot tea from valved beakers while they waited for the nightly poker game to begin. Blackborow had come out of the galley. She gave Ruby an embarrassed look. Dr. Eyestone whispered something to Dr. Curley and slipped out, presumably back to the robotics lab. Ruby half expected Blackborow to go with him. Her chores were done for the evening, and she spent as much time as she could with the robots. But she remained where she was.

"What's this doofus up to, I wonder?" Nielson asked.

Ruby followed his gaze and wondered the same thing with kinder words. Dr. Curley floated at the end of the mess where the talent shows took place. *No banjo. Thank God.*

He cleared his throat and called out, "Your attention, please!" He reddened as everyone looked at him. He had played music on several occasions, but he rarely spoke in front of the group. He cleared his throat and continued. "For your listening pleasure, allow me to present, in their debut performance — the Doo-Bots!"

Dr. Eyestone herded all seven robots out of the airlock and into the mess. He winked at Blackborow. "Thank you, thank you, thank you! Ready, bots?" The robots formed a semi-circle. "One — two — one, two, three, four!"

The one called Hercules — Ruby couldn't tell them apart, but someone had painted their names above the forward sensor — began to hoot a series of low tones. As she tried to understand what this was supposed to demonstrate, the others joined in, in other registers. Ruby's mouth dropped open in amazement. They were *singing* in close harmony! At the same time, they executed a series of coordinated movements. The one called Mrs. Chippy danced — that was the only word for it — with more spirit than the others.

Stunned silence turned to laughter and applause. Even Blackborow cheered up, and Gunner shook with silent mirth. His camera floated forgotten at his side.

Ruby moved closer and nudged him. "Aren't you going to film this?"

His eyes widened and he nodded, though he seemed beyond speech. He raised the camera. Ruby smiled broadly. She was glad this delightful performance would be part of the doc.

As the bots began their second number, Gunner swung the camera to capture Ruby.

"Hey!" she protested.

He lowered the camera and grinned at her. "You have a wonderful smile, Boss. I couldn't help myself. The camera loves you."

The smile froze on her face. Here he came again, with his compliments and charm and precise little mustache, trying to get her to talk. "Fine. Just remember, this doc isn't about me."

"It's too soon to know what it's about."

"That's right. Maybe it's about them." She waved toward the singing, dancing robots.

"I doubt that, but I'm happy to include this footage. It captures the spirit of the expedition so far — optimism, cooperation, and hard work with a cheerful attitude."

His words startled Ruby, and her smile turned real again. "I couldn't have said it better. That's exactly what I want to see."

"For the most part, you've got it. Even Nielson is coming around. Interesting guy. What were you talking about just now?"

"Just ... working out a detail in the chain of command."

"Uh huh. He was a jerk to Blackborow and you called him on it."

"That is none of your business."

"As long as you put him in his place. How'd he take it?"

"The Doo-Bots came along in time to distract him. I really hope he's not angry — I need everyone working together. If something important breaks, he's the only one who could fix it."

Gunner raised an eyebrow. "Don't be too sure about that. But don't worry, either. He's a grownup, and Blackborow's resilient. They'll be fine."

He was probably right. Nielson loved machines too much to let anything happen to the ship, and Blackborow was young and optimistic enough to bounce back from much worse than hurt feelings. But an unexpected thought jarred Ruby. She knew who the crew and science staff answered to, but what about Gunner? Did he answer to her? Or to someone higher? If the need arose, did she have the authority to put him in his place?

Harte returned to his quarters soon after the robots' performance ended. He reviewed the footage, and if anything, was even happier to have it for the doc. It didn't require any text to explain it. It was a delightful surprise.

He looked over the rest of the day's shots and added captions where needed. The interaction between Nielson and Mrs. Chippy drew a smile. He acted tough, but Harte suspected he was a softy underneath. Audiences would love him.

He came to the shot of the Boss with her big grin. He captioned it, "Commander Ruby Ladd enjoys the debut performance by the Doo-Bots." Then he backed everything up on the external drive. He also sent the whole file to a secure server at his studio back home, a painfully slow process. It took almost fifteen minutes to ping the server and receive the confirmation reply, not including the time to send the images. Gamers back home spoke of "moon ping," but they had nothing on this. But it was an important failsafe. All the images would be waiting there when he returned, even if his equipment were damaged or lost. No one else would see them until he released them to the public.

He was about to clear the images from the camera, but he delayed over that smiling shot of the commander. How did such a small, relatively young woman achieve this level of leadership? Harte had nothing against short people, or women, for that matter, but you rarely saw them rise to the heights, whether in business, politics, academia, or the military. How had Ruby Ladd managed it against those odds?

She would say by showing up and working hard. That's what she'd told him the first night. He doubted he'd get a different answer if he asked her now. She refused to be considered exceptional, which was very special indeed. She didn't issue many orders — she had pulled rank on Nielson after dinner, but that was an anomaly. She didn't go around reminding people that she was the Boss; she just *was*.

When she entered a room, the atmosphere changed, becoming more positive by the strength of her optimism. Early in the mission, Harte had suspected this effect would wear off before long. Although shipmates bickered and chafed at their confinement, their admiration and respect for their commander had grown through the whole first month and showed no signs of waning. Her brand of optimism wasn't a passive hope that things would turn out well. It was active; she *made* things turn out well. He doubted she had ever in her life just waited for things to go her way.

She also managed to seem interested in everyone and their work, from the captain and the science staff, all the way down to the cook. She conveyed confidence in each shipmate's abilities, and the confidence rubbed off. Again, she was subtle and discreet about it, but in his line of work, Harte had to be observant. He was particularly touched by her care of their young stowaway. At first glance, Harte had taken Amelia Blackborow for a skinny, troubled teenager who had no place on a spaceship, though he appreciated the drama she added to his doc. He was sure he wasn't alone in that assessment. The commander had seen past the surface to the girl's hidden strength. And she was right — Blackborow was now as much a member of the expedition as anyone, capable and reliable beyond her years. The Boss still provided a subtle protection, but

Harte doubted it would be needed much longer. And when it wasn't, Ruby Ladd would gracefully withdraw.

And that was only one shipmate. He had seen over and over how her warmth and interest buoyed someone's confidence just when they needed a boost. In fact, the only person who didn't get this treatment was ... Harte Gunner. It wasn't that she didn't believe in his abilities. She praised his work and even asked his opinion regularly. But in most of their interactions, he had felt a chill. Her words were cordial; probably no one else detected the brittleness underneath. True, he didn't need his self-confidence bolstered. He didn't need her approval or her permission, only her cooperation in getting the shots he required for his project. He hadn't come on this jaunt to make friends. But a little warmth would have been nice.

He finished clearing the camera and plugged it into its charger, then zipped himself into his bag for the night. Before his mind's eye, he still saw the Commander's smiling face. That was one of few shots of her alone. He had told her he didn't yet know what the doc was about. It was supposed to be about the whole expedition, but it kept coming back to Ruby Ladd. She was the center, and he wanted to know more. What was she really like? What made her that way? What really happened on the Chickering Expedition?

And what did she have against Harte Gunner?

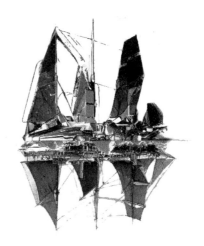

Chapter 10

2124/10/11: I thought I was making a space doc, but instead I'm making one about people living in a can. I need to get outside.

> *— Harte Gunner's Production Journal*

Exterior Shot:
Empty space. Stars shine in the background. Endurance passes majestically from left to right …

Harte paused and looked up from his imagined scene. Left to right was wrong. With no sunlight falling on its reflective surface, the ship wouldn't be visible against the black of space, and the backlighting would overpower any stars. He began again.

Exterior Shot:

Empty space. Stars shine in the background. Endurance passes majestically from right to left ...

He frowned. The sun side of the ship might be too bright to look at. He'd have to filter the shot. He also had doubts about majestically.

Captain Anderson drifted from the galley into the messroom, sipping from a beaker of coffee.

"Skipper, how fast are we going?"

Anderson grabbed a handhold to stop himself near Harte. "Right now, or on average?"

"Either."

"Our average looks to be 27,000 kilometers per hour. Right now, faster than that — I'd say 30K, but we'll have to decelerate soon or miss Mars entirely."

Harte pictured his exterior shot again. At 30,000 kph, the ship would be visible for about one frame. There wasn't even any point in generating that scene. He sighed and closed his comm without saving the aborted work.

Although he'd been aboard an orbital craft before, he hadn't imagined his great space epic would be so cramped. Just to have some elbow room, he preferred to work in the mess rather than in his little slot of a cabin, though neither had a view. You couldn't expect that kind of luxury in a refitted cargo vessel. He appreciated the little plants in his quarters, but a pot of succulents was no replacement for a forest ... or a window. The viewport on the bridge offered a good view of space, but that view didn't include the ship. He'd recorded plenty of good material over the first six weeks of the expedition, but aside from the weightlessness, there was nothing to differentiate this doc from any studio picture made on Earth. He needed an exterior shot to establish context for the activity within the ship.

There was no practical way to set up the fixed camera he imagined. He was willing to use a computer-generated image, but it had to be faithful to reality. He opened one of the stills he had captured on the Moon, before he boarded the ship. Looking at the image confirmed his doubts about majestic. Endurance wasn't graceful or elegant enough for that. It was a sturdy tub of a vessel, encrusted with antennas, panels, and gizmos — like giant barnacles on the hull of seagoing ship. Harte didn't know what everything was, only that each object had a purpose. And at least one person aboard who knew what that purpose was.

If he used this image against a background of stars and added the solar sail, it would be close to his imagined shot. He doubted Commander Ladd would allow false drama, and he didn't want to use one, anyway. Just the ship moving through space. But he saw now that the physics of it were absurd. For the ship to appear in the shot for any appreciable time, he'd have to set his imagined camera so far away that Endurance would be little more than a moving dot. Such a shot might be useful to demonstrate their incredible speed and the even more incredible distance, but it would come off comical, not majestic.

"I need to get outside."

"Hah!" Anderson barked. "Two chances of that — fat, and very, very slim."

"Then what's the point of all that training?"

"Emergency, Mr. Gunner." The Boss's voice startled Harte. She had come in without his noticing. "Only in an emergency. And then it wouldn't be you."

"Thank you, Boss," Anderson said. "I didn't want to be the one to break the news."

Harte opened his mouth to argue.

"Make way, make way!" John Eyestone interrupted before Harte could get a word out. Eyestone and Lee Keith pulled game boards from their locker and attached them to the table. Blackborow, Nguyen, Crean, Curley, and Wild joined them.

"Crean, you're with Nguyen at checkers," Mr. Keith said. "Curley and Blackborow, backgammon. Wild and Eyestone, chess."

The players took their places and set up the magnetic playing pieces. At a signal from Keith, they began to play, and Harte turned his camera on the activity. He didn't know how he would explain it in the doc, but he recorded the images, anyway.

Tabletop games had been popular entertainment since the first days of the expedition, but in recent weeks, Lee Keith had started a highly involved tournament consisting of simultaneous matches of checkers, backgammon, and chess. After a time determined by some algorithm Keith had developed, he gave a signal and everybody moved one place to the left and continued to play, either at a different game or on the opposing side of the same game. As far as Harte could tell, nobody really understood the scoring, but

Keith tracked something, and used it to assign positions in the next round.

As time went on, this and other aspects of shipboard life reminded Harte of nothing so much as his years in arts and media school. So maybe the Boss was right: they were running their own little college. They lived, ate, and socialized together in their space-traveling dormitory. Cliques formed around interests — robotics club: Eyestone, Curley, and Blackborow; chess club: Curley and Keith; band: Curley and Nielson — or status: officers; crew; scientists. None of the cliques were exclusive, though, a benefit to Harte who didn't naturally fit into any of them.

In addition to the games tournament and a running poker game, they had a book club, regular performances, and a prayer meeting that often turned into a discussion of theology or philosophy. On top of professional space training, experts on board now offered a surprising variety of electives. Aaron Curley had been giving banjo lessons for weeks. Eyestone was teaching advanced algebra to Amelia Blackborow, who offered lessons in conversational Spanish. Eyestone also offered a popular class called "Theoretical Bartending," his expertise coming from a job he'd held while in grad school. The SkyComms, and even Blackborow's cheap consumer MyComm, included a decent camera, so Harte offered weekly photography classes. His students didn't have his range of lenses, but they were improving their eyes and enjoying their new skills.

The Doo-Bots were popular photography subjects, both as a group and as individuals. Samson and Slag actively sought attention, seeming to pose for the camera. Mrs. Chippy didn't pose, exactly, but she was rarely far from her human shipmates. She seemed to like Nielson best — no accounting for robot taste — but also often joined Blackborow in the galley. Just now, the bot was following her around the game table.

Nielson came in. "Where's my robot?"

Keith gave the signal and the players changed places again. Blackborow and Curley had now come around to opposite sides of the backgammon game where they started.

"Your robot, Mr. Nielson?" Dr. Eyestone asked as he jumped several of Wild's checkers.

"She's helping me." Blackborow smirked at Nielson. "What are you going to do about it?"

"Are you winning?" Nielson asked.

Keith gave another signal. The shifts seemed to be coming closer together, but Harte still couldn't figure out the pattern. Now Blackborow and Eyestone were playing checkers.

"Who knows?" She laughed.

Nielson shook his head. "If your checkers is as good as your poker, you probably are." He joined the spectators.

Harte enjoyed witnessing the change in relationship between these two. Nielson had been the least willing to accept Blackborow onto the crew, even making her cry that one time with the ice cream a couple of weeks back. But during the DooBots' first performance, he had whispered something to her that made her smile. An apology, perhaps? Now they had an almost sibling-like bantering relationship, with Mrs. Chippy as a point of connection. He expected to feature them prominently in the finished doc.

After an hour, Keith called a halt to play and everyone went back to work for the rest of the afternoon, the rules of the tournament still a mystery. Harte suspected the process was more important than the product ... if there even was one. The same could not be said of his project. It was interesting to gather material, but he looked forward to the moment when it all came together into a coherent whole. It would be a gigahit ... if he could pin down the narrative. And if he could get outside.

"The audacity of it!" Ruby hissed to Anderson. Gunner had gone with Blackborow to the galley, leaving them free to talk about him if they kept their voices low.

The Skipper chuckled. "He has a point. There's no notion, in here, of how big space is."

"I should know better than to expect good sense from you."

"You said he did well in training. Maybe you should let him out — it might scare the arrogance out of him."

She smiled at the thought. "No, it would be too tempting to just leave him there and pick him up on the way home."

"He still rubs you wrong, does he?"

It was an unfortunate choice of verb, in light of the rules about appropriate contact. Her face grew hot at the idea of an attractive celebrity massaging her skin. She cleared her throat. "Nothing I can't handle. I'll let him out when we get to Mars, same as everybody else."

Anderson twitched an eyebrow. "We'll be there soon enough."

"February does not seem soon."

"The way this sail is working, it could be January."

She expressed her hope in a long sigh. "I could live with that."

After supper that evening, Nielson made his way to the performance area. He had played his harmonica with other musicians before, but Ruby had never seen him perform on his own. And he didn't appear to have his instrument with him.

"How many spacers does it take to screw in a lightbulb?" he asked. Silence. "C'mon, it's a joke! I say, 'How many spacers does it take to screw in a lightbulb,' and you say ..."

"What's a lightbulb?" Blackborow asked.

"You know, like an LED, but bigger," Dr. Eyestone said.

"Oh! Like in old cartoons, when someone gets an idea?"

"That's it — the Edison thing."

136

She frowned. "What's *screw* about it, though?"

"Ergh! No!" Nielson interrupted. "How thick are you people? You're supposed to say, 'How many?'"

"Oh. How many?" Blackborow asked.

"None! We're not allowed to screw!"

A few people laughed uncomfortably, some groaned, and Blackborow turned red. From there, the material failed to improve. His timing was all right, but the jokes themselves became more personal but no less vulgar, including one that indirectly questioned the parentage of the Skipper's children.

Before he or Ruby could object, Lee Keith called out, "You're not funny!"

Ruby started. It seemed that Keith, like Blackborow, had figured out Nielson was not actually a threat. The engineer faced his heckler and swallowed. "I suppose you could do better."

"Me? *I'm* not funny!" Keith protested, which got a laugh. "But you need better material."

Nielson threw up his hands and didn't attempt any more jokes. It was the shortest performance the *Endurance* party had witnessed, but no one seemed sorry to see it end. Ruby worried that Keith might come in for renewed bullying, though on second thought, it didn't seem likely. The victim who stands up isn't a victim anymore.

Chapter 11

2124/11/13: We are closer to Mars than to Earth, yet I feel I am at home and with my family. Where better to spend this day?

— Ruby Ladd's private diary

Ruby woke to an unexpected alarm — the unmistakable hoots and beeps of the Doo-Bots. The tune was familiar, but it took a moment to place it: "Happy Birthday to You." She grinned. Somebody knew what day it was.

At least two somebodies — how else would Dr. Eyestone know to teach the robots a new song? Ruby picked up her comm and found a birthday message from Wild. It was a picture of the two of them, captioned *Ruby & Pete, best friends 4ever. Happy birthday, teammate!* They were wearing basketball uniforms in the photo and had their long hair in ponytails. So they were fifteen; they'd both cut their hair short the next year. They made silly faces for the camera, their arms over each other's shoulders. She didn't remember who had taken the photo, but the occasion was a regional tournament. Their team was knocked out in the semi-finals that year. The next year, with Ruby as team captain, they took the championship.

The comm pinged with a call from the bridge.

"Good morning, Boss, and happy birthday," Anderson said. "I have some news I think you'll agree is worth celebrating. See you at breakfast."

She hurried to clean and dress herself. News of any kind broke the monotony of a long space journey, though she sometimes wished she could turn off the feeds about the pandemic, the destructive hurricane season, and the brewing civil war in the Confederate States of America. But the Skipper's message implied especially good news. She was always ready for that.

As Ruby pulled on her uniform jacket and prepared to leave her quarters, her comm notified her of an incoming call. Her heart sped up, hoping against hope for birthday greetings from her father. It was Wesley James.

"Happy birthday, Commander. I guess we can't call you a prodigy anymore, now that you're in your thirties. Over."

"Thank you, sir. I'll try to behave like a grownup. Over." She waited through several seconds' delay. At least the call was audio only. Video took more bandwidth and tended to break up.

"The ship appears to be making good progress, too. Ahead of schedule? Over."

"So they tell me. The solar sail is performing admirably. Captain Anderson says it might save us as much as four weeks. Over." She tapped her fingers against her leg. Why did it have to be a live call? She wanted her breakfast.

"Excellent. The sooner we can get places in a reasonable time, the sooner we can begin colonizing. Well, I won't keep you from your celebration. James out."

At least he'd kept it relatively brief. But his eagerness to colonize was frustrating. Five months rather than six was still an extremely long trip, especially for amateurs.

When she finally got there, breakfast was peanut butter and jelly between two waffles, eaten like a sandwich. "It's the closest I could get to birthday cake," Blackborow explained. "No ice cream, though." She glanced at Nielson with a mischievous smile.

He scowled back, but Ruby suspected he was trying not to laugh.

"I wish I could put candles in it," the cook added.

Ruby laughed. "We can't spare the oxygen for thirty candles!" She turned to Anderson. "So, Skipper, what's your news?"

He usually wore a cheery expression, but this morning, his smile seemed to reach around his head. He leaned close to Ruby's ear, his excitement unmistakable through his quiet voice. "Dr. Crean went over the data from the solar sail. It's working even better than expected — we recalculated our ETA, and we should get to Mars ... by Christmas."

Next to him, Jamie Crean looked as pleased and proud as a new father. "We're going to adjust course, then take in the sail today."

She stared at them both, struck mute by this news. He'd said maybe January! "But ... but that's a full two months ahead of schedule." She beamed. "Are you sure?"

"Pretty sure. We went over the figures three times."

"Let's share the news. Dr. Crean, please do the honors."

He made the announcement. After a moment's hush, the mess resounded with cheers. "And for anyone who didn't know already, it's Commander Ladd's birthday."

Their over-acted surprise was a clue they'd known for a while and probably had something planned. She didn't find out what until after supper.

In honor of the occasion, they presented a more elaborate talent show, featuring every possible talent aboard. With Curley on banjo and Nielson on harmonica, Gunner led a sing-along to warm things up. Ruby didn't mind the instruments so much when there was singing to go with them. Dr. Eyestone presented the Doo-Bots again, and then performed magic tricks, with Blackborow as his assistant. Dr. Mack sang a jazzy, funny standard about swinging on a star. Ruby didn't know the song, but Gunner must have; with permission, he joined in and made it a duet. Betty Nguyen did an interpretive mid-air dance while Dr. Crean gave a mock lecture that ended up proving by logic that 1 + 1 = 3.

Even Captain Anderson took a turn. "Sorry to get serious after that. This is something I learned in high school that I like to keep fresh." He proceeded to recite Hamlet's to-be-or-not-to-be soliloquy.

"Cheery selection," Gunner whispered.

Ruby started. He had an unnerving way of appearing right next to her. "He does it well."

Gunner nodded in agreement. "'The undiscovered country' — that sounds like where we're going."

She shuddered. "I sincerely hope not."

Last of all, Nielson took the makeshift stage. Shipmates glanced uneasily at each other, and some actually groaned at the memory of his bad jokes. Then Keith joined Nielson and played the straight man. Although most of the jokes poked fun at some member or other of the expedition — Anderson was the favorite target — the teasing was gentler than before, and the punchlines drew humor from truth. The two were much funnier as a team than Nielson alone, and he seemed to know it. They received a rousing ovation.

As a final celebration, Ruby opened the morale locker and allowed a bottle of Cabernet to be shared among the entire party. It was only a few sips apiece, but they had been without alcohol long enough that even that little was a treat.

Gunner had filmed the talent show but put the camera aside to savor his drink. He raised his beaker to Ruby. "Happy birthday, Boss. May you have fifty or sixty more. Good news about the new ETA, isn't it?"

He seemed to approach her with sincere friendliness. Maybe the wine had mellowed her, but she decided to accept his greetings in that spirit. "It's great news, especially if we get the same results between Mars and the Belt. I never imagined we might be tagging asteroids by April." She sipped from her beaker.

"You'll have to show me the sights on Mars."

She laughed out a mouthful of wine and had to recapture the drops from the air. "There's not that much to see at the research base."

"It's my first time on another planet," he reminded her.

She relented. "There is a good view from the surrounding hills. And you'll want to see Chickering's memorial." The Pearl ached a little, but she resisted the urge to touch it. The gesture didn't help, and she wanted to break the habit.

"Are you ever going to tell me what really happened?"

She gazed at him. She almost felt like talking, but that was probably the wine, too. "I won't say no. Ask me again when we get there."

Harte had begun to feel as if he had always traveled in this ship and always would. The revised ETA reinvigorated him and the entire party. The routine did not change, but everything gained new purpose. Dr. Curley and Dr. Eyestone were planning a training regimen for the robots on the Martian surface. Shipmates who had been skipping workouts immediately got back in the habit, to make sure their bodies were prepared for increased gravity. Most of them put their labs and personal space in shipshape order every day, as if they would be landing tomorrow. Or as if they were children and Santa was coming tonight. Well, if the Skipper's estimate was correct, that wasn't so far off.

Harte filmed through the forward viewport for a few minutes every day, the closest he was going to get to outside. As they drew nearer, Mars changed from reddish dot to disc to orb. For days, it seemed they must be close enough to land, only to get closer but not yet close enough. Just when it seemed they would never get there, they passed through the orbit of the moon Phobos, and it suddenly felt real — they were actually going to land on Mars.

In preparation, he looked up information about the base there. He found a map that made it look like a small boarding school, with dormitories for staff and occasional visitors, offices, kitchen, dining hall, infirmary, chapel, and gymnasium. The population was small — only thirty at this time, mostly researchers and administrators — but with plans for gradual increase. Hundreds of young adults applied for a handful of intern slots. Those accepted received a stipend and college credit for doing whatever grunt and gofer work was required. The experience would look good on a resume. Harte had applied himself when he was younger but had not been accepted.

Extensive greenhouses produced mushrooms, roots and tubers, legumes, including peanuts and soy, a variety of greens and other vegetables, and several kinds of berries. Hemp and bamboo provided fibers for textiles, as well as plant-based polymers for 3D printing a range of useful items, such as basic shoes and handles for tools. All organic waste was composted and returned to the soil to grow more food.

The mining and manufacturing facilities were still small in scale — more proof-of-concept than anything, meant to demonstrate that a community of humans could provide for itself. Using resources extracted or grown on-site, they produced their own building materials, furniture, tools, and some clothing. The base was nearing self-sufficiency, though some equipment and supplies were still sent from Earth. *Endurance* carried several pallets of flour; it was not practical to grow the quantities of grain required.

The staff, pros and interns alike, were on a two-year rotation. A new superintendent, Baird Rogers, had taken over the previous January. From Harte's scant administrative experience, he figured this would give the man just enough time to learn the job before he rotated out. But if he liked the work, perhaps he would get to come back.

He was about to read up on the history of the place when Commander Ladd spoke. "Good job, Skipper — it's Christmas Eve, just like you said." She patted the captain on the back.

Harte had encountered her on the bridge almost every time he went there, as if she, too, could hardly wait. Her manner toward him had thawed a trifle, and he was tempted to remind her of her near promise to talk about the past. But he didn't want to press his luck.

He stuck to innocuous topics and did what he could to remain in her good graces. "Nielson had a pool on when we'd get here," he said. "I lost fifty ivars."

The commander laughed. "I'm no gambler, but I'd have won. Frank Anderson is a superb intuitive navigator; if he says 'by Christmas,' it's gospel."

Harte gazed through his camera at the lumpy little moon. "That's a sight. It doesn't even look like a moon. It's more like ... a spud the size of Idaho!" He hoped he was right about the name. As he recalled, the former Mountain states aimed to keep their names as they joined up with former Plains states and provinces under the governance of a league of Indigenous tribes.

"Nowhere near that big," Ruby replied. "You could wrap it in a piece of foil the size of Ada County."

Harte grinned at this unexpected bit of trivia. "You sure know your geography, Boss. Any chance of stopping off?"

"Too late now," Anderson said. "It's closer to its planet than any other moon in the solar system. It zips around so fast, it rises in the west."

"That's hard to picture. I may have to include an animation, just to explain it."

Commander Ladd nodded. "Not a bad idea. Did you know it's hollow? Part of it, anyway."

"I hadn't heard that."

"There's a whole network of little caverns. SCEI enlarged a couple of them. You can't see it from this distance, but there's an emergency supply depot, right ... there." She pointed.

He continued to film, though he couldn't tell what exactly she was pointing at. "If you can't see it, how do you know?"

"I supplied it. Chickering let me have that assignment for myself, and I like to think I considered every need."

"Why would such a thing be needed at all, so close to the planet?"

"Perhaps a ship arrives too damaged to land in atmosphere — it can safely dock here and await rescue from the surface, or effect repairs. A large party could subsist for at least a week."

"Is that likely?"

She shrugged. "It's never been used. We've been sending humans for only a few years, after all. And the planet's atmosphere is still pretty thin, though if the terraforming succeeds, that will change. I like to plan for all possibilities."

"So I see." He took care with the phrasing of his next comment. "Commander Chickering must have really known your strengths, to give you an assignment that fit so well."

"A distraction," Anderson said.

"That's enough, Skipper." She didn't raise her voice or even glance at him, but it was the sharpest tone Harte had ever heard her use with the captain. "We were a good team. Working for that man really honed my organizational skills." Her left arm twitched upward, then dropped to her side. She squeezed her fingers into a fist.

"He was especially organized?" Harte asked.

Captain Anderson snorted.

She frowned in Anderson's direction, but he wasn't looking. "Anything but. He was an idea man. Actually, he was a lot like you, Mr. Gunner — and you, Skipper — wildly creative, not afraid of risks. He'd try anything. People adored him — they'd do any crazy thing he asked."

"But not you, I'll bet."

"I adored him, too. Maybe more than anyone else. My job was to take his impossible dreams and make them reality. I didn't want him to fail." She turned away, as if she considered the conversation finished, but Harte suspected it was just beginning.

"Huh. So what happened with Olympus Mons?"

She turned with a sharp glance and swallowed visibly. When she replied, her voice was a hoarse whisper. "I was too late."

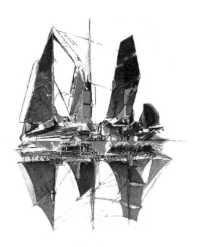

Chapter 12

2124/12/24: I can't believe we're spending Christmas on Mars! The Boss has practically promised to tell me about the Chickering Expedition — the best present I could hope for.

— Harte Gunner's Production Journal

They entered orbit around the Red Planet. The Skipper alerted Columbia Base of their approach and estimated arrival time. Ruby couldn't deny the thrill about this tangible progress in the expedition. The real work was about to begin. But it grew increasingly difficult to maintain her customary optimism, this close to the scene of too many bad memories.

At that moment, her comm alerted her to a message — a text from Wesley James, not a live call. She was grateful for that, lacking the serenity to tolerate the lag.

Congratulations on reaching Mars ahead of schedule! Momentous achievement; a triumph of human ingenuity and spirit. If this keeps up, we will be colonizing other worlds in no time.

"Hey, Skipper, Wesley James is already calling our expedition a triumph. He's ready to start sending colonists."

He glanced over his shoulder at her. "Maybe wait to answer him until we're on the ground."

"You don't believe we might crash, do you?"

"Never tempt fate," Anderson replied. "But let's save the celebration until we know everyone can walk off the ship. We may have knocked weeks off our ETA but we've still been in zero G for four months."

Ruby turned and found Harte Gunner back on the bridge with his camera, like a well-groomed stalker, asking gentle, considered questions that concealed sharp blades. He filmed as they orbited. "Will we be able to see Olympus Mons from here?"

She flinched. She couldn't help it. With effort, she quelled her rising anxiety. "From orbit? Easy. It's bigger than huge. We won't get close to it on the surface, though."

"That's too bad."

"Not really. You'll get a better picture from up here. It's so big, it's hard to see from the ground — it disappears over the curve of the planet."

"Wow," he breathed.

She couldn't help smiling at that. He had an almost childlike sense of awe, which probably helped make him so good at his work. And until today, he had mostly refrained from asking about Chickering. Now that they were close to the site of that disaster, she doubted he would continue to respect her silence on the subject. She'd said too much already.

Harte continued to film as they orbited. The Boss was quiet, but Captain Anderson pointed out Olympus Mons as they passed over. She was right — it was no trouble at all to see it from orbit. Its broad shield covered a huge area like a vast, rumpled circus tent.

"Biggest volcano in the solar system," Anderson said. "Considering that, it has a pretty small death toll."

"Don't," the commander said.

Anderson glanced at her. "I'm sorry, Ruby, but —" She glared. He closed his eyes and began again. "I'm sorry, Boss. You're right. It wasn't the mountain's fault."

She turned away. Harte wasn't sure what to make of the near conflict growing between these two.

The captain went on, with an obvious change of subject. "You're lucky, Gunner — it's an unusually clear day for Mars."

"Will you land *Endurance*, or do we have to take the shuttle?" Harte wasn't looking forward to cramming into that dinky craft with eleven other people and only eight seats.

"With this puny atmosphere?" the captain said. "We'll go down in style. Be sure to film it, though — it's quite the light show."

"But not dangerous?" Harte asked.

"Well, this whole jaunt is dangerous, isn't it?" Anderson said. "But *Endurance* is a well put-together little ship. Magnetic shielding protects us from radiation, and a carbon composite heat shield keeps us cool on re-entry."

Harte made a quick note of this information in his production journal before he joined the others for lunch. After the meal, they suited up and strapped in. Anderson applied the braking thrusters. They hit the atmosphere and glowing plasma streamed over the nose of the ship, an unexpected special effect Harte was pleased to capture. But he would have recorded the landing, regardless. It was the first thing to really *happen* in months.

They came in low over the large Gusev Crater, near a range of small hills. Anderson brought *Endurance* to a flawless landing just outside the research base. Most of the base was underground and easy to overlook from the air. Here and there, windows and skylights winked in the sunshine. With the calm winds, there was relatively little dust in the air.

"Nicely done, Skipper," the Boss said. She unstrapped herself and stood, and the rest of the party followed suit. "Collect your gear and meet by the airlock. Take care walking until you get your planet legs."

After months in zero G, Harte found it odd to have his feet on the floor, to know the floor was down, to *stand*. Odd, but good. It was a pleasure to walk again. He felt the gravity, but it wasn't bad. He'd done his workouts.

"How long can we stay?" Blackborow asked.

Commander Ladd smiled at her. "I've arranged for us to bunk here till New Year's Day. You all deserve a Christmas break. But I'm most interested in sleeping in a real bed tonight."

A bed? Now there was a novel idea! Harte gathered with the others by the airlock, his duffel over his shoulder and his camera in his gloved hand.

As they left the ship at last, the Commander reminded everyone to lower the gold visor. She watched each member of the party walk past and questioned anyone who seemed off-balance. Harte hung back and walked with her toward the welcoming committee of three spacesuited figures. Although she had answered a few of his questions, she had been visibly tense since before they entered orbit. She was still awfully quiet.

"I feel like I weigh a ton!" he said, to lighten the mood.

"It's only about a third of a G," she replied. "It feels good. And I'm glad to see everyone leaving the ship under their own power. The last time I was here, a few of the rookie officers had to be carried off. Excuse me, will you? One of these people must be Superintendent Rogers." She moved forward through the little crowd to greet him.

Harte filmed the meeting, but he was still thinking about what she'd said. "The last time I was here ..." She was getting close to telling him details about that expedition. Now that they were here, maybe she'd feel more like talking.

A pair of technicians from the base returned with Nielson to the ship to go over what was needed to prepare it for launch. The superintendent led the rest of the party into a large tunnel opening, through an airlock, and into the base proper. It was a relief to remove the helmet at last. Rogers was revealed to be a tall dark-skinned man in his forties, his short hair beginning to recede but still dark.

"Dormitories are down this passage." Rogers gestured to Harte's right. "The doors are marked with your names, and the bathrooms should be obvious. Commander, I've put you in the VIP suite. Is there anything else you need?"

"Thank you, Superintendent. I think we can manage."

"Very well. I'll expect you in the dining hall at 1900 for a festive supper. You'll be our honored guests."

He left them and the party began to move into the passage toward their rooms. Harte caught up with the Commander.

"Don't forget your promise to show me the sights," he said. "Tomorrow?"

"Fine. Think of it as a Christmas present."

"Thank you. Maybe we can finally have that interview."

She turned and glared at him. "Oh, we'll have an interview, all right. One on one. Stow your gear and meet me in the gym."

She strode past him, toward her quarters. He didn't know what to make of her statement or her attitude. He headed down the corridor and found his assigned room. He would be sharing a small double room with Lee Keith. In this extensive base, there would be less privacy than on the ship. How did the Commander rate a VIP suite, and he didn't? Nowhere else in the world was he not a VIP. But this wasn't that world.

He set his duffel and camera on one of the beds and removed his spacesuit.

"What's going on with the Boss?" Keith asked.

"I'm not sure." Harte changed into workout clothes and picked up the camera. "I hope to find out."

"I don't think you'll need the camera. She said 'gym' and 'one-on-one.'" Keith shook his head. "I wouldn't want to be in your shoes." With that glum pronouncement, he left the room.

Harte reluctantly left the camera behind and followed signs to the gymnasium. He hoped to meet the Commander in private but found the entire expedition party gathered near the basketball court.

She was already there, a ball in her hands. "I issued the challenge, so you can have the ball first." When he stepped onto the court, she passed it to him, hard.

"Oof!" He caught it, but the impact forced the breath from his lungs. "Are we playing H-O-R-S-E?" It had been a while since he went one-on-one against anybody, but he remembered the basics. Each basket earned the shooter a letter of the word. The first to spell "horse" was the winner. He would go easy on her, let her work out some of this unexplained anger.

"No, we're playing E-N-D-U-R-A-N-C-E. Go!"

He quickly learned there was no need or even possibility of *going easy*. He had the height advantage, but she was quicker and a better ball handler. The low gravity probably helped, but she also had a killer outside shot. Soon, they were both puffing and sweating, but if anything, the play grew more aggressive. Harte blocked a shot and knocked the commander down. He took her hand to help her up.

"Sorry, Boss."

"Don't be. A third of a G won't do any harm."

Harte wasn't so sure about that. He expected to have bruises, some from the floor, some from her elbows. After he missed his next shot and she made hers, he had E-N-D-U-R to her E-N-D-U-R-A-N. He picked up the ball and called a time out. He was exhausted. In spite of all his hard work aboard ship, he wasn't in as good shape as he'd thought.

"Come on, Gunner, let's play!" She clapped her hands and assumed a defensive stance, balanced on the balls of her feet with knees bent and her hands out. She was breathing hard, but otherwise, didn't appear tired.

He watched her and tried to catch his breath. "Why are we doing this?"

"You asked for an interview."

"I know, but —"

"If you win, I'll talk."

"I wish you'd mentioned that earlier," he puffed.

"So that wasn't your A game?"

"It was, but ..." He didn't see much chance of winning now. "What do you have against me, Boss?"

She stared at him, then blinked. She left the court and sank onto a bench at the sidelines opposite the spectators. She picked up a towel to wipe her face and took a pull from a water bottle. He sat next to her, still holding the ball. She glanced at him sidelong. "I don't know."

"Well, try this — I don't work for you. You didn't choose me." He forced himself to keep his gaze fixed on her.

Her lips twisted into a half smile. She nodded. "That's part of it. They didn't even ask my opinion."

"Who would you have suggested? There isn't anyone else for a job like this."

She puffed a breath through her nose. "And there's the rest of it — you're so full of yourself!"

"I call it confidence."

"Semantics," she said. "The real issue is this: you call me Boss, but you're not really a member of the party. You're just a ... a spectator!"

He sighed. "I'd be a member of the party if you'd let me. I may not work for you, but I would love to work *with* you." She rolled her eyes. "They didn't tell you, did they?" he asked.

"Who didn't tell me what?" she asked.

"SCEI didn't choose me, either. I offered my services."

"Wait. *You* went to *them*?"

He shrugged. "Yeah. Think about it — what do I do? I take the audience to dangerous places they'd never see otherwise. I've done mountain-climbing docs, undersea, in orbit. This seemed like the next logical step, and I wanted it — the ultimate thrill."

She narrowed her eyes at him. "I really don't need a daredevil thrill-seeker endangering my mission."

"I would never do that! I don't ask anyone to take a risk I wouldn't take. But you were taking this ride, anyway, so I volunteered to come along. Frankly, it hasn't seemed all that dangerous — until now. You almost gave me a heart attack!"

He half-expected her to finish the job, but she chuckled and handed him the towel. "Sorry. You brought out my competitive streak. You're not a bad ball player." She folded her arms. "And I don't think you can really call yourself a *volunteer*. You'll make a fortune when this doc comes out, whether I talk to you or not."

"No, *we* will. My contract stipulates that all members of the expedition party will share in the profits."

That shut her up for a moment. "Very ... noble of you. Shall we finish our game?"

He handed her the ball. "I'm finished already. You win."

"No, you do."

He frowned. "You had more points."

"You asked me a question I couldn't answer. Maybe ... maybe this interview is just what I need."

It was his turn to be at a loss for words. This was what he wanted, more than the thrill, more even than the stunning images. She was going to give him her side of the story — the untold side. Just like that. It seemed almost too easy. Except for the bruises.

He glanced at the spectators on the other side of the court. They watched with rapt attention. For all the intensity of their conversation, he and the commander had kept their voices down. He doubted anyone had heard, though they probably suspected something important had happened. He turned back to her.

"Here's what we do," he said in an undertone. "We act as if we've finished the game. No one needs to know anything more."

"Agreed."

They stood and exchanged a sportsmanlike handshake. They were saved awkward questions by the much more important announcement that dinner would be served in ten minutes.

Ruby returned to the so-called VIP suite. It was a small single room with a bed, a chair, a built-in desk, and a small closet. But it had its own bathroom, like her cabin aboard ship, only with running water and a complimentary bathrobe. The others had to share common facilities down the hall. There was just time to shower and change. A real hot water shower — the height of luxury after months aboard ship, even if it was metered to only five minutes. Ruby enjoyed every one of them, then put on her dress uniform and joined the others.

Superintendent Rogers provided a festive Christmas Eve supper, vegetarian but enhanced by some additions from *Endurance* — real whiskey and some good chocolate. Ruby was seated to Rogers' right, with Anderson on her other side and Wild and Crean across the table. Gunner was a few places down, on the other side of Anderson and Dr. Mack. Ruby was glad to have a little distance from him. Their talk in the gym had left her feeling raw. The celebration helped. It distracted everyone and delayed any further conversation on the lines he wanted to pursue.

There were gingerbread cookies for dessert, a comforting, homey touch. Ruby was about to take another when Gunner caught her eye with a hopeful smile. Rather than continue their talk, she left the dining hall and hurried down the first passage she came to. She intended to return to her room, but when she slowed down enough to read the signs, she discovered she was headed away from the dormitory, toward the chapel and infirmary.

A tall woman in black with short graying curls approached from the other end of the passage. As they neared each other, she brightened as if she recognized Ruby, and quickened her pace. She looked familiar, but Ruby couldn't place her, especially when she saw the clerical collar. Ruby didn't know any clergy these days.

The other woman smiled and held out her hand. "Commander Ladd? Chaplain Anne Ingram. I don't know whether you remember me, but I flew out with you and Commander Chickering."

Ruby shook her hand. "I knew you looked familiar. I didn't realize your stint would be so long. Everyone else from that crew is gone by now."

"I extended it — twice. Not everyone gets to have a whole planet as their parish!" They both chuckled at that, Ruby a little uneasily. "This is lucky, running into you like this," Chaplain Ingram continued. "I wanted to invite your party to our Christmas Eve service in the chapel. It's a nice time — lots of music."

"I'll … let them know. I'm sure you'll get several takers."

"2300 hours. I hope to see you there."

Ruby shook her head. "You won't. I have … a low tolerance for God talk."

The chaplain smiled. "It won't be just practicing Christians, you know. Way out here, we all observe everything, just to break the monotony."

"It's not that. Five years ago, I would have been first in line. But I haven't been inside a house of worship since …" Ruby swallowed. "You know. The funeral."

"Commander Chickering's? That was a great tragedy," Chaplain Ingram said.

Ruby frowned. "I think somebody has to learn something for it to qualify as a tragedy. Otherwise, it's just a pathetic waste."

"What did you learn, Commander?"

Ruby shook her head. She couldn't speak.

"It was a hard time for all of us. But God did not kill those men."

"Didn't save them either," Ruby muttered.

"No. I know you tried."

Ruby didn't answer. Few besides Anderson knew about that last failed act of disobedience.

The chaplain wasn't done. "But I believe God was present. The Lord is no stranger to grief, you know. So if you want to talk about it —"

"I really do not."

"All right. Maybe another time. I'm also a certified mental health provider, so it doesn't have to be God talk. I will tell you this — the only way out is through."

"Thanks." Ruby didn't want to think or talk about any of this. She couldn't seem to escape it, but at least she could put it off. She gave the chaplain a tight smile and turned back to the dining hall. Most of the party was still at the table. She wished she could be so light-hearted, but then she probably wouldn't be the Boss. "Mr. Wild, please let everyone know there will be a Christmas Eve service in the chapel at 2300, and all who wish to may attend."

He grinned. "It'll feel like it's really Christmas. I'll spread the word." In a quieter voice, he added, "You going?"

"What do you think?"

"I'll see you at 2230."

"Yeah, right," she said under her breath, and left the dining hall again. This time, she found the correct passage to get to her room. It was early, but she was worn out from the basketball game and the gravity and thoughts of Chickering. She undressed and crawled into bed.

She woke to a quiet tapping. She pulled on her robe and stumbled to the door. "Whoever you are, you'd better have a good reason for waking me. It's the middle of the night, for Christ's sake."

"Interesting choice of words, Boss."

"Wild? What are you doing here?"

"It's 2230. I thought you'd be awake."

"I'm awake now, so you might as well come in." She turned on the light and opened the door. "What is it?"

"I can't believe you went to bed early on Christmas Eve! I came to get you for the service."

She stared at him. "You were serious about that?"

"Get dressed, Boss. Let's go."

"You can't tell me what to do."

He grinned. "Well, who could? I'm *asking* you, as your old friend Pete, to come to the service with me. It was always your favorite."

He knew her too well. He knew she didn't want to go, and why, but he also knew how she used to be, before all that.

"I give up. Give me five minutes."

She put her uniform back on and joined him in the passage. Although they got there in plenty of time, the tiny chapel was already packed. It looked like the entire base had turned out, plus the whole *Endurance* party. They probably had to bring in extra chairs. The only decorations in the plain room were a small artificial tree and lighted electric candles, but that was enough. Wild pointed out two free seats at the end of the second row. Ruby slid into her place and only then saw that her seat was next to Gunner's. It was too late to move; Wild had already taken his place on her other side.

Gunner smiled. "Glad you could make it," he whispered.

At least he wouldn't expect her to talk about Chickering. She was grateful for that alone but enjoyed the service for its own merits. It was good to sing the familiar old carols, accompanied by guitars … and Curley's banjo, but she was warming even to that. It helped to have Gunner's confident voice in her ear. The music and candlelight gave her a cozy glow. Even the Pearl seemed to loosen a bit.

She listened with new ears to the story of love coming to imperfect people in an imperfect world. Whether she believed it or not, she'd always liked the story, the idea of it. But could that love reach to *this* world, where she had suffered so much humiliation and loss? Maybe it could. They were a long way from Bethlehem, but even here there were plenty of imperfect people in need of love.

So she was in a charitable mood when Gunner fell into step beside her on the way back to the dormitories.

"No camera?" she asked.

"I snuck in early and took some shots with my comm, but it didn't seem right to record the service. I'm glad I went, though. There's something about singing carols by candlelight on Christmas Eve …"

"I'm sure they appreciated your strong voice, too," Ruby said. "More of your professional training, I assume?"

He laughed. "No, but my parents got me into a children's choir when I was nine or ten. I sang with them for years before I found out it was an elite ensemble and I was on scholarship. I thought it was for fun! It was good training, though, and it helped my voice change smoothly. I just went from alto to baritone with barely a crack."

"Because heaven forbid the great Harte Gunner have a gawky adolescence."

"I found plenty of other ways to be gawky. Any athleticism I have developed later." He smiled down at Ruby. "And I still don't come up to your level. Well, here's where we part ways. Merry Christmas, Commander." He gave a mock salute and headed down the passage to his room.

"Merry Christmas, Mr. Gunner," Ruby murmured, too low to be heard.

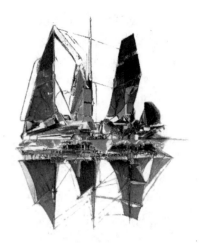

Chapter 13

2124/12/25: Our arrival couldn't have been better timed. Morale has been good, but a little gravity, more space, and a larger society come as a much-deserved gift.

— Commander Ladd's Expedition Journal

Harte didn't hear any reindeer during the night, but he saw Commander Ladd slip out during breakfast and return with a bag and a Santa hat in her hand. No one else seemed to notice, but he was eager for the promised interview, and kept an eye on her for any sign that she was ready to begin. Still, there was no need to ruin the lavish and jolly meal with business.

As they left the table, the Boss put on the hat and presented each member of the expedition party with a small package. She had a smile and a "Merry Christmas" for each one.

"Good morning, Mr. Gunner. Merry Christmas." She glanced at him, then away. She gave him a package, but no smile.

He would have preferred the smile and no package. After their basketball game, he thought they had at least come to an understanding, even if they weren't best pals. Why else would she sit with him at the chapel service? And they'd had a civil conversation afterward. Clearly, he still had work to do. He tore off the wrapping to reveal a detailed little model of *Endurance*, the perfect size to hang on a Christmas tree. "This is very nice. But I didn't get you anything."

She laughed harshly. "I didn't get you anything, either. I didn't know you were coming until after I had those made. That one was mine."

"Thank you. Maybe we can share it."

"That won't be necessary." She glanced around, though by now no one else was nearby. "I'm going for a walk outside. Get your suit on and come along if you want. Bring your camera."

Harte hurried to his room and struggled into his spacesuit. It was easier with a decent amount of gravity, but the whole business was entirely more trouble than he was used to for a mere walk outside. He hoped the pictures would be worth it.

He met the Boss at the airlock a short time later. They put on their helmets and stepped inside. Before the outer doors opened, she reached up and lowered his gold visor.

"Hey!" he protested. He could barely see.

"Do you value your eyeballs, Mr. Gunner?"

"They're insured for a million ivars. Each."

"Of course they are." The door slid open, and they stepped outside. "Mars has no ionosphere, no magnetosphere, barely any atmosphere. There's nothing but that visor to keep solar radiation from melting your retinas."

"Oh. I knew that," he bluffed. The sun was high in the sky. It seemed too small and too bright, even with the visor.

She strode away, toward a trail into the hills under which the base lay. She was a fast walker, but his longer legs made it easy to keep up. He fell into step beside her. "Thanks for letting me come along. I thought you might still be angry."

"Don't waste your air. We're climbing."

She *was* still angry. At least she remembered her promise to show him the sights. In silence, they climbed to the pass between two of the low hills. If he'd been accustomed to Earth gravity, Harte suspected he could have run to the top. As it was, it was not a difficult climb, but he felt it.

At the top, Commander Ladd leaned on something that looked like an informational sign while he filmed the Gusev Crater. It was another calm day. The dark blue sky contrasted sharply with the butterscotch-colored landscape of rocks and smaller craters.

"Not much of a promised land," he said.

"I've always thought Mars looked more desolate than the Moon," the commander replied. "Why is that?"

He'd been thinking the same thing. "Because … it has a sky. It's a world, but it's dead."

"It might have been alive once," she said. "It might be again."

"It's hard to imagine anyone living here permanently." He panned across the crater, searching for any color variation or sign of life.

"Humans have adapted to some pretty harsh environments," she said. "It won't be Puget Sound country, but if the planet can hold enough of an atmosphere —"

"Maybe we should work harder at fixing the planet we have, before we start mucking up another one."

"Or maybe what we learn out here will help fix it."

That was a good point. Experimentation on a dead rock was safer than on a living world. He tried to imagine this crater as a lake, these hills as islands …

He shivered. "Cold up here. I thought these suits were insulated."

"They are, but they're really meant for hard vacuum. They reflect the sunlight, so you don't get much radiant heat. The air is thin, but extremely cold — around 210 Kelvin."

"Two hundred ten sounds hot."

She snorted. "That's minus sixty-three Celsius. We won't be out here long enough to freeze, but we'll lose a little body heat. Unless you want to go back in?"

"I'm fine." He tried to ignore the chill and turned to film back the way they'd come. *Endurance* sat on the flat landing field, small in the distance. It wasn't the exterior shot he'd been dreaming of, but it was better than nothing. "From here, it looks like one of your little models. Hard to believe we came all this way in that!"

"And she'll carry us much farther still." He heard genuine affection in her voice. Even the ship got more warmth than he did. "The real expedition hasn't even begun yet."

"I'm ready." He tilted the camera up the slope of the larger hill and ventured what he hoped was a safe question. "So you know now what I'm doing here. If you don't mind my asking, how did you get this command?"

To his relief and amazement, she answered. "Probably because I was the only one qualified." She paused. "Or insane enough."

"How do you figure?"

"Initially, SCEI asked me to head the planning team. So I assembled a good group, and we planned every detail we could think of. Once Director James had the plan in hand, he attempted to find a commander who ... wasn't me."

"Why?"

"You'd have to ask him. I'm not sure he trusts me. But nobody else had the right combination of experience, organizational skills, and temperament. It had to be me."

"And you say *I'm* full of myself!"

"I call it confidence," she replied.

He snorted. "Let me guess who else was on the planning team — Wild?"

"Very good."

"Anderson?"

"No, but I wasn't going to attempt this without him. Dr. Crean and Dr. Mack were part of it, though."

Things were going well, but it seemed prudent to pull back to generic topics. "I meant to research the history of the base, but I didn't get very far. Do these hills have a name?"

A tinny laugh filled the headset. It was a delightful sound; he wished he was recording their conversation, but she hadn't seemed inclined to grant the interview when they set out. Now it was too late to set up the equipment. "Is there anything left in the solar system that doesn't? They're called the Columbia Hills."

That seemed familiar. "Are they named for the hills back home?"

"No. Those hills were named for the Columbia River, which was named for a sailing ship." She paused. "These hills were named for a different ship. It broke up in the atmosphere."

"Here, on Mars?" He didn't remember hearing about any such accident.

"No, on Earth, a long time ago. Seven astronauts died; they named a hill for each one. They never got out of Earth orbit, but I'm sure they would have appreciated the thought. But that's not why I brought you here. There's ... another memorial."

She swept the dust off the sign and stepped back. It was a memorial to Commander Chickering and the five members of his party who perished on Olympus Mons. It included a group photograph, with each member named, but there were odd gaps in the grouping.

"This picture was edited."

"You have a good eye, Mr. Gunner."

"Of course I do. That's why they're insured."

She made an impatient noise. "It was taken from a portrait of the entire party. Frank Anderson was here at the end. Nielson was there. And I used to be there." She pointed to the gap on Chickering's right.

"So you were his right hand."

"He was my friend. They all were, but especially the Boss."

Harte hid his surprise at hearing someone else honored with that title. "Are they buried here?"

"No." She was silent a long time, then cleared her throat. "No, they're not. It seemed important to have a memorial on the planet, and this is still the only human outpost."

"Will you tell me what happened?"

She touched her chest. "How much do you already know?"

"That Robert Chickering led an expedition to Mars in 2119, with the purpose of surveying potential Skysteader sites, as well as convenient mineral resources." This was public information that anybody could look up, but she didn't interrupt. He continued. "This base was already partly completed, and the expedition delivered technicians and support staff."

"You make it sound so dull."

"The public record is dull. That's why I'm talking to you."

"Fair enough. When did it turn interesting?"

"Late in the mission, Chickering and some of the officers climbed Olympus Mons without vehicles or robotic assistance. They made the summit but perished on the descent."

"And where was I in all this?"

"That's what I hope to find out. Although you were Chickering's First Officer, you didn't participate in the climb, so you survived. An investigation cleared you of wrongdoing. The official record is silent after that, so that's all I know, except that you were grounded until this expedition."

"The *official record*," she said, her voice heavy with scorn. "Which rumors have you heard?"

"Everything from incompetence to mutiny to envy-fueled murder." Before he met her, Harte had been willing to give these rumors some credence. It was hard to take them seriously now. On the rare occasions she spoke of Chickering, it was with affection and respect. And yet … "They say you didn't cry at the funeral."

"Ask me if I cried at my mother's funeral."

"Did you?"

"No. See what a cold-hearted bitch I am?"

Her bitter tone startled him. "I'm sorry I brought it up."

"No, I am. That was a trick question. Mom requested no service." She blew out an audible breath. "I thought I could do this, but I can't."

He considered letting it go, but something bothered him. "May I ask one more intrusive question?"

"I can't stop you asking."

"It must have been rough, losing so many friends at once. Were you treated for post-traumatic stress?"

She nodded. "All the survivors were. It's automatic after an event like that."

"Did it help?"

She was quiet for a long time. "Maybe not as much as I thought it did. I still self-medicate."

Harte nearly hyperventilated. This wasn't the story he expected.

"Calm down, or you'll waste too much air," she commanded. "My drugs of choice are exercise and work."

"Oh."

"I can usually sleep through the night now. I hardly ever have nightmares anymore. And I trust … most people."

"You mean the people you know." He thought about this expedition. It was made up almost entirely of people she knew well, or people recruited by one of her closest friends. "I wish you trusted me."

"I may yet, unless you give me good reason not to. Come on, we should go back while we still have air."

Harte glanced at his HUD. He still had plenty, but it wasn't worth an argument. "That's all right. You don't have to talk more until you're ready."

She laid her hand on the sign, over the empty place where she once sat next to Commander Chickering. "What if I'm never ready?"

"Take as much time as you need. I'm in no hurry."

He was encouraged to hear a lighter tone when she answered. "Yeah, it's not like I can get away from you. You and that damned little mustache." She started down the trail.

He hurried to follow. "What's wrong with my mustache?"

"It's too perfect. It's hard to respect a man who's vain about his appearance."

"I'm not vain!"

She snorted. "Right."

"I work in an industry where the visual aspect outweighs everything else. How I look is part of my brand, all right? Besides, it's easy for you. You always look great."

"I ... what?" She stopped and turned to face him. She didn't sound angry — more startled. He couldn't see her face through the reflective visor, but he could imagine it well enough. Boy, could he imagine it ...

"I've seen you in the morning before coffee. Hell, I've seen you when you've been on watch all night. I've never seen you look bad."

She shook her head and laughed as she continued the descent. "He asks me to trust him, then tries to flatter me. I don't even know what to do with that."

Harte knew what he *wanted* to do with it. Unfortunately, it was against a whole bunch of rules. Plus, she'd probably pitch him out an airlock if he suggested it. "Never mind. Forget about it. Forget my mustache, too."

"If you'll take my advice," she said, "you'll grow a beard to go with it."

Ruby Ladd had been in a lot of perilous situations in her life, but she couldn't remember ever feeling as uneasy as she did about this interview she had promised Harte Gunner. The Chickering Memorial had seemed like the perfect spot to finally unburden herself. Once there, it was like it had just happened, and she was back in the thick of reporters and investigators who wanted to know the real story. And there was her old boss, gazing out at her from the past. With reproach or encouragement? She would never know, but she fully expected the old nightmare to recur — the one in which she climbed a dark slope in a hopeless attempt to bring him an oxygen tank. She thought about the memorial sign. She preferred the original picture, with everyone in their places, as they were Before. The altered version seemed to imply that only the dead were worth remembering. Then again, the survivors had a chance to be remembered for something else.

Ruby smiled to herself. It was twisted, but she had found the positive. And it wasn't as if she had trouble talking to Gunner at all. It was alarming how easily she talked with him about everything but Chickering. Why had she said that about his mustache, of all things? That alone was something to be uneasy about. They had parted on good terms when they returned to the base, but she was just as happy to avoid him the rest of the day.

And it was a good day. Christmas on Mars was just the holiday everyone needed. Lunch was an informal buffet, but at suppertime, they all feasted together in the dining hall again, then retired to a comfortable commons for synthetic eggnog and a carol sing. The Doo-Bots performed to great acclaim. Baird Rogers came over during their second number, a swinging arrangement of "Jingle Bells."

"How much for one of the robots? We could use something this entertaining."

"I'm sorry," Ruby said. "Dr. Eyestone would never let me break up the band. You'll just have to program one of your own."

He laughed. "Figured as much, but I thought it couldn't hurt to ask." He moved up closer to the stage.

"Hey, Boss, there you are!" Anderson sat down next to Ruby. "How's your Christmas?"

She hadn't spoken to him since she gave him his present at breakfast. "Mostly good. Did you call your family?"

"I chatted with Marie and Frannie for almost two hours! Rubin was there for a while, too, but he's only three; he doesn't have the patience for the delay." He grinned. "Frannie was disappointed that you missed Thanksgiving."

"I'm surprised she remembers me!"

"Aunt Ruby is pretty hard to forget. So where'd you get to this morning? I was looking for you — I wanted to apologize for yesterday. I went too far."

In the excitement of their arrival, she had almost forgotten that moment of conflict. "Thank you; it means a lot, coming from you. But it's all right. You're entitled to your own opinions."

"Still, it wasn't fair to bring it up in front of Gunner."

"*He* brought it up, remember?"

"And you took your hostility out on him instead of me. I guess I should thank one of you for that. So, where were you this morning?"

The Pearl twinged, and her holiday spirits drained away. "I took Gunner up to the memorial. It should be in his doc."

"Ah." They listened as the Doo-Bots swung into "White Christmas." "So you're giving him your side of the story?"

"I said I would."

"But you haven't yet?"

"It's ... difficult to start." She sipped her drink.

"Understood. For what it's worth, I think it's time."

"It's your story, too, Skipper."

"I know, but I'm not going to say anything without your OK."

She shivered. "Has he asked you to?"

"Nope. He may be conceited, but I think this guy has principles. And I think he prefers your face."

"That's ridiculous!" But what had Gunner said? That she always looked good. No, great. She figured he was just trying to sweet-talk her. If it was anything else … she didn't want to think about it.

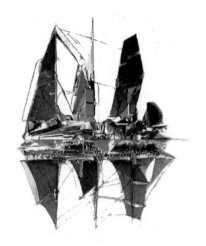

Chapter 14

2124/12/26: The Boss's past remains a mystery, our future lies in the Asteroid Belt. Still no clear narrative about the present, beyond the affection the party has for their commander.

— Holden Gunner's Production Journal

Once Christmas Day had passed, Ruby was eager to get on with the expedition. But her people had earned their full week of R and R. They deserved to enjoy the luxury of a little more elbow room and a lot more gravity. As much as they were all getting along well now, it was good for them to socialize with other people while they had the chance. They would get plenty of each other's company in the coming months. Their presence acted as a tonic to the research colony, too. Visitors were a rare treat. She hid her impatience and set her sights on a New Year's Day launch.

Wind kicked up overnight on December 30, and by morning the sky was pink with dust. It wasn't a storm yet, but the base meteorologist predicted it soon would be.

"What do you think, Skipper?" Ruby asked at breakfast.

He sucked his teeth thoughtfully. "I'd rather not leave the ship out in a dust storm. She's tough, but it won't do her electronics any good. Nguyen and I were talking about taking her into orbit and bringing the shuttle down when you're ready to go."

"Or we could just go now, a day early. Is she ready for launch?"

He grinned. "As soon as you give the word."

With a decisive nod, Ruby rose to her feet. "*Endurance* party, your attention, please. Finish your breakfast, then gather your gear and meet at the airlock in one hour. We launch in ...?" She turned to Anderson.

"Ninety minutes."

As much as she'd enjoyed spending a few days at the base, Ruby was glad to leave Mars. At least no one besides Gunner had seen her reaction to the Chickering memorial. Anderson already knew how she felt, and Wild probably guessed, but there was no reason to spoil anyone else's holiday. If they were disappointed to have their planet break cut short by a day, nobody complained. This was the part they'd signed on for. The true expedition was about to begin.

Within hours, they were in orbit again. Details of the surface were blurred by the strengthening dust storm. Leaving now was the right decision. Anderson and Nguyen adjusted some calculations based on new observations, deployed the solar sail, and set a course for a comparatively busy area of the Asteroid Belt. It was back to months of weightlessness and passing the time, but Ruby wouldn't have had it any other way.

As a bonus, her space sickness didn't recur. When lunchtime rolled around, she was ready for it. She made her way to the galley to check on lunch, quietly singing to herself.

"... three French hens, two turtledoves, and a —" She broke off. The galley was empty. No reliable Blackborow in sight.

Ruby used the handholds to turn around and propel herself back out, just as Harte Gunner propelled himself in. The collision dispersed their energy and left them floating motionless, and closer together than seemed polite or necessary.

"Watch it!" It came out sharper than she intended, but he flustered her like no one else. Ruby grabbed a handhold and pushed back a little.

"Pardon me." Gunner stayed where he was. "No lunch yet?" He looked amused and perfectly coiffed, as usual. After months of keeping his hair precisely at the four-centimeter limit, he'd now let it grow longer. A challenge? An acknowledgement that he didn't work for her? But it was thoroughly contained. Just how much styling gel was required to maintain that look in zero gravity?

Ruby pulled herself together. "Apparently not. I suspect Ms. Blackborow isn't feeling well."

"Then it's up to us." He began opening supply lockers.

"That's the simplest solution," she said, though she didn't want to spend any more time alone with him than she had to. But he was a volunteer — he didn't have to be here at all, let alone make lunch. She would try to be a good sport. "I should check on Blackborow first, but I'll come right back and give you a hand."

"Before you go, can I ask you something?"

The Pearl throbbed once. "If it's all the same to you, I'm not ready to talk yet."

"No, it's not that." He glanced around, though no one else had come in yet. Still, he lowered his voice. "I hoped you might reconsider my request for EVA — any chance?" His eyebrows did a hopeful little jig.

She stared at him. "Out of the question. It's too big a risk except in an emergency."

"But I hate to waste your expert training. And my pictures would be so much clearer."

"That isn't an emergency."

"Please? The audience will love it, and I wouldn't ask anyone else to go."

She huffed impatiently. Such a spoiled child! "Mr. Gunner, look at me. The answer is no."

"You know, for a space commander, you don't have much sense of adventure."

She glared at him. "Adventure is your job, not mine. My job is to do this mission and bring everyone home safe — including you." She pushed past him and floated out of the galley before he could ask again.

Ruby found Blackborow in her quarters, huddled in her bag, though not asleep. She started to get out. "I know, I'm late! I'll be out in a moment, I promise!"

"That isn't necessary." Ruby gently pushed her back into the bag. She recognized the misery written on the cook's pale face even before she spoke. "Mr. Gunner is in the galley now, and I'm going to help him."

"But … he's famous, and you're the Boss!"

"And we volunteered." Ruby already wished she hadn't promised her help, but it was too late now. "It's no trouble once in a while."

"Thank you. I don't want to think about what will happen if I move."

"Shall I send Dr. Mack to see you?" Ruby asked.

"No, if it's like last time, I'll be fine in a few hours. But maybe I'm not cut out for this line of work."

"You're young. If this isn't your thing, you'll have plenty of time to pick something else. But remember who else gets spacesick." Ruby made a wry face and pointed to herself. "You just have to decide if it's worth it."

"I'll keep that in mind. Thanks for coming to check on me. Don't worry, I'll be all right."

"Then I'll get back to the galley. The famous man is waiting for me." Ruby grimaced.

Blackborow managed a wan smile. "He's much nicer than I thought he'd be. Not snobbish at all. We're lucky to have someone so talented with us."

"We are," Ruby agreed. "But we have many talented people aboard, you among them. Don't forget that."

Harte watched the commander leave the galley. Once again, he'd miffed her with what he thought was an innocent comment. He wouldn't press his point about EVA. At least, not yet. There wasn't much to look at outside the ship. But he was sure the view would improve, and when it did, he would ask again. For now, he would record daily shipboard life, help out in the galley, and be as agreeable as possible. She'd change her mind.

He lost some of his certainty when she returned to help with lunch. She barely spoke to him and left the galley as soon as she could. She must have been more than just miffed with his comment about her sense of adventure, though he didn't know why such a small thing should make her so angry.

Or did he? Of course — it all went back to Chickering and Olympus Mons. She had every right to be upset and he'd been a jerk without meaning to. And an apology might only make things worse.

Harte stopped by the galley again in the late afternoon and found Blackborow, already recovered from her bout of space sickness.

"I'm glad you're feeling better," he said. "I know you don't need my help, but I thought between us, we could put together a festive supper for New Year's Eve." He secretly hoped the commander might check in. She admired Blackborow's growing competence as much as he did. But she didn't appear, as if she were avoiding him. He would never get that interview at this rate.

"Thank you! We should use the fresh produce we got from the base."

"Yes, OK." Harte got out the sealed tubs of spinach, strawberries, and ripe avocados.

Blackborow produced a vacuum-sealed package of smoked salmon. "This seems fancy enough for a celebration. I've been wanting to use it, but there's not enough for an entree."

"Are there any of those pepper-jack cheese slices left?"

"Yeah, lots, in the freezer."

"When I was in cooking school, we used to make an omelet with smoked salmon and pepper-jack. We called it the Seattle Fire."

"No eggs, though. Can't make an omelet without eggs."

"Do quesadillas. Mash the avocados and mix in the salmon and spinach. Spread that on the tortillas, two per serving, and put them together with cheese in between. Into the sandwich press to toast the outside and melt the cheese; the melted cheese and mashed avocado should hold it together. What do you think?"

She grinned. "Sounds delicious! And strawberries for dessert — simple."

They got busy preparing this colorful meal. It had a mouthwatering aroma. "That's a relief — no one can complain about this," Blackborow said. "It looks like a party."

"Are you sorry we didn't stay on Mars one more night?"

She laughed. "We would have had more ingredients to choose from! But no, not really. It's better with just our group, out here. When was the last time you did anything really *new* in the New Year?"

She had a good point. For someone who liked risk, he'd fallen into a safe, predictable rhythm. He filmed different exotic locations or extreme activities, but the schedule was the same. New Year's Eve generally meant the same group of associates and acquaintances, with an interchangeable selection of pretty people added to the mix. He drank and danced with these attractive strangers all night but couldn't recall their names in the morning — not even those he'd slept with. It was kind of nice to know ahead of time that he wouldn't wake up with a stranger and a hangover.

Blackborow began to hull the strawberries. "Did the Boss talk to you yet?"

Harte stiffened. "What makes you think she's not talking to me?"

"What? No, I thought she was supposed to give you a story about Chickering."

"Oh, yes, that. She started it. We're ... doing the interview in segments."

"It must be a long story."

"It may be. Mostly, the Boss is ... busy."

Blackborow looked pensive. "It must be lonely for her when she's home."

"Why do you say that?"

"She doesn't seem to have friends or interests outside of ... this."

"How would you know that? She might have a very active social life — probably beats guys off with a stick."

Blackborow laughed. "She could hurt someone that way! But I asked her once — I don't think there's anyone she really cares for." She frowned. "Except maybe one. I think she and Mr. Wild were lovers once."

"She told you *that*?"

"No, I just guessed based on something else she said. And they wouldn't be now, anyway. Although maybe when this is over ..."

Harte's mouth went dry and he had a strange, unpleasant feeling in the pit of his stomach. The Boss and Mr. Wild? They had the easy familiarity of old friends, though no obvious chemistry. But she had all but admitted having no sense of adventure. And why should he care? All he wanted was his pictures, and the story to go with them. He cleared his throat. "Do you really think it's appropriate for us to gossip about our commander?"

"Is it gossip if you just want the person to be happy?"

"What makes you think she's not?"

Blackborow cocked her head and pursed her lips thoughtfully. "I think she loves her work. She seems pleased with the mission, and the personnel. But something is making her very unhappy."

Harte sighed. "That would be me."

"You? Why?"

"Because she promised me an interview, but there's something she doesn't want to tell me."

The girl frowned, looking older and wiser than her eighteen years. "It isn't always about you. Maybe she doesn't want to tell *anyone*."

That was a new way of looking at it, and the end of the conversation. It was time to serve the holiday supper. The colorful quesadillas went over well, though they were wrong about one thing. Lee Keith complained that they'd used more of the supplies than he'd allotted for the day. Blackborow looked chagrined, but Dr. Eyestone rose to her defense.

"It's New Year's Eve — loosen up a little! We'll make up for it by sleeping through breakfast tomorrow."

That night, the Doo-Bots put on their most polished performance to date, and Harte made sure to record them. He wouldn't be able to use all his footage, but it was good to have a record of their unique style.

He zoomed in on the commander where she bobbed between Anderson and Wild. Like everyone, they were all smiles. Then the commander sighed. She turned to Wild and said, "I'm going to miss those little guys."

"Have you developed affection for machines, Boss?" Wild asked, plainly amused.

"Of course not! But ... they're good for morale. Every little bit helps."

Just then, Eyestone and Blackborow walked through the door behind the Doo-Bots. It looked like they were going to repeat their magic act. Then Harte realized what he was seeing — they were *walking* on the floor. He had barely absorbed this when they walked up the wall and across the ceiling, where they paused to perform a brief dance step as the robots finished their song.

The crowd laughed and applauded as they descended to the floor again. Blackborow lifted her foot. "Gecko boots!"

"Where'd you get those?" Keith cried.

"From the supply locker," Dr. Eyestone replied. "What are you going to do about it?"

Harte recognized the boots now. They'd practiced with them once during space training. It was clear these two had practiced more, and more recently. Harte didn't join in the general clamor for a pair. No reason to add to the confusion, though he wanted some, too.

"Boss?" Keith pleaded.

"All right, calm down, everyone." She had barely raised her voice, yet they settled down almost immediately. Eyestone and Blackborow looked sheepish. "That was very entertaining, you two. Thank you. But you know those boots are meant primarily for extra-vehicular activity." Harte perked up at these words, but she ignored him. "They need to be kept clean. If they get too dusty, they won't grip, and that could be dangerous."

"We'll make sure they're clean before we put them back," Blackborow said.

The commander smiled. "I know you will. Now, then, I think it's time to break out a little New Year's libation."

The Boss wouldn't allow enough alcohol for anyone to get really drunk, but there was enough to lend a certain mellowness. At midnight, a cheer went up. Dr.

Eyestone, wearing a mischievous grin, grabbed Blackborow and kissed her. She blushed but didn't appear to object. Harte hadn't thought about it before, but the two were only a few years apart in age. Though they came from different backgrounds, they made a believable couple.

Commander Ladd circulated around the room to greet each member of the party.

"Happy New Year, Mr. Gunner," she said when she came to him. She shook his hand.

"What — no kiss?"

"It wouldn't be appropriate. Did you see me kiss anyone else?"

"No." And he'd been watching. "But remember — I don't work for you."

She smiled, it seemed against her will. "It still wouldn't be appropriate."

"I suppose you're right," he said, content with the smile. "Happy New Year, Commander." He squeezed her hand and reluctantly let go.

Everyone but the Boss got out their comms to send greetings to Earth. Harte dawdled over his, uncertain.

"Who's waiting for you back home?" the commander asked.

"No one, really. My staff celebrates when I leave them alone."

"Family?"

"Well, my folks, I guess, but I've kind of drifted away from them."

"Write them," she ordered. "Let them know how far."

KAREN EISENBREY

"80 million kilometers," the Skipper said.

Harte ignored him and focused on the Boss. "You sound like you know something about that."

She met his gaze. "My dad's still living, but … we don't talk."

"Never?"

"Not since Mom died. Remember what I said about not crying? That was true, even though she didn't have a funeral. I just … couldn't. Not after Chickering. Dad thought I didn't care, and I didn't know how to explain. He cut me loose. I let him know about this expedition, but I didn't get a response."

"I'm sorry." Harte didn't know what else to say, but it made him think. He began to compose a message.

Dear Mom and Dad, you'll never guess where I am this New Year's …

Commander Ladd looked around the mess and managed a smile. "Everyone I care about is right here."

Captain Anderson looked up. "My kids would be insulted to hear that. She eats Thanksgiving dinner with us whenever we're both at home," he explained. "I think they missed her more than they did me."

"That seems like a stretch," she said.

Anderson grinned. "You might not believe me, but she's very good with children."

"I have no trouble believing that," Harte said. "See how she takes care of all of us!"

She looked startled but pleased. "I have to. You can't have a successful expedition with a discontented crew."

"And the commander is only as happy as her least happy shipmate?" Harte paraphrased. Before she could reply, he turned to Anderson. "We shouldn't call her Boss — we should call her Mom!"

"I wouldn't try that if I were you," Wild put in.

"I think what my kids like is that she doesn't treat them like children," Anderson went on.

"I don't?"

"Well, obviously, you talk at their level, but not *down*. You give them respect. And then there's the stories."

"Stories?" Harte asked with interest. "I thought you must bring them presents or something."

"She tells wild tales."

"All true, I swear it," the Boss said.

"That's why they're so good."

"That's a present I wouldn't mind getting," Harte said. She glanced at him, then away, shaking her head. He smiled. His intuition was right. If they ever finished that interview, it would *make* the doc.

Chapter 15

2125/04/23: The asteroid chase has begun! We will begin deploying robots as soon as possible.
— *From Commander Ladd's monthly report to SCEI Director Wesley James*

After the New Year's Eve festivities, the expedition continued much as before. Except with Mars behind them, there was nothing of interest for Harte to film through the forward viewport. Stars and more stars, impossibly far away. But they encountered their first asteroid only a few days into the New Year. As soon as he heard the report, Harte hurried to the bridge to record the momentous event.

"I had no idea it would be this soon!" He pointed his camera at the viewport. "Where is it?"

"Just off to port," the captain replied. "It doesn't look like much, though."

Harte finally found it, a small, irregular chunk. It wasn't reflective and barely showed up at all when he reviewed the image. "Well, that's a letdown. I pictured the Asteroid Belt as a lot more impressive."

Anderson laughed. "This is just the inner fringe. The Belt is tens of millions of kilometers wide. We've a ways to go before we get into the thick of it."

"So we're not just looking for the closest asteroids for mining?"

"The ultimate plan is to build large space stations to facilitate mining and manufacture. Our hope is to find a number of resource-rich asteroids relatively close together to make it worth the trouble." Anderson grinned. "It'll take time but be patient; I believe you'll see a picture worth capturing."

As Harte turned to leave, the commander entered the bridge. She nodded. "Mr. Gunner."

"Commander."

He no longer suspected her of actively avoiding him, but she had been formal and guarded since their aborted interview on Christmas Day. He had learned the hard way not to push her; his bruises from the basketball game had only just healed. He was tempted to forget about a face-to-face interview and submit written questions. But he wanted more than her answers — he wanted her voice.

At least it was book-club day. These weekly meetings helped pass the time and keep things lively. Harte joined the rest of the club in the mess. The Boss never participated and the Skipper, rarely. Almost everyone else was present.

Dr. Crean called the meeting to order. "Dr. Curley asks us to go ahead without him today. He has some new data to review."

"That asteroid?" Harte asked. "It doesn't look like much."

"To him, it does. It's the first one we've seen."

The book club had never become what Dr. Crean originally envisioned, where they all read and discussed the same book. They continued to report on a wide variety of works, but everyone's tastes had been influenced by everyone else's. Blackborow and Nielson were reading different volumes in the same wizard-detective series.

Mr. Keith had discovered a previously unexplored taste for poetry — not Byron so much as Service. "This is from 'Call of the Wild'."

"I've heard of that!" Blackborow interrupted. "Isn't that a dog story?"

"You're thinking of *The Call of the Wild*, by Jack London," Betty Nguyen said. "But London probably knew Service's work."

Mr. Keith cleared his throat and began to read. "*'Have you suffered, starved and triumphed, groveled down, yet grasped at glory, grown bigger in the bigness of the whole?'* Maybe that's us — we're doing something big, out here in the hugeness of space."

"Except for the suffering and starving part," Nielson said.

Keith smiled a little. "I hope we've planned better than that."

"What about you, Gunner?" Dr. Crean asked. "Anything new this week?"

"As a matter of fact, yes. I took Mr. Nielson's suggestion and looked at some old comics. The stories are OK, but I'm more taken with the visual style."

Nielson grinned. "Like the costumes on the superheroines?"

"Among other things," Harte allowed. The outfits were arresting, but impossible. Although maybe in zero-G ... "But some of the writing is pretty good, too," he hastened to add. "Who's next?"

Ruby didn't recognize the alarm's song fragment, a relentlessly cheery duet that kept repeating. That was this expedition, one day exactly like another since the first of the year. A whole month. She groaned and unzipped her sleeping bag. Her head hurt and she couldn't remember where she'd left her can-do attitude.

Washing her face and brushing her teeth were usually enough to snap Ruby out of the worst mood. She willed herself to smile. She was commanding a space mission, her dream job — what could be more exciting than that?

She drifted into the galley for coffee and a NutriCube — Citrus Medley flavor, and all the breakfast she could handle. Blackborow greeted her with a grunt, and Ruby answered in kind. In the mess, Wild lifted his cup to her. Though she knew him to be a regular sleeper and it was first thing in the morning, he had the look of someone who had pulled an all-nighter. Before she could comment, Anderson dragged himself in.

"What happened, Skipper?" Wild asked. "Did you see your shadow and climb back into your burrow?"

Anderson stared for several seconds before he answered. "What?"

"You know, Groundhog Day? February 2?"

Ruby frowned. "I've never understood what a marmot has to do with weather forecasting. Especially on a spaceship."

"Would you people shut up?" Nguyen muttered. "Some of us are trying to sleep."

"What the fuck is wrong with everybody?" Nielson snarled.

The tears Ruby hadn't been able to shed for five years threatened to burst out all at once. Sure, there had been some friction in the early weeks, but they had all come together as a team, especially since Christmas. And now they were bickering — the *officers* were bickering — about Groundhog Day?

Wait. Sluggishness, headache, short tempers …

Ruby locked eyes with Nielson. They spoke as one. "The CO_2 scrubbers."

Nielson nodded. "On it." He left the mess.

The others looked at each other with understanding and dismay. Apologies followed.

"I think we can all put off trying to be productive until this problem is fixed," Ruby said. "If I know Nielson, it shouldn't take long."

"I had something to tell you," Anderson said. "I think it was important. Something about ..." He looked at Dr. Crean. "About the solar sail?"

Crean considered for several seconds. Ruby couldn't get over how slow everyone was this morning. Finally, he nodded. "That was probably it. I sent you the latest figures last night."

Anderson drew out his comm and hunted for the information. "Of course. It's right here. Everything's so much harder than it should be! But this should cheer everyone up. I predict arrival in the Belt proper by Easter."

"And when is that, exactly?" Ruby asked.

"It's late this year — April 22," Anderson replied. "But look at it this way: most of the trip out is behind us now."

Finally, the real work of the expedition!

As soon as the ship's sensors indicated multiple asteroids in the vicinity, Gunner took to filming daily through the main forward viewport, just as in the approach to Mars. There usually wasn't much to see, though his persistence paid off once. He captured good images of a reflective chunk of rock shining in the light of the faraway sun, and showed it to everyone who would look. He hadn't repeated his request for extra-vehicular activity, and Ruby hoped he'd accepted her refusal. She could see how it might improve his doc, but it wasn't something to be taken lightly. One little accident, and they'd be performing a rescue — or retrieving a body.

Once again, Anderson's estimate proved alarmingly good. By April 23, the day after Easter, they were in a relatively thick zone of the Asteroid Belt. A large, spherical body was visible in the distance, beyond a collection of rocky lumps, an "asteroid family," no doubt the result of some long-ago collision. *Endurance* joined the orbiting objects, moving in the same direction, but a little faster. The asteroid chase was on.

"I thought you would have furled the solar sail," Ruby said to the captain and Dr. Crean. "I can't imagine an asteroid would be too kind to it."

"I'm still testing its functionality," Dr. Crean replied.

"We've turned the sail so I can use it for steering," Anderson said. "It should be safe enough for now, though we'll take it in before we enter any major debris fields."

Over the next few days, they approached several asteroids. Dr. Curley assessed each one's size and likely composition. The first few, he rejected as too small to be worth mining.

"So when we find one that looks promising, you'll send out a robot," Gunner said as he filmed. "We came all this way to tag seven asteroids?"

"Six — Mrs. Chippy won't be leaving the ship. But once all the bots have been deployed, the Skipper will turn the ship around so we can retrieve them and send them out again."

The next morning after breakfast, Dr. Curley finally identified a good-sized asteroid that seemed likely to contain valuable metals. Anderson used the solar sail and steering engines to maneuver the ship. When they were close enough, the entire party gathered to watch as Hercules shot away on his — its — first mission. The robot looked unbelievably small and vulnerable, away from the safety of the ship. Ruby had to remind herself, it was a machine doing the job it was built for.

She wrote up the robot launch in her expedition journal and sent the monthly digest to SCEI. It was a few days early, but she suspected they would be as excited as she was about the first event of the expedition.

Dr. Eyestone was unusually quiet after the launch. Ruby accompanied him back to the robotics lab. "How soon do you expect data?"

"We're getting a signal already, but he won't have anything really informative until tomorrow at the earliest." In spite of this, he gazed at his screen with rapt attention.

The other robots wandered around the lab in no apparent pattern. Some of them bumped against Ruby and Dr. Eyestone, as if seeking attention. "Do you think they know?" she asked.

The roboticist looked up. "Know what?"

"That one of them is gone."

He watched them mill around. "Probably. Hercules was well liked." He reddened. "Anyway, that's how it seemed to me. It's difficult not to anthropomorphize."

As Ruby watched, the robot called Sir Ernest moved in a more deliberate way. It herded the others into a tight group, then began to hoot the opening of one of their songs, a lively party number. Haltingly, the others joined in, Slag took lead, and before long, they sounded just like they always had. The casual listener would never notice that one of the basses was missing.

Dr. Eyestone smiled. "That one always knows how to cheer us up. A good thing — Hercules isn't the only one with work to do."

A loud bang echoed through the ship. "What the — ?" Ruby said.

The Skipper's voice came over the speakers. "No cause for alarm. A small chunk of debris struck the hull, but that's what she's built to take." After a pause, he continued. "Commander Ladd and Mr. Nielson, please report to the bridge."

It took a lot to upset Captain Anderson, but even through the PA, Ruby thought his voice sounded strained. She made her way to the bridge as quickly as she could. "What's the trouble, Skipper?"

"Maybe nothing. We're coming up on a major debris field. I'll try to avoid the worst of it but we should furl the sail before we get into it."

"Then do it. You don't need my permission for that."

"No, but — it won't come down. It's stuck somehow, and the video feed doesn't show me the problem. I need you to order an EVA to see what's wrong."

"Done." In this situation, EVA made sense.

Nielson entered the bridge. "Did I miss it?"

"Just the man I wanted to see," Anderson replied. "Mr. Nielson, I need you to go out and see if you can fix the solar sail mechanism. It's stuck."

Before Ruby's eyes, Nielson lost all his bluster. "If it's all the same to you, Captain, I'd rather not. I came on this trip to fix engines, systems, things like that. Not to go … out there."

"You may have to," Anderson said.

"And if I refuse?"

"That sounds like insubordination, Mr. Nielson."

"Just a moment, Skipper," Ruby broke in. She recognized Nielson's fear as valid, even if she didn't share it. "I think I know who might be willing to help you."

"Who?"

"Gunner. He did very well in training. He'll try anything, and he's handy with tools."

Nielson nodded vigorously. "Absolutely. He'd be much better than me."

Anderson looked thoughtful. "That could work. He might even like to film a little out there."

Ruby smiled. "I think he could be persuaded."

Chapter 16

2125/04/26: After a bumpy beginning, my first-ever EVA yielded the most awe-inspiring footage I have ever recorded, and that's saying something. This doc will be gorgeous, with or without a narrative.

— Harte Gunner's Production Journal

Ruby could have sent Gunner a private message, but she wanted to see the look on his face when she proved she could change her mind for a good enough reason. She found him in his quarters, preparing a batch of images to send home. "Mr. Gunner, may I come in?"

He turned with a surprised smile. "Of course, Boss. To what do I owe the pleasure?"

"I've approved your EVA."

He grinned. "Ha! Good one. What do you really want?"

"I'm not joking. We need someone to look at the solar sail's retracting mechanism. It's stuck."

"Why not Nielson?"

"He ... thought you were better qualified in this case." It was the truth and saved her from casting a crewmember in a bad light. "I'm inclined to agree. But while you're out there, you might as well take a few pictures." She handed him a pair of gecko boots that she'd requisitioned from Mr. Keith. "Here. You'll need these."

"Wow, you're really serious! Does this mean I can go out now?"

She chuckled at his enthusiasm. "Yes, the sooner, the better. Get ready. I'll send along a buddy to keep an eye on you."

As soon as the commander closed the door behind her, Harte struggled into his space gear. It was getting easier, but that wasn't saying much. He pulled on the gecko boots and practiced walking. When he slid his foot or pulled it straight up, it stuck fast. With practice, he soon mastered the rolling heel-toe step that peeled up the grippy pads. It felt odd to walk on the floor while still being weightless. His feet gripped the floor, but his arms floated up and out unless he consciously held them at his sides.

He wondered who his "buddy" would be. Probably Wild. Everyone had undergone training, but it would have to be someone experienced, and Wild never lost his cool. Besides, the Boss trusted him completely. Harte ground his teeth. But as he neared the airlock, another suited figure in gecko boots approached — too short to be Wild. Much too short.

Ruby was glad she didn't have to wait around for Gunner. She wanted to get this thing over with. She didn't share Nielson's fear of EVA, but the pressure suit was uncomfortable, and while novel, the gecko boots were disorienting.

"This is quite an honor," Gunner said. "I didn't expect the Expedition Commander to oversee my little space walk."

"You're my responsibility." They donned their helmets and checked the seals, then entered the airlock. The doors closed behind them.

She reached to lower his gold visor, but he had already done it. "See? I was paying attention."

"Glad to hear it. Grab a harness from the locker and get a tether on. When the outer doors open, back out and push gently away from the hull. Remember, small, controlled movements, just like we practiced. Float out to the end of your tether and get some pictures of the ship first, then pull yourself back along the tether. Once you have your feet on the hull, you'll be able to walk over and take a close look at the sail."

"Got it." He selected a harness and had it on, tether attached, in no time at all. For an amateur, his skills were impressive. She didn't say so aloud; his ego was big enough already.

Captain Anderson's voice came over the helmet speakers. "All ready back there?"

"Yes!" Gunner confirmed. The outer doors began to slide open. As soon as there was enough space, he backed through and pushed away — maybe harder than strictly necessary, but he had his movement under control. He drifted out from the ship, the tether trailing after him. Ruby watched from the opening to assist if he needed it, but that wasn't likely. He had a natural talent for this sort of thing and seemed to remember his training. Then the end of his tether drifted past her.

She dived for it despite being untethered herself. She trusted the gecko boots would hold. Leaning out from the ship like a ski jumper, she fumbled the magnet end of the tether just before it floated out of reach. It caught as the line passed between her gloved fingers. She closed her fist around it. A training tether? What was that doing here?

It took effort to stop Gunner's movement away from the ship, a long moment that stretched out forever. Sure, he was weightless, but he had mass and momentum. One heel started to peel up, but Ruby forced it back down. Her legs ached with the strain. A man's life depended on a pair of boots and her Achilles tendons. A shipmate's life.

"Hey!" he protested as he started to move back toward the ship. She didn't have the breath to waste on explanation. She slowly straightened herself, then drew him back into the airlock. When he was close enough, she grabbed him by both arms and held him as his boots adhered to the floor.

"What were you thinking?" she demanded.

"Me? What about you?" He rested his gloved hands on her shoulders. "Boss, you're shaking. What's wrong?"

"You just scared me to death." She held up the end of his tether. "What are you doing with a training tether?"

He started. "Training — oh. That's why the harness already had a tether locked on."

"And you didn't think that was odd?"

"It seemed — convenient. I thought maybe they were stored that way."

"Convenient. I see. Who put the harnesses away after the last training session?"

"Um ... I think I did, but I didn't notice the tether, what with all the other parts."

She released him and turned away. "Goddamn you, Gunner, I should just kill you myself and save the rest of the universe the trouble!"

"Boss?" For the first time, Gunner sounded unsure of himself.

The Skipper's voice interrupted. "OK, you two, don't make me come out there. Play nice."

Ruby gulped several deep breaths to calm herself, though she hated to waste the air. In spite of his training and native skill, Gunner didn't really know what he was doing; if anyone deserved a scolding, she did. "I read you, Skipper. We'll go to a private channel." She held up three fingers and watched as Gunner switched his radio. "Skipper? Did … anyone else hear that?"

"I don't think so; it's book club day. Are you sure everything's all right?"

"It is now. Just a little mix-up, but no permanent harm done. We'll try to make this brief." She switched to channel 3.

"Are you OK, Boss?" Gunner asked.

"Why wouldn't I be?"

"I never heard you swear before. If it makes any difference, I'm really sorry."

"I'm sorry, too. Just … please be more careful."

"I promise. So I can still go out?"

"We don't have any other volunteers, but you're not going anywhere without a babysitter." She fastened a real tether to his harness and geared herself up, too. "I'm coming with you."

Harte drifted backward away from the ship, filming as he went. His heart thumped from the recent accident, but capturing a stunning image was the surest way to calm down. In spite of everything, he remembered his training, making only small movements. It was jaw-dropping to have stars at his feet, impressive enough that he couldn't be disappointed in the lack of dramatic asteroids. This area was supposed to be crowded with them, but that seemed to be a relative term. He felt lucky to have more than one creating a backdrop behind the ship. The big spherical one was visible in the distance, while nearer were two odd-shaped lumps, dark voids against the stars.

And then there was the ship. This was the exterior shot he'd dreamed of, only better. The reflective hull would have been too bright to look at without the gold visor. His camera lens had a similar filter. With the solar sail and communications masts, he could picture *Endurance* as a seagoing vessel of long ago. The ship shone against black space, obscuring the stars. *Endurance* was the star of this show.

Or one of them. The commander walked across the hull with casual ease. The distant sun shone on her. He couldn't see her face through the reflective visor, but he soon heard her voice in his helmet.

"How are you doing out there?"

"Fantastic! It's like the world's greatest matte painting!"

"Glad to hear it."

"I thought it would be cold, like on Mars, but it isn't. In fact, I'm pretty warm."

"You're in a vacuum flask the size of the universe; what did you expect? That's why the suit has a cooling system."

"I wonder — could we re-enact you rescuing me? It would add drama."

"No. If you didn't document it the first time, I'm not about to fake it."

"In spite of that, I take back what I said about your sense of adventure. Your quick action saved my life."

"Oh, somebody would have come for you eventually," she said. "And you were right the first time — I left my sense of adventure on Olympus Mons. Now get back here before your air runs out. We have a job to do."

"Thanks for including me in it. This is so worth the risk!" He pulled himself back along his tether to join her on the ship.

"You'll never convince me. How can a picture be worth almost dying?"

"The key word is *almost*."

"I have little patience with foolish risks."

"And the risk you just took?" he asked.

"Unavoidable," she said. "And I know what I'm doing."

"I've noticed. But I don't think the risks I take are foolish." He walked over the hull to the sail. He was getting used to the gecko boots; it felt almost natural. He filmed the mechanism and sent a feed to Anderson on the bridge. Pinkish Mars dust was packed around the retractable mast — an obvious design flaw in the prototype, considering the whole assembly was closed inside the housing while the ship was on the surface. Harte pushed the mast gently, but it barely moved. At least nothing was damaged; it was just stuck. He pulled himself to the top of the mast and managed to collapse the top two sections. "I'm always — OK, *usually* —

safety conscious in the extreme. And even when I have a full crew, I generally do the dangerous stuff myself. It's worked out well so far." He returned to the base of the mast and tried to dig out some of the dust, but he didn't have a narrow enough tool for the job. Maybe the robots could do it. He took a few more shots of the problem area.

"It only takes once. I can't afford to lose you." She released a shuddering breath. "Or anyone. I will not put at pointless risk the people under my command."

Harte turned to face her and lowered the camera. "No. You're not Robert Chickering." Her head jerked up and he heard a gasp over the speaker. "The Olympus Mons climb was a publicity stunt, wasn't it?"

She crouched on the hull and rubbed it with her gloved finger. "One of Chickering's impossible dreams. I often thought he belonged to another age, back when there were still places on Earth to conquer. Well, if he couldn't be Amundsen or Hillary, he'd find someplace to conquer that wasn't on Earth — and SCEI loved it. People were losing interest in the program, and a major sponsor was threatening to pull funding. Chickering's stunt, as you aptly called it, was just the boost they needed. But it wasn't fair."

"It never is."

"He was hailed a hero for dying in the pursuit of a meaningless accomplishment. Maybe if they hadn't encouraged him, he'd still be alive."

"That's why you should tell your side."

"That's not fair, either. He isn't around to defend himself. I don't want to sully a friend's reputation."

"But why keep protecting him now?"

"It's what I do."

Harte smiled. That was certainly true. He'd seen it from the start, with Lee Keith, with Amelia Blackborow, and with himself just now. "And you're outstanding at it. But it sounds like he got the glory, while your reputation suffered for something you didn't do. That's not right."

"I'm alive — I already got the better part of the deal."

"I guess I can understand if you don't want to let down a father figure."

"I still have a father!" she snapped.

"Who, if I remember correctly, did not understand your ambition, and is currently not speaking to you."

"Fine. Most of what I know about leadership, I learned from Chickering, so if that makes him a father figure, I'll accept that."

"I can't imagine he had your ... collaborative style," Harte said, carefully bland.

"That's one of the things I learned. He was more the charismatic, benevolent-dictator type." She sighed. "He could get his people to do anything, even if it didn't make any sense."

"Didn't you tell me it was your job to make it make sense?"

"Except that last time." She gazed at something off to her right. "He wouldn't let me. He decided to plan the whole climb himself. He laughed about it, said he had to learn to do it himself before I went on to greater things. But he wouldn't let me see his plan until it was too late to change anything. Why would he do that?"

"Perhaps he was beginning to see you as competition," Harte said. "I know it would cross my mind if I had a protegee as talented as you."

"So he thought I'd try to poach the credit? I would never —"

"That, or brain lesions," Harte muttered.

"What?"

"Just thinking out loud. Maybe he had brain damage that changed his personality."

She sighed. "And I'm supposed to be comforted by that?"

"Fine, what about this? He had a terminal condition and decided to go out in a blaze of glory. Is that heroic enough?"

"That's worse! He took five of our best people with him!"

"He didn't take you. He left someone capable enough to finish his work."

"I don't know where you get this stuff, Gunner. You're just making things up."

"I'm a creative thinker. I look for the narrative."

"But does it have to be so cruel? The real story is hard enough to tell without your embellishments. Do you want to hear it or not?"

Harte's mouth went dry. He hadn't even seen it, but she really planned to tell him everything, right here, stuck to the outside of the ship in the middle of the Asteroid Belt. She never wanted to talk when it was easy to record, but he wasn't likely to forget any of this. He could write it up later, have her check it for accuracy, maybe use it as voiceover in the finished doc ...

"I want to hear it." His voice barely sounded like his own.

She was quiet so long, he wasn't sure she'd heard him. Then she picked up the story as if he had never interrupted. "He finally let me see the plan the night before, and it was mostly all right. He'd selected a good starting point, and a decent route that shouldn't have taken more than three days up and down. The food and water numbers added up. But the air was off. They'd be able to carry six tanks apiece in their life-support rigs, enough for seventy-two hours in ordinary conditions. But I don't think he accounted for the strenuous nature of the undertaking, and he didn't plan a cushion — extra tanks in a pack, a supply cache at the top, something ..."

"So you told him and he didn't like it," Harte guessed.

"Understatement of the century." She drew an audible breath. "Remember the rumor about mutiny?"

He stared at her. "Really?"

She nodded. "I tried to relieve him of his command. It was a last resort, the strongest tool in the box, but he left me no choice when he wouldn't listen to reason. Unfortunately, most of the other officers thought I had some hidden agenda. They stood with the Boss instead of me."

"Most?"

"Frank Anderson was the navigator. He was with me, God bless him. I lost one friend and gained a better one." She shook her head. "Maybe I was naive, but I really thought Chickering would thank me for trying to save his life. You said it before — I was his right hand." She thumped her right glove into her left. "I was as loyal to him as Wild is to me. But he took it as a personal insult and a sign of disloyalty. In front of everybody, he charged me with mutiny, removed me from the climbing party and confined me to quarters at Columbia. Anderson delivered the party to their base camp, but then volunteered to stay with me. That freed up a few more air tanks, but Chickering wouldn't take them. He was going to stick to his plan or ..."

Or die trying, Harte finished for her, though not aloud. He didn't trust his own voice when hers trailed off like that.

After a moment, she continued. "I calculated when they would be likely to have used up half their air and called Chickering, but he wouldn't take my calls, and he wouldn't let anyone else take them." She slowly shook her head. "He had to know by then."

"But he couldn't back down without losing face." Harte recognized the macho impulse.

"You've seen the video they made at the top."

"It's a great moment," he said. "They're so jubilant. But it always seemed awfully short. If I had been there ..."

"Don't wish that."

He eyed her. He still couldn't see her face, but he could imagine the hard look. "I guess not. But maybe you wish I had been."

"No." Her voice sounded softer, almost broken. She pressed a hand to her chest. He recognized the gesture as something she did almost every time her old commander was mentioned.

"You don't have to do this."

"Yes, I do," she said. "The only way out is through."

He wasn't sure what that meant, but it was clear this was much more than a story. Maybe it helped her, knowing he couldn't see her face, but she was completely unguarded. His earlier assessment — prettier than a diamond, and almost as hard — was completely wrong. She wasn't hard at all. Strong, yes; tough; armored at times, out of necessity. But not hard. She was showing him a wound that was only half healed, trusting he wouldn't make it worse. "I'm listening."

She nodded. "Before they reached the top, they probably knew they were in a race against time. That's why they didn't hang around. And when Anderson and I saw that video live, I counted only five climbers, when there should have been six."

"One of them must have been recording."

"That's what I hoped. But the image was too steady. I don't think even you could hold a camera that still under the circumstances." She let him absorb that, then continued. "It was already going bad. So for the second time ever, I disobeyed a direct order. What did I have to lose?"

"Your career?"

"But to save a friend? I'd do it again, in a heartbeat. I ordered Anderson to take me to them. They'd made the summit; the descent wasn't important. If we could just get to them in time —"

"But you didn't."

"Time was against us, too. We had a lot of distance to cover, and I'd left it too late. I had a pretty good idea when the air would run out. Five minutes before that, we were still thirty minutes away. So that's when I cried. Not at the funeral, but while they were still alive. Because we were too late. Because Chickering and I never got to make up. He was my friend, and his last words to me were, '*I expected more loyalty from you, Ladd. Stay here with the crew.*' Six good officers died for nothing — for vanity."

"Are they ... still there?"

"No. I assumed command of the expedition to do the one job left to me — to get everyone home. Including the dead. I retrieved the bodies myself. But I had no tears left. Not for them. Not for Mom. Not for anyone."

They faced each other in silence. Harte now understood her obsession with not running out of air, as well as her loathing for stunts. She had risked her reputation and the job she loved to do something real. She was still haunted by that failure. But as Harte saw it, the failure wasn't hers. It fell squarely on the man who had risked lives for his own empty glory.

"There was an investigation of the incident," she continued. "I wasn't formally charged with anything but the mutiny, though I was under suspicion for a lot more. There was abundant evidence that I wasn't involved with planning the climb and had tried to communicate the flaws. SCEI stopped short of blaming Chickering; they had already acclaimed him a hero, and they needed a hero. They couldn't blame me, so they left it inconclusive — a tragic accident, how terrible, but the Initiative must go on so their sacrifice wouldn't be in vain."

"With you grounded, stuck at a desk," Harte said. "Where's the sense in that?"

"They portrayed it as a favor — I'd been through a traumatic experience, and I needed time to recover. But I suspect they saw me as a loose cannon. Remember when I said Wesley James didn't trust me? Well ..."

Harte laughed. He couldn't help it, though he stifled the impulse as quickly as he could. "Sorry, I'm not laughing at you. But with all due respect, Boss, you're the most firmly-bolted cannon I've ever met."

"Thank you, I think."

"What about the climber who was missing from the video?"

"I found his body apart from the others. From the position, it looked like he'd died on the way up. And his sixth air tank was missing. There was no way to know whether he'd given it up voluntarily, and nothing to be gained even if I did know — they were all dead, so if someone was a murderer, they hadn't gained much." She paused. "I've never told that story to anyone."

Harte nodded. "And I didn't record it." He raised the camera and filmed. Crouched on the ship, she looked small, yet still in command. The asteroids were strange and lovely in the background. Between them, one bright star shone. "Beautiful!" he breathed.

"What? Should I move out of the way?"

"Stay right where you are. That's the publicity poster."

"With me in it? I don't think —"

"You have to be in it."

"You can't even see my face. No one will know it's me."

"I'll know. And I can add your face. I'd rather have you smiling, anyway."

Anderson's voice interrupted. "It's time for you lovebirds to come in now. We're approaching the debris field, and I want everyone strapped in, just in case."

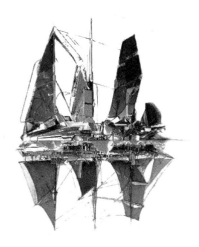

Chapter 17

2125/04/26: The Boss isn't afraid, so I won't be, either.

> — *Amelia Blackborow's private diary*

Ruby and Gunner walked over the hull to the open airlock. The outer doors closed, and Ruby raised her gold visor. As Gunner followed her example, she turned away. She had told him everything but wasn't ready to look him in the eye without a filter. They waited in silence while the chamber pressurized.

He was the first to speak. "That was ... quite a story. Thanks."

She forced herself to look at him. It was easier than she expected. "Do you still want to use it in the doc?"

"I don't know. It doesn't have much to do with this expedition — except that it has everything to do with the expedition commander." He cocked his head to the side. "I'm even more impressed now by your positive attitude. Unless the optimism is just an act?"

"It's not. That's my temperament, I guess. If my father figures have let me down, at least I've had better luck with sibling figures."

"Could I be one?"

Ruby gave him a long look but didn't answer. She had trusted him with her story, and now waited to find out whether that was a wise or foolish move. She couldn't see who would be helped by making the information public. At least he hadn't recorded her rescuing him. The doc didn't need that kind of cheap heroism.

The doors slid back, and they re-entered the ship. He started to remove his helmet. She placed her gloved hand on his arm. "Leave it on."

"Do you believe there's any real danger?" he asked. "We've been hit by debris before, and it didn't do any harm."

"I don't know, but the Skipper sounded worried. That alone is enough to make me pay attention."

They joined the rest of the party on the bridge and strapped into their seats. Only a small fraction of the debris was visible, but at a glimpse of the radar display, Ruby understood the Skipper's concern. At some time in the past, something big had been pulverized by something bigger, leaving behind pieces ranging in size from gravel to boulders as large as *Endurance*. There was no easy way around.

The first impact reverberated through the ship. Something rattled over the hull like hailstones. Nguyen engaged the steering engines to avoid the larger chunks, but there was no way to miss everything. Anderson tried to furl the solar sail. It moved a little, but in spite of Gunner's best efforts, it was still jammed.

"Skipper, we don't want to be here," Ruby said.

"I'm beginning to agree with you." There was nothing carefree in his tone. "Everyone strapped in? Good, because you're about to feel some Gs."

He engaged the braking thrusters, canceling forward momentum and effectively backing them out of the debris field. The ship shuddered under one more big impact. The lights went out for a moment, and somebody yelped — Ruby thought it was Lee Keith. They came back on almost immediately. Anderson swung the ship around and engaged the main engines. There was an ominous thunk from deep in the ship. They lurched to one side, then stabilized.

"What the —?" Anderson muttered. He studied the instrument panel.

"Captain, we've lost the communication laser and antenna," Nguyen reported.

"Systems report," Anderson ordered. He sounded calm again, but Ruby could hear the strain.

"The hull is dented but intact. Life support is fully functional. Air pressure, normal. Photovoltaics are at fifty percent. There isn't much left of the solar sail. Radar is down. And we're on backup power. The reactor is offline."

"Mr. Nielson, head down to the power plant and see if you can fix it," Anderson said. "Dr. Crean and Mr. Gunner, go with him."

"Perhaps we should head back to where we left Hercules," Ruby suggested. "We don't want to use up our stored power maneuvering around debris, or risk being hit by something we can't see."

"Already on it," Anderson replied. "Dr. Eyestone, home in on the little guy's beacon."

Harte accompanied the physicist and engineer into the depths of the ship. He hadn't thought much about the small reactor since the installation of the new turbine at the beginning of the expedition. Since then, it had been reliably powering ... well, everything. Including the engines. How far could they get on back-up power?

"That must have been some impact, to trigger a complete shutdown," Dr. Crean said. He held a Geiger counter, which emitted a few random clicks. "At least there's no radiation leak."

"Maybe we can just start it back up, then," Harte said.

"Easier said than done," Crean replied. "A fusion reaction is a delicate balance. If anything is out of balance, the reaction stops. That's what makes it so safe, but it means we won't be able to start it until everything is right again."

He and Nielson began to assess the damage. "Well, shit," Nielson muttered. "It's the damn turbine again. It got knocked off balance and spun itself to pieces."

"How bad is it?" Harte asked.

"Not as bad as it could be," Dr. Crean said. "The reactor itself is intact and potentially functional."

"But bad enough," Nielson said, "because this was already the spare turbine. The spare for the spare was flawed enough to be recalled."

"You can't fix this one?" Harte asked.

"Won't know until I try. We can run lighting and life-support systems on emergency power, but we may need to convert the propulsion. But when the backup batteries run out …"

"What about a mechanical generator?" Harte asked.

Nielson grinned. "I like your thinking, Gunner. We don't have one, but we could build one."

Crean looked from one to the other and nodded. "The exercise equipment?"

"You got it," Nielson said. "Let's put these people to work."

The fitness equipment used mechanical resistance to simulate gravity. With a few modifications, the efforts of their shipmates could be converted into electrical energy. It wouldn't replace a fusion reactor, but together with the remaining photovoltaics, it would keep some of the storage batteries charged. They would not suffocate in the dark.

The robot Hercules was equipped with a beacon so they could find him again. Unfortunately, with the ship's communications array knocked out, they had to be close for Dr. Eyestone's receiver to pick it up.

"What if we can't find him?" the roboticist asked. "What if we miss him because we're too far away?"

"Don't worry," Ruby assured him. "You'll never meet a better navigator than Frank Anderson."

She wasn't faking confidence. She had no doubt they would find Hercules again. But then what? Nobody was willing to say it, but the situation looked dire. They couldn't call for help. Even if they could, there was no practical way for help to reach them. They had only themselves to rely on. That said, if she had to rely on anyone, this was the group she'd choose.

Hercules had launched right after breakfast. Only a few hours had passed, but it seemed like a distant event after all that had happened since. During lunch, Ruby tried to devise a plan for their severely altered expedition.

"Hey, Boss, aren't you going to change out of your spacesuit?" Wild asked. Everyone else had changed before lunch, once they were sure there was little danger of depressurization. "Or do you know something we don't?"

Ruby glanced down at her suit. She'd removed her gloves and helmet but hadn't found a moment to change. She still wore the gecko boots. "I'll get to it. Food takes priority."

She was surprised at how hungry she was, but EVA was like swimming that way. She dug into lunch with a will … and felt guilty for enjoying it. But it was especially good — Blackborow had combined the ingredients of two or three different MessPaks and some fresh herbs to make a chicken and pasta casserole. The others praised it extravagantly, perhaps to avoid talking about the situation. Dr. Eyestone alone was quiet. He didn't eat until Blackborow coaxed him personally.

Endurance traveled more slowly toward Hercules' asteroid than it had away. Anderson kept the engines on low-power mode to conserve batteries. Fortunately, the asteroid traveled to meet them, and by the end of the day, they were back where they'd started. Anderson directed them without error to Hercules' position, which buoyed everyone's spirits. With skillful use of the braking thrusters and steering engines, he set down on the asteroid and anchored the ship to the surface. The rock was only about twice the size of the ship, but psychologically, it felt good to be *on* something, even if the gravity was still near zero.

The whole party made a fuss over the little bot as Dr. Eyestone brought it aboard, and the Doo-Bots performed after supper. Following the performance, Ruby kept everyone in the mess to deliver her news.

"Due to damage to the ship, I am forced to indefinitely suspend our primary mission. We will remain on this asteroid to make repairs. The robots will go into storage to preserve their power cells." A disappointed groan ran through the gathering. "I share the feeling. They have been excellent for morale, and we will all miss their performances. We can only hope they return to duty soon. Meanwhile, we have our own duties to perform. Dr. Mack, Dr. Crean, and Dr. Curley, feel free to continue your research, as much as possible. Mr. Nielson has permission to draft anyone he needs to help with repairs. In the meantime, to reduce power needs we will confine our living and working space to this level of the ship. The cargo deck will be sealed off."

Betty Nguyen sputtered. "But … our quarters?"

"We will all have to sacrifice a little privacy. You may sleep in your own cabins tonight. In the morning, gather what you need of your belongings. My quarters will serve as the women's dormitory. Captain Anderson and Mr. Wild have agreed to take in the other men. We will move whatever we can of the laboratory and fitness equipment into the mess. It'll be tight, but we'll manage. Any questions?"

If there were, they went unspoken. But as the meeting broke up, she overheard one.

"What's the point?" Lee Keith muttered. "We're all going to die!"

He was the first to say it, but he couldn't be the first to think it. Blackborow's eyes were wide with barely contained fear. The thought had crossed Ruby's own mind, but she refused to allow room for it. She made her way over to him. "Mr. Keith, I will need an updated inventory of all food supplies, cross-referenced to daily caloric intake at both full and reduced rations. Ms. Blackborow, please assist him."

"Yes, ma'am," Blackborow replied immediately.

It took Keith a bit longer, but he nodded assent. The look of panic began to leave his face.

"When you've finished that, start on all other supplies. It will be a real help to know at the beginning what we're working with."

Ruby left them and went straight to her quarters. It was early, but she was physically and mentally worn out. And she wanted a little time alone before the enforced togetherness, though she didn't regret offering to share. They had to be united in this, and physical togetherness would demonstrate that. There were no officers or crew now — just twelve humans who wanted to survive.

Once she was alone, the first thing she wanted was to get out of her spacesuit. She removed the gecko boots, the outer suit, and the life-support rig. She was about to peel off the pressure suit when she heard a tap at the door.

"Who's there?"

"Gunner. May I come in?"

Her heart thumped hard as the flight response kicked in. But she'd told him her story. He had no power over her now. She slid the door open. "Sure. To what do I owe the pleasure?" That was how he had greeted her before EVA, but he missed the joke.

"Nielson asked me to —" His eyes widened. He cleared his throat and looked away. "Pardon me. That's … a good color for you. Should I come back later?"

She glanced down at the form-fitting pressure suit. It covered everything but left nothing to the imagination.

She didn't really care, but his discomfort was amusing. "Please, Mr. Gunner — it's not as revealing as what you'd see at the beach."

"I've never seen you at the beach, Boss."

"Can you believe I've had this on most of the day?" More for his modesty than her own, she pulled on a uniform jacket. "This is the first chance I've had to change. Now, what did Nielson ask you to do?"

"He sent me to take some measurements, to make sure we can fit four sleeping bags in here." He pushed himself in, his toes skimming the floor. She slid the door closed. He pulled out a tape measure. "Wow! Your room's way nicer than mine! Want to switch — or share?"

"Not a chance. You'll be with the Skipper, Nielson, and Eyestone."

"Excellent — the party cabin."

"I'll be right next door, so keep the noise down."

"Yes, ma'am." He began to measure every available surface. An advantage of microgravity — the sleeping bags could be fastened literally wherever there was room. "That was quite a speech. I don't think I could have delivered it so calmly."

She was glad her effort to stay calm hadn't shown. "What would panic achieve?"

He snorted. "I don't believe you know the meaning of the word. But that's good — they look to your example, and it sounds like you've got it all planned out."

"I have to think about contingencies; this is a basic emergency plan, with some minor modifications."

"Uh-huh. You just don't want to admit you're a genius."

She smiled at that. "Just thinking as far ahead as I can. Will you still be able to film?"

"Sure, as long as I can charge my equipment. Do you think it's a good idea, though? It might seem like a waste of power."

"I want to maintain as much normality as I can," she said, though the fact of an attractive man in her quarters was about as abnormal as could be. "If you're still making your doc, that means you expect to show it someday."

"I see your point. And the story just got a lot more dramatic." He grinned, then grew serious. "I'll do whatever I can to help. I can do more than take pictures."

"I'm well aware of that. You're at the top of Nielson's list for the repair crew."

"Good, I wouldn't want to have to fight for my spot. Well, good night, Boss. Sleep well." He held out his hand.

"Thank you, Mr. Gunner. You, too." She gripped his hand more heartily than she meant to, imparting enough momentum to cause a collision between them. "Whoa!" Rather than bounce off, she grabbed his shoulder with her free hand. This succeeded only in adding spin. She hummed a few bars of "The Beautiful Blue Danube."

"Grab something!" he exclaimed.

"I did — you!" It seemed like the funniest thing she'd ever heard, and soon they were both laughing too hard to talk.

"What are we doing?" he gasped.

"I'd say about forty-five rpm." She snickered, but his laughter died away.

"No, I mean why are we laughing? It doesn't seem right."

She grew serious, too, and squeezed her eyes shut. "To keep from screaming."

"Boss, are *you* afraid?"

She sighed and forced herself to look at him. "Apparently, I no longer have any secrets from you."

"Actually, I'm surprised. I didn't think you were afraid of anything."

"Are you saying I'm an emotionless robot?"

"That might be an insult to the robots."

Ruby no longer felt like laughing, but she had to smile at that. "Point taken. But anyone who isn't unnerved by this situation is not sane enough for leadership." She sighed. "A few hours ago, the worst thing I could imagine was telling you what happened with Chickering. Hardly seems like anything now." She pressed her forehead against his shoulder. It was a relief to lean on someone solid and warm.

He patted her back just above the shoulder blades, then straightened his arm to put some distance between them. "Careful, there, Boss. A man might think you were starting to not hate him."

"Oh. Right." She released his hand and touched the wall to stop her spin.

"Don't worry. I won't tell Wild." He found a handhold and turned toward the door.

"About what? A moment of silliness at the end of a stressful day? And why would he care? Neither of us answers to him."

"I just thought he … you … the two of you …"

"Who told you that?"

"No one. It just seemed … likely."

"Mr. Gunner, do you realize you're talking about something that happened when I was sixteen? It's less a part of this story than Chickering."

"No, I —"

"I suppose if you're really interested, you'd have my blessing. You're more his type than I am."

Gunner stared at her a moment with his mouth open. He blinked and closed it. "Let's start over. You're acting kind of weird, Boss. Have you been drinking?"

She rubbed her face and sighed. "I almost wish I had been. I think we can agree this whole day has been kind of weird."

He smiled and nodded. "I won't tell *anyone*. Are you all right?"

"No. But I will be." She still wasn't sure how much she could trust him, but his presence was helping. She felt steadier. "We all will be. Thank you for asking. It's good to have someone … objective to talk to."

"Hey, my life's at stake, too!"

"OK, not objective. But you don't work for me. It makes a difference."

With a grin and one of his mocking salutes, Gunner left her. Ruby brushed her teeth, finished undressing and zipped into her bag. As the lights went down, she gazed out the viewport at glittering space. One gleaming star seemed especially big and bright. Although not superstitious by nature, she made a wish on it, for the continued safety of her shipmates. They were under her care as well as her command. Nothing bad would happen to them if she could help it.

She didn't wish anything for herself, though she couldn't get her mind off how good it felt to hold Gunner. Why did it have to be him? But it couldn't be anyone else. Appropriate physical contact between a commander and her people was limited to a handshake, a pat on the back, and the occasional assistive boost in zero gravity. She loved this group like family, but as long as they worked for her, she couldn't even hug them. It was an acceptable trade-off to do this work. But Gunner didn't work for her. She was so starved for touch that she might have done something really foolish if he hadn't pushed away. This wasn't the time or place for any of that. She had really dodged a bullet.

But she couldn't help feeling she'd missed an opportunity.

Chapter 18

2125/04/27: Unit cohesion is proven in adversity. Morale remains high and everyone is hard at work. I couldn't ask for a better team.

— Ruby Ladd's Expedition Journal

Harte couldn't sleep. He tried, if only to fully appreciate his last night in private quarters. Although he wasn't a natural worrier, he had qualms over the situation — marooned in space with no communications, far from help or even advice. But it didn't seem real yet. Maybe it wasn't that bad; Nielson could probably fix whatever was wrong, and then they could finish their mission and go home.

Something else kept him from his rest. His mind returned again and again to that odd, clumsy moment with the Commander. No doubt the hug, or whatever it was, had been unintended at first, but they had both let it go on longer than necessary. He wondered now how much he could have gotten away with. A grope? A kiss? More? Someone that fit could probably go for hours! In the bright blue pressure suit, she resembled the barely costumed heroines in the old comics he'd been reading. Only better; the Boss was real. All she needed was a cape and high-heeled boots. Then he had a better idea — the pressure suit left nothing to the imagination, so why not imagine her without it?

Harte rubbed his eyes to try to erase that compelling picture. What was the point? He wasn't convinced anymore that she'd pitch him out an airlock, but this was the last place to plan a seduction. Still, he couldn't forget her vulnerability while she told her story, and again in her cabin. Just for a blink, she had shown him another side. He could almost believe she trusted him. Maybe even liked him. He hadn't come on this expedition to make friends, but his heart fizzed with delight at the possibility.

After a while, he quit trying to sleep, grabbed his camera and went to the bridge. Watch was invariably dull, and whoever was on duty appreciated visitors. The lights were off to save power, but by the glow of the instrument panel, Harte recognized Captain Anderson.

"Evening, Skipper. May I join you?"

"Gunner? I think it's technically morning, but come on in. So, sleep wouldn't come?"

"You got it. I usually hope for the best, but I feel like I'm waiting for the situation to get worse."

"Lord, how could it?" Anderson shook his head. "I was kind of glad it was my turn on watch, so I didn't have to try to sleep."

"Are you worried?"

"It doesn't look so hot right now, but with the Boss in charge, we stand a better chance. I just keep thinking about Marie and the kids. They'll be fine, I know, but I don't like to worry them."

"No one even knows we're in trouble," Harte objected.

"Not yet. But in a month or so, someone will notice we've stopped communicating." He gazed out the viewport. "You couldn't ask for a better view, though."

Harte strapped into the navigator's seat to admire the panorama. He could pick out many of the same features he had filmed during his EVA. "That star sure is big. It didn't seem as bright when I was outside."

"Dr. Crean could probably tell us why that happens."

Harte chuckled. "Let's not wake him." He turned on his camera and filmed for a while. "I've often wondered — what are you watching *for*?"

"It was my turn."

Harte glanced at the Skipper to see if he was kidding. "No, I mean, in the old days, on a ship at sea, they'd be watching for pirates or submarines or something. There's nobody out here but us."

The captain grinned. "So you don't think we're likely to meet a shipload of little green guys?"

"If we do, I hope my camera's charged."

Anderson nodded. "Sailors have always set a watch, to keep alert for danger, or anything unusual. Not just other ships, but icebergs, or land, or a change in the weather. Sometimes it's comforting just to know there's someone awake."

"So the watch is the designated grown-up?"

"Something like that."

A voice called from the doorway, "Hey, Skipper, are girls allowed in this clubhouse?"

"Speaking of …" Anderson turned with a smile. "We'll make an exception for you, Boss. Join the Insomniacs' Club."

Harte's stomach flipped. He'd been picturing her naked, and now he had to be cool in front of Captain Anderson. He swallowed hard and tried to think unsexy thoughts. *Marooned on an asteroid* just about did the trick.

Commander Ladd entered with two beakers. She handed one to Anderson. "Who's *we*?"

Harte turned in his seat. She flinched. "Mr. Gunner! I … didn't realize you were here."

"I hope it isn't a problem."

"No, of course not," she sputtered in a way that told him it was. She had her uniform on again, but her tone was more effective at chilling his ardor. As she gave him the drink, her fingers touched his and he jerked back as if it were an electric shock. "Careful, that's the last of the cocoa."

"You should have it," Harte said.

"I don't need any. I just wanted to keep the Skipper company. What were you looking at?"

"That big, bright star." He pointed it out. "We were talking about asking Dr. Crean why it seems brighter than it did earlier."

She nodded. "I noticed it, too." She stared at it, then turned to Harte with a frown. "Did you happen to get any shots of it earlier, during our EVA?"

"I think so. Why?"

"No reason. Dr. Crean might find it helpful."

"In that case, I'll take a few more shots now, in case we turn away from it."

Anderson laughed. "You can count on that. This rock just keeps tumbling, and we tumble with it. I wouldn't mind, but it turns the solar panels away from the sun."

"Nielson and I had an idea to rig a generator to some of the exercise equipment," Harte said. "It could at least keep our comms charged while we work on the reactor." The Boss gave him a hard stare. "I know it's not much, but —"

"It's an excellent idea," she said. "We'll need the exercise, games, reading material, and journals — all good for morale." She considered. "I'd say the bike, wouldn't you?"

He grinned. Maybe they could be friends, after all. "That's what I was thinking. It's the most compact."

"And efficient. Find a place for it in the mess tomorrow."

With that, she turned away to stare at the bright object in space. This left Harte free to watch her while he sipped his cocoa. It was warm and comforting. Her presence had much the same effect. He wasn't thinking about seducing her now; not much, anyway. She had become brisk and efficient again. He just wanted to sit close to the warmth of her confidence and believe that somehow, they would come through this alive.

The asteroid rolled over and the bright star disappeared from view. Now the sun, small but brighter by far, shone on them. The viewport darkened to protect them from its rays. "It must be morning," Ruby joked. By the ship's clock it was about 0400, two hours to rise-and-shine. "I'm going to see if I can get a little sleep before breakfast."

Gunner yawned and stretched. "I think I'll try a little of that myself."

Anderson grinned. "I'll see you slackers later."

Ruby left the bridge ahead of Gunner, acutely aware of his presence though he had the good sense to keep his mouth shut. She couldn't shed the memory of holding him in her quarters, or the fantasy of doing more. Was he thinking the same? That distraction was the last thing she needed right now. She bid him a terse goodnight and returned to her quarters, where she managed a fitful nap before the alarm sounded.

By sheer habit, she emerged from the bag and went to breakfast. Blackborow was in the galley. Lee Keith hovered as she prepared the meal.

"No need to go overboard," he said.

"Nonsense," Ruby cut in. "We have a lot to do today. We're going to need a full meal."

"But the supplies —"

"Talk to me about supplies later. Breakfast first." She left the galley before he could say more.

She was surprised to see Gunner at breakfast. He couldn't have slept any more than she did. Neither of them had much to say, which she chose to blame on fatigue, though she didn't actually feel tired now. There was too much to do. The Skipper came off watch and joined them.

"Morning," he yawned. "I'm here to do my part."

"Your part is to finish your breakfast and get some sleep."

"You were up most of the night, too," he objected.

"I took a nap." She smiled. "And I'm the Boss. To bed with you, Captain. That's an order."

He turned to Gunner. "I know when I'm licked." He swallowed the last mouthful and trailed off to his quarters.

Everyone else got to work installing velcro and sleeping bags in the three cabins and moving personal items and lab equipment from the cargo deck. Nielson was occupied with the damaged power turbine and the stalled reactor. Ruby took a break from helping everyone else to get his report.

"Well, how does it look?"

He eyed her. "Not good. Even if we can restart the reactor, we won't be able to generate power with this busted turbine. No power, no launch. Or a launch that drains all our backup power."

"Can you swap in the spare turbine?"

"The recalled unit, you mean?"

"Is that a no?"

"It's a big fucking maybe."

"If that fails, could we convert to a different propulsion system? Chemical rockets?"

"The shuttle uses hydrogen, but I doubt there's enough fuel for these big engines."

"All right. Do what you can with the turbine and keep me posted."

She returned to the others, a little shaken. She was used to Nielson's foul mouth and negative attitude, but to have him doubt he could fix something — that was new. Time to develop a back-up plan.

Gunner recruited Dr. Eyestone to help bring up the exercise bike. In microgravity, it weighed almost nothing, but it was awkward to move. They bolted it into place in a corner of the mess. With hardware from the robotics lab and Nielson's supply locker, they rigged up a generator that could charge a small power cell or feed back into the grid. They finished just before lunch.

After so much bad news, Ruby jumped on the chance for a celebration, however slight. She ordered a full lunch and ignored Keith, who was obviously biting back a remark.

"You've all worked hard, and you're going to keep working hard," she said. "We're going to take turns riding that bike. We still have to keep our muscles and bones in shape for when we return to normal gravity. Now we'll also be keeping the lights on and the air flowing."

She took the first ride and charged her comm. When she climbed off, Lee Keith was waiting for her. "Commander, I've got an initial report on the food supplies."

She sighed. There was no putting it off. "Well done, Mr. Keith. What's the word?"

"On full rations, we have enough bulk provisions and MessPaks for three months, plus about four months' worth of NutriCubes."

"That's … not bad. Even if we end up camping here awhile. Thank you." She smiled until he turned away. Seven or eight months. It would have been plenty of time, if they could launch and if they still had the solar sail. As it was, even if they launched immediately, eight months wouldn't bring them close to Earth. It might not even get them all the way to Mars. They would have to go to half rations, or less … but not yet.

Chapter 19

*2125/04/27: Just when you think it can't get any
fucking worse — it's worse. I don't believe even the
Boss can get us out of this one.*

— Chip Nielson's private diary

Dr. Crean pulled Harte out of the line for the exercise
bike. "The Boss says you have something to show me."

It was difficult to hide his surprise. He knew what
Crean was talking about, but she hadn't seemed
particularly intrigued at the time. "It's kind of
interesting, I guess."

"Interesting, how?"

"A ... phenomenon. Something I hope you can
explain. I'm not sure if it's astronomical or optical or
what." He displayed an image. "I took this during my
EVA yesterday."

"Nice shootin', Tex," the physicist murmured. "What's the question?"

"This star. When I saw it again later from inside the ship, it seemed brighter. Did it actually change, or is it an illusion?"

The Commander drifted over to look, too. She stopped her movement with a light touch on Harte's shoulder, almost too brief to feel. Yet the sensation lingered long after she'd lifted her hand. He controlled his breathing and deliberately did not look at her.

Crean had him flip back and forth between the two images. "Hard to say for sure. I can tell you one thing — that's not a star." He pulled out his comm and opened a chart of the solar system. Harte flipped down his AR lens so it would appear as a three-dimensional projection. "It might be a planet. Where did you see it?" When Harte answered, Crean did some calculations. "It's bright enough to be Jupiter or Saturn, but they're not in the right position. How good is your resolution?" Harte gave him a withering look. "OK, OK, sorry," Crean said with a laugh. "Zoom in as far as you can." He gazed some more. "Wow. That is good."

"Of course it is. Can you answer the question?"

He frowned. "I ... think I need to see this thing for myself. Come with me to the bridge. Boss, will you join us?"

"You know I'm always up for a science lesson."

"We might want to wake the captain."

Harte couldn't see how this was important enough to wake Anderson, but Crean looked more serious than he'd ever seen him. The Boss looked troubled, too, but she had a lot on her shoulders. The captain was not in his quarters. They found him on the bridge. Nguyen was on duty, and Anderson was asleep in his seat. He roused when they entered.

"What are you doing here?" Commander Ladd asked. "I sent you to your quarters."

"Too noisy in there with all the remodeling. What are *you* doing here?"

"Dr. Crean is about to solve a mystery for us."

The asteroid had rolled over a few more times since the previous night, and the bright object was visible again. "Is it just me, or does it look bigger now, too?" Harte asked.

Dr. Crean stared at it. "Not bigger. Closer. It's another asteroid, and it's headed this way."

Nguyen gasped. Gunner and Anderson exchanged startled glances. Ruby shook her head. Dr. Crean had confirmed her fear.

"But it's not going to hit us, right?" Gunner said.

"I need to collect more data. Based on our observations, all I can tell right now is that it's moving toward us, and it's moving faster than we are."

Ruby rubbed her eyes. Now she felt tired. All she'd wanted was a successful expedition where people worked together, got the job done, and went home. But everything was going wrong before the real work of the expedition could even begin. It had been going wrong from the start, when she fired Lloyd Green and gained a stowaway. The mission was a failure. *She* was a failure.

None of that, she told herself. *You are still in command. As long as your people are safe, you haven't failed.*

She looked straight at Dr. Crean. "When will you know if that thing poses a threat?"

"I should have a rough idea by the end of the day."

"Good. That's your assignment. Gunner, I suspect Nielson could use your help. Nguyen, as you were. Skipper, go back to sleep."

"Fat chance," he muttered, and gazed at the bright spot in space.

Harte returned to the reactor compartment. People were still moving gear from the cargo deck, so that part of the ship hadn't been sealed off yet, but it soon would be. He found Nielson pulling the damaged turbine.

"The Boss sent me to help."

"Good. I need a hand installing the replacement turbine."

"Wasn't this the spare?" Harte asked. "The other one was recalled."

"Tough, it's what we have, and it was working when we launched. I'll take my chances."

Harte had expected Nielson to try repairing the damaged one, until he got a close look at it. The housing was banged up, and many of the blades were shattered or bent. There weren't enough left to repair. He secured it out of the way and helped install the replacement.

"That wasn't so hard. What now?" he asked.

"Just a simple matter of restarting the reactor." Nielson rolled his eyes. "The way our luck's been running, I wouldn't be too goddamned hopeful."

"I appreciate your positive attitude," Harte said, but Nielson missed the sarcasm. He tried again. "Is it hopeless?"

Nielson glanced up. "We have to try." He pressed his cheek to the bulkhead. "I hate to see her like this."

"Who? The Boss?"

Nielson glowered. "The ship, you idiot! She's all beat up and hurt, and we're the only ones who can help her."

"*If* we can."

"Yeah. *If*." Nielson sighed, then shook himself. "I hope we can finish before this area is depressurized. Can you imagine doing this kind of work in gloves?"

Before Harte could answer, Commander Ladd joined them. Dr. Crean was with her, and they both looked grim. "Sorry to interrupt," she said. "I've asked Dr. Crean to help you restart the reactor. If that can't be done in ... let's say four days, put all your efforts into alternative options for launch. We need to get off this rock."

"What's the hurry all of a sudden?" Nielson asked.

"We are in the path of a larger, faster asteroid," Crean said. "In three weeks, give or take a couple of days, this rock, and everything on it, is going to be destroyed."

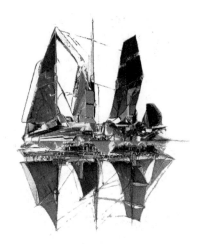

Chapter 20

2125/04/28: What was I thinking? "My turn" to go on tour. I'm so sorry, my dear one. So sorry.
— Betty Nguyen's private diary

The Boss left and the three men gathered around the reactor. Nielson muttered and swore as he pulled up the instruction manual.

"'Stable and foolproof,'" he mocked. "Just not fucking asteroid proof."

"Well, to be fair, what were the odds of that?" Harte asked. What had Dr. Crean said at the party's first meeting? *Asteroids collide every million years or so ...*

"Astrofuckin'nomical. But what are the odds of getting plastered by an asteroid where we sit? We're cursed."

"No such thing," Dr. Crean said. "We'll improve our chances —"

"Our shitty chances," Nielson muttered.

Crean gave him a long look before continuing. "We'll improve our chances if we get busy fixing this mess. The magnetic containment was disrupted, so we need to restore that first."

It sounded simple. It wasn't. Even an amateur like Harte quickly grasped that restoring containment was theoretically easier than restarting the reaction, but it didn't matter because both were likely impossible with the tools they had at hand.

After ninety minutes that accomplished nothing more than frustration, Nielson called off the effort for the day.

"I say we sleep on it and give it one more try tomorrow. But unless we get a damn miracle, we'll be converting the engines."

Ruby's heart wasn't in the singalong that evening but she faked as much enthusiasm as she could. No one else seemed openly worried yet, though they might have been faking, too. But this first night in crowded conditions had a festive, slumber-party atmosphere about it. No need to depress morale while it was still good.

Wild was on watch, the only one who didn't stay for the singalong. Anderson retreated to his quarters as soon as the music ended. Gunner and Nielson soon followed so they could be fresh and rested when they returned to work on the reactor. Blackborow went with Dr. Eyestone to make sure the robots were fully charged.

"It's been a long day," Dr. Mack said. "Time to turn in."

Betty Nguyen started to follow her out, then turned back. "Coming, Boss?"

Ruby waved them off. "You two go get settled. I'll be along."

She took an extra turn on the bike to charge her comm and generate power for the ship. It kept the worry at bay and helped her think, though she really did not like her backup plan. It had to be a last resort. But maybe the exercise would help her sleep better than she had the night before. Not likely with three extra people in her quarters, but it couldn't hurt.

Dr. Curley also stayed in the mess after he put his banjo away, studying something on his comm.

"I'm not ready to turn in yet," Ruby said. "How about a quick game of chess?"

He looked up with a smile. "Sure. How fast do you think you can beat me?"

She set up the board and let him have the first move. "Have you learned anything about the composition of our new friend?"

"It could be ice," Dr. Curley said. "It's certainly reflective enough. I wanted to find an ice asteroid, but I never dreamed it would come to us."

"Seems like anything can happen out here. Careful what you wish for."

"Whatever data we collect should be helpful to whoever comes after us," he said.

"I like your attitude," Ruby said.

"Facts and figures soothe my anxiety."

Ruby recognized that trait. "I have every reason to believe we'll come through this. Ooh, check!"

He got out of it. They went back and forth until it was clear they were in stalemate, and neither would win.

"You should know that doesn't happen very often." Ruby held out her hand.

He grinned and shook it. "Well, you have a lot on your mind. I take my little victories where I can. Good night, Boss. Tomorrow's another day."

Ruby slipped into her quarters quietly so as not to wake the others. A wasted effort because they were not asleep.

"... think I needed an adventure after all this time?" Nguyen was saying. "What was wrong with teaching others to pilot spacecraft?"

"We all had our reasons, Betty," Dr. Mack said, her voice gentle and soothing. "You're here because you wanted to be here. I'm glad you are. We're better off with you."

"It's OK to be worried," Ruby said as she joined them. "There's an element of danger even on a short hop or a test flight. On a jaunt this long? It's almost guaranteed. But we'll get through it."

"What's the plan?" Dr. Mack asked.

"Best case? Nielson restarts the reactor and we finish the mission," Ruby replied with all the certainty she could muster. "If that isn't possible, we still have time to try out plans B and C. They're not completely formed yet, but I'll tell everyone when they are. But now it's time to get some sleep."

She tucked into her bag and was about to doze off when Blackborow came in. Ruby feigned sleep to avoid further conversation. The others were either already asleep or also faking. Wide awake again, Ruby waited until Blackborow was settled, then slipped out to the bridge to keep the watch company. Although it was Wild's turn, Anderson was there, too, his gaze fixed on the nearing asteroid.

"Shouldn't you get some sleep, Skipper?" she asked.

"Look who's talking. I can sleep just as easily here as in that crowd."

"I sympathize," she sighed. "Maybe I shouldn't have put all the quiet men in Wild's cabin."

A slow smile spread over Wild's face. "I'm glad I have some peace to look forward to."

"You're welcome. And I'm glad for some quality time with my two favorite guys."

Wild raised an eyebrow. "I was beginning to wonder about that. Gunner's been monopolizing a lot of your time."

She reached over and squeezed his hand. That much was allowed. "Actually, I think he's jealous of our *intimate association*."

He chuckled. "Such as it was. How'd he hear about that?"

"Made it up out of his own head, I think. He 'looks for the narrative.' I told him he could pursue you with my blessing."

"That's very thoughtful of you, Boss, but I don't think it's me he wants."

She held her head with both hands. "God help him if he wants more from me than my story."

"Does he have it yet?"

"The whole sorry tale. I told him things I've never told anyone else."

Wild's eyebrows shot up and he stared straight at her. "Was that wise?"

"I don't know." She thought about it for a moment. "I feel better with it out."

"And he's still pitching in around here. I don't think the documentary is his total focus anymore — if you'll pardon the expression. It's like he's one of us."

Ruby nodded slowly. "That's what he said he wanted. Maybe it's true."

The Skipper stirred. "Will you two please can it? I'm trying to sleep here."

"Sorry, Skipper. I'll go. Maybe I can sleep now, too."

Her cabin was quiet when she returned, and she managed a brief doze before the alarm sounded to begin another day. She was encouraged to find almost everyone still in a positive frame of mind. The only low-spirited member of the party was Dr. Eyestone, who had been without a job since the bots were powered down. He welcomed her suggestion that he help Nielson with the reactor. She wished she could work on the repair herself, but she lacked those skills, and it wouldn't help to hover.

Ruby had her own work and plans to occupy her, plus a few extra rides on the exercise bike. If nothing else, it tired her out enough to go to bed on time. She assumed this night would be quieter. No such luck. Nguyen was on watch, but Blackborow and Dr. Mack were especially chatty. They took forever to fall asleep. By then, Ruby was wide awake, staring out the viewport at the approaching asteroid. She got up and joined Nguyen on the bridge.

Anderson was there again, too — or still. "I didn't see you at a single meal today, Skipper. What's going on?"

"Blackborow's been bringing them to me here."

"You sleep here, you eat here — I hope you leave to go to the head."

He gave her a tight smile. "Yeah. But I feel guilty about it. This is my ship — I should be able to get her off this rock!"

"She's my ship, too, Skipper."

Nguyen gave them an uneasy look. Ruby doubted her presence was helping, and this visit wasn't doing anything to calm her own racing thoughts.

"I'll sleep on it," Ruby said at last. "See you tomorrow."

The captain didn't appear at breakfast the next day, and Ruby didn't see him when she came to lunch, either. She went to the galley and found Blackborow counting out twelve MessPaks.

"What have you got in the way of comfort food?" Ruby asked.

"How about mac and cheese?"

"Sounds good. Give me one for the captain, too."

Blackborow extracted two meals from the storage locker. "He seems ... worried." Her voice shook a little.

"No, he just thinks better away from the crowd," Ruby bluffed. "We'll be fine."

Ruby returned to the bridge. She activated the heating units on the MessPaks and handed one to Anderson. "Thought you might like some company."

"Thanks." He peeled back the cover, squeezed the entire packet of hot sauce over his macaroni and stirred it in. He returned his attention to the viewport, where the approaching asteroid was clearly visible. He shoveled down his lunch without looking at it or appearing to taste it, though his ears turned red from the pepper sauce.

Ruby ate with a little more attention to the meal, but it didn't offer the comfort she was looking for. "I don't think staring at it will make it go away, Skipper."

He sighed. "I've never lost a ship."

"Well, don't start now! We'll think of something — it's not too late."

He didn't answer. Ruby gathered their trays and utensils for composting. "I'm going. Will I see you at supper?" He waved a hand but didn't speak as she left the bridge.

Ruby met Dr. Mack in the passage between the bridge and the mess. "Doctor, am I glad to see you! Can you do something for the captain? He's really not himself."

"Actually, I hoped I might do something for you, Boss." Dr. Mack didn't even try to hide her concern. "You look terrible. When was the last time you slept?"

"Before breakfast." It wasn't a total lie. She *had* slept, at some point, before breakfast. She just wasn't sure how many days ago.

Dr. Mack folded her arms. "Ruby, you're exhausted. You need to rest before you start hallucinating."

"I'm fine! How can I just go off and sleep at a time like this?"

"At a time like this, we need you sharp. You're no good to us if you start seeing things. As your friend, I advise you to get some rest; as your doctor, I order it. To your quarters. Now."

"But —"

"Anyway, I need to draw some blood for my study. Come on." Dr. Mack took Ruby's arm and propelled her to their shared cabin, now empty and quiet. She waited while Ruby undressed, then zipped her into the bag.

"But what if I can't sleep?"

"Don't worry." The doctor swabbed Ruby's arm with disinfectant. She inserted a needle into the vein, so skillfully that Ruby barely felt it. But instead of drawing blood, she injected something.

"Hey! What ...?" Ruby lost the ability to talk before she could finish the sentence. Her eyes closed against her best efforts.

"You'll thank me later," Dr. Mack said. "Sweet dreams, Boss."

Harte ate a quick lunch and took a turn on the bike. They were close to giving up the effort to restart the reactor, so the mechanically generated power was even more precious. It also got him away from the other nigh impossible project, converting the engines to allow launch.

It didn't help that Commander Ladd was apparently determined to work herself into the ground. He'd seen her only briefly before lunch, when she picked up two MessPaks and left again. That glimpse showed dark circles under her eyes and worry lines creasing her brow. At least she was eating, and making sure the Skipper did, too.

No one had said anything aloud, but he assumed the whole party was worried about her. It seemed wrong; it was *her* job to worry about *them*. But if she wasn't able to function, they would be in more trouble than they already were.

As he got off the bike and prepared to return to work, Harte overheard Dr. Mack ordering the Boss to get some sleep. He hoped the doctor had enough authority to make the order stick, because he doubted the commander would listen to anyone else.

When Ruby woke, the cabin was still empty. If the others hadn't come to bed yet, she guessed she hadn't missed supper. She hoped not — she was starving. She got out of her bag to relieve herself, clean up, and dress again. She had to admit, the nap had done her good. Her head felt clear for the first time in days.

In the mess, a few people were finishing a meal, while others were starting to work again. Gunner, Nielson, Crean, and Eyestone weren't there; she assumed they were back to working on the reactor. They usually took it easy after supper, but she admired their diligence.

"There you are, Boss!" Blackborow handed her a dish. "I saved you some breakfast."

"Breakfast? What —?"

"How do you feel?" Dr. Mack asked.

"Better."

"You should," the doctor said with a smile. "You slept for seventeen hours."

Ruby glared at her. "What did you give me?"

"Just a mild sedative."

"You call that mild? It knocked me out for most of a day!"

"No, it just got you past the insomnia. The rest was all you." Dr. Mack cocked her head to one side. "Although a side effect can be vivid dreams. I'd say you had some good ones."

"Why, did I talk in my sleep?"

"Not in words. But you sounded ... happy."

Ruby tried to remember her dreams. They had been vivid and detailed, though they scattered on waking. But one had been more memorable, involving pleasant naked activity with someone. Someone with a mustache. She could still feel it. Her face burned.

Dr. Mack grinned. "Anyone we know?"

"Oh, shut up. And don't ever pull a stunt like that again."

"I won't if you won't."

Ruby sighed. This wasn't getting anywhere, and she felt too good to be really angry. "What did I miss?"

"Nothing. We haven't been crushed yet, but they still haven't fixed the reactor."

That news blunted her appetite, but she forced herself to eat. Dr. Mack was right: they needed her sharp, and they needed her healthy. And it was time for a hard decision.

She put on her suit and helmet and went through the depressurized cargo area to the reactor compartment. Four helmeted figures were staring at the reactor and didn't appear to notice her until she was with them.

"Dr. Eyestone, I have a favor to ask," she said. "I think we've all earned some entertainment. Please power up the Doo-Bots and get them ready to perform."

He lit up and immediately went to the lab to get the bots out of storage.

Ruby turned to the others. "Well, what's the prognosis?"

Nielson looked from the reactor to her face. "In my expert opinion, we are fucked."

She glanced at Gunner. "Fucked is the one thing we most definitely aren't," she muttered. Both men stared at her — she'd spoken aloud over the public channel. Gunner actually looked embarrassed. "What I mean is, if we can't get out the door, we'll climb through the window. This isn't over yet."

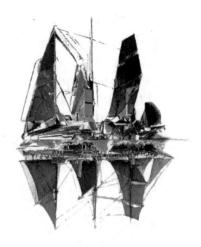

Chapter 21

2125/04/30: I don't even want to tell them what I have in mind. But is there any other choice? Our whole purpose has shifted.

— Commander Ladd's Expedition Journal

Harte didn't know what had changed, but the Boss was herself again. She was back in charge and she had a plan. Maybe that was all he needed to know. Seeing her rested only made it more obvious how exhausted she'd grown in the days after their EVA. They'd gotten along without her for a day, but they missed her. Now she was back, and the relief was palpable. Even if she was starting to talk like Nielson.

"I'm glad you're feeling better, Boss," he said. "I was afraid you might be sick."

She barely glanced at him through her visor. "I can't afford to be. Mr. Gunner, get your camera. I want you to get as many shots as you can of the ship as she is now."

"I can do that." There was something poignant about the request. Something urgent. "You mean right now?"

"Right now."

Through his gecko boots, Harte felt a vibration like many small impacts, and Mrs. Chippy emerged from the robotics lab with her strange loose-jointed trot. She bumped Nielson's leg.

"There you are, my darlin'! What a pest you are!" The engineer patted the robot with his gloved hand. Commander Ladd turned her face away.

"Mr. Nielson, we need to talk to the captain. Come with me." Maybe it was the helmet speakers, but her voice sounded thick and strained.

"I'm right behind you." Nielson gave the bot a gentle shove. "Go on back to your boss now. I'll see you later. No? Come along, then, but it'll probably be dullsville." The bot trotted along after Nielson and the commander.

Harte was the last to leave the cargo deck. His moment of relief and restored cheer was short-lived. The Boss had a plan, which should have been encouraging, except she clearly didn't like it. Harte didn't know what was going on, but he had a feeling he wasn't going to like it, either.

Ruby and Nielson re-entered the pressurized section of the ship and removed their helmets and gloves. Anderson was still on the bridge when they got there. He gazed out the viewport, toward the bright spot that seemed too small to be their doom. Ruby laid a hand on his shoulder.

He turned and gave her a weak smile, as if he already knew. "Well, Boss."

"Well, Skipper. I think we have to face it. There's no way to get the ship off this rock. This is the end."

He nodded and looked away. "The end of our endurance."

She moved in front of him and gripped his hand so he had to look at her. He had tears in his eyes, and she had to swallow hard before she could speak. "No, Frank, not ours. Only the ship."

"How can you say *only* the ship?" He caressed the instrument panel in front of him as if it were a living thing. "She's been a good ship, a strong ship. Our home. Without this ship, there's no expedition. No us."

"She has been a good ship, and I'll miss her," Ruby agreed. "But we still have a mission, you and I. A new one. We have ten people with us who want to go home. We're going to get them there."

He stared at her. "Make that all twelve of us. But get them home in what? The ship's about to be pulverized."

"In the shuttle."

"The *shuttle*? Are you crazy?" he exclaimed. "That's like putting out to sea in a rowboat. It's a landing craft, not an interplanetary ship."

"That's what it was designed for, but it can be redesigned. More to the point, it can get off this rock and keep *us* from being pulverized." Ruby smiled. "With you at the controls, I have faith that it can get us where we need to go."

He continued to stare in disbelief, then allowed a little smile to creep onto his face. "Anybody else, I'd tell 'em to get lost. Coming from you, I can almost believe it."

"So you're with me?"

Anderson lifted his hands in surrender. "Sure. What have we got to lose?"

"Thank you." Ruby turned to the engineer. "Mr. Nielson, you have charge of all work on the shuttle. Recruit anyone you think might be helpful. Make it spaceworthy. Make any modifications necessary."

"I can make it spaceworthy, but there's only so much I can do to increase its speed," Nielson said. "And the fuel in the tanks is all there is. Sure wish we had a spare propulsion system." He looked down when Mrs. Chippy bumped his leg. "Are you volunteering yours?" He chuckled, then grew serious again. "You know, that might work."

"What might?" Ruby asked.

"The robots have their own propulsion," he replied. "It's not much, but there are seven of them. In a pinch, it could be just enough to get us where we need to go. Or at least pointed in the right direction."

"Figure it out with Eyestone," Ruby said. "You have two weeks."

He grinned and saluted smartly. "Yes, ma'am!"

Harte was filming in the mess when Nielson suddenly appeared in the frame. "Gunner! With me!" He jerked his thumb toward the airlock to the cargo deck.

Harte lowered the camera. "We just came from there. I thought both the reactor and the conversion were lost causes."

"They are. The Boss just gave me a new assignment, and I want you to be my chief assistant. We're takin' to the boats."

Harte shook his head. He must have misheard. "Sorry, we're what?"

"Abandoning ship and making our getaway in the shuttle."

Crean and Curley turned to stare at Nielson. Blackborow and Keith emerged from the galley, where they had been working on the supply inventory. All four began to talk at once.

"That's insane!"

"What was she thinking?"

"There must be some mistake!"

"The Boss knows what she's doing," Wild said in his slow, deep voice. The panicked speculation ceased.

At that moment, the commander appeared from the bridge. "Thank you, Mr. Wild. I hope I do." She turned to the others. "I'll explain more fully when we have everyone together. For now, continue as you were, but give Mr. Nielson your full cooperation if he asks for help."

She smiled, and when her gaze rested a moment on him, Harte's confidence soared. He would try anything she suggested.

There wasn't room in the shuttle bay to do the needed exterior work, so they hauled the little ship out and anchored it to the surface of the asteroid. It looked like a toy next to *Endurance*. Harte couldn't believe they were thinking of crossing the solar system in it, but it was all they had. And it was kind of nice to work on something that wasn't already broken.

Nielson checked every seam and rivet to make sure the exterior was sealed. Contrary to most of their recent luck, the shuttle remained undamaged. They climbed inside and powered it up. The lights worked and the small cabin was soon pressurized.

The engineer took off his helmet and grinned as he looked around. "We have a lot of work to do." He spoke with relish.

Harte didn't need to be told, and he wasn't as thrilled at the prospect. "How are we going to travel anywhere in this?" If anything, the shuttle seemed smaller than it had during drills. Its modular design could be rearranged to accommodate passengers, cargo, or some combination. In its current configuration, it had a small cargo area in the back, a two-seat cockpit up front, and seats for six passengers — three down each side, upholstered in a rusty orange. There was no head, no galley, no sleeping quarters. It was completely unworkable for any trip longer than a few hours.

"We reconfigure," Nielson said. "We pull four seats out of *Endurance*, put two at each end, like sitting around the dining table. Right? The upholstery won't match and we'll have to sleep in our seats, but I can think of worse things. We can install a head back here, and still have space for supplies. We'll make a little closet, keep stuff from breaking loose. Let's see, what else?"

Over the next several days, he recruited more help to move items, though he and Harte did most of the actual installation. Mrs. Chippy was with them much of the time, mostly underfoot, but occasionally useful by accident. Nielson patted and teased her, joking and whistling while he worked. He was in the best mood Harte could remember from the whole trip.

They added armor to the hull and wiring for the functioning solar panels so they could be moved from *Endurance* before launch. They took precise measurements to determine how many of the large storage batteries would fit — far from all but better than none. The air supply was more important. There wasn't even close to room for the exercise bike, but Harte rigged a hand-cranked generator that could keep their comms alive.

They built a private cubicle and installed one of the toilets and waste-disposal units from the main ship. They included a rack to hold individual attachments for each member of the party — the last thing they needed was a bladder infection. Nielson decided it was important enough to cram in the water-reclamation system and the smaller CO_2 scrubber, though they took up precious space. There was no need for an actual galley — they would have to leave all the bulk provisions. They walled off a small storage area for the food and other supplies, with racks to hold the bins. Once the space was stocked, there was barely room inside to turn around. It held most of the crates of NutriCubes. They squeezed a few MessPaks and packaged cookies into odd-sized gaps, for the sake of morale and variety. One gap, too narrow for a food crate, turned out to be exactly the right size for the hot drinks dispenser. There would be some comfort in that tiny miracle.

While this work was underway, Harte also filmed as much as he could: the crowded mess, the dorm-like cabins, the dimly lit bridge and its permanent occupant, Captain Anderson. The Doo-Bots performed every night, and the Boss insisted that he get more footage of them. His lens often strayed to her face. She didn't look worried, exactly, but there was a new sternness to her features. She rarely smiled. That picture haunted him whenever he closed his eyes.

Nielson optimized the shuttle's engines for maximum thrust. At the last possible moment, they transferred the storage batteries and the magnetic shield generator, which would protect them from cosmic radiation. The little ship was as ready as it would ever be. The Boss had given them two weeks, and they used every day.

"What'll we call her?" Nielson asked. He held the airbrush Eyestone had used to ID the robots.

"Why call it anything?" Harte said.

"A ship needs a name." Nielson looked thoughtful for a moment. "And I know just the one."

Harte assumed it would be something vulgar, but when Nielson lowered his brush, tidy letters read *Ruby Marie*.

"She'll get us home," the engineer said.

Ruby wore her dress uniform that evening. That final night aboard *Endurance* needed to be an occasion. And she wouldn't wear it again. The fitted white jacket and slim black pants were not durable enough for the voyage ahead. But she would wear the polished black boots.

She instructed Blackborow to use as much of the remaining provisions as she could for a last, festive supper. After they'd eaten, she produced the last container of booze on board, a cheap, synthetic tequila. She could almost hear Lloyd Green laughing at her. Looking back on it, she wondered if she should have taken that initial problem more seriously — the first sign that the expedition was doomed. But Ruby had never been superstitious, and they weren't doomed yet. She doled out the liquor. If ever they would need it, now was the time.

She lifted her beaker. "My friends, we have been through a lot together, and we are not done yet. Tomorrow we embark on a great adventure like no space traveler has attempted before. Our only aim is to survive. We may find it isn't possible, but at least we will have tried. If I die in the attempt, then I will say now, there is no group with whom I would rather have spent my final months. And if we survive, which I believe we have every chance to, it will be because of this courageous crew. To you."

They drank. It tasted like disinfectant, but it was better than nothing. Then Wild lifted his beaker. "I beg to differ. If we survive, it's all down to you, Boss. You brought us this far, and you will bring us home."

She accepted his faith with as much grace as she could. If they believed in her, it helped her believe in the plan. "Thank you. On a more mundane topic, we should have adequate water aboard, but for drinking only. We'll have a dispenser of hygiene gel for our skin, but we'll just have to let our clothes get dirty. And we will have to be careful not to overtax the waste disposal systems. Necessary use only — no shaving or haircuts."

Gunner fingered his mustache. "I guess I'll have to grow that beard, after all."

For a moment, Ruby felt all funny inside. She swallowed and tried to hide her discomfort.

"How much stuff can we bring?" Blackborow asked.

"One spacesuit, one sleeping bag and one small duffel apiece. So only a couple sets of clothing. We'll stink, but we'll all stink together."

"Camera bag?" Gunner asked.

She couldn't help smiling at that. "Absolutely. Document everything. I want the world to know what we've done."

They ended with a musical evening. It was like so many others, but the whole time the Doo-Bots performed, Ruby had a lump in her throat. On the positive side, there had been no complaints from the Pearl in a long time.

When the performance was over, she approached Dr. Eyestone and spoke quietly.

"Whatever you need to do to get them ready, now's the time."

"I guess I should clean the gecko pads so they can cling to the shuttle." He closed his eyes. "I just had a terrible thought. We can't have them thinking independently out there, can we?"

"If we need their propulsion, it'll be best if they're under your control," Ruby said.

"Ugh. I'll have to reset them to default."

"They won't be the DooBots anymore?"

Dr. Eyestone shook his head and swallowed hard. "I have backups, but ..." He blinked rapidly and his lips twitched.

Ruby remembered then just how young he was. She laid a hand on his back and tried to keep her voice from breaking. "I'm sorry, John."

"Maybe it's better this way," he said. "If we have to use them for propulsion, it's one and done. No sense carrying them along the rest of the way. Better if they're not our little friends anymore."

"I'll help you clean them up," Ruby said.

They suited up and returned the robots to their lab. Dr. Eyestone attached them to their charging station and put them into sleep mode. Ruby went to each one and laid her gloved hand on its dome, above the painted names. She wanted to thank them for their sacrifice, but it seemed silly to talk to machines. So she helped clean their feet.

When they were fully charged, Dr. Eyestone reset each one to default mode.

As he came to the last one, Nielson burst in. "What's happening? What's he doing?"

"He's returning them to their default setting, Mr. Nielson. So they don't get any ideas while they're on the outside of the shuttle."

"But Mrs. Chippy's riding with us, isn't she?"

"I'm sorry. There's no room inside," Ruby said.. "She'll be outside with the rest, in case we need the extra propulsion. Remember, she did volunteer."

"You can't do that! You can't kill Mrs. Chippy." He propelled himself across the lab and put himself between Dr. Eyestone and the robot.

"Mr. Nielson, please," the roboticist protested. "This is hard enough."

"Then at least let me say goodbye." Nielson switched off his comm, but Ruby could see his lips moving through the visor. He pressed his gloved hands to the little bot. He patted it gently and left the lab without a word to either of them.

Chapter 22

2125/05/15: Our "home" is smaller, our supplies more limited, our mission non-existent. We are happy just to be alive. Sooner or later, the loss will sink in ...

— Commander Ladd's Expedition Journal

In the morning, Ruby inspected the shuttle. It was stuffed; there would be room for twelve people, their spacesuits, and a couple changes of clothes. Nothing more. In spite of cramped quarters, she was pleased to see the hot drinks dispenser. It and the magnetic tabletop games would be needed more than ever to boost morale. The party had also downloaded as many books as possible from the ship's computer, dividing up the library among their comms. As long as the power cells held out, they wouldn't lack reading material.

She shook her head at the name painted on the shuttle. *Ruby Marie.* If they'd asked, she would have told them to leave her name out of it. At least they had included the Skipper's partner, too, though Nielson was too much of a traditionalist to include Wild's. Ruby wouldn't have expected him to be so thoughtful, but she was getting used to surprises.

When her inspection was complete, she gave the rest of the party permission to file aboard. She offered each one a handshake and a word of encouragement. She pulled Dr. Curley out of line.

"No banjo?"

"I didn't think there would be space, and I know you don't care for it."

"I've come around," she said. "Music may be as essential to our survival as food. Stow your gear and go get that banjo."

While the others got settled, she returned to *Endurance*'s bridge. Captain Anderson stared out the viewport. The asteroid looked near enough to touch, an uneven gray-white chunk a bit larger than their rock.

"Skipper?"

He turned with a strained smile. "It's Frannie's birthday today."

Ruby laid her hand over her heart. "So it is. How old is she, six?"

Anderson swallowed. "Seven."

"Wow, already? Seven's supposed to be a lucky number. So this bodes well for our launch."

"They might be wondering about us by now. Worried. I hate to spoil Frannie's birthday."

"Then don't, Frank. Take us home."

He closed his eyes but nodded. "Home, or near enough." Earth and Mars were at similar distances, but not in the same direction. Mars was close enough to make a difference, considering their limited supplies, so it was their chosen destination. Anderson opened his eyes, squared his shoulders, and flicked a series of switches. The lights on the bridge brightened. "We won't leave her dark."

Ruby waited while he extracted the data recorder and changed into his spacesuit. They went out and boarded the *Ruby Marie* together.

Harte helped Nielson take in the anchors that secured the shuttle to the surface, then entered the ship and strapped into a seat. It felt good to be going somewhere again, not just waiting — even if the outcome was anything but assured.

The Boss rode shotgun beside Captain Anderson. The others took seats as they pleased. Blackborow sat next to Dr. Eyestone in the end seats nearest to the galley, as she had dubbed the screened-off storage space. The roboticist looked like he hadn't slept at all. He didn't speak but managed a smile for Blackborow. Harte had one of the side seats next to them, with Betty Nguyen on his right and Nielson across the way. Keith, Curley, Crean, Mack, and Wild claimed the remaining seats.

There was enough space under each seat for a sleeping bag and a duffel, and a supply of space-sickness bags in a pocket at the end of each row. Harte strapped his camera bag to his left armrest, to make use of the open corner space between his seat and Blackborow's.

They launched toward the oncoming asteroid, angled to starboard to be out of the path of debris when it hit. Blackborow gripped Eyestone's hand. He didn't seem to notice. Harte aimed his camera forward and recorded. The shuttle vibrated more on launch than *Endurance* had, whether because of the difference in size or propulsion, he didn't know. He hoped the footage would at least be usable.

As they rocketed past the ice asteroid, Anderson cut the thrusters and the ride smoothed out. Then he engaged the steering engines to turn the ship back the way they'd come. Harte would capture clear images of *Endurance's* demise.

From a distance, the damage to the ship wasn't apparent. All the viewports gleamed with light from within. She looked welcoming, like home. How could they leave her? Then the larger asteroid pushed into the smaller, crushing the brightly lit ship between them. The small, rocky asteroid cracked apart. The ship was gone. And it all happened without a sound.

Harte lowered the camera and blinked back tears. Nielson stared out the viewport, slowly shaking his head. Dr. Mack closed her eyes and clasped her hands together, perhaps in prayer.

Blackborow gasped and pressed her face into Eyestone's shoulder. He squeezed her knee and murmured, "At least the robots are safe with us," then kissed her cheek.

How had Harte missed it? He'd noticed they were close enough in age to be a plausible couple, but those two really were more than shipmates. More than friends. He could have focused the doc on this budding romance — a great narrative. Maybe in edits ...

"This was not how I wanted to find an ice asteroid," Dr. Curley muttered.

Dr. Crean nodded in agreement and patted him on the back. Nguyen looked stunned, but so did everyone else. Except for Keith, who tapped furiously at something on his comm. Had he even watched the destruction? Maybe this was his way of coping.

In the cockpit, the Boss had her arm around the Skipper. She rarely touched anyone, beyond a handshake, apparently due to some strict regulation. Maybe they were past rules now, though it was hard to believe she'd relax discipline, even in a crisis. This was Ruby Ladd being not a boss, but a friend. Harte considered including the scene in the doc. No, better to leave it private. He would remember.

The commander removed her helmet and unbuckled her harness. She turned and propelled herself into the passenger area. "Ms. Nguyen, change clothes if you like; then join the Skipper up front. Time to set a course for Mars."

Nguyen got out of her seat next to Harte and made her way to the galley or storage closet or whatever it was. It was the only private space large enough to change clothes.

The Boss hesitated before assuming Nguyen's seat. "I hope you got pictures of that, because we'll never see anything like that again."

"I got it. There won't be a dry eye in the house — except maybe yours."

"Maybe not even mine." She glanced toward the cockpit. "I'd appreciate it if you delete the Skipper's reaction. He's never lost a ship before, and he's taking it hard."

"I didn't record it."

She nearly smiled. "Good man."

Just as Nguyen strapped into her seat in the cockpit, an impact rocked the ship.

"Skipper?" The Boss sounded as tense as Harte felt.

"Just a parting shot, I think," Anderson replied.

"The hull's intact and all systems, functioning," Nguyen added.

They both fell silent as they studied the instrument panel. "Damn," Anderson muttered. "It ruptured the auxiliary fuel tank."

"Are we in danger?" Commander Ladd asked.

"Not unless we light up the thrusters — or try to land in atmo. But we're not planning either of those anytime soon, so we're OK ... for now."

"Do we have enough fuel?"

"None to waste, but there'll be enough as long as we don't have to make too many course corrections."

The Boss tapped her fingers together and frowned. "We should plan to stop at the Phobos emergency depot, just to be safe."

"It's about time someone used it," he replied.

After that last bit of excitement, they settled into their new routine. One by one, they changed out of their spacesuits and stowed them in a rack at the back of the passenger area. If possible, it made the cramped space seem even more crowded. Harte filmed a little of their new home. He was careful not to invade the commander's space, small as it was. She flinched whenever he moved toward her. He tried not to take it personally. Whatever trust they had established during the EVA didn't seem to be a permanent change. She was still wary of him, and he wished he had discovered the reason back when they had a hint of privacy. It was unlikely to come out now.

She called for everyone's attention, an easy matter when they were all within a few meters of each other. "Thank you all for your hard work and cooperation these past few weeks. Our escape was a close one, but without everyone's efforts, it wouldn't have happened at all. I'm going to try to keep that in mind in the coming weeks, whenever I grow impatient with the close quarters." She smiled around the group, almost but not quite at Harte. "Unfortunately, we'll be confined to our seats most of the time. Mr. Keith, I'd like you to make a schedule so everyone gets equal opportunity to stretch, go to the head, and so on. Dr. Mack has offered to teach us some exercises we can do in our seats to prevent too much bone and muscle loss. And we can all take turns cranking Mr. Gunner's generator."

"I'll crank my own generator, thanks very much," Nielson grumbled.

Harte swallowed hard and bit his lip to keep from laughing. It was an unfortunate turn of phrase, spoken in innocence. Anyway, there was only one person he wanted cranking his generator. And she was the least likely to oblige.

Strapped into her seat, Ruby clasped her hands in her lap to hide their shaking. Her mind kept replaying the unwanted image of *Endurance* crushed between two asteroids that then reduced each other to rubble. The disaster tested Ruby's optimism, but of course there was an obvious bright side: she and her shipmates had escaped the destruction. They had cut it closer than she would have liked, but their departure had been orderly, not panicked. The auxiliary fuel tank was an unfortunate loss, but this insane scheme could really work … if the little ship held together and if they could maintain high morale. Two big ifs, but so far, so good.

"There. Finished," Keith said.

"The schedule I asked for?" Ruby said. "That was fast."

"No, the final supply numbers. I'm sending them now."

She opened the report as soon as it arrived. Unlike the earlier estimates, this report was based on the exact numbers of rations and other supplies packed onto the shuttle.

"Skipper," she said. "We need to go over your time estimates in light of Mr. Keith's revised supply inventory." She unbuckled her harness and made her way to the cockpit. It was crowded with three of them in there, but she slid the door shut behind her.

"Is it better or worse?" Nguyen asked.

"See for yourselves," Ruby said, casting the report to the display screen.

They spent the next hour working through a complicated math problem involving food, water, air, fuel, and distance. Without the solar sail, the *Ruby Marie* would gain acceleration only from burning fuel, of which they now had less than expected. They had fired the rockets to launch from the asteroid and again to set course on their current trajectory. Now they were coasting. At this velocity, they would encounter Mars again in no less than seven months.

"On full rations, we have only five months' worth of food," Ruby said. "A little less."

"The auxiliary tank is empty now," Anderson said. "I could safely fire the rockets again and get there faster, but we'd have to make another course correction. That takes fuel, too; can we spare it?"

"What about the robots?" Ruby asked. "Would their propulsion be enough for the course correction?"

Anderson looked at their figures again. "It might be. Ms. Nguyen can recalculate our course after we get up to speed."

Ruby left them discussing how long of a burn they could afford and resumed her seat next to Gunner. She didn't want that seat, but it was the only one available.

Most of the group had staked out territory on boarding. Ruby, Anderson, Wild, and Nguyen would rotate through the cockpit on a regular schedule and trade off the same two seats in the passenger area.

"All well?" Gunner asked.

Ruby didn't look at him when she answered but tried to keep her voice neutral. "Sure. Just a minor course modification. We might feel some Gs." She chose not to mention the potential food shortage. In spite of having to leave the bulkier food items behind, they had a storage closet stuffed to bursting with rations, and everyone was in good health and spirits. There was no need to worry anyone else about that yet. "Dr. Eyestone, it's time. Ms. Nguyen will send you the trajectory."

"Oh," the roboticist said. "So soon?" He sighed heavily. "All right, I'll get them ready."

Harte reviewed his footage of the destruction of *Endurance*. He wasn't sure he would ever get over the shock and sorrow of it, but even with the loss still fresh, he couldn't deny the beauty of the images. Would it be more effective in silence, or with the recorded reactions of his shipmates? Maybe he could make two versions.

The shuttle vibrated and G-forces pressed him against his armrest. Before long, they were coasting smoothly again. A faint thud reverberated through the hull, followed by a second.

"Did something else hit us?" Dr. Mack asked.

"No," Dr. Eyestone said, his voice quiet and hoarse. "The bots are using their propulsion to adjust our course. When they run out of fuel, they'll release from the hull. Based on location, that was Delilah and Samson."

"Releasing from the …" Harte said. "They're not coming with us?"

Dr. Crean nodded slowly. "We don't need the extra mass. They're helping us get where we're going."

At the next small thud, Eyestone said, "Hercules." Thud. "Slag." Thud. Thud. "Sally and Sir Ernest."

"No," Nielson whispered. "NO! You can't! Not …"

Thud. "Mrs. Chippy."

Chapter 23

2125/05/18: Our Commander has the biggest heart I have ever encountered. Who else would allow, let alone suggest, a funeral for robots? But she always knows what the party needs most. Perhaps that's my narrative …

— Holden Gunner's Production Journal

Ruby slept poorly the first night. Adrenaline from their narrow escape plus the loss of not only the ship but also the robots plus trying to sleep strapped into a seat added up to racing thoughts and insomnia. She managed to doze off just before the alarm sounded. From the drawn faces around her, she assumed no one else had slept much better. Ruby had no appetite for breakfast. Hot coffee helped a little, but as soon it was finished, Nielson turned to Dr. Eyestone and muttered something. Ruby couldn't make out all the words, but the tone was snide, and she caught something about robots. Eyestone ignored him with admirable restraint, physically turning away as much as possible as Nielson continued to whisper.

A sullen crewmate was the last thing she — they — needed. Nielson had been cheerful and engaged while he was readying the *Ruby Marie*, but it seemed too much to hope the mood would last. Ruby sympathized with his loss, but after less than an hour, she could take no more.

"Mr. Keith, just this once, I'm going to cut in line — I need a stretch." She unstrapped from her seat. "Mr. Nielson, please join me."

He gave her a "Who, me?" look, but left his seat and followed as she made her way to the storeroom at the back. She closed the door behind them.

"Is this your office now, Boss?"

She glanced around the tiny space. It was like having a meeting in a closet, but it would have to do. "Unless you'd rather have this conversation in front of everyone."

"What conversation is that? Are you offering to crank my generator?" He grinned.

The blood rose in her cheeks. She kept her face impassive, though it took all her restraint not to sock him. She had never struck a subordinate, and she didn't plan to start now. Besides, it was her own fault for making the stupid remark in the first place. "Mr. Nielson, have I ever disrespected you?"

"Not to my knowledge."

"Then would you like to rethink that suggestion?" She stared him down.

He blinked first. "Yes, ma'am, I would. Pardon me. Don't know what I was thinking."

He seemed sincere, though she was never sure with him. "We've been casual on this expedition. I prefer casual, but I will not accept disrespect."

"Right. So, what can I do for you?"

"I want you to stop muttering at Dr. Eyestone."

"I don't know what you're talking about. I never muttered at nobody."

"Mr. Nielson, you are so full of shit." His eyes widened when she spoke his language. "It's not that big a ship — everyone heard you. If there's a problem, I wish you'd tell me rather than act like a nine-year-old."

His jaw worked. "He … he killed Mrs. Chippy." He blinked fast and rubbed a fist against moist eyes.

"That isn't true. Who pressed reset on her?"

Nielson looked at his feet. "I did."

"And I know it wasn't easy for you." Ruby spoke as gently as she could. He had bonded with the little robot, and his loss was real. "It took courage. But it was the right thing to do."

"Eyestone would have done it if I hadn't."

"Yes, he would. Because I told him to get them ready, and that was part of it. You can blame me if you want to but leave Dr. Eyestone out of it. He built those robots and lost all seven."

"Yeah, but he's got his little girlfriend, and I … Well, anyway, we shouldn't have dumped them. It's not right."

"I don't like it, either. But there was no room inside. What could we have left instead? Seven crates of rations? The water recycler? The emergency air supply?"

Nielson shook his head but didn't answer.

"They did something important for us, riding on the outside. Without their mass, we're more likely to get where we're going." Ruby took a chance and laid her hand on his shoulder. He didn't shrug it off, which gave her courage to continue. "You worked a genuine miracle getting this ship ready. If we survive, it's at least as much your doing as mine. But we all miss the Doo-Bots. Now that we have nothing but time, maybe we should have a ... a funeral for them."

"A funeral? For machines?"

"Well, we can't have a wake; we drank all the booze already."

He cracked a smile. "All right, I see what you mean. Still seems weird."

"I can't disagree with you. But if you think you can speak civilly to Dr. Eyestone, I'd like you two to plan it. You ... knew them best."

"I might be able to manage that."

She thought about his rapport with the bot. "Is there anyone waiting for you, back home? Family? A partner?"

He waved a hand. "I was almost married once, a long time ago, but we split up before it was too late."

"I'm sorry."

"Don't be. We were young and dumb; it wasn't a good match."

"Still — nobody else?"

"Aw, you know — other engineers, drinking buddies …"

It sounded like a lonely life, not unlike her own. But at least she had Anderson and his family. "Maybe when we get home, you could … get a pet of some kind. Something alive."

"Machines are easier."

"Are they?"

He puckered his face the way he did when he thought hard. "I see what you mean. Are we done?"

She forced a smile and tried to make it sincere. "I hope so. Thank you, Mr. Nielson."

Ruby remained in the small storeroom to compose herself. A funeral for robots? She expected some funny looks from the rest of the party. Her own mother didn't have one! But Ruby had always felt strange about that. They had honored the dead woman's request, but it still seemed wrong. Too late, she understood the ritual was more for those left behind. Wherever the idea had sprung from, if it distracted Nielson for a few days, it would be worth the raised eyebrows. It might even help him work through his grief. It might help all of them. They had suffered a great loss — not only the robots, but the whole purpose of the expedition. Maybe a funeral was exactly what they needed.

"You're planning a what?"

The Boss had worked one of her miracles. Nielson not only had a purpose again, he was voluntarily cooperating with Dr. Eyestone on some kind of project. Harte had no idea what it was until the two of them called him into the little storage space, which had become the de facto conference room.

"A funeral. For Mrs. Chippy," Nielson said.

"For all the robots," Eyestone amended.

"A robot funeral?" Harte managed not to laugh; the two men looked so earnest. "Whose idea was that?"

Nielson glanced at Eyestone. "The Boss suggested it. So we could … you know … as a group."

"Grieve?" Just saying the word produced a lump in Harte's throat. But he wasn't surprised that this was the commander's idea. She understood people. Many times, he'd witnessed her warmth toward the others. Just not toward him.

"Yeah, grieve or whatever." Although acutely embarrassed, Nielson was determined to see this through. It meant something to him. "She asked us to plan it, however we want. And we hoped you might put together a whadayoucallem …"

"A montage," Eyestone supplied.

"That's the one. A montage, for the service. I know you have lots of pictures."

Harte smiled. It wouldn't hurt him to have a project, too. "That I do, and it may be a while before I get to do anything else with all those images. Why not?"

They held the service a few days later. After lunch — the last of the MessPaks — Dr. Eyestone asked for everyone's attention. They all knew he'd been working on something with Nielson, but not what. Hard as it was to conceal anything in such close quarters, they had managed to keep the details of their project quiet. A ripple of anticipation ran through the group, and all eyes turned expectantly to the roboticist.

"Friends," he said, "we are going to take a moment today to remember those of our number who aren't with us anymore." He paused to clear his throat. "We began this venture with seven apparently identical machines that had one specific job to do. Over time, they developed personalities, for want of a better word. I gave them names and in a moment of boredom, taught them to sing. They never had a chance to do their intended job, but as we got to know them and they got to know us, they brought a lot of joy to our lives. Most of you didn't get to say goodbye before they ... gave their all for us. So anybody who wants to, you'll have a chance to say something today."

"I'll start," Nielson said. "Mrs. Chippy was no damn use as a robot, except by accident. She was usually underfoot and in the way, demanding attention. I don't know why she decided to follow me around and pester me, but she could always cheer me up. It just doesn't feel right that she's gone." His voice failed on the last word, but he gathered himself to continue. "I'd like to read a poem. This is Byron, not me." He acknowledged Aaron Curley with a nod, then cleared his throat and opened his comm. "'There have been tears, and breaking hearts for thee ...'" He swallowed and wiped his eyes, unable to go on.

Blackborow took his comm and continued the reading in a clear voice. "'*And mine were nothing, had I such to give. But when I stood beneath the fresh green tree, which, living, waves where thou didst cease to live, and saw around me the wild field revive with fruits and fertile promise, and the Spring come forth her work of gladness to contrive, with all her reckless birds upon the wing …*'"

Dr. Curley joined her on the final line, from memory. "'*I turn'd from all she brought to those she could not bring!*'" They exchanged a sad smile.

Although Byron was a tough act to follow, everyone said a few words, including the Boss. "We are lucky to be alive," she said. "No, not *lucky*, because our escape came through hard work and sacrifice. Our survival came at a price, and it is right to acknowledge that price, accept that we have suffered loss. Hercules … Sally … Samson … Delilah … Slag … Sir Ernest … Mrs. Chippy." She spoke the names slowly, not with hesitation or mockery, but with solemn respect. Harte heard a little pause at the end, as if she wanted to say one more name. Her mother's? Chickering's? "They served us well, even if they didn't get to perform the job they were designed for. Their sacrifice may be the thing that saves our lives. I salute them."

Harte allowed a moment of silence before he took his turn. "I'm a picture person, so I'll keep my words brief. I hope this montage will help us remember our little friends at their best."

The monitor at the front of the cabin came on. The first clip showed the Doo-Bots at their first performance, without audio; the party songs seemed inappropriate. There were other performance shots, but also some of Mrs. Chippy with Nielson, and one of Hercules rocketing away on his one actual mission. Harte had watched the whole thing before, but it still brought a lump to his throat. He was glad he had so much footage of the robots. He had never expected it to be more than comic relief.

He had also included shots of the ship: on Mars back on Christmas Day; floating in space with the Boss small and commanding on the hull; and bravely lit up in her last moments. Next to him, the Commander gasped and gripped his hand. It was pure reflex, but still — she was touching him skin to skin. They were all united in this looming, unspoken loss. Now he knew the name she wanted to say: *Endurance.*

The montage concluded with the Doo-Bots performing a soulful ballad, complete with audio. Soon, the whole party was singing along. Eyestone, Curley, and Blackborow knew the words, while everyone else hummed or sang nonsense. An unusual funeral song, and through it, the Boss held Harte's hand. He didn't want to do anything to break contact, not even breathe.

As the montage ended, she released his hand with a jerk, but looked him in the eye and smiled. He thought he might have a heart attack. "That was well done. Not too long, and just the right images."

"After all, I have cut together a film or two before," he said. "I think I know what I'm doing."

The smile died away and her eyes narrowed. "This is a very small ship, Mr. Gunner. I suggest you scale back your ego, or there won't be room for the rest of us."

"You misunderstand ... I didn't mean ..."

Captain Anderson passed them on his way back to the cockpit. His face was wet with tears, but he was in control of himself. "I'll meet you up there, Skipper." The Boss followed him, all business again.

In silence, Harte watched her go. Her smile and her praise meant more to him than any of the awards he'd won, and he'd spoiled it. He hadn't meant to boast. He'd stated the obvious as a joke, but the humor had failed utterly. He would have to work harder to win the Boss's regard. Well, he needed a new project.

Ruby accompanied the Skipper into the cockpit and strapped into the navigator's seat. He slid the door closed behind them, though they generally left it open during the day.

"You were a bit rough with Gunner just now."

She sighed. "I know." She already regretted her remarks. Gunner had a healthy ego but was not as full of himself as she had once believed. Throughout the expedition, he had been unfailingly kind, helpful, and diligent, volunteering for responsibilities unrelated to his primary function. "He ... gets on my nerves."

Anderson chuckled. "We'll all do that if we're not careful. But he did a beautiful job just now. All of them did. Thanks for thinking of it."

"How are you doing?" she asked.

"Feeling lucky to be alive," he replied. "Every day I can say that is another day closer to home."

When Ruby rotated back out of the cockpit, the only open seat was once again the one next to Gunner. She nodded in greeting but otherwise did her best to ignore him.

"Boss?"

She jerked and turned to face him. "What?" It came out more sharply than she intended.

He flinched as if she'd struck him. "I ... want you to have this." He held out the small model of *Endurance* she had given him on Christmas. "Everyone has one but you."

"They brought them along?"

"I think so. It was easy for me — I had room in my camera case. But I think everyone made space."

She took it from him, careful not to touch his fingers. "Thank you, Mr. Gunner. That ... means a lot." She wished she knew how to apologize for all the times she'd snapped at him. "She was a good ship."

He smiled. "'By endurance, we conquer.'"

"Sounds like a good motto. Are you sure you want to give this up?"

"I have my pictures of the real thing."

Chapter 24

2125/06/21 Morale surprisingly good in spite of reduced rations. Will a banjo and a book club be enough to sustain us in the months to come? They will have to be — we have no one but ourselves to rely on.

— Commander Ladd's Expedition Journal

After the robots' funeral, they turned off interior lights to save electricity for life support and navigational instruments. As the days and weeks passed, they established a new routine. Ruby relaxed discipline a little, allowing a later wake-up time, though she insisted that sleeping bags be stowed neatly before breakfast. One by one, they went to the head, according to a rotating daily schedule devised by Mr. Keith. Water was now for drinking only, but they cleaned themselves with hygiene gel. It worked well on skin, less so on hair, of which they had more and more as time passed. The Skipper soon resembled a yak in shagginess. Wild looked like a Norwegian fisherman. Gunner's carefully groomed mustache grew bushy, and he must have run out of styling product because his longer hair now stood up like everyone else's. His scruffy new beard made him look rugged and outdoorsy.

Although there was no longer any actual cooking to be done, Blackborow continued to act as cook, with assistance from Dr. Eyestone, distributing NutriCubes at mealtime. Breakfast consisted of a single cube, with coffee to wash it down. Supper was the same, but with tea. Each cube contained the calories and nutrients of a full meal. They were dense and chewy and tasted mostly of vitamins. They filled the stomach and fed the body but failed to satisfy. No one complained that they ate only two meals a day. They weren't active enough to need all the calories of a third meal, which made a good excuse for the reduction.

They performed Dr. Mack's isometric exercises twice a day. They needed to maintain what they could of muscle and bone, and it helped pass the time. Ruby squeezed in a few extra sets each day. She continued to note her observations of morale. The science staff analyzed data and wrote reports. Nielson maintained the ship. And the book club continued in a new form. Rather than meet weekly to report on their various favorite books, they now spent time each day reading aloud to each other. This provided entertainment while preserving most of the power cells. The prayer meeting now met daily, too. Dr. Mack was kind enough to schedule it when Ruby was in the cockpit.

The *Ruby Marie* had never been intended to travel far from its mother ship or a planetary base. It had only a low-power radio transmitter, as opposed to the microwave laser aboard *Endurance*. Those who were adept at such things tried to boost the power of the transmitter, without draining every power cell on the ship. They sent regular SOS signals, but never received a reply. Over the distance the signal had to travel, it would likely be lost in the background noise by the time it reached a receiver.

After supper, Dr. Curley often brought out his banjo and led a sing-along. Then Ruby didn't mind her seat next to Gunner — everyone was happy to sing with him, and she was no exception. But the sing-alongs always ended. Whoever was on watch reported to the cockpit and everyone else unpacked sleeping bags. The five-point harnesses that held them in their seats meant they couldn't get into the bags. They tucked and fastened them so they wouldn't drift away during the night.

Ruby usually managed a few hours of sleep each night, but it took a long time to get there. She looked forward to her nights on watch, when she didn't have to try to sleep. She had all the worries of the expedition on her mind, and after bedtime, it was hard to be optimistic. And then there was Gunner, sleeping beside her. The enforced intimacy was difficult to tolerate. At least in zero gravity, he couldn't snore.

Several weeks after the loss of *Endurance*, Harte began to wonder if he had ever really had any other life than this aboard the *Ruby Marie*. Documentary footage to the contrary, it seemed unlikely. Every day was filled with activity, though little of it had any obvious purpose. It was a tolerable life — dull, but pleasant enough. They were on reduced rations and had run out of toothpaste, but no one was suffering. Neither did there seem much to live for. It was all just habit.

He wished now that the Boss hadn't already told him about the Chickering Expedition. It would have been something to look forward to. He considered asking for a formal interview so he could record her answers this time. But would she be willing to speak openly in front of the whole party? And how could he ask, when she had so much on her mind already? She had responded to their altered circumstances with her trademark steadiness and optimism. He didn't want to rock that by probing an old wound. Although she had opened up to him once, she remained guarded. After all this time, he had failed to earn her trust.

When July 9th came, it didn't feel enough like a birthday to mention it. Thirty-one didn't mean anything, anyway. They passed the afternoon as usual, as the book club. It was Blackborow's turn, and she chose something she'd gotten from Lloyd Green before they left the Moon: *Mastering the Art of French Cooking*. The main characters seemed to be butter and cream. As she read the detailed recipes, people chuckled and murmured appreciatively. Harte's mouth watered. They weren't starving by any stretch, but it was a long time since they'd had any variety or abundance in their diet. The cookbook was like something from a dream.

"It's a kind of pornography, isn't it?" he whispered to the commander.

She didn't answer but unfastened her harness and pushed out of her seat. She propelled herself, not to the head, but into the supply closet, and closed the door behind her.

Blackborow stopped reading and looked up. "Is she all right?"

"She's been edgy — not like herself at all," Dr. Mack said.

"She doesn't always eat her dice," Blackborow said. "She thinks no one notices, but I keep track."

"Knowing the Boss, she imagines someone else needs the food more," Wild put in. "That's how she is."

Harte suspected she hadn't been sleeping, either, but didn't know *how* he knew. It wasn't like she talked to him about it. Or much of anything else. "Maybe your reading finally made her hungry." He unbuckled his harness. "I'll check on her. Blackborow, don't stop; that's the best meal we've had in ages."

He slipped into the storeroom and closed the door behind him. The commander was at the far end with her back to him. She gripped the rack of supply bins and took deep breaths.

"Hey, Boss — everything OK?"

"I'm fine, Mr. Gunner." Her voice was calm but brittle, with a hint of tremor.

He maneuvered next to her. She didn't turn to face him, but her striking profile was rigid with tension. "You don't sound fine. What's wrong?"

"I just needed a moment to myself." She glanced up with a smile he didn't believe.

He nodded sympathetically. "I guess the pressure of leadership can weigh pretty heavily, even on your strong shoulders."

She shook her head. "That isn't it. Sometimes I just need a break from … the togetherness."

He chuckled. "It's not easy, but it sure beats the alternative. You got us out of a tight spot." He shivered as a new thought occurred to him. "Is something wrong with the ship? Are we going to run out of something critical?"

"It'll be close, but we should make it."

"That's a relief." Laughter filtered through the partition. "You should be happy — everyone's doing remarkably well. Even Nielson has mellowed. And Blackborow was just getting to the part about the souffle."

The Boss laughed, too, but it sounded like a sob. "Yes, they are doing well. I couldn't be prouder of this group."

"They're worried about you, Boss."

"They don't need to be. Did someone ask you to check on me?"

"I volunteered." He cleared his throat. "I … worry about you, too."

"Well, don't. You'll still get to make your doc."

"You think that's all I care about?" She threw him a sharp, sidelong glance, but didn't say anything. "I figured it might be easier for you to tell me your troubles, since I don't work for you."

"Thank you, Mr. Gunner, but I think I've told you enough troubles for one lifetime. I'll deal with this alone."

"I believe you'll try," he said. "I'm not convinced you'll succeed. But you have to — this whole crazy venture is riding on the strength of your optimism. So please tell me — what's the problem?"

She drew a breath and huffed it out through her nose. "You are, Mr. Gunner."

"Me? What did I do?"

"It's not anything you *did*. It's something you can't do." She turned away again.

"Aw, c'mon, Boss — you should know by now there's nothing I can't do."

She didn't laugh at his joke. "Please go away," she whispered. Her shoulders were hunched and shaking. It was the strangest thing Harte had seen in a career of seeing strange things.

"If that's what you want. I can't go very far, though. It might be easier just to tell me how I'm ruining your life now. Maybe I'll stop." He laid a tentative hand on her shoulder.

She swatted his hand away and made that strange sob-laugh sound again. Without warning, she turned and launched herself at him, knocking him into the rack of supplies behind him. He steadied himself. This was it — he'd gone too far somehow and now she was going to kill him with her bare hands. She could probably do it, too.

She twisted her fingers into his hair and wrapped her legs around his waist. She squeezed the breath out of him, but what a way to go. Then ... she kissed him. He couldn't breathe, his scalp was on fire, and she seemed intent on devouring his face. It was Heaven. It didn't matter that he hadn't changed clothes in more than a month. Neither had she; if they smelled, they smelled alike. She tasted sweet, savory, warm — like life.

Before he could respond the way he wanted to, she pushed away. "That's how you're ruining my life. Now please forget that ever happened."

"I couldn't forget a kiss like that if I lived to be a hundred." He reached out and drew her close. She pressed her head against his chest. "So where did that come from? You never seem to want to be near me."

"Because I can't be near enough. I have to sit out there day after day, looking at you, hearing your voice, but I can't touch you, can't ..."

He stroked her hair, a slightly sticky corona of short chestnut clumps — but not all chestnut anymore. He hoped he hadn't contributed to too much of the gray. "Shh, it's all right. This is a good thing."

"Ha!"

"No, really. I will confess that I've been entertaining impure thoughts about you for a long time. I had no idea the feeling was mutual."

"I couldn't afford to think about it, let alone say anything. Very bad discipline, especially under these circumstances."

"True. But if I'd known you cared —"

"I don't *care*. I just … want your body."

"Likewise, Boss, with sugar on top. Had I known, I'd have made a move months ago."

She shuddered. "That would have been a very bad idea."

"That's what I thought at the time, though I was mostly afraid you'd hit me."

"I would never strike a subordinate."

"What about an equal?" She didn't answer, so he continued. "You always think of everyone else, but has it occurred to you, someone might want to help you?" He ran his hand over her remarkably firm buttocks.

"No." She grasped his hand firmly and moved it away, though she didn't let it go. "Not here. Not now."

"Are you sure? It would be an honor to relieve your tension. And we've got all this great privacy."

She laughed at that, a real laugh. "I appreciate the thought, but not here."

He glanced around. "The only other choice is out there."

"That isn't what I meant. It's still bad discipline, and worse hygiene. Besides, I don't want to be a test subject."

"Understood. But if we live through this, get someplace where it would be right —"

"With a bed, and some gravity," she put in.

"At the very least. But are you saying you want me to … crank your generator?"

She smiled and looked at him with her clear-eyed gaze. "Yes, Mr. Gunner, I guess that is what I'm saying."

"And yet you still don't like me."

"Only when you're being an arrogant know-it-all."

He chuckled. "Guilty as charged. But you don't trust me."

"I ... try. I want to, but —"

"Maybe it would help if you called me Harte."

"Not until this is over. For now, discipline must be maintained."

"Fair enough. You've given me a reason for living. I can wait a little longer if you can." She relaxed in his arms. Maybe she did trust him. "I might see a problem in the short term."

She groaned. "Oh, no. Now what?"

"We've been in here awhile. If we come out together as red-faced as I imagine we are, people will guess what's up and assume a whole lot more. We need a cover." He looked around the storeroom and his gaze landed on the hot drinks dispenser. "Tea."

"What?"

"We'll make tea for everyone. I don't suppose there's any kind of treat to have with it."

"There should be a package of cookies, if we can find them. I squirreled them away for a future morale boost." She stroked his beard. "I like your thinking, Mr. Gunner."

"Who do you think I learned it from?"

Ruby emerged with the last package of cookies while Gunner filled beakers with tea.

"... and barbecue so monumentally greasy, I ate half the fuckin' plate before I noticed it was paper and not meat!"

The group roared at Nielson's account. "So then what did you do?" Dr. Eyestone asked.

"I ate the other half!"

"When we get back to the world," Wild said, "I'm going to have an entire fried chicken and a whole tub of potato salad. And a pie. Apple."

"I want soup," Blackborow said.

"What kind?" Dr. Mack asked.

"I don't care! Any kind, as long as it's in a bowl, with a spoon."

Nguyen nodded. "You have to taste my dad's pho."

"This isn't any of those things," Ruby interrupted, "but I thought you might appreciate a little treat." She handed the package to Blackborow. "It's Gunner's birthday." She glanced at him and grinned at his obvious surprise. "I'm sorry, Mr. Gunner, was it a secret?"

"No, I just didn't think you knew. Thank you for the party." He winked.

She was reasonably sure he didn't mean the cookies and tea.

Blackborow held the package with obvious relish. "Oh, yum, are these the dark chocolate ones? I thought they were all gone!"

"You were in there so long, I was expecting a full turkey dinner," Nielson said.

"The cookies were well hidden." Ruby didn't have to fake her smile. It was such a relief to have confessed her desire. Kissing Gunner had left her a little giddy, and she could still feel his facial hair around her lips. Hard as it was to wait, from now on she would have to maintain discipline and decorum. But she had something to live for. They both did.

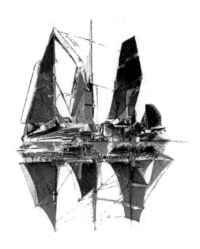

Chapter 25

2125/09/30: I feel useless. What can be causing this symptom? Persistent nausea, but no pain, fever, or other sign of infection. And I can't run any tests. I had to leave all my research equipment behind. I can only comfort the patient and hope this malady will cure itself.

— Dr. Yvonne Mack's Research Diary

Harte filmed less as the days, weeks, months blurred together. He had already interviewed everyone at least once and rarely saw a shot he hadn't already captured. He limited himself to a few frames a day to extend his camera batteries.

At least he had something to look forward to, though he couldn't speak of it. If he understood correctly, at the end of this ordeal, the Boss promised a night of carnal abandon. Maybe if he pleased her, she'd consider making it a habit. Just thinking about it was compelling enough to drive worry from his mind, and much more pleasant — even if it was all in his head. They had agreed not to act on their attraction, or even discuss it. Exchanging a glance was thrilling, and a fleeting touch, incandescent.

The party went about their other activities almost by rote — exercises, book club, sing-along, prayer meeting. They reduced rations to one meal a day to make the NutriCubes last, so the energy level was low, but morale remained good. Now, out of the sameness, something for everyone to look forward to: they expected to reach Mars in less than a month. They were going to make it.

When it was her turn to go to the head, Blackborow unclipped her duffel from under her seat. "Time for a clean shirt."

"Lucky you. How do you have a clean shirt?" Harte asked. He'd been alternating his two sets of black turtlenecks and jeans, so all his clothes were equally filthy.

"I've worn this one the whole time. There's not much left." She extended her arm to show the ragged condition of her green uniform top.

She went to change and came back wearing a new shirt. Bright red.

"You can't wear that!" Nielson exclaimed. "It's bad luck!"

"Take it off right now!" Nguyen added.

"I don't have anything else. Besides, I like it. I got it at the launch loop visitors' center, just before I met Mr.

Green. It's been at the bottom of my bag the whole time, so it's brand new."

Harte had to admit, for a souvenir, it had tasteful style, with just a small SCEI logo above the chest pocket. The color was good on her, too. It was a nice change to see something bright and clean.

The others obviously did not agree. They continued to harass her until she burst into tears and fled to the galley. After a moment, Dr. Eyestone grabbed his bag and followed her.

"He'll get it off her," Nielson muttered.

"Oh, shut up," Harte said. "She's just a kid — why should she know about your superstitions?"

"Because we told her the first day out!"

He vaguely remembered that conversation, from a lifetime ago. "You were serious? Anyway, she wasn't there, remember? We didn't find her until later."

"Yeah, well, even so —" Nielson said.

Commander Ladd drifted back from the cockpit and the bickering ceased. She gestured with her chin, and Wild took her place up front. She joined the group. "I won't have it." She spoke quietly and didn't look angry, but no one dared be the first to meet her gaze.

"Won't have what, Boss?" Nielson ducked his head, and Harte was sure he would have shuffled if there were gravity.

"After all we've been through, do you think the color of someone's shirt has any importance at all? I will not have superstition divide this expedition."

"What expedition is that, Boss?" Nielson looked up at last. "We never got to do the job we signed on for."

"I know that better than anyone, Mr. Nielson. But it doesn't help us a bit if we fall apart now. If we are to survive this, we will survive together."

When Blackborow returned, she was wearing a multi-colored tropical-print shirt, far too big for her but with no red. Nobody mentioned the red shirt again.

Perhaps because they couldn't do much else, the Boss finally agreed to play chess with Harte. As Wild had warned early on, she could plan eight or ten moves ahead, and change tack at lightspeed. But Harte's creative, intuitive style of play challenged her. They played almost every night after supper. Usually, she won.

Maybe two weeks after the red-shirt episode, Harte finally prevailed. "I should have bet something this time!" he exclaimed.

"It's not like you have any use for money out here," she teased. "You already have a lot more than I do, anyway." She gathered the pieces and returned them to their case.

"I'm sure I could think of something else. What do you want when you win?"

"Home-baked rhubarb pie," she replied without hesitation. "You owe me ten."

Blackborow groaned and grabbed a space-sickness bag from the pocket on the side of her seat. She got it to her mouth barely in time to contain the upheaval. It didn't amount to much; none of them had eaten for hours. Afterward, she sat back, shaking and pale. "Well, that was … unexpected. Yuck."

"Sometimes space sickness comes back," Dr. Mack explained. "We don't really know why."

"We'll talk about something besides food," Harte said. "Come on, Boss, think of something more ... imaginative."

The commander raised an eyebrow and smiled. It was an electric look. They didn't have to discuss this any further. From then on, the loser promised unspoken things for the winner to imagine, to be delivered if — when — they finally had their night alone, with a bed and some gravity. It didn't really matter who won, because as he saw it, they both did.

As the days passed, Harte needed that occasion in the future to take his mind off what was happening in the here and now. Blackborow did not recover. If anything, the nausea became more persistent. Most days, she couldn't even look at food, let alone eat it. The Boss took over food distribution duties, and Blackborow was allowed to rest. By nibbling slowly, she was able to keep down half a NutriCube per day. She grew weaker and did not seem to improve.

Dr. Mack consulted her medical references but found no definitive answer. "No fever, so not a viral infection. No pain, so probably not bacterial. And we shouldn't have any pathogens with us unless something was hiding out in the shuttle." She looked up from her comm. "Is anyone else feeling queasy?" No one was. "Nausea and fatigue. Under normal circumstances, Amelia, I'd give you a pregnancy test, just to rule it out. But I don't have one and it's not likely, anyway. I'm starting to think you're suffering from anxiety."

"I never had that before. And aren't we all anxious?" Blackborow asked.

"It manifests in all kinds of ways: insomnia, intrusive thoughts, heightened alertness ... and nausea. Not like your life is all smooth and easy right now."

"I can't argue with that," Blackborow said. "I wish I could, though. I don't like this!"

"I'll teach you some breathing and meditation techniques that might help," Dr. Mack promised.

That evening after Blackborow dozed off, Nielson whispered, "It's because she wore red. She's gonna die."

They all pretended not to hear him. But Harte wondered, was it true? And who would be next?

Ruby's sleep had improved after her confession to Gunner. It still wasn't great, but it was better. But after Blackborow got sick, the improvement evaporated. She sat in the darkened shuttle and stared out at star-filled space. It was hard to be hopeful, even so close to their goal. She pulled the little ship model from her pocket and floated it in front of her. A pang from something other than the Pearl nearly brought her to tears, but looking at the model of *Endurance* was a good reminder that things were not as bad as they might have been.

She changed position and found herself looking into Gunner's open eyes. She started but managed to keep her voice to a whisper. "I didn't know you were awake."

"I knew you were. What's the trouble?"

"Pick one. What's making Blackborow sick? Are the rest of us going to catch it? Is it serious? Will there be enough food? Are we going to survive this? What was I thinking, bringing all of you out here? We have no business traveling so far from home."

"Wow. You even worry in detail. That actually makes me feel better."

"That makes one of us."

"May I make a correction, though? You didn't *bring* us out here. We came voluntarily. You just did the job you were hired for."

She frowned and crossed her arms. "I should have said no."

"Then the rest of us would likely be out here under someone else. Except we'd all be dead by now."

"You don't know that."

"I believe it."

"Thank you." She sighed. "I'll be brave again by morning."

"I believe that, too. You're the bravest person I ever met. And the most competent."

She chuckled. "I have to give you credit — you've finally figured out the type of compliment that works on me."

"Well, now that I know it might get me somewhere ..."

She shook her head, but the worry was dissipating. "Remember when we were on Mars, and you said you wished I trusted you?"

"That's a day I'll never forget."

"I'm sorry it took so long. You're a stronger person than I took you for at first. I need all the strength on my side I can get." She swallowed. "I don't think I ever thanked you for getting me to talk about Chickering."

"Thank me? I thought you'd never forgive me."

"I needed to forgive someone, but it wasn't you."

"It wasn't you, either. You didn't do anything wrong."

"All these years, I've been blaming myself for failing someone I admired. I couldn't blame Chickering — he was dead. But that meant I couldn't forgive him, either. I didn't realize how much grief I was carrying. There was never a good time to deal with it. I wrapped it up and shoved it aside, tried to work my way out of it instead of feeling it."

"Until a nosy filmmaker came along and pestered you into spilling your story. Why don't you hate me?"

"Who says I didn't? But telling you about it, I saw things more clearly. The only way I failed Chickering was in not disobeying him sooner. *He* failed *me*. He made a boneheaded mistake, and he was too proud to admit it."

"He had the classic tragic flaw — too much pride in his own abilities."

Ruby frowned. "Someone else called it a tragedy. But did anyone learn a lesson from it?"

"I'd say you learned plenty, and that's why we're still alive to have this conversation."

"We're not out of this yet. What if I have a tragic flaw of my own?"

"It wouldn't be hubris. If anything, you're too willing to sacrifice yourself for people who don't deserve it."

"These are my friends! Who doesn't deserve it?"

"Maybe me?"

She smiled. "I have designs on you, Mr. Gunner. You have to survive, too."

He gazed out the viewport. "A good tragedy is supposed to make its audience feel pity and fear, to give them catharsis. Is this it?"

"I don't know. Maybe," Ruby said. The Pearl gave a weak throb, but the pain was diffuse. "Chickering died through his own fault. I have to live with that, and it will always hurt because he was a good friend. But I think he would have owned his mistake in the end, if he'd had a chance. I have to forgive him, and myself, and let it go."

"Just like that?"

"No, not just like that. But I've made a start. I have more important things to do than let that episode hold me back."

"I could have told you that."

"You're such a know-it-all," she said, but without any rancor. "Even if you didn't intend to help me with my load of unprocessed grief, I'm glad you were persistent."

"I didn't intend to *at first*. I wanted a great, untold story. But then I saw how much you were hurting, and yet you were so competent and functional in spite of it. It — wasn't about me anymore."

"I thought everything was about you."

He smiled. "Not everything. So does this mean I can use the Chickering story in the doc?"

"If it's necessary."

"Thank you, Boss. You won't be sorry. Try to sleep now."

"If only ..."

He frowned. "Should I wake Dr. Mack? Maybe she could give you something —"

"No! I won't have the whole party eavesdropping on my dreams. What if I say a name this time?"

"As long as it's mine ..."

"Oh, hush!"

"Is there anything I can do?"

She thought hard. What could he do that would relax her, that wouldn't be a breach of discipline? She reached over and held his hand. "Would you ... sing to me?"

He kissed her knuckles. "I would be delighted."

"Just don't wake the others."

"I don't think that's likely. Look at them — like little angels." He grinned. "Our babies."

She shook with suppressed laughter at that image. They were under her care, though. She was happy to do all the worrying for them so they could sleep. She returned the model to her pocket. Gunner kissed the top of her head. Even holding hands felt transgressive, right there in front of everyone. It was thrilling to do that much and get away with it.

He began to hum a gentle melody. She couldn't quite place it, though it sounded familiar. Maybe the Doo-Bots had done it. She closed her eyes and listened as he quietly sang the chorus, something about standing by each other when things were bad.

That was it — the song at the end of the funeral montage. She relaxed and drifted on the music. That's what she would do: stand by this brave crew who had endured so much for so little. They would stand together. They would make it. They would survive. They had to.

Harte listened as the commander's breathing grew deep and regular. Her hand was warm in his, and he wished — not for the first time — that they were alone and free to follow their desires. The one kiss she'd given him hinted at what she was like when she relinquished control. He could hardly wait. All the hardship would be worth it for that one night. On this night, he would have been happy just to hold her in his arms and rock her to sleep, but the seats and harnesses didn't allow for that. Handholding had to stand in for everything else.

He leaned back and watched her sleep until he joined her.

The morning alarm woke him, followed by the commander's voice. "Mr. Gunner, please release my hand."

He pretended to start awake. He stared at their hands, then let hers go. "Sorry, Boss. I … think I had a nightmare." Their eyes met, and it was almost impossible not to laugh.

"I told you he liked you," Blackborow said in a loud whisper.

"He's lucky I'm merciful when I've slept well," the Boss said. "Don't let it happen again, or I'll give you nightmares."

He nodded and put on a contrite face. Nightmares? If she was in his dreams, he had nothing to fear.

Chapter 26

2125/10/15 Supplies nearly gone. Energy low. Morale better than expected. We're so close.

— Commander Ladd's Expedition Journal

Gunner hung filming through the cockpit viewport. Ruby maneuvered around him with a light touch on his shoulder.

He jerked at her touch but smiled. "Sorry, Boss. Am I in your way?"

"Just reporting for duty," she replied. "But you're working, too. Wouldn't want to miss that view." Mars tantalized, once again growing from dot to disc to orb, so close but out of reach.

"I keep thinking we're almost there," he said. "When's our ETA?"

"Another two weeks," Captain Anderson said. He released from his seat and left the cockpit to visit the head.

Gunner lifted his camera again. "Two weeks. Doesn't sound so bad, does it?"

Ruby slid into the copilot's seat and buckled in. He was right; two weeks didn't sound like a long time to travel. Not after five months aboard the *Ruby Marie*. This close to safety, she didn't dare entertain the idea that they might not make it. They would; they had to! But it wasn't going to be comfortable.

The supplies of coffee and tea had run out a week or so ago. Not critical items, certainly, but without caffeine, the party's energy level slumped further than it already had. Sometimes they drank hot water for the small comfort, but it wasn't stimulating. Behind Ruby in the darkened cabin, most of the others dozed. When the Skipper returned, he closed his eyes for a nap.

More importantly, food supplies were running low. They were already down to one NutriCube per person per day, but at that level of consumption, there were enough left for only twelve days. Ruby wished they could fire the engines, but the fuel supply was barely enough for the braking and steering maneuvers needed to dock at the Phobos depot. Ruby was resigned to fasting for a few days. She regretted inflicting it on anyone else.

Harte didn't expect to feel the difference between one meal a day and no meals at all. The first day, he had hunger pangs around when they would have eaten, but he hadn't felt *not hungry* in weeks. On the second day, he only wanted to sleep. He forced himself to film his companions and the planet now looming out the viewport.

The worst part was, he knew there was one NutriCube left. He'd filmed the empty galley, to illustrate one of many hardships, and discovered the lonely ration in its case. He didn't know why the supply had not come out even. Probably they'd started out with a partly used crate. Or the commander had put hers back at some point, sure someone else needed it more. Now they all needed it, but no one was willing to take it. Harte dreamed about it — that he had eaten it and would be punished, or that someone else had and he resented it.

The Boss emerged from the empty galley. "My friends, we're going to make it. Skipper says we're on schedule to dock at the Phobos depot tomorrow." She held up the remaining NutriCube. "This isn't the celebratory feast I wish I could offer you, but I say we share this as we've shared everything these past few months."

Those who had been sleeping stirred in their seats. Dr. Eyestone went to the galley and returned with beakers of hot water for everyone. Dr. Mack said a silent blessing over the NutriCube before the Boss broke it and distributed a piece to each member of the party. When everyone had some, they ate together.

It was nothing, barely a mouthful. The flavor was strong after days of no food. The carbs and vitamins hit with a jolt of energy. Harte had almost forgotten what it felt like to be wide awake. He wanted more, but he was glad they had shared this last thing. Tomorrow, they would be safe.

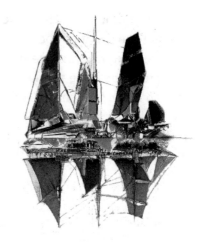

Chapter 27

2125/10/30: We have reached the Phobos supply depot, battered but unbeaten. Our continued survival depends on alerting Columbia Base to our presence. I can't believe what I have in mind.

— Commander Ladd's Expedition Journal

At last, they entered Mars orbit. They were on the last of the big power cells. Even the transmitter was disconnected. It didn't seem to work, anyway, and they didn't require it for docking. There was a communications center at the Phobos supply depot that they could use to call for help. They still had air and water, so they wouldn't die yet. That was the most positive way to put it, but Ruby remained optimistic. They had come this far ...

Captain Anderson used a little of their dwindling fuel supply to get into orbit around the dark little moon. Two at a time, they crowded into the storeroom and changed into spacesuits, a process that took over an hour. Ruby packed her good boots into her duffel with her clothes, then helped Blackborow with her spacesuit. The young cook was pale and wasted with her illness but seemed to have regained a little energy.

"We did it!" she said. "We got here. It's going to be all right now."

"Of course it is," Ruby replied, though obstacles still stood between her people and safety. "We're going to the Promised Land."

"I thought you weren't religious."

"Doesn't mean I can't talk the talk. And I did promise to bring you all to safety. There's a medical staff at Columbia Base — they'll take care of you."

"That's good, but I don't mean it's all right only for me."

"Neither do I, but you're the one I'm most worried about. We're all weakened, but you've been sick, too."

"I feel bad — I haven't kept up with my exercises."

"I don't think you're the only one," Ruby said. "You had an excuse."

"You never stopped."

"It helps me think." She assisted Blackborow with her gloves and helmet. "There's a physical therapist at the base. Half the staff turns over every two years, so there's always a need for rehab and training."

"That's good planning. Whose idea was that?"

Ruby thought back and smiled. "Mine, I think. A few of my shipmates arrived in poor condition, and it fell to me to shape them up. I'd had some experience with athletic trainers, but I'm not a professional."

"I'd trust you," Blackborow said. "How did it turn out?"

"In the short run? Great. They were in good enough shape to climb Olympus Mons."

Blackborow puzzled over this for a moment. Her eyes widened. "I'm sorry, Boss. I shouldn't have asked."

Ruby gave her a sad smile. "It's all right. I need to talk about it. I just wish I'd done a poorer job with the PT." She swallowed the lump in her throat. "You're the youngest of our party — how would you like the honor of the first step on Phobos?"

"I'm not the first," Blackborow argued.

"We'll be the first to use the depot as I intended. That's close enough."

A beacon marked the opening to the cavern that held the depot. It began to broadcast as they came in range.

"At least our receiver works," Anderson said. "Ready? We're going in."

He judged the speed and angle perfectly. They slid into the opening as if the ship were on a rail, and a burst from the braking thrusters brought them to a halt in the correct position to dock at the end of a hangar-like cave. The weary crew gave a ragged cheer.

They rose from their seats. At first, even the microgravity of the tiny moon felt oppressive to their weakened limbs. With sleeping bags and duffels full of dirty laundry in hand, they lined up to leave the *Ruby Marie*.

Blackborow tottered to the exit, then paused. Ruby gave her an encouraging nudge, and she collapsed in a heap. Ruby and Eyestone reached her at the same moment.

"I'm sorry!" Ruby whispered. "Are you all right?"

Blackborow smiled. "I'm fine. I just forgot about falling. I see what you mean about physical therapy."

Dr. Eyestone helped her up. The rest of the party joined them, and they approached the entrance to the depot. Ruby looked up the entry code, punched it in, and the doors slid back. They were in. Things were looking better.

"Mr. Gunner, turn on the power. Mr. Nielson, get the air supply going. Everyone else, let's see if we can find something to eat."

By the lights on their helmets, they examined the supplies. It was mostly NutriCubes, as well as some NutriGel, a liquid ration formulated for maximum absorption and minimal waste, meant to be carried inside a spacesuit on lengthy EVA or planetary exploration. A crate of toothpaste and brushes caused unexpected excitement. There was plenty of water, along with coffee, cocoa, and tea, two comfort stations, a stack of cots, and the communications center — still in crates.

"What? No, this was supposed to be ready for use!" Ruby cried.

"Don't worry, Boss. We'll get it going," Wild said.

They cheered when the lights came on, though they had to squint in the unaccustomed brightness. The untidy scatter of bags made it look like they'd been there longer than a few minutes, but Ruby chose not to mention the mess yet. There would be time to clean up later. The compact space didn't take long to pressurize. Helmets came off, Ruby and Dr. Eyestone distributed rations, and conversation dwindled to wordless appreciation of their first full meal in days. The dice didn't taste so bad, after all.

After the meal, most of the party changed out of spacesuits. Anderson took Nielson and Gunner out to remove the damaged fuel tank and see if the shuttle could make one more trip. They came in hauling most of the seats.

"She'll probably hold together, if we lighten the load," the Skipper reported. "If necessary, she could take a rescue party to the surface, but not everyone — three at most. And she's not coming back here."

Ruby considered. If the communications center had been assembled and functional, they could alert the base immediately and ask for help to come to them. As it was, it might take days to set up and activate. She glanced at Blackborow, who lay on a cot with Dr. Eyestone hovering over her. Dr. Mack didn't have the equipment to determine what was wrong with her or to treat it. The girl needed an infirmary. Probably they all did. And the supplies wouldn't last forever.

"This is the plan," she announced. "Captain Anderson and I will take the *Ruby Marie* and try to reach

Columbia Base. They'll be able to provide suitable transport to collect everyone else."

"You should take Amelia with you," Dr. Mack said.

Ruby shook her head. "There's a chance we'll have to set down at a distance from the base and walk the rest of the way — possibly for hours. She couldn't walk more than a few meters. I want you to care for her here, and we'll send help as soon as possible. Mr. Nielson, do what you can to get the ship ready."

"Yes, Boss." He was still suited up and went out immediately. Gunner went with him.

Wild approached her. "I'll go with you, Boss."

"Thank you, Mr. Wild. A commander never had a more loyal first officer." He smiled, but she shook her head. "That's why you need to stay here, Pete. You'll be in command while I'm gone. I'm counting on you to keep up morale. It shouldn't be more than a few days, but — if something should happen, you'll have the comm center. As soon as it's working, put out a call for help."

"If that's what you want." If he was disappointed, he didn't show it.

Ruby busied herself with preparations for departure. They couldn't take much — enough air, water, and NutriGel for about three days. If it took any longer than that, the whole plan was a botch, anyway, and the rest of the group was on its own.

Nielson and Gunner came back in and removed helmets and gloves. "She's ready for you, Boss," Nielson said. "There isn't much fuel left, but enough to get to the surface."

"Thank you, Mr. Nielson. I trust your judgment."

He looked at his feet and smiled. Then he met her gaze. "Am I to go with you, Boss?"

She had not previously thought about taking him, but if the ship needed repair mid-flight, he was the man to do it. "I'm not sure we could make it without you." Nielson seemed pleased as he walked away, though Gunner did not. "Do you have something to say, Mr. Gunner?"

"I should go with you," he said in a low voice. "I'm nearly the mechanic he is, and much more pleasant company."

"I know." Her throat ached. "I don't need that distraction. And I'd rather keep Nielson with me than leave him here; he's potentially corrosive to morale. You'll support Wild. Be strong and set the right example. Besides, you need to keep your pictures safe." He didn't look happy, but he didn't argue, either. She reached into her pocket and pulled out the little ship model. She'd been carrying it since he gave it back to her, after the robot funeral. She pressed it into his hand. "Keep this safe for me, too."

He nodded and accepted the model in silence.

They timed their departure to reach the surface early in the morning, base time. Ruby, Anderson, and Nielson suited up after a meal with the whole group, except Blackborow. She slept on her cot.

"I'd like to say a prayer before you go, if that's all right," Dr. Mack said.

Ruby braced for a complaint from the Pearl. It didn't come. She hadn't prayed in years, but under the circumstances … "I think that would be very appropriate. Thank you."

They gathered in a circle. Dr. Mack took Ruby's hand in hers, and the others joined up likewise. Gunner contrived to be on Ruby's other side, which improved her attitude, even if holding his hand conjured the polar opposite of prayerful thoughts. She trusted God would understand.

"Precious Lord, thank you for bringing us to this refuge and for your continued protection. Thank you for the gifts and skills that have brought us safely this far: our engineer, who can fix anything; our captain, who can fly a ship through a needle's eye; and our commander, who has the vision to see possibilities where others see only obstacles. Hold them in your care and walk with them as they seek help for us. Amen."

"Amen," Ruby said, and squeezed Gunner's hand. She did not want to let go. She wanted to kiss him, but now was not the time. She gave him what she hoped was an encouraging smile and dropped his hand. "This isn't goodbye," she whispered. "We have unfinished business."

Most of the party suited up and went out to the hangar to see the rescue party off. Harte filmed their departure. He longed to be with them, and not only for the images he might capture. But if Anderson and

KAREN EISENBREY

Nielson couldn't keep the Boss safe, how could he? He was pleased with the images he did have, and once again impressed with Anderson's skill in maneuvering the shuttle out of the restricted space. He imagined how they would complete his doc. But even if he hadn't liked them, he felt good about having taken them. As he had promised the Boss at the beginning of their desperate run from the Asteroid Belt, he was still making his doc. It had started as a way to keep up morale, as well as a sign of his faith in her leadership — "If I keep collecting images, it is because I believe we will make it to safety." It was still that, but it had taken on a talismanic quality — "If I keep collecting images, we *will* make it to safety." Even so close to the end, he was determined to take at least a few shots every day.

After the *Ruby Marie* had disappeared from view, the group drifted aimlessly back into the supply depot. Blackborow sat up on her cot. She looked a little less pale, but she didn't try to get up. Dr. Mack stayed near her, though there didn't seem to be much she could do. And if she couldn't help, Harte certainly couldn't.

Except the Boss had assigned him to help keep up morale. He put a smile on his face and joined them. "How are you feeling, Amelia?"

"Better, I think. A little gravity goes a long way." She gave a weak smile.

"Space sickness or anxiety, it must help to be safe here," Dr. Mack said. "I'll feel better when we can get you to the infirmary, though."

"I think we all agree on that," Harte said. "Well, I have a job to do."

No one else had concrete duties to attend to. Harte was glad he had an assignment. He pushed his worry for the Boss's safety to the back of his mind and began to examine the dismantled comm center.

Wild joined him. "What's the prognosis?"

"I can't find an instruction manual, so that'll slow things down. But the components look familiar. I think I can get it working."

"You might invite Dr. Eyestone to help you. He could use a project." Wild glanced toward Blackborow's cot, where the roboticist hovered.

Harte smiled. "Spoken like the Boss herself. I'll ask him."

"I see the way you look at her," Wild said in a quieter voice.

"I … what?"

"You have my blessing, but if you hurt her, I *will* have to kill you."

Harte stared at him. Wild had such a deadpan delivery, Harte never knew when he was joking. "If *I* hurt *her*?" he said at last.

Wild grinned. "Good point. She'd probably do the job herself."

"Anyway, I'm not even sure she likes me, so I don't think it'll turn into anything serious. It's just … a physical thing we need to deal with."

Wild's eyebrows twitched. "Lucky man. You still have my blessing."

Harte laughed. "What are you, her brother?"

"Her teammate — always."

"Maybe you're the lucky one, Wild."

Wild gave a quick smile like he knew it. He turned toward the others. "Your attention, please. I know I'm not the Boss, but she left me in command. We don't know how long we'll be here — it could be one day, or seven, or more. We should expect that the Boss will come any day but accept that maybe she won't. Let's arrange this place as comfortably as possible. We don't have a lot of space, so we'll have to keep it shipshape. But once we've done our chores, maybe Dr. Curley will get out his banjo."

This speech put new life into the group. Harte invited Dr. Eyestone to help tinker with the comm center. The others arranged the seats from the ship into a neat sitting area. They moved the cots to the other side of the room and stacked the supply bins to create a partition between sitting and sleeping areas. They rolled up the sleeping bags and stowed them out of the way. By the time the job was done, everyone was chattering about who they wanted to see and what they wanted to eat when they got home. Home seemed real again. Of course the Boss would get them out of this! She had never failed them yet.

It helped to be back on full rations. Harte hadn't realized how undernourished he was until he suddenly had energy again. After supper, they had more music and read aloud to each other. Even Blackborow sat up with them. She had eaten a little, though she declined to read from her cookbook.

As they sang what Wild declared to be the last song before bed, Blackborow groaned and clutched her abdomen.

"What is it?" Dr. Mack asked. "Do you feel sick again?"

Blackborow shook her head, her face contorted. "It hurts!"

Dr. Mack glanced at Eyestone. "Let's get her onto a cot."

Eyestone lifted Blackborow from her seat and carried her to the sleeping area. Harte followed and helped rearrange some of the bins to form a more private cubicle for her. There was nothing more he could do. He wasn't sleepy, so he returned to the comm center. He didn't make a lot of progress, but at least it was something to do.

He couldn't help hearing Blackborow's groans and sobs, and the quiet comfort of Dr. Mack's voice. Maybe this new symptom would give her the clue she needed. He just hoped it wasn't a burst appendix or infected gallbladder. Dr. Mack was skilled, but Harte was pretty sure she didn't want to do surgery under these conditions.

Hurry back, Boss. We need help now.

"It's going to be a rough landing!" Anderson shouted. "Hang on!"

Ruby gripped her armrests. Surely they were coming in too low, too fast. But she trusted the Skipper. He'd rarely given her any reason not to. And now they were in the Gusev Crater, a long way from the base, but still — not bad. He hit the retro rockets, but they cut out soon after. The *Ruby Marie* hit the ground, bounced, and slid across the rocky surface. So much for the landing gear.

Ruby had her harness unfastened as soon as they stopped moving. "Do you think she'll explode?" Anderson stared at her a moment, then laughed long and hard. "What's so funny?"

"There's nothing left to explode — we're completely out of fuel."

"Then I guess we'd better start walking."

Nielson was still strapped into the one remaining seat in the passenger area, where he'd been since they entered the atmosphere. He had made a number of small repairs and adjustments during the short flight. He was probably as responsible as Anderson for the relative success of the landing. Now he stared, wide-eyed and silent.

"Mr. Nielson?" Ruby shook his shoulder. When he didn't respond, she knocked on his helmet, which got his attention. "Mr. Nielson, we're going to have to walk the rest of the way. Come on, get up now."

He nodded and unfastened the straps. He tried to stand but fell back into the seat. "I can't. It's too much gravity."

"I know, we're all weaker than we should be. We'll get used to it, but we need to go now, while it's light."

Between them, she and Anderson got Nielson onto his feet. They stepped out onto the Martian surface, the unaccustomed pull of a planet's gravity dragging them down. It was a calm, clear day. The flat, butterscotch-colored crater bottom stretched off in front of them, the Columbia Hills visible in the distance.

"See, this isn't so bad," she said. "We just head for those hills. How far would you say it is, Skipper?"

He eyed the hills, then held up his hand to judge the angle. "Maybe ninety clicks."

"OK. We have air, water, and food for three days. No problem."

After two steps, Nielson fell again. Ruby wanted to join him, but by force of will kept herself up.

"Leave me with the ship," Nielson begged. "I can't walk that far."

"I'm not leaving anyone alone," Ruby replied. "We don't have to go fast. We just have to keep moving."

"What if a dust storm comes up?" he asked. "We won't be able to see where we're going."

"We'll hunker down together and wait it out. Conditions are good now, so let's go. Skipper, you lead."

Ruby fell in behind Nielson to make sure they didn't lose him. She listened to his muttered complaints for a few minutes before she cut in. "We can't afford to waste air on unnecessary talk."

He fell silent, though she assumed the complaints continued in his head. They trudged for fifteen minutes, covering a few hundred meters, then rested for five, then trudged another fifteen. During rest breaks, they sipped water and NutriGel through tubes threaded from the life support packs into their helmets. They needed all the strength they could get. She considered letting her companions sleep after the sun went down, but they still had so far to go. They could get by for a time without food and water, but when the air ran out, that would be it.

"Look, there's a beacon on top of Husband Hill," she said, pointing to the blinking light in the distance. "We just need to keep walking toward it."

She took the lead and let Anderson follow Nielson. They continued their slow, steady pace all night. Ruby didn't even want to think about the air temperature. The cold, thin air of Mars would steal their body heat even through their suits. All the more reason to keep moving, and to consume as many calories as possible.

They kept conversation to a minimum to conserve air, but Ruby gave Nielson an encouraging word whenever he lagged. The movement was enough to keep them awake, though Ruby often found herself half dreaming. She looked forward to a real bed at the end. When the sun rose, the weather was still calm, so they pressed on. It didn't seem they had made much progress, but when she looked back, the shuttle was barely visible. There was no choice but to go on.

They plodded on at the same slow pace, and the view ahead hardly seemed to change. But Ruby had the sense that something was different — there were four of them, not three. Perhaps someone from the base had come to help! But when she looked around, she couldn't see anyone else. Still, the feeling persisted of a fourth person walking near her, just out of view. At one point, she squawked in surprise as she felt a strong, encouraging hand on her shoulder.

Anderson spun to face her. "What is it? Are you all right?"

"Yes, I … just stumbled. I'll be fine as long as I remember to pick up my feet." They didn't need to know she was losing it. This presence meant them no harm.

On the morning of the third day, they reached the base of the hills. Ruby allowed a longer rest break while they planned their route. Nielson sank to the ground. To judge by the snoring that came over the comm, he fell asleep instantly.

"We could go around and avoid a climb," Anderson said.

"It'll be a lot longer; I'm not sure we'll make it. But if we go up and over this pass, we come down right by the entrance to the base. It's not that steep."

Between the two of them, they finally agreed the shorter route made more sense. The wind was starting to rise, and they didn't want to get caught out in a dust storm so close to their goal. Ruby woke Nielson and they began to climb. It was much harder than it looked. When fit, she could have run up this slope, but now they did most of it on all fours with many stops. But after three grueling hours, they reached the top and rested beside the Chickering memorial.

"We did it, friends," Ruby said, and shook hands with her two visible companions. Their once-white suits were grubby with dust, but still intact, though Neilson's mission patch hung by a few threads. "We're almost there."

She gazed at the picture on the memorial sign. *I did it, Boss. My people survived*. She indulged for a moment in a feeling of triumph, of vindication, but did not wallow. It was too soon for that.

But they were close. The base was just below them. They started down on weak and shaking legs. They fell and slid more than they walked, but eventually reached the bottom. Anderson helped Nielson up from his latest fall.

"Boss! Something's wrong — I think Nielson's out of air!"

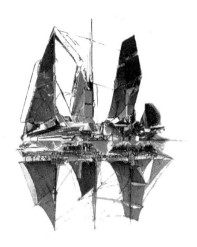

Chapter 28

2125/11/02: I know this will come as a shock: I am alive.

> — *Message from Ruby Ladd to SCEI Director Wesley James*

This was Ruby's nightmare, ever since Chickering. Nielson gasped but his tanks were empty. A quick glance at her HUD revealed that Ruby's air supply, while low, was far from gone. But Nielson wasn't in as good condition, or as experienced with how to ration air. All it took was a few extra moments of panic. She and Anderson draped his arms over their shoulders and supported him to the entrance. He moved his feet a little, but he wasn't really walking.

Ruby radioed the base. "Open the main airlock."

KAREN EISENBREY

"What are you doing out there? Everyone's supposed to be inside. Don't you know there's a storm coming?"

"Then open the goddamned airlock so we can *be* inside!"

After what seemed like forever, the doors slid open, and they dragged Nielson in. She hadn't heard a gasp from him in a long time. As soon as the inner doors opened, they laid him on the floor and Ruby wrestled his helmet off. He was limp, his eyes closed and his lips blue. "No, no, no! Damn you, Nielson, don't do this to me. Not now. Not after all this." She yanked off her glove and felt his neck for a pulse. Weak, yes, but there. He jerked and sucked in a breath.

Ruby took off her own helmet. A passing intern stared at them. No wonder, if they all looked as bad as Nielson.

"Don't just stand there!" Ruby snapped. "This man needs medical attention!"

"I … I …" The intern continued to stare.

Ruby let loose a string of profanity. "Help us! Now!" She slapped the floor for further emphasis.

That got his attention. He got on the comm, then hurried away, looking badly spooked.

Anderson fought a smile. "We don't hear language like that from you too often, Boss."

"Well, it's Nielson, isn't it? He taught me well."

Soon a small vehicle hummed up with a pair of medics aboard. They hid their shock better than the intern, but not completely.

The driver, her curly red hair in a ponytail, stared at Ruby. "Aren't you...?"

"Later," Ruby said. "Take care of him first."

"Of course." They loaded Nielson onto a stretcher. "We'll take him to the infirmary. What's the problem?"

"His air ran out before we could get inside."

"Name?"

"Nielson. Chip Nielson."

"You're ... not base staff, obviously," the other medic said. "How did you get here? No ships have landed recently."

"We walked." She stared at him, and he seemed disinclined to ask more questions. The intern must have warned them about the foul-mouthed crazy woman. As they were about to leave, she had a thought. "Do you go near the superintendent's office?"

"Yes, it's on the way."

"Take us there." She climbed onto the little vehicle and motioned for Anderson to do likewise.

The driver opened her mouth, then closed it without saying anything and drove off. The ride seemed the height of luxury. Ruby was sorry it had to end so soon.

The little ambulance slowed outside Rogers' office. "Are you sure? Maybe we should take you to the infirmary, too."

"Later," Ruby said. "We have a job to do."

They entered the office. A bored-looking young man at the reception desk wrinkled his nose as they approached but did not look up from his screen.

"Excuse me," Ruby said. "I need to see Superintendent Rogers."

"Name?" the assistant asked, still without looking up.

"Commander Ruby Ladd of the *Endurance*."

He snapped to attention and stared. "But you're … that's … I …"

Baird Rogers sprang out of his office. "Commander Ladd? My God! And is that hairy creature Frank Anderson? You're alive!"

Ruby managed a smile for him. "Apparently so. I need your help."

"Anything! What can I do for you?"

Her knees buckled and she gripped the edge of the desk. "Let's start with a seat and some solid food."

"I can do that. Come in."

They hobbled into his office. He seated them in comfortable armchairs and ordered sandwiches from the kitchen. He didn't even mention the smell, though they both had to be extremely ripe.

"I can't tell you how good it is to see you alive," Rogers said. "With no communications for months, we feared the worst. Wesley James has been losing his mind."

Ruby snorted. "I'll bet. Anything that delays his dreams of colonization wouldn't go over too well."

Rogers cleared his throat. "Not to mention the loss of life and a good ship. Speaking of which …"

Before he could finish, the food arrived. He held whatever he was going to say and allowed Ruby and Anderson to eat undisturbed. They demolished the pile in minutes. PBJs had never tasted so good. *Endurance* had probably delivered the flour for the bread. An uprush of pride and grief took Ruby by surprise. She swallowed the bite of food past a lump in her throat.

"As I was about to say, I don't know how you managed to sneak up on us," Rogers said. "I wasn't even aware your ship had entered orbit, let alone landed."

"*Endurance* was destroyed in an asteroid collision in May." Ruby swallowed hard. "We made our escape on the landing shuttle."

"On the *shuttle*?"

"It was all we had. We crashed it on the other side of the crater and walked the rest of the way."

"This is amazing!" Rogers shook his head in disbelief. "No one has heard from you in months; you were presumed dead. There was even a memorial service. Quite beautiful, really. You should see the recording."

"Let me guess, colonization efforts must continue so our deaths weren't for nothing. I'll be sure to contact SCEI to clear up any confusion," Ruby said. "But first, showers and clean clothes."

"You should see Dr. Fairfax, too."

Ruby nodded. "We just sent a man to the infirmary. Most of all, we need a ship."

"The big staff transport comes in January. You can be my guests until then. I'm rotating out, so I'll be leaving with you."

"That's good to know," Ruby said. "But I mean a small ship, immediately. The rest of our party is camped on Phobos."

"The rest of your party? How many?"

"Nine."

Rogers did the math. "You two, your man in the infirmary, and nine more? Twelve — then you didn't lose any?"

"No. Not a one. I didn't lose a one." And Ruby smiled, really smiled, for the first time in days.

"That's good news," Rogers said. "Perhaps the best news we've had since you left us. We have a shuttle that can pick them up, but the *Aurora* doesn't get much use. It'll take a day or so to get her ready."

"My people need urgent medical care," Ruby said. "One in particular has been seriously ill."

"All right, I'll have the maintenance crew start immediately."

"So, did we miss anything important while we were away?" Anderson asked.

Rogers gave him a strange look. "Anything … important?"

"He means news," Ruby said. "We lost communications months ago. Did the Confederates resolve their differences while we were gone?"

Rogers blew out a breath. "In a manner of speaking. Religious extremists staged a coup and overthrew their government — terrible, bloody conflict. It's the Holy Confederate Empire now, and all hot to conquer a few neighbors. Even the Northwest Union closed its borders as a precaution." He frowned. "Or maybe that was about the pandemic. Not that it helped much, but at least there was a vaccine by the time it got there. The HCE didn't have much chance to flex its muscles, though. They've had a hell of a storm season along the Gulf, and the fighting knocked out most of the early-warning system. The hurricane losses outnumber the fighting three to one."

Ruby let this news sink in. "So, any good news?"

He nodded. "An eco-tech company, Leviathan, out of Seattle — that's your hometown, isn't it?"

"Yes. What about it?"

"They've developed a technology to stabilize the climate relatively quickly. They expect to return greenhouse gasses to 2010 levels within just a few years. Of course, that's no comfort to those billions of people; too late for them, poor souls." He shook his head sadly.

"Wait, what millions of people? You mean from the war and the hurricanes —?"

"Not millions — at least a *billion*; probably more."

Ruby felt dizzy. "What happened to them?"

"You name it — war, famine, pestilence, along with a few big earthquakes and a nasty series of storms. I wouldn't blame some of the survivors if they want to join us out here. We're not ready for them, of course, but ..."

Anderson stared at him, struck mute by the enormity of this news. Ruby covered her face with her hand. It would have been bad enough to learn of these disasters as they happened. Received all at once, the news was more than she could process. It would take time to come to terms with it. At least a billion people ...

"I'm sorry to be the bearer of bad tidings," Rogers said. "We're all used to it, but you didn't know. Still, your own survival is a miracle — it gives me hope. Let me see what we can do in the way of showers and clothes."

Another vehicle drove them to the shower rooms, and someone from the laundry met them.

"Just leave your space gear; we'll return it when it's clean." She distributed clean clothes and basic, 3D-printed shoes. The underwear and Anderson's uniform were regulation blue. "I hope it's all right," she said of the beige technician's uniform she held out for Ruby. "We don't have an officer's uniform in your size."

"Clean is more important than color," Ruby assured her.

The shower, though metered, was hot, wet, and reviving. It felt as close to heaven as Ruby could imagine at the moment. She got out and got back in so she could have another five minutes. Afterward, she finally looked in a mirror. No wonder the people at the base had looked so horrified. The puffiness of zero gravity had masked the gauntness of her face. Her cheekbones jutted over hollows, and her eyes were sunken and dark. She had thought her hair was long and wild before, but wet and with gravity pulling it down, it drooped almost to her collar. At least it was clean now.

She dressed and stepped into the shoes. They were stiff and too large. Anything more than tiny, shuffling steps, and she walked right out of them. She made her slow way to the infirmary, but she couldn't keep her hands out of her hair. It kept falling into her eyes and tickling her neck.

"Need a haircut?" She turned toward the voice. A woman with green eyes and curly red hair greeted her with a smile. "The chair's free. And I'd consider it an honor, Commander." She gestured toward the doorway behind her. "I'm Lucy, by the way."

Ruby shook her hand. "Do I know you?"

"No, but I know you."

"News travels fast."

"You better believe it does! There are only thirty of us, and nothing much really happens here." Lucy grinned. "Also, I gave you a ride to Rogers's office."

"Thanks for that. So which is your side gig?" Ruby asked.

"I already had my cosmetology license when I came out here," Lucy said. "I'm working on EMT certification while I'm here."

"A woman after my own heart. Get in touch when you get back to Earth if you need a job." Ruby sighed. "It's been ages since someone else cut my hair. Sure, let's do it." She followed the stylist into the one-chair salon, squeezed between the infirmary and the chapel. She hadn't even noticed it before.

Lucy ran her fingers through Ruby's damp hair with professional interest. "It's not really that long. When did you last cut it?"

"I have no idea," Ruby replied, and dropped into the chair. "April, maybe?"

Lucy fastened a cape over her and got out a comb. "I'm here from 1100 to 1300 every day. Some days, nobody wants a haircut, and then others, I'll have five in a row! The rest of the time, I'm an aide in the infirmary. I guess I'm just a people person! I always liked to ..."

The shower had been stimulating, but Lucy's pleasant chatter lulled Ruby. She closed her eyes and listened without much attention until the voice faded. It was dark, but she had to keep going. She crawled up the slope toward the pass. She was bringing oxygen to the man at the top. Without it, he'd die. Not Chickering; he was already dead. His own fault. No, this was another man. She had something to tell him, too. His name was —

Ruby jerked awake.

"There, all done," Lucy said. "What do you think?"

Ruby tried to calm her racing heart as she examined her new look. The skeletal face was still a shock. Her hair was longer than she would have asked for, but she was grateful enough for the nap that she didn't complain.

"I look like a girl!"

"The word you're looking for is *woman*," Lucy corrected. "Is it all right?"

"I'm not complaining," Ruby said. She ran her fingers through the new 'do. "I haven't worn bangs since I was twelve, but they cover the worry lines. This is good."

Lucy grinned. "Your boyfriend will like it, I think."

"I don't have a —" Ruby's heart sped up again. Or did she? She hadn't thought of Gunner, apart from the group, since leaving the depot. But he was all right. He had to be. It was only a dream. But she had to tell him … something. "It's wavier than I remembered. And the color …" Although it was still mostly chestnut, a substantial amount had turned gray. She looked like she'd aged twenty years.

"Do you want to dye it, too?" Lucy asked.

"No. I earned this. I'll keep it."

By the time she got to the infirmary, Dr. Charlotte Fairfax had finished examining Anderson and was ready for her. She pronounced them undernourished and significantly weakened, but otherwise in good health.

"How far did you say you walked?" she asked Ruby.

"About ninety kilometers. But we took over fifty hours to do it."

"In your condition, you shouldn't have been able to walk one kilometer!"

Ruby smiled. "We had no other choice."

"There's no medical reason to keep you here," Dr. Fairfax said. "But you need to sleep." She called the administrative office about rooms. "Do you mind sharing for one night? They're painting some of the dorms and there won't be two singles available until tomorrow, but there's a double that's open now."

"I don't mind sharing. Do you, Skipper?"

"Not at all. To tell the truth, I'm not sure I want to be alone. At least, not until everyone is safe."

"I'm with you on that," Ruby said. "We'll take the double for now."

Dr. Fairfax called for a driver to deliver them to their room. Once there, Ruby plugged her SkyComm into the charger and recorded a message. She didn't feel like putting up with the time delay of a live transmission.

"To: Director Wesley James, SCEI HQ, from: Commander Ruby Ladd, late of the *Endurance*. I know this will come as a shock: I am alive. The ship is lost, along with the robots and nearly all the equipment, but all hands survived and will soon be safe at Columbia

Base on Mars." She paused, then added, "Sorry about the ship. She was a good one and we were grieved to lose her."

Twenty minutes later, she received a response — as close to immediate as possible. It was unrehearsed and recorded in haste, the most spontaneous effort she had ever seen from the SCEI director. "Commander, I can say only that I am stunned by your news. You were recently honored for your heroic sacrifice in the name of the Initiative. Needless to say, we're … I'm … well, we're stunned, but much happier, of course, to honor your heroic survival. I will schedule a live call for tomorrow, to begin your debrief. When you get home, I'm sure we can arrange a parade. And of course, you will be our first choice to lead missions in the future. Welcome home, Commander."

It was almost worth the hardship to see James fall all over himself in her praise. But a parade? That seemed a bit much.

Anderson shaved off his beard and combed his hair before he placed a live call home. "How do I look?"

"You look alive, Skipper. It's enough."

He placed the call and waited. Eventually, a sad-looking woman answered. She stared at the screen at her end. "Frank?" she asked in a small voice.

"Hello, Marie. Am I ever glad to see you."

After another interminable wait, she said, "You're safe? All of you? Ruby, too?"

Ruby leaned down to be in the picture. "Hello, Marie. Yes, we're all safe now. Give Frannie and Rubin my love."

She left the room to give Anderson his privacy and returned to the infirmary.

Nielson lifted a weak hand in greeting. "Hello, Boss."

"Mr. Nielson, I'm glad to see you conscious again. How do you feel?"

"Like I damn near died and didn't."

"I'm sorry I had to put you through that."

He shook his head. "I probably would've really died if you'd left me with the shuttle like I asked. Chickering would have left me. But you didn't."

"We don't know what Chickering would have done."

"We can guess. I prefer your way, Boss."

She smiled. "I let SCEI know that news of our demise was premature."

He grinned back at her. "How'd they take that?"

"Apparently we were big heroes when we were dead, and now we're bigger heroes because we're not dead." She rolled her eyes. "They want to give us a parade."

"We're not heroes, Boss. We're survivors, is all."

"I know that, Nielson."

"Except for you. You are the biggest goddamned hero I ever met, even if you did kill Mrs. Chippy."

"For what it's worth, I'm still sorry about that."

He nodded once. "It's worth a lot. I forgive you. You saved all our lives."

She returned to the dormitory on dragging feet. Besides her nap during the haircut, she had been awake for most of three days and didn't have much left, now that the adrenaline had worn off. Anderson was already in his bed, and she crawled into hers quietly so as not to wake him. It felt strange to lie down in a real bed, but in a good way. She was so tired she could have slept anywhere.

"Hey, Boss," Anderson murmured. He rolled over to face her.

"I thought you were asleep."

"Almost. I can't stop thinking about it."

"About what?" she asked.

"We really *did* something, didn't we?"

"You won't get any argument from me."

He rolled onto his back with his hands behind his head. "And not just you and me these last couple of days, but all of us. It feels like the most *real* thing I was ever part of."

She knew what he meant, though it was difficult to put into words. It was so far beyond the ordinary, as far as space travel beyond life on Earth. "We'll never top it — at least, I hope not. But I know I'll never forget any of it. We cut through the surface, to the heart and soul of things."

"That almost sounds like God talk, Boss."

"Does it?"

"Can I tell you something spooky?" he asked.

"Go ahead." She arranged herself comfortably to listen.

"When we were walking yesterday, sometimes I felt like there were … four of us."

Her spine prickled. "Really?"

"I never saw anybody. I figured it must be a hallucination, but …"

She took a deep breath and expelled it slowly. "I felt it, too." She rolled onto her back and tried to be the voice of reason. "We were both pretty exhausted. The mind can play tricks sometimes."

"Yes. But it seemed really … solid."

"I know." She recalled that comforting hand on her shoulder. She could have done with more hallucinations like that on this trip.

"Who do you suppose it was?" he asked.

"Whoever it was, they were no stranger to desert places. Or to grief."

"I think that's how we kept going," Anderson said. "We had help. We've had help the whole time."

She considered that. One miracle after another, and a lot of hard work and suffering. "It's not quite over yet. What if Blackborow is still getting worse? I won't feel easy until everyone is here with us."

"True. But that hardly seems like any kind of challenge, now. So what are you going to do when it *is* over?"

The words were out before she could stop herself. "I'm going to sleep with Gunner."

Anderson chuckled. "Good for you, Boss. You deserve it."

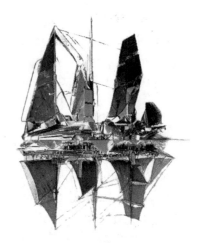

Chapter 29

2125/11/04: This morning, I told the team the Boss might come today. She has never failed us and did not disappoint.

— Peter Wild's private diary

Ruby woke gradually and naturally — no alarm sounds, no looming disaster, no one holding her hand. When she checked her comm, she discovered it wasn't the day after she'd gone to sleep, but the day after that. No wonder she felt rested. She couldn't even be too irritated over the seven missed calls from Wesley James.

As she crawled out of bed, Frank Anderson returned from the shower room. "Looks like you needed sleep as much as I did. Grab a shower and then we can find some breakfast."

"I don't know which sounds better. I'll make it quick."

Ruby pulled on a robe and shoved her feet into the ill-fitting shoes for the walk to the showers down the hall. Although she walked like an old woman, the face in the mirror looked less like a zombie. Washed and dressed, she felt almost completely human again. A substantial meal completed the process — though it was almost noon, the breakfast buffet in the dining hall was still open.

Superintendent Rogers found them at the table. "Good to see you both up and around!"

"What's the word?" Ruby asked.

"The weather has calmed and the shuttle's ready to go to Phobos for the others," Superintendent Rogers said. "You take it easy today. I'll let you know as soon as they arrive."

"Oh no, you don't. These are my people. We're going along, aren't we, Skipper?"

"Damn straight."

"In fact, Captain Anderson could pilot the ship," Ruby said.

"That's going too far, Commander. You may go along as passengers, but that's all."

She didn't argue. She was too eager to get going. Five days had passed since she'd left the party on Phobos, several days longer than she'd hoped the rescue would take. What if —?

"By the way, Commander, we heard from them last night."

That was good news. It meant Gunner had gotten the comm center working. "Are they all right?"

"I'm sorry, it wasn't a strong signal and they moved out of range before the message was complete. They managed to say they were there and wanted to be here."

"It's still good news. What are we waiting for? Let's go!"

They got back into their newly cleaned spacesuits and boarded the shuttle with a pilot, a navigator, and a pair of medical technicians for Blackborow. One of them was red-haired Lucy, starstruck to the point of silence when she learned she was about to meet Harte Gunner. The ship was larger than the *Ruby Marie*; there was room for four in the cockpit, with passenger seats for more than the nine they were going to collect.

Just before they launched, Ruby received a live call from Wesley James.

"I've been trying to reach you. What's going on? Over."

"Hello, sir. I had to sleep off a nonstop, three-day, ninety-kilometer hike. Over."

"Oh. Well, I'll let it go this time. But it's important that we get your report. Your experience will be key to plans for colonization. Over."

"Sorry, sir, I can't talk now. We're about to pick up the rest of our party. We can talk later. Ladd out." She ended the call and ignored his attempts to reconnect. There was no point in reporting on her experience until she knew everyone was safe. Even at that, she wasn't eager to talk about it. The only way it could inform colonization efforts would be to delay or even cancel them. And she was sure that wasn't what James had in mind.

As they flew over the crater, Ruby saw a tractor towing the crashed shuttle back toward the base.

"I can't believe you traveled all the way from the Asteroid Belt in *that*," the pilot said.

"You do what you have to," Anderson said. "I'll bet it's a tight fit docking this ship at the Phobos depot. How many times have you done it?"

The pilot glanced around. "Never; why would I? Your group is the first to use it. But how hard can it be?"

"This should be fun," Anderson whispered to Ruby.

When they got close and the pilot saw the narrow opening, he paled. They orbited several times, and Ruby began to worry they would run out of fuel before he was satisfied with the approach. At last, the pilot turned to the Skipper. "Captain Anderson, I'm going to let you have the honor of docking."

The Skipper smiled. "Thank you." They changed seats. Anderson got on the comm. "*Endurance* party, this is the shuttle *Aurora* from Columbia Base. Come in, please. Over."

Dr. Curley's bearded face appeared on the screen. He grinned at first, but then his face fell. "We're glad to see you, *Aurora*. We sort of hoped our own people would come for us."

"What?" Anderson stared at Curley, a baffled look on his face.

"We thought the Boss would come for us, or anyway, Captain Anderson. That's all."

"Dr. Curley, who do you think I am?" Anderson exploded.

Ruby moved the camera to point at her. "Dr. Curley, put Mr. Wild on, please."

Dr. Curley's jaw dropped open. "Boss!"

Wild took his place. "I told them you might come today."

"All well, Mr. Wild?"

"All well, Boss."

She moved the camera to point at Anderson again and turned her face away from the others in the cockpit. All well. For the first time in over five years, Ruby Ladd wept.

Things happened quickly after that. It was a tight fit, but Anderson maneuvered the *Aurora* into the cavern with his usual calm skill, as if he did this every day. Because Wild had told them the Boss might come, the party's few belongings were ready for departure. Lee Keith had even made an inventory of the supplies used, so the depot could be restocked. All but Blackborow were in spacesuits by the time the shuttle docked.

Dr. Mack met Ruby at the airlock. "She's better," the doctor said before Ruby could ask. "But —"

"But what? What was wrong with her?"

"I couldn't test to be sure, but the best I can tell, she was pregnant — probably no more than six or seven weeks. Remember when I said I wished I could give her a test to rule it out? I was mostly joking! The injection shouldn't have worn off yet. And anyway, when? How?"

Ruby pictured the little storage closet at the back of the *Ruby Marie*. She had rejected it herself, but it would do in a pinch, if you were young and in love. And Blackborow and Dr. Eyestone had spent a certain amount of time alone in there. At least somebody was getting some.

"Wait — you said *was* pregnant?"

Dr. Mack nodded. "She lost it, about a day after you left."

Ruby closed her eyes. Was that better or worse? "Because of low gravity?"

"Could have been that, or the stress, or the short rations. Maybe it would have happened anyway. We may never know. I plan to mention it in my report, anecdotally, as something to be aware of in the future."

She led Ruby behind a partition of supply bins. Blackborow rested on a cot with Dr. Eyestone by her side. Ruby knelt beside her and took her hand.

"Ms. Blackborow — Amelia — I'm so sorry."

"It isn't your fault."

"Maybe it is. I made you fall when we got here."

"I didn't fall that hard. Besides, you told me to be careful, and I didn't listen."

Ruby shook her head. This was no time for placing blame. "It's a hard way to learn a lesson. Did you ... know?"

"I was as surprised as anybody." She glanced up at John Eyestone. "We fooled around, but we never really

... Anyway. I don't feel like I've *lost* anything, if that's what you mean. Or not yet."

"Still, you weren't even supposed to be here. I should have taken you back to Armstrong as soon as we found you. Then none of this would have happened."

"But then I wouldn't have met John!" She smiled up at Dr. Eyestone.

"I'll take the blame," he said. "I knew better, but after we left the robots …"

"I understand," Ruby said. "Complete abstinence may be too much to ask on long space journeys. SCEI will have to find another way."

"We've been talking about getting married, or whatever we're supposed to call it now," Blackborow said. "And I'm going to go to school and make something of myself."

"With that attitude I'm sure you'll succeed. Do you still want to fly spaceships?"

"Not so much. Maybe I'll teach Spanish. Or go to cooking school and open a restaurant!"

"With singing robot waiters," Dr. Eyestone added, a dreamy look in his eye.

The medical technicians brought a pressurized stretcher so Blackborow wouldn't have to struggle into a space suit. While they were loading her into it, Ruby caught sight of Gunner across the room. Her heart stuttered and her stomach fizzed when their eyes met. He smiled and held up her duffel.

She crossed to him. Now would have been a good time to kiss him, but she had her helmet on, and he put on his while she watched. She held out her hand and he shook it.

"Hello, Boss." He handed her the duffel. "What took you so long?"

"Nice to see you, too, Mr. Gunner." They were on the public channel, so she kept it innocuous. "We made a hard landing in the crater and had to walk to the base, about fifty hours. Nielson almost didn't make it."

Gunner's eyes widened. "Then you guessed right, leaving us here."

Wild joined them. "Of course she did. Boss, we're about to shut off the air supply and the power, and then we can get out of here."

"I imagine you're all ready to see the last of it."

He glanced around. "It wasn't bad. You thought of everything — no surprise there. And nobody even made the 'living in fear' joke. But it was a load off my mind when Gunner got the comm center working."

"We barely got to use it," Gunner protested.

Ruby smiled. "Still — I like a man who can get the job done."

As soon as they got back to Columbia Base, the new arrivals were whisked away to the infirmary. Most of them couldn't even walk off the shuttle. Gunner managed a few steps, but then even he needed a wheelchair. Ruby wanted to hurry after them, but she was still weak herself. By the time she shuffled to the infirmary, they had been taken to the exam area. A nurse — his badge ID'd him as Jeff Lansford — stopped her when she tried to enter.

"Sorry, Commander, that area's off limits."

"But are they all right? Blackborow needs immediate care, and —"

Nurse Lansford smiled and laid a hand on her shoulder. "OK, Mother Hen, calm down. We'll take good care of your brood. Ms. Blackborow lost some blood, so we're giving her extra fluids, and an antibiotic to prevent infection. The rest of them just need rest, feeding, and physical therapy."

Ruby bristled a little at the "mother hen" comment until she saw how well it fit. "It's hard to turn off the worry."

"I understand. You did well, but we'll take it from here." He glanced at the clock. "It's late — have you eaten?"

"No, not yet. Not since breakfast."

"Go have dinner, then get some sleep. We'll see you tomorrow — you have a PT appointment at 1100 hours. And Dr. Fairfax left instructions that once they're out of the exam room, you should have full access to your people, at any hour. I think she's a little in awe."

It was difficult to turn away, though it helped to meet Anderson at the door. He'd been even slower to catch up.

"We can't see anyone right now, Skipper. Let's get out of these suits, find something to eat, and hit the sack."

They returned to their shared room to change, turned backs the only concession to modesty. The borrowed uniform was in better shape than any of Ruby's own clothes, so she put that back on. She opened the duffel and lifted out her good boots. They'd lost some of their shine, but they were still in excellent shape. She pulled them on, relishing the comfort of footwear that actually fit.

By the time they got there, the dining hall was about to close, but the servers seemed happy to provide for the visiting celebrities. Ruby still marveled at the taste of real food. She began to feel better.

Superintendent Rogers found them there and sat with them. "Now that your whole party is here, it seems more appropriate for you two to have separate quarters. The VIP suite is ready for you, Commander."

Ruby didn't mind sharing, but he was probably right, if only for appearance's sake. And he seemed to feel he was doing her an honor. After supper, she bade Anderson goodnight and went to her new room. It was the same she'd had at Christmas, freshly painted, and similar to other rooms she had slept in — small, unadorned, a single bed, a single chair. She sank onto the bed. She thought of her quarters aboard *Endurance* and how hard it had been, at first, to share them. She recalled the difficulty she'd had sleeping on the *Ruby Marie*, with everyone around her. This was an honor, a treat, a luxury. She gazed at that quiet, empty room and couldn't bear to be alone.

Don't be such a baby, she chastised herself. *Everyone is safe and you'll see them tomorrow. Don't fall apart now.*

She didn't want to do anything, even sleep. But there was something. She folded her hands and tried to pray. It had never been easy, even when she still had some faith. Her mind had always wandered to plans and to-do lists.

She waited for the Pearl to twinge, but it seemed to be gone for good. Tears came before words. All she could think of was all that *had* gone wrong, all that *could have* gone wrong and didn't, all that was now past. The tears flowed, tears of grief and relief, longing and release. The hardship was at an end. So was the expedition. But everyone was safe.

"Thank you," she whispered.

She felt warm, and not so alone. She drew her legs up onto the bed and leaned back against the pillow. Everyone was safe. All was well. The loosening that had begun on Christmas Eve was complete, and she could let go.

She knew what day it was, but not what time, either at home or here at the base. Her clock still told her the time on a ship crushed in the Asteroid Belt almost six months ago. She hadn't changed it aboard the *Ruby Marie*; there had been no reason then, and it felt … disloyal.

No. I'm through living in the past.

Once she'd synchronized her comm to the time at Columbia Base, she composed a message that was long overdue.

Dad,

   Contrary to reports, I am alive. I hope you are happy to hear this. The expedition was an unmitigated failure, but all survived, at least in part due to my efforts. I hope to see you when I get back, if you will. I know you think I wasn't there for you the way you needed when Mom died, but …

She started to explain that it wasn't her fault, then deleted the words. It wasn't his fault, either. She had been trapped in the web of her grief, while he drowned in his own. Each had let the other down, but it didn't have to stay that way.

   I wasn't there for you the way you needed when Mom died. I'm sorry about that, and I hope we can try again. I miss her. I miss you, too.
      Love, Ruby

She thought for a moment, then erased her name. She had to make sure he knew this message was real, not a cruel hoax. With a smile, she signed it "Sapphire." Not even Wild knew about that old nickname.

   She didn't know whether to expect a reply, but eighteen minutes later, it came.

My Gem, I will see you! When? It is already too long a wait.
   -Dad

She closed her eyes. Little by little, things were working out. She felt again the presence that had walked with her. All well, Boss. All well.

In the morning, Ruby stopped at the chaplain's office before breakfast.

"Chaplain Ingram? Do you have a moment?"

The chaplain beamed. "Ruby Ladd? It is wonderful to see you, though this is the last place I would have expected you. What can I do for you?"

"I ... expect my people will need mental health counseling. Maybe spiritual, too."

"Yes, I've had a chance to speak with a few of them already. Anything else?"

"No. Well, yes. I ... need your help, too. Is now a good time?" Better to dive right in rather than chicken out.

"We can at least start. Has a lost lamb returned to the fold, then?"

"More like the shepherd came and got me."

The chaplain nodded. "I've been talking to some of your people. They're in remarkable shape, emotionally. Seems like you're a pretty good shepherd yourself, Commander."

The tears returned. Embarrassed, Ruby smiled as she wiped them away. "I haven't cried in years and now I can't seem to stop. It's like something broke in me. Or melted."

"I think you're entitled. You've been carrying eleven other people for months. But you brought them over and they're in good hands. You don't have to be strong anymore. You can finally let go."

That made sense. Ruby felt lighter and freer, if a little empty. "That's harder than it sounds. I'm glad it's over, but … part of me wishes it wasn't."

"Don't you want your people to be safe?"

"Of course I do. I just hate to break up the team."

The chaplain smiled gently. "You can't protect them forever."

Ruby knew that, and yet she had been imagining something very like it. "No. You're right. But I don't know what I'm going to do for a follow-up. I don't think I could bear another mission like this one, but what else do I know how to do?"

"You know how to lead. Don't worry about it. When was the last time you had a vacation?"

Ruby laughed. "Would you believe, never? I don't even know how, but maybe I should learn."

"Enjoy this time. You've had your great moment, and eleven people are extremely grateful. For once, you have the luxury to live in the present. There must be something that kept you going, that you looked forward to at the end."

Ruby smiled. There was something …

"You're young, with courage and talent. Something will call to you," the chaplain continued. "When it does, you'll be ready to say yes. Just remember, you don't have to do it alone."

Chapter 30

2125/11/05: I have come to a difficult decision. I think I have to give up space travel. I'm still on Mars and I miss it already. But SCEI is rushing into something that we're not ready for. I can't be part of it.

— Ruby Ladd's private diary

Ruby had hoped to spend the day with the *Endurance* party, but Superintendent Rogers called her into his office after breakfast to deal with administrative chores that ended up taking most of the morning.

"I'm sorry about this," he apologized. "We're happy to have you here, but it causes a significant bump in our population and resource usage. If you can fill in the details, it will help justify the supply requisition."

"I understand," she said. "I just wish Mr. Keith was in condition to do it for me."

By the time she finished, it was almost time for physical therapy. She got to the infirmary with a few minutes to spare. Wild, in pajamas and a robe, sat in a chair next to the first bed.

"The Boss is here! Hip, hip!"

"Hooray!"

The cheer sounded ragged but sincere. Ruby's exhausted spirits lifted.

Wild leaned on a cane and pushed himself to a standing position. It broke her heart to see her friend in such frail condition. At least he could stand; the others were all in bed. He grinned and held out his hand. "Boss, you're out of uniform."

"So are you, Mr. Wild." She gripped his hand, then wrapped her arms around him and held him a moment. "Change is good. I might even start wearing red."

He squeezed her tight. "Isn't this against regs?"

"Fine, you're all fired." She went down the line of beds and embraced every member of the party, including a startled Nielson.

"Something in my eyes," he said, and rubbed them.

"Mine, too."

Blackborow was the most difficult to hug, with an IV in her arm and various monitors blinking around her bed, but she was awake and alert. Although extremely pale, she managed a smile. "It's good to see you, Boss."

"It's better to see all of you. But I have one hug left — where's Mr. Gunner?" She tried to keep her tone nonchalant.

Wild pointed with his thumb toward a curtained cubicle. "End bed. They're doing something medical with him."

"Is he all right?"

"As much as any of us. I think this is the first time they've had all the beds full, so the medical staff is making the most of it." Wild gave her a sly smile. "I'll tell him you asked about him. Too bad he had to miss the hug."

"It'll keep. He doesn't work for me," she replied. "You're all re-hired."

An authoritative voice cut short the visit. "Are you Ruby Ladd?"

Ruby turned to face a woman not much taller than she was, but of a stockier build. "I'm Commander Ladd."

"Pearl Adams. You're late for your appointment. This way, please."

"Meet your new boss, Boss!" Wild called after her.

So she had traded one Pearl for another. Ruby preferred the no-nonsense physical therapist to the tight ball of loss. Even if both made her ache. Ms. Adams administered an array of strength and flexibility tests and assigned an exercise regimen using resistance bands.

"You'll need to do those every day and meet with me once a week."

"Not a problem," Ruby said. "I can do more, if you like."

"Later. You need to rebuild muscle and bone without hurting yourself. You should be in good shape by the time you head home, but you'll have to keep it up aboard ship or you'll lose it all again."

"Trust me, I know."

"I must admit, I was eager to meet the miracle worker," Ms. Adams commented as Ruby walked on a treadmill. "I agree with Dr. Fairfax — there shouldn't be any way you could have walked that far in your condition."

"With faith all things are possible," Ruby said.

The physical therapist frowned. "I didn't realize you were a religious person."

"I'm not. I wasn't." She thought carefully about the rest of her response. "I guess I'm going to give it another chance. At the time, I just believed I had a duty to fulfill, and I didn't know any better than to try."

"Well, whatever the reason, Dr. Fairfax reports you and Captain Anderson aren't nearly as weakened as the others. My tests show the same. Whether you maintained more strength somehow, or had supernatural help, I couldn't say. But … it's an honor to work with you."

Following her appointment, Ruby went to lunch with the Skipper, with a notion of trying to visit the infirmary again afterward. A live call from SCEI Director James preempted all her plans. With the delay, even a simple conversation would take a long time. And this wasn't a simple conversation. She took it in her room while Anderson had his PT appointment.

She gave James a more detailed explanation of events and sent some of the scientific data her staff had derived. "We still don't know if there's enough material in the Belt to make asteroid mining feasible," she said. "We'd have to build one or more full-support stations for it to work at all, but there might not be enough resources to make it worthwhile. I think you'll agree we're a long way from colonization of space. There are too many variables with a large group of people — among others, their response to prolonged low gravity conditions. And without proven, reliable hibernation technology, the long travel time is too much to ask."

"I disagree — you've shown that people can endure long space journeys; even extreme hardship."

"This was a select group of talented professionals," she argued. "And we barely survived. You'd have a hard time repeating our experience with a group of colonists." She hoped he would be persuaded, but while she waited for his reply, she started making notes in support of her argument.

"But what if you were leading them?" She felt an automatic thrill at the offer ... and hated herself for it. He didn't wait for her response. "Don't answer now — we can have this discussion another time. I, for one, can hardly wait to see Mr. Gunner's images. Can you send us a sample?"

"I don't have access to his files. He'll send them himself when he's ready."

After the call ended, she continued writing up all her arguments against the rush to colonize space, even if no one wanted to listen. James's apparent trust was flattering, but in spite of the physical therapist's words, Ruby wasn't a miracle-worker. It wouldn't have taken much to turn their hardship into a complete disaster. It was against her natural optimism to list a lot of negatives, but she was also a planner, which required foreseeing possible pitfalls. She knew firsthand many of the dangers involved in space travel, though it was impossible to predict all the ways things could go wrong. But just because something hadn't happened yet, didn't mean it wouldn't or couldn't.

It was nearly suppertime when she finished her report. She would have a full debrief when she got home, but she didn't want to wait. She sent it immediately. Maybe it would make somebody think. Before she went to supper, she drafted another message. She didn't send this one. Not yet. It would require more cool-headed thought.

It had been a long day. The physical therapy, on top of everything else, left her aching and exhausted. Everyone she saw told her to rest, so she dutifully returned to her room soon after supper. She had appreciated the privacy during the SCEI call, but now it felt empty and lonely again. Not that she wanted to be with just any people. She wanted *her* people. If they were still hers. The expedition was effectively over. But those eleven people were her whole world now. Being alone in this room was like being alone on the Moon. Or worse — at least on the Moon, she had friends.

It wasn't likely any of her people were even awake. It would be cruel to keep them from their rest just because she was feeling lonely and vulnerable. She'd gotten through the previous night alone. She could do it again.

She undressed but couldn't make herself climb into bed. She did her PT exercises first, lunges and squats with stretchy bands that mimicked Earth's gravity. Pearl Adams had assigned her one set of five reps each, which hardly sounded like any kind of workout. Ruby set a goal of ten reps, but by four, her legs were shaking, and it was all she could manage to finish five. Some miracle worker.

She still couldn't settle down to sleep. She paced up and down in her dark blue briefs and camisole until her feet got cold. She had regulation officer's underwear, but no slippers. Her good boots seemed like overkill, but they were better than the too-large plastic shoes. She pulled them on and continued to pace. All day, she'd been doing what she was told, something she hadn't had to deal with in a long time. She didn't even have the ship model in her pocket, which had so often calmed her aboard the *Ruby Marie.* Did Gunner still have it? He must. Even if he didn't, the thought of him hit her like a punch in the chest. She needed to tell him ... something.

Nurse Jeff had said she had full access to her people, at any hour. If they were all asleep, she wouldn't bother them. But now seemed like a good time to test whether she was still the Boss.

Harte crept back to bed, leaning heavily on a walker. The walker pricked his pride, but others in the group weren't even doing that well. At least he was able to go to the toilet on his own; a walker beat a bedpan every time.

Everyone else was asleep, and he tried to be quiet as he creaked past their beds. He was wide awake. He drew the curtain around his bed so he could leave the light on and worked his way back under the covers. With the head of the bed raised, he sat up and began to send image files to his Earth-based server. He had a several-month backlog, so the process would take hours, but it seemed more important than ever to secure the images. It was good to have something to do.

He couldn't believe he'd missed the Boss's visit, a disappointment even if she had come to see the whole group, not him alone. He'd heard there were hugs, too. He wanted a lot more than that, but he would have taken a hug. All along he had fantasized that as soon as they got to the base and had a bed and some gravity, they'd get right down to business. It never occurred to him that he wouldn't even be able to walk unassisted. He could still imagine all kinds of things, but even if he had the strength to try them, he'd probably fracture several important bones in the attempt.

He could wait. He was happy to be alive. It felt good just to wear clean clothes, even if they were hospital pajamas. And the stylist who cut his hair had cheered him up. She was cute and bubbly and said nice things about his work — and his mustache! But she wasn't Ruby Ladd. He missed her and wanted to see her, even if they couldn't do anything but hold hands. There were things he wanted to tell her, things he needed to ask her. But maybe now that the crisis was over, the Boss was regretting her promise. Maybe she didn't even have so much as a hug for him now.

He picked up the *Endurance* model from his nightstand. They had ended up sharing it, as he proposed on Christmas, but he would get it back to her somehow. It meant more to her, and he had plenty of pictures of the real thing. He opened a file of older images, not of the ship but of the commander, the first shot he took of her smiling. It wasn't just the camera that loved her ...

Footsteps tapped through the infirmary. It seemed late for a nursing visit, but he hadn't stayed overnight in a hospital since he was nineteen, after he'd broken ribs and a kneecap in a rock-climbing accident. Maybe one of the others had signaled for something. The steps stopped on the other side of his curtain. He looked up from the image of the Boss as a hand drew the curtain back. Smiling, in a bathrobe, blue underwear, and low-heeled boots, stood the real thing.

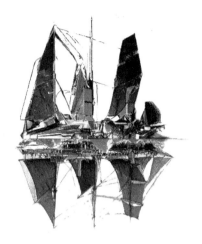

Chapter 31

2125/11/05: Is it over? Must I write The End*? But maybe not* Goodbye.

           — *Holden Gunner's Production Journal*

To Ruby's disappointment, everyone in the infirmary was asleep. But a light glowed behind the curtain around the last bed. She tiptoed through the darkened infirmary and peeked around the curtain. Gunner was awake — working, even. He'd had a haircut and trimmed his mustache to its former precise contours. And he'd kept the beard, neatly trimmed to match. He was gaunt and worn, like all of them, but to her hungry eyes, he looked like a banquet.

    He glanced up from his comm. His eyes widened and his mouth dropped open in a smile so delighted, it was one step from laughing out loud. "Boss? Do you know what time it is?"

"No, and I don't care. I'm glad you're awake. I need to talk to someone who —"

"— doesn't work for you?"

She frowned. "No. Who I don't work for."

"Whatever the reason, it's good to see you. I thought ... I ..."

Before he could finish, she crossed the distance between them and kissed him. "I've wanted to do that since I left you on Phobos, but it was never the right time."

The only other time she'd kissed him, his facial hair had been grown-out and comparatively soft. Newly trimmed, it was bristly and burned her lips — a sensation she wanted to get used to. He held her, and that felt good, too. Only the position was awkward. She turned around and leaned against the bed to pull off her boots, then shucked her robe, and climbed in beside him.

"Nice pjs," she commented as she lifted the blanket.

"Um — likewise? But it *really* isn't the right time for that."

"I know. I demand more stamina than either of us has tonight. I just need to know you're alive." He made room for her, and she rested her head on his chest. His heartbeat thumped strong and steady in her ear. She raised herself up on one elbow. "Mr. Gunner, your heart-rate seems a little elevated."

"I think your outfit did that, Boss. You look like someone with superpowers."

"It's still less revealing than what you'd see at the beach."

"Then maybe it's just you."

"Should I go?"

"No. I want to know you're alive, too." He held her tight, as if he feared she might try to escape. "I thought maybe you'd gotten tired of me."

"I haven't even had you yet! I've been trying to see you all day, but it's like a conspiracy around here — always some task to keep me away."

He grinned. "That physical therapist is a drill sergeant, isn't she?"

She gave him a wry smile. "You should thank her. With her help, you'll be able to ditch the walker soon."

"Oh. You saw that?"

"Couldn't miss it. Be thankful you can get out of bed at all."

"I am, but —"

"It wounds your ego to admit physical weakness? Mine, too. Get over it. You're strong where it matters, Mr. Gunner —" she patted his chest "— and your body will be strong again." She licked his Adam's apple. "Personally, I can hardly wait."

He gulped and the object of her attention rose and fell. "You're not making it any easier. I wish I could be more use to you, but for now, I walk like an old man, and I feel like I weigh a ton."

"It's only a third of a G. Earth would crush us both."

He opened his mouth as if to object, then closed it again, shaking his head. "I think I'm done complaining."

"Good. My turn. I was talking about SCEI. I'm not used to having bosses."

"It's hard to imagine you meekly following orders."

"I guess I'll have to get used to it, though; it's not like I have much of a command left."

He caressed her shoulder. "I can think of a bunch of people who would beg to differ. I don't even work for you, and I'll always think of you as the Boss."

She squeezed her eyes shut to hold back tears. "I don't know what's happened to me, but I can't stop crying."

He kissed her eyelids. "About time." They lay quietly together, and Ruby relaxed enough to imagine sleeping. "Do you plan to stay here all night?" he asked.

"If you're OK with it. My room is too … empty."

"I'm more than OK with it. But I never would have imagined the great Ruby Ladd was afraid to sleep alone."

"I slept alone last night," she defended herself. "After I said my prayers and everything."

"You're full of surprises tonight, Boss."

"That's more or less what the chaplain said when we talked this morning. She gave me some wise advice."

"Is this the result?"

She chuckled softly. "Not exactly, though I don't think she'd disapprove. She told me not to worry too much about my next move and just focus on the thing that kept me going during our experience. So I'm here, focusing."

"Mm. Wild gave us his blessing."

"You told him?"

"He guessed on his own. Maybe we weren't as sneaky as we thought."

"I don't care anymore. I told Anderson, too. He seemed happy for me, though I'm not sure he was actually awake."

Gunner was quiet for a while. "I heard from SCEI today, too."

"I figured as much. They asked me for your images."

"They sent me a long message. They can't wait to produce the doc — they think it will be just the kind of inspiring, feel-good picture people need right now."

She snorted. "Feel-good? We nearly died."

"They want me to omit the images of hardship. We'll have to mention it in passing, I suppose, but we can't show it."

"But it's a survival story!"

"That's why it's so inspiring. But it's not the picture I want to make."

"Did you tell them that?"

"Not yet. But I'm thinking of breaking my contract."

She sat up and stared at him. "Won't they just get someone else to make the doc with your images?"

He grinned. "They can't. They don't have my images. I have them with me, and on a secure server at my studio."

"But doesn't SCEI own them?"

"They would if I were a SCEI employee. But I'm an independent contractor. And I have a very good contract."

For the first time, she did not dislike his smug grin. She let him draw her back down beside him. "You mentioned this amazing contract before. You must have some fine negotiating skills."

He laughed. "I have a fine legal department."

"Even so, won't you have to pay back a lot of money?"

"I don't owe SCEI anything. I used my own equipment. I waived any advance in exchange for a larger percentage of earnings from the finished doc. And I retained all rights to the images."

"So you came on this little ride for free?"

"That's one way of looking at it." He held her closer. "You might have to give me a second night to make up for it."

She chuckled. "I'll decide that after we've had the first night."

"It's good to hear you laugh again."

"I have been a little grim recently, haven't I?"

"With reason. You had the world on your shoulders."

"No. Not the world. Only twelve people." She sighed. "At least you and I still have something to look forward to. The expedition's over, the escape's over ... What will it be like to go back to the world, with more than just the twelve of us? A world that has suffered more than we have? Will they even care? More than a billion people ..."

"Even you could not have saved them, Boss. It's not your fault."

"I know. But who's going to want to hear about our little group?"

"In the worst times, people need good stories. They need —"

She covered her ears. "Don't say it!"

He said it anyway. "— heroes."

"But we're not —"

"You are," he interrupted. "You could be. You will be, if I have anything to say about it."

She sat up again and crossed her arms over her bent knees. "Wesley James wants to give us a parade."

"Parades are nice."

"A 'welcome-home-thank-God-you're-alive' parade would be nice, but I don't think that's how it will play out," she said. "It's Chickering all over again."

"A publicity stunt?"

"He wants me to lead the colonization effort. He wants to use us to sell it. It stinks." She pressed her forehead against her arms. "I wrote a resignation letter."

"Can you do that?"

She looked around at him. "I'm back from the dead — I can do anything I want."

"My God, you're sexy when you talk tough. But that's not what I meant. Could you give up a career you love?"

"It hurts to even think about it. But, yeah, if it comes to that; if it's my choice."

"That seems like a rash move for you."

"I didn't say I'd *sent* the letter. I'll do the debrief, give them a chance to prove me wrong. But I'm not optimistic."

"What'll you do then? I assume you have a plan or three."

"For once, no plan. Flying completely blind."

"Then come and help me."

"Help you, how?" She lay back down and snuggled up to him.

KAREN EISENBREY

"We'll make the doc together. I was going to ask Dr. Mack to do the narration, but I've changed my mind. It needs to be you. It really is your story. We'll tell the whole story, let folks make their own decision."

"I'll think about it. Then what?" She liked the idea of spending more time with him, even if it only delayed the inevitable.

"We could travel around and make appearances — us, and any of the others who want to be part of it. Show the doc, have a Q and A, maybe agitate to fix our planet before we mess with the others."

"My dad can finally be proud of me." She beamed at the thought. Their reconciliation already seemed complete. "Something like this might even bring him out of retirement."

"I think people will want to meet the heroes of the *Endurance*."

"You keep saying that! We're not heroes. We're survivors."

"We'd all be dead without you, Boss."

"That just means I did my job."

"Exactly. That's the story I want to tell. What do you say?"

"OK, maybe. And … after that?"

"Would you consider sticking around?"

"Sticking around for …?"

"I'm thinking about starting a non-profit arm of the studio, making docs to call attention to important issues and raise funds for them. Natural and man-made disasters, injustice, maybe the conflict in the HCE. I could sure use someone with your experience, organizational skills, and temperament. I would love to focus on the artistic and technical side of things; let someone else look after the organizational details and the ... the *people.* Including the people who might take issue with what we plan on doing"

She slumped. "You want me to work for you?"

"*I* want to work for *you*. With you. Whatever."

"I see. A business partnership." It was better than nothing. At least she wouldn't have to say goodbye. She wouldn't be able to keep him safe from dangerous situations, but she would be supporting something that might make the solar system a better place. "Didn't you ask me this once before? I thought you were joking."

"That was before you liked me. So is it a warm day on Mars?"

She had to smile about that, snug in his arms. "It is for me. This could be what I need — something new."

"Yeah, me, too. We're both back from the dead, right? Maybe you can teach me to lead."

"I've been trying — weren't you watching?"

"I haven't taken my eyes off you since the day we met."

"That used to bother me." She pondered. This was a major career change, yet the decision had practically made itself. "Do I do the hiring?"

"Absolutely. You've proven your abilities there. I wouldn't even mind having Nielson around."

She sighed. "It won't be the same, though."

"What could be? Would you really want to do *this* again?"

"No, but ... God, Gunner, we swung on a star!"

"You're my star. May I kiss you, Boss?"

He didn't wait for permission. He pressed his mouth to hers in a way that promised everything, and more.

She laughed. "I thought this was supposed to be a business partnership."

"Excuse me, who came and climbed into my bed?" He stroked her hair. "It wouldn't have to be all business. I've never been settled, but now I think I'm finally ready to plant that garden — maybe start a family."

She barked a surprised laugh, then stifled it in consideration of the others sleeping nearby. "Start a family? What, with me?"

"Who else? You told me your deepest secrets, we did extra-vehicular activity together, you saved my life at least twice, *and* you asked me to crank your generator."

"It's still a big jump from one night of passion to starting a family."

"Two nights, remember? Or as many as you want. You won't be disappointed."

She didn't want to feed his ego too much, but she suspected he was right — the sex would be amazing, *if* they ever got to have any. That expedition wasn't over yet. "It's still a leap."

"That's what I do best. Here goes: I want to marry you."

"We're not using that word anymore, remember?" She tried to sound cool and unruffled, but her voice shook. Why was she hesitating? Not only would he have hygiene and stamina covered, he was smart, talented, creative, and strong enough to stand up to her. An equal. But she'd come in without a plan. She had only her heart and her gut to guide her.

He frowned. "I don't know how else to say it. I want us to be a team. I want my children to be like you."

"Are you sure about that? You called me a striver with no sense of adventure."

"Adventure is overrated. You have a sense of what's *right*. And I love you, Boss."

She swallowed. "In that case, shouldn't you call me by my name?"

"I'll try … *Ruby,* but I told you, you'll always be the Boss to me."

"No, I won't. How can we fight if I'm your boss?"

"We won't fight."

She laughed again. She had to. "Two strong personalities, living together? We'll fight." She kissed him. "But then we'll make up."

"That's a relief. After everything you've been through, I don't want to hurt you."

She squeezed her eyes shut. "That's unavoidable. But you get points in advance for helping heal some old wounds." Now she knew what she needed to tell him. It hit her again, like a punch in the chest. "I love you, too, Mr. Gunner. Harte. Name the day. Tomorrow, if you like."

"Really? You don't want to try out the merchandise first?" He grinned, new smile lines creasing his face.

She traced one of the lines with her finger. "I'll wait if you want to, but it's not required. And just think, how many people get to honeymoon on Mars?"

"It'll be your birthday soon," he said.

"I'm surprised you remember! But yes, it's a week away."

"Let's do it then, so I only have to remember one date," he said.

She laughed at that. "Smart man. Whenever we do it, I can learn from you, too, starting now."

"What could I possibly teach you?"

"How to find the story I need to tell," she said. "How to leap."

THE END

Afterword

This work of fiction was inspired by the remarkable true story of the failed Imperial Transantarctic Expedition of 1914-17, and it is dedicated with deepest admiration and respect to the memories of Sir Ernest Shackleton, Mr. Frank Hurley, and the men, dogs, and cat of the *Endurance.*

About the Author

Karen Eisenbrey lives in Seattle, WA, where she leads a quiet, orderly life and invents stories to make up for it. Although she intended to be a writer from an early age, until her mid-30s she had nothing to say. A little bit of free time and a vivid dream about a wizard changed all that. Karen writes fantasy and science  fiction novels, as well as short fiction in a variety of genres and the occasional song or poem if it insists. She also sings in a church choir and plays drums in a garage band. She shares her life with her husband, two young adult sons, and four feline ghosts. Find more info on Karen's books and short fiction, follow her band-name blog, and sign up for her quarterly newsletter at kareneisenbreywriter.com